For A.R.

**Act of Charity**

Hawkwood Books 2011
**www.hawkwoodbooks.co.uk**

# Act of Charity

*We have just enough religion to make us hate, but not enough to make us love one another.*
Jonathan Swift

# 1:  Witness

She saw him standing beneath the brick-roofed passage about fifty metres away, leaning against one of the walls, arms folded, watching her. She slowed her pace, stopped, appeared to reach some inescapable conclusion then walked on, resolute or desperate, she wasn't quite sure which; probably both. He'd had no doubts as to what she would do, though; principled people were easy targets.

'Silly girl!' he thought.

Around them, the lights of Homerton cast a gloomy pallor over an already night-engulfed streetscape. Gloomiest of all was this railway underpass, once a route for brash, excited pupils, now a forbidding conduit linking resilient little pockets of urban survival. She was light in the shadow with her sparkling eyes, colourful track suit and gentle gait, all so pitifully out of place.

He waited patiently, going over the rules – no contact, no touching, no trace at all. He was safe and she was not, this was the truth of it and nothing else need bother him.

She stopped, trying and failing to hold his gaze, unaware of what she was up against, only of a deepening foreboding. She was nervous, more than she thought reasonable, but a fierce determination guided her. Why had she come? She'd thought she could handle it alone, but this was misguided. She felt the strength ebb from her legs and her heart beat faster. She could barely control her breathing and was afraid of faltering. Everything that she was, everything that she had forced herself to become in her young, troubled, wonderful life began to crumble. But she did not flinch. She had to do this. There was still hope!

Face to face. She forced herself to speak. He listened but didn't answer. With a smooth, relaxed motion he pushed himself away from the wall and stood in front of her, a nemesis in total control of the moment.

She moved to her right, he moved to his left, a mirror movement impeding her way. She moved back, he moved with her. She said something but he didn't answer.

And at last she realized her mistake, a terrible, fatal, unredeemable mistake. She'd assumed that she was dealing with reason and conscience whereas what confronted her was an utterly alien absence of both. She almost collapsed with the sudden insight, but did what she could to hide her fear.

With one finger pointing at her chest, he manoeuvred her against a wall of the arch. She challenged him, but he said nothing. She felt anger rise inside her, a fierce thing, indignation that this should be happening to her, that so much good would be undone by this... this...

She didn't have time to finish the thought.

With the hand that wasn't pinning her to the wall, he whipped out something bright of faerie silver. She had only a moment to register the knife before she felt the cold, razor sharp cut across her throat. The movement was too fast to allow for any reaction. She just stood there, disbelieving. She felt her neck and looked at her hand, drenched in blood. She stared at him and he stared back, still saying nothing, calm and composed as if they were the oldest and best of friends. His expression revealed nothing but the utter, terrifying absence of conscience.

She tried to speak but only gurgled like a child. A sickening faintness spread through her and the pain began to dig in. The world spun and she spun with it, staggering then falling to her knees. Still he did nothing but watch.

Dizziness overwhelmed her and she fell, one arm, in a vain and flailing effort, seeking support, the other holding her torn neck. The ground slipped away, became the wall, became the sky. Her darling love, her darling brother, what would they do? Oh, how she wanted to see them, one last time, to explain all, to touch them, to comfort them. Who would give them comfort now?

Thoughts vanished as all that was experience and life and love ebbed away in a pool of spilt blood. He made no gesture whatsoever, wholly unmoved and unaffected, silently marking the vanishing moments.

Something caught his eye. He turned, squinted, waited.

Nothing.

Except...

He peered into the darkness. A shadow, a movement? No, not at this hour, it couldn't be.

Just the stillness of a Hackney night.

He relaxed and turned back, realised it was almost over and cleaned the knife with a cloth, put it into a polythene bag and slipped it into an inside pocket. From another pocket, unbelievably, even with a touch of pride in his preparations, he took out a camera. Calmly, he focused it on her and started to film. A pool of muddy crimson had formed around her. He thought he could hear the word 'Why?' but he doubted she could even think now, let alone speak. He could have finished things off quickly and quietly but he had no desire for more violence, not with the

2

risk of leaving an atom of evidence. Besides, he wasn't a beast. The deed was done now and there was no need for exaggeration.

She clutched at air, or at something he couldn't see, but there was no strength in her grip and her hand slid down onto the ground, twitching. Still he watched, growing more fascinated by the moment. Every part of her body trembled, fighting for the only thing it knew, life.

She slipped onto her back, facing upwards, mouthing what might have been a question, but he had nothing to offer, neither explanation nor absolution.

He took a step back as the blood flowed towards him, an almost hypnotic sight. He fancied he might see a spirit leaving the earthly realm, but all he saw was the physical, no evidence of anything more.

She was still quivering, not yet dead.

He paused the film, leaned over, thinking her eyes still followed him, but he wasn't sure how much of him she could see, probably nothing. He resumed filming.

The moment of death was unmistakeable, a complete change in substance, a transfiguration, instantaneous and marvellous to behold. In one sense, it hardly seemed worth noting, a tiny alteration from sound to silence, awareness to oblivion, movement to marble. It was everything he imagined and more.

He shut down the camera, slipped it inside his jacket and, without a glance behind, walked away.

# 2:    The Twinkling Lights of Hackney

## 1

"You know," said Michael, studying the night horizon from their bedroom window, "I think I like this place."

Naila wedged herself up in bed and studied him, countless curls falling over her shoulder in a sleek, rich waterfall of darkness. Michael could see her reflection in the window pane as if she were an angel floating over the bejewelled nightscape.

"You're very sweet when you go all romantic on me," she said.

"I'm serious," Michael answered. "Every area has its own character. You could take me to any London street and I'd know where I was."

"I'm sure you would too, Michael. Won't you come back to bed and convince me? You're so far away."

Michael didn't budge. He wanted to savour the moment of making love that had been so good and to soak up this city which so attracted him. He couldn't be hurried. Every second was precious and you had to time life carefully. Naila understood. She'd taught him, deepened his understanding and perception, she of all people would know his mind.

"Come and see," he said.

As gracefully as any dancer, Naila eased out of the duvet, wrapping it around her shoulders to keep in the warmth. She tiptoed to the window and curled up to him, enclosing them both in its folds.

"Many cities are romantic by night," she said, looking out at the astonishing array of lights.

"Yes, I know, and I wouldn't hold this up as a cultural icon. It isn't Prague," he said, "or Paris..."

"...or Tehran," Naila said.

She said it with a faint hint of nostalgia and an even fainter hint of an accent not yet totally absorbed into a London lilt.

"...or Tehran," Michael agreed, "or any of a million wonderful places, but it is what it is. There's a mystery about it."

Naila held him closer and put her hand in his thigh, feeling him.

"My poet!" she laughed.

"I am," he said. "But I mean it. I like it here. There's so much happening, so much variety, energy and change."

"For the better?" she kept stroking him and though he responded he seemed equally fascinated by the skyline and the mysterious East London night.

"Why not? There's hope and design and good will. It could so easily be a dismal, depressing place but it isn't, you just have to look."

Naila peeked under the duvet and he heard her say, "I am looking."

"I suppose it isn't much to you, Naily, is it?"

She squeezed him and said, "If it's much to you, it's much to me. That's the way I work, Michael."

He knew this. She loved him most generously. His fears were her fears, his passions were her passions. He wondered if he knew how rare this was and how lost he would be if it were ever taken away.

"Yes, but be honest, Naila, Tehran! I know you want to adore Hackney..." She pinched him. "...but it doesn't quite match up, does it?"

"It matches up fine," said Naila, kissing his shoulder and his arm. "I see it with your eyes, my love."

He took her in his arms and hugged her. Whenever she called him 'my love' he had no choice but to hold her as if he would pull her soul into his.

"Yes, but if it weren't for me, how would you see it?"

She shook her head and thought. She always thought before she spoke, even for a moment. It was one of infinite characteristics that fascinated him, this sensibility and generous intelligence.

"I think I might see it as a crowded place, too busy, too frantic, with people from all nations struggling to live the Western Dream. It has all the things you say, but so do many parts of London. I'm not sure what singles one out from the other, perhaps it is just familiarity. You have been in London much of your life, Michael; I for only a few years."

He looked down, almost downcast.

"Much of my life!" he repeated. "Doesn't that put you off me, Naily?"

"No. Why should it?"

He stroked her face and said, "I haven't done much, have I? Haven't seen the world."

"No matter Michael, travel doesn't always broaden the mind. There are many well-travelled fools."

He didn't look satisfied.

"You know what I mean. People move on. Live elsewhere. You did. I didn't."

"This is nothing," she said. Her voice, with its unique, subtle inflexion transfixed and excited him, but he listened too because what she said was always direct, honest, wise and true. "It is your roots I love," she said, "and this..." She held him again, and again he felt that completeness which he longed for when she released him. "You know," she whispered, "we are still in front of the window. People can see us."

He wouldn't move back to the bed, resting against the window sill, fascinated by the city lights. This was the best time to appreciate their home, two rooms on the top floor of a worn out estate building off the Upper Clapton Road, a potentially human disaster given light and hope by Naila's presence – and her paintings. They brought to the unimaginative space a rich, colourful and joyful air. There were exotic landscapes, mysterious portraits and a beautiful image of a boy throwing pebbles into the sea. All were wonderfully colourful, full of passionate intensity, giving the room a Bohemian feel.

Along with Naila's Art were papers scattered here and there - Michael's poetry. This was what had drawn her to him in the first place, a window into his soul. She liked them; she liked them a lot even though the world cared nothing for his efforts, even despised him for it, but she loved him for it. She'd read everything he'd ever written, talked about his work, suggested changes, taken up the better ideas, challenged him and comforted him, saw what made him write the things he wrote, and he adored her for this – but also, he had to admit, because she was astonishingly lovely, an Eastern treasure in downtown Clapton.

"I look out and I'm full of ideas." he said. "If you think about it too long, it's overwhelming."

"Then don't think too long," she joked. "Besides, bad things happen out there."

"I know, but not now, surely?"

"Why not?" she said. "This is life. Such a ...what do you say ... juxtaposition, all things, on top of each other, good and bad. It's only a little geography that separates heaven and hell, Michael."

This made him turn his head from the twinkling lights of Hackney into the twinkling light of her eyes.

"That's wonderful," he said. "I wish I'd come up with that."

"You can use the line," she said. "I'll let you."

They kissed and this time they moved as one towards the bed.

He never knew what to make of it. He couldn't understand this wonderful woman loving him so much. It made no sense and at times he wondered if he should doubt her, but he couldn't. He trusted her with all his unrewarded poetical heart. And when he lost himself inside her he felt, as ever, that he'd found so much more than he'd lost.

"I ought to work," he said, as they lay together afterwards.

"Must you?" she asked.

"Can't help it," he answered. "I get inspired – or restless, I don't know which. I need to write something."

Naila sighed and let him go. She watched as he put on his dressing gown, sat at the desk and began to write. Then she leaned over the side of the bed, found her own drawing pad and pencil and started sketching him.

"I know what you're doing," he said, without turning around.

"Ssh, genius!" she whispered. "Don't staunch the flow."

He carried on writing, she carried on drawing, he with the serious look of the artist, she with the smile of a contented lover. At times she felt they were in danger of falling into cliché, but they had their own dreams, and nothing, they were still passionate enough to believe, could take those away from them.

She drew, as she'd drawn many times before, his wonderful head, his untidy black hair and his open, enquiring brown eyes. By any standards he was a handsome young man, but his spirit excited her as much as his looks. Did he love her as she loved him? Naila doubted that men could love as deeply as women, and her good looks were sometimes an obstacle, but she had faith in him and his feelings. Her beauty had been both the blessing and the bane of her life. All beautiful women knew this; perhaps all women knew this whether or not they were beautiful.

She drew each line with care. She'd never drawn a portrait of him without care because that would have been blasphemous; he was, after all, touched by a certain divine innocence and it was a duty to do this justice. Close by, in a battered, leather briefcase, she had more images of him, some sleeping, some reading, some worrying or smiling; some – like this one – writing. She thought she could find an infinite number of poses for him and never be satisfied. She adored them all and often took them out to study, as if there was a secret that she might discover if she had enough time just to keep staring. She would happily have stared at him for hours on end, but he got embarrassed which made her love him even more.

"Are you making me angelic again?" he asked, again without turning.

She didn't answer, but focused intently on the drawing, etching the shoulders, the shadow behind his ear, the fall of every hair on his head, trying to capture an essence that she knew was there and wanted others could see. They never did and never would, but that didn't stop her seeing him as she did, which was how she knew him to be. It made no difference what others saw or failed to see, but if she could invest the tiniest fraction of her love in these portraits, then she'd be satisfied. And if she could somehow invest her life and energy with that same emotion, then surely someone, somewhere would understand, and that, in the end, was what Art was all about, otherwise it was worthless. But she doubted anything could ever come between them, certain that they'd found something untouchable, even by this often brutish world.

They'd met at a college where Naila taught art, both history and practical. Michael, just a few years younger, had been a student. Such liaisons weren't uncommon, but Michael and Naila were uncommon. They were their own universe and carried with them something which most mortals only dreamed about. Kathryn, Michael's sister, was delighted he'd met a kindred spirit and fervently hoped that Naila would never tire of her rare, fragile brother.

"I'm done," said Michael, standing and stretching.

"Can I see?" Naila asked.

"Not yet," he said. "I'm only done for now. The thing itself isn't done."

"Oh," she said. "Well, I'm done too," and she showed him the portrait. He didn't know what to say. He shook his head. "You don't like it?" she asked.

"I love it," he said.

It really was wonderful, so much more than the lines and shades that filled the page.

"I look like a proper poet," he said.

"You are a 'proper' poet!" she said.

He put the portrait down on the bedside table and sat beside her, feeling her shoulders, her neck, her arms, all so wonderfully sculpted and full of mystery. Nothing he'd ever written could capture that mystery, though he'd tried, yet she captured him with a few sweeps of a pencil.

They made love for the third time that night, once again losing themselves in each other and only reluctantly accepting the gradual return of consciousness.

"Don't tell me you want to work again?" she said.

"No," said Michael. "Inspiration's over for today."

"I'd be happy to read..." but he shook his head and looked sad. She put her forefinger to his eyes and gently ran them around the rim as if she were drawing him again. She traced his features, all the time looking into his eyes as if she could see as deeply as it was possible to see, studying him in that peculiar way which always threw him completely.

"What are you thinking?" he asked her.

This time it was she who shook her head.

"Secret," she whispered. "Isn't a lady entitled to her secrets?"

"I suppose."

"Michael?"

"Yes?"

"I'm still needy."

He slid his legs around her, clasping her tightly, and she did the same, facing him as he faced her. "My love," she whispered.

"Always?" he asked.

She wanted to say yes, always, yes, yes, yes! She wanted to fall into bliss yet again and stay there forever, but the moment was taken from her.

A harsh sound cut through the tenderness of their love; a bell, banal, intrusive and unwanted.

Someone was at the door.

**2**

Margaret Hargreaves settled her ancient bones into the ancient armchair, stared at the telephone and wondered - should she or should she not call Nell? She was anxious for many reasons but, oddly enough, the least of these was dying. Maggie was 91 years old and although she'd spent a decade or so in mid-life worrying about death, now, when it was imminent, she couldn't care a monkey about it. She worried about very little, not even her immortal soul which she assumed she'd lost when − well, that was private, but the little which still bothered her included Nell. She could have done with a chat and to see the bright, beautiful girl, but she'd promised herself not to keep phoning . She knew what young people were like, busy, busy, busy.

She brushed the arm of the chair with her fingers. Dust again. The house need a little TLC and Nell was just the one for that. All Maggie had to do was ask and help would be freely given, but she was careful not to overdo it. 'Don't take advantage,' she told herself. The alternative, calling social services, was out the question; they'd start poking around, taking more interest in her than was necessary. Besides, they did it because it was their job; Nell did it because she had a heart of gold.

She stood up carefully as her ninety-one year old body began complaining again. She wandered around the lounge, having a quick word with the people inside the photographs, trying not to feel too foolish as she did so, then flitted around the room fiddling with the relics of her puzzlingly long life. This had always been her home. She'd been born and still lived in Powerscroft Road. Around her, Hackney had shed its skin a dozen times, but the remembered borough was much more real to her than the new. She recalled true Hackney Carriages, when Mare Street was a thoroughfare for horses and when the area was a retreat for the well-to-do. She seemed to recall the past in countless fragments and it was only Nell's interest that had begun threading the history together. Maggie's memory was a frustrating thing, it let her down so many times, and yet the one thing she really wanted to forget plagued her every second of every day. Life was like that, a bit of a bitch, really.

Nell wasn't the girl's real name, but she reminded Maggie of that Dickens story ... what the devil was it? ... The Old Something or Other... Curiosity Shop! Yes, that was it! Maggie had met Nell in a local supermarket some months earlier when Maggie had her purse stolen. Angry and in tears she had sat sobbing in the manager's office, looking distinctly unwell. Nell, being a nurse, asked if she could help. She persuaded the manager to fork out some replacement money for Maggie which seemed to pain him somewhat, then took Maggie home and had visited her once a week ever since, helping to keep her home shipshape and listening to her stories about the 'old days'.

"We'll make a book, Maggie," Nell had said, "all about your life."

"My life's not worth a fart," said Maggie, which rather threw Nell, but she convinced Maggie that it was much more than that. Maggie was still hesitant, rightly so, for there were things no one knew and no one ought to know, especially Nell.

"I can't tell you everything," she'd said.

"That's okay," Nell replied, "just tell me whatever you like, but I'm sure you've never done anything bad, Maggie," at which Maggie sniffed but didn't answer. No amount of prodding would make her tell Nell everything because, if she did, Nell would drop the book, bomb out the door and never be seen again.

Maggie slid open a drawer from an oak cabinet and took out the manuscript which now filled over a hundred pages. It was a mixture of Nell's writing and Maggie's notes. Maggie glanced at it with mixed feelings, wishing she could include the one event which haunted her but knowing that she mustn't. Without it, the book was empty, but with it – well, it was the devil's own witness. Ah, but it would be such a relief to tell after all this time, only not to Nell, not to Nell!

She replaced the book and walked over to the radiogram, taking out a record Nell had bought her from Islington Market, Caruso singing Verdi, a seventy-eight rpm version which was the only speed the machine could handle. Nell had laughed aloud when she'd first seen the giant turntable in action.

"It isn't supposed to be funny, dear," Maggie had said. "It's opera!"

"I know," said Nell, "it's just that I've never heard a seventy-eight played before. It's weird."

"What do you call this, then?" Maggie had asked, pointing at the device hanging round Nell's neck. Maggie remembered Nell's expression listening to the gritty recording. If there were angels on Earth, Nell was one of them.

She glanced at the time on a grandfather clock ticking away interminably in the corner of the room. It looked as though Nell wasn't going to call. Maggie decided it was time for a little buck-me-up so she bustled into the kitchen, humming along with Caruso. The kitchen had nothing of the twenty-first century about it; not even much of the twentieth. There was an abundance of wood, as there was in the whole house. Wood gave a sense of permanence and Maggie was nothing if not permanent. She hadn't capitulated to the Formica Age or the Age of Melamine and fitted furniture. She switched on the strip light which flickered for half a minute before filling the room with a dull yellow glow, then opened the larder, poked around and took out a half empty bottle of gin. She cradled it gently, wiped the outside with a grubby cloth, found a tiny tumbler and poured herself a thimbleful of fire.

She tried not to think about the past but it crept up on her. She would sometimes stop whatever she was doing and shout "Piss off, why don't you!" which would have shocked those who saw her as a gentle old biddy, but it never did leave her alone, or not for long. And what was there to think about if not that?

Well, there was Nell, of course... but also Jerome, the mysterious cousin fifteen times removed who had turned up a few months ago. He lived, he told her, in Richmond Road to the west of the borough. She didn't know what to make of it when he'd said that she and he were distantly related. He was charming and broke up the loneliness. At first. It was when he started talking about her will that she got a touch suspicious and ended up banishing him, the fraud, but he'd turned up one evening unexpectedly at the same time as Nell. She saw straight away that he'd taken a shine to the girl, but that just wouldn't do. Nell was an item, and a happy one, and though Jerome had pressed Maggie for Nell's telephone number, she'd refused, of course, but had worried ever since that he'd found the girl and been pestering her. Tosspot!

Maggie sat on a rickety wooden stool at an even more rickety table, sipping the liquid fire which normally did the trick, but tonight she couldn't relax. Something in the air was wrong. Caruso stopped singing but the radiogram hummed away in the other room, its ancient electronics apparently unwilling to resume total silence.

Maggie opened a drawer full of kitchen paraphernalia and took out a well-worn leather bound address book bought from Woolworths on her 35th birthday a few lost lifetimes ago. She'd never crossed out any names or numbers so it was full of ghosts as well as the living, one of which was Nell. After deliberating a while, she took the book into the lounge, sat down, flicked through the pages, ignoring the arthritic aches in her fingers, found the number, pulled the phone towards her and dialled, holding the phone against her good ear.

"Hello?"

"Hello. This is Margaret Hargreaves of 27 Powerscroft Road."

"Who?"

"Maggie," said Maggie in a petulant voice as if the speaker was inordinately thick, "the old biddy?"

"Oh Maggie, yes, Kathryn's told us about you. What's up?"

"What's up where, dear?"

"No. I mean, is everything all right?"

"My dear, there's a lot of noise coming down the phone. I can't hear you very well."

"Oh, right, it's the stereo. Just a second...." The voice disappeared for a moment and when it returned the line was clearer. "Is that better Mrs Hargreaves?"

"Much, thank you. Do you have an accent, my dear?"

"I'm Australian."

"Ah well, that explains it."

"I was asking if everything was alright."

"I don't know dear. Is Nell... I mean Kathryn, there?"

"No, she isn't. She's a busy girl, Mrs Hargreaves. Shall I ask her to call you when she gets back?"

"If it isn't too late, yes please. I'm going to bed now but I have a phone by my bedside. Can't get around like I used to, not a spring chicken, you see. Who am I talking to please?"

"I'm Ursula."

"That's a lovely name. D.H.Lawrence used it in Sons and Lovers, you know."

"Did he?"

"Yes. You should read it. Tell Nell that I called. She can call me any time, as long as she's alright."

"I'll tell her Mrs Hargreaves. Is that all?"

"That's all, dear. Good night."

She hung up and sat for a while staring at the address book as if it had hidden within it the great secret of her life, and in a way it did.

After a few moments she closed it, slipped it back into the kitchen drawer and wondered whether there was ever going to come a day when she'd find some peace after this long and troubled stay on Earth. She should tell Nell, she really ought to. You couldn't keep a secret like that from someone like her, it wasn't right.

Agitated and not a little grumpy, she switched off the lights and headed up to bed.

## 3

"Who was it?" a voice called down the stairs.

"Kath's old lady friend," said Ursula. "Wanted to know where she was."

"Where is she?"

"I don't know! Am I my flatmate's keeper? I hope she's not going to phone every time Kath is late home. It'll get out of hand, like having a mum watching out for us all the time."

Four of them shared a flat near the River Lea, a pretty location on a redeveloped quay, out of the way a little from the boiling point of Hackney life, reasonably priced, and they had two cars, both family presents, so that helped, but the main advantage of being there, and the reason for choosing it in the first place, was that they were all rowers and their home was within a breath of the Lea Marina.

They had a room each, Ursula, Jasmine, Elena and Kathryn, and had managed, quite remarkably, never to get on each other's nerves. They weren't sure why, but they suspected it was because Kathryn was the focal point and seemed able to channel the house energy in a positive way. She was also the only with a boyfriend, and not just any boyfriend, but the love of her life, and this seemed to shine a ray of hope on their sometimes sad singles lifestyles. They had routines which dovetailed pretty well, considering they were each so different. Ursula, on loan from her native Australia, was a graphics designer, Jasmine the ruthless commanding officer of a telephone sales team, Elena a junior teacher and Kathryn a nurse. Considering each career path required very different skills and characteristics, the way they worked together was impressive.

Ursula and Jasmine were about to head out for a drink leaving Elena, not unusually, to finish a mountain of marking.

"Elly?"

"What?"

"Last chance. Come with."

"I can't."

"Come on, give it a rest. No one works that hard that long."

"I can't, really."

"Only for a couple of hours, Elly, it'll freshen you up, babe."

Elena poked her head out from the bedroom where she'd been immersed in countless unreadable stories. It always amazed her to think that children changed from illiterate barbarians to do grown-up things like running telephone sales teams and graphics design. It didn't seem possible, like a puppy morphing into a tiger, or a kitten into a wolf; children and adults were two different species.

"Oh, I don't know..."

"Not long, Elly, promise. Come on! We all need a break. I need you," and she broken into a Beatles chorus in the way of persuasion. Elena sighed and capitulated.

Five minutes later the three of them were squeezing into Ursula's car heading towards Upper Clapton.

"Give Kath a call," said Elena. "Maybe she can meet us there."

Jasmine called but the phone was not switched on.

"She's on early mornings, isn't she?" Ursula asked, checking as she turned towards Stamford Hill. "She'll probably be tucked up by the time we get back."

"Where're we going?" Elena asked. "I thought you said this was local."

"City's local, girl," said Jasmine. "Don't panic. Somewhere new for a change."

The roads were unusually easy to navigate. Normally there was enough traffic to provide an army's worth of carbon footprints, but it was mid-evening and the driving wasn't too onerous. Lights shone everywhere. There was hardly a black patch from their quayside home to the city. Everywhere was built up, but until they reached Shoreditch there weren't too many cultural hotspots - The Rio was the one oasis of hope in an otherwise functional landscape of shops, homes, homes and shops.

"Do you ever wonder why we're here?" Elena asked.

"Is that a deeply philosophical question," Jasmine said, "or just rhetorical?"

"Both," said Elena. "There must be other places to kill time."

"We're not killing time love," said Ursula, driving and talking with equal energy, "we're living. This is life."

"And we're not doing badly," said Jasmine. "You're just tired, Elly. I can see it in the bags under your eyes and the wrinkles..."

"Enough," said Elena. "Thank you kindly."

"How's it going in the monkey house?" Ursula asked.

"Me or her?" Jasmine said.

"Her."

"Oh, usual mayhem," said Elena. "What's the matter with kids today, eh?"

They laughed. Ten years ago they'd all been locked away in the monkey house themselves, kids of eleven at the end of their junior school education. Now they were all grown up and fending for themselves in the big bad world. It was a bit much to take in, especially as Elena had feet in both worlds, which was doubly unsettling.

"Let me tell you about my day," said Jasmine. "Something interesting happened."

"Wow! Something interesting!" said Ursula. "In telephone marketing? What's the world coming to? Tell us," she said, slowing to avoid a cat ambling across Dalston High Street.

"It was Jill. Her waters broke."

There was a moment's silence as if they were all taking on board the meaning of this peculiar statement. They'd been expecting something like "we hit our targets for the fourth week in a row" or "there was this abusive client", but Jill's waters weren't in the frame. Ursula nearly had to pull over and stop, she was laughing so much and Elena smiled, despite tired jaw muscles.

"It's true," said Jasmine. "She shouldn't have been in, and she was supposed to finish the end of the week, but she came in and the little baby almost popped out."

"What, while she was on the phone?"

"Yeh."

"Blimey."

"What did the client say?"

"I took over, didn't I? No one else free."

"Seriously?"

"Yeh."

"You told her what had happened?"

"Him. It was a him."

"Oh. What did you say then, 'Excuse me sir, we'll have to interrupt this marketing pitch as the lady at the other end of the phone is about to give birth?'"

"Pretty much."

A scream of delight from Ursula.

"Wait till Kath hears about that," she said. "It wasn't her hospital, was it?"

"As a matter of fact it was. Not much choice around here, is there?"

Although full of impressive, often oppressive, buildings built to last forever but now in constant need of tender loving care, Homerton Hospital was a more modern vision, an attempt to lift the borough into the twentieth and twenty-first centuries. Not a moment too soon either, the old hospital having lasted long beyond its sell-by date. It may not have been perfect, but it was light years ahead of the miserable buildings it replaced. Evidence of this Victorian and Edwardian heritage was still very visible around the borough, a heritage which might have graced the best horror films of the day. Kathryn had told them horror stories of her own about her life as a nurse, after which none of them felt much like moaning about their own daily grind.

"Want to give her another ring?" said Ursula.

Jasmine tried, but the phone was still off.

"Probably necking Daniel whilst we sad souls go man-hunting in Sin City."

"We're not man hunting," objected Elena. "At least I'm not. Are you two?"

"Not sure what I'm hunting," said Ursula. "How about you, Jas?"

Jasmine thought for a moment and said, "If a suitable boy comes my way, I won't say no. He'd have to match my high standards though."

"You mean two legs and something in between?" Elena asked.

"Oh, teacher! Really!" said Jasmine.

"We shouldn't have persuaded her to come with," said Ursula. "She'll lower the tone of the evening, you'll see."

"Always does," said Jasmine.

Elena poked her lightly in the shoulders then slouched in the back seat, sinking into exhausted teacher mode, humming a song she'd been singing with the children. The others asked her to sing it louder, and she did, and they joined in.

"This is great!" said Jasmine. "I feel young again!"

"You are young," said Ursula.

"I'm twenty-two. Is that still young?"

"Not as young as twenty-one, but you're not past it yet, girl."

"Feel it," said Jasmine. "Think I need a shot in the arm. New job maybe."

"Yawn," said Ursula and Elena in unison.

"Sex?" suggested Jasmine.

"Um, yummy. Now you're talking," said Ursula.

"At least you two have semi-decent meaningful jobs," said Jasmine, "but Elena you're fagged out every night and Ursula, your eyes are going to be worn out by the time you're thirty. My job might be crap, but it doesn't aspire to be anything else, does it? We're here because we're here because we're here. There's no reason for any of it, so there's no point hunting something that isn't there."

"Blimey Jasmine, that's a bit heavy. Lighten up, lighten up."

"I'm light as a feather," said Jasmine. She started tapping a tune out on the dashboard and singing Elena's banal song to a rock beat. Ursula joined in and Elena did her best too, wondering what the children would make of it if they saw their respected teacher slouched in the back of a car wrecking their wonderful music.

"Girls," said Ursula. "I have news. We're here."

Hackney had suddenly turned into the City of London. It was always a surprisingly fast transition. You could see the precise spot where the trouble ended and the money began. Hackney's chequered background and troubled present stopped exactly where the immeasurable wealth of the city began. Run-down buildings ended and the fabulous cityscape of Midas began. It was extraordinary and spoke volumes for the priorities of the modern world. Despite the rhetoric and posturing, despite even the Olympic dream, Hackney remained a shadow of its illustrious neighbour, poorer in most ways except in spirit and variety of life, which were surely more important, at least in some cosmic scale of measurement.

They parked in a small side street and headed into a wine bar which was heaving. A few heads turned as they came in, but turned back quickly to the conversations in which they seemed to be fully engrossed.

"My treat," said Ursula. They found a square metre of space and she ordered them drinks, limiting herself to orange juice as she was chauffeur for the evening.

"So," said Elena. "What now?"

"Now we wait to be accosted," said Ursula.

It didn't take long. About three seconds, in fact.

"I am willing to accost you," a man said, turning towards them.

"You are?" said Ursula.

"Frederick Stromberg from Sweden. How do you do. And this is my friend Steven from the good City of London."

He put his arms around a young and not unattractive man who nodded at them. The two men seemed, in their unmistakeable male way, to be ticking the check boxes.

"Oh look," said Ursula, "there's a table .. for three, I think. Girls? Excuse us, Frederick of Sweden and Steven of London."

Ursula hurriedly sat down at the table before anyone else took it.

"That was a bit of a rush," said Jasmine. "Didn't even get to know Freddie Kruger and his friend."

"No point," said Ursula. "Not our types."

"Now hold on a minute," said Jasmine. "I was almost interested."

"There were only two of them," said Ursula. "And they weren't our types. I could tell."

"Oh you could, could you? Well I'm not so sure about that. And anyway, who did you expect to meet here? Melvyn Bragg?"

"Don't know," said Jasmine looking at the two men who were deciding whether or not to follow them to the table. "Nothing ventured. What about you Elena?"

"What about me?"

"Fancy them?"

"I don't think so. Let's make this a quick visit, ladies."

"Elly, come on! Don't be a grouch," said Jasmine.

"I'm not a grouch!"

Jasmine put her arm around her.

"Sorry, Elly, really. You're not a grouch at all. You're a sweety-pie."

Frederick of Sweden made another attempt at rallying his troops and storming the castle, as it were, but Ursula gently yet firmly told them to vanish. It wasn't that the men looked socially inept or embarrassing in any way, but just unutterably shallow. Probably not even entertaining. And there were only two of them. If they could rustle up number three, however...

"Tell us about your day then, Elly," said Jasmine.

"Not likely. Social catastrophe."

"What, one happened, you mean?"

"No. It would be a social catastrophe to talk about it."

" I don't think so," said Ursula. "Social catastrophe is global warming or economic meltdown. Get things in perspective, Elly."

"Where's Kathryn?" Jasmine said, impatiently. "If she were here we'd be accosted and pulled by now."

"Oh, why's that?" asked Ursula.

"Well, it's all to do with numbers," said Jasmine. "There are three of us, right?"

"One, two, three," Ursula checked, counting conscientiously. "All present and correct."

"Well, if there were only two of us, Frederick of Sweden and Steven of London could have had their way with us."

"So I'm in the way?" said Elena.

"No, no, no," said Jasmine. "They really aren't our type. No, it's just to illustrate a point."

"Which is?"

"Even numbers good, odd numbers bad. Simple. Look around. Everyone's in even numbered groups."

They looked, but it was impossible to tell who was with who.

"Where did you get that statistic from, Jas?" asked Ursula.

"I counted. I'm good at numbers. And it's obvious. So, if two men come for us and there's two of us, we're okay. And if two men come for us and there's four of us, we're still okay because the other two can natter away together."

"And feel unwanted?" said Elena.

"Just concentrate on the numbers," said Jasmine.

"Supposing there are two of us," said Ursula, "and four men come hunting. What then?"

"Hmm," said Jasmine. "Lucky us!"

Ursula smiled but Elena looked heavenwards and said, "This is all a bit demeaning, Jas. Whatever happened to women's liberation?"

"We're not **that** liberated, Elly. You mean we should make the first move?"

"Why not?"

Jasmine thought for a moment and said, "Because **that** would be demeaning. Anyway, we *can* make the first move. It's all a question of subtlety."

"Really? Show me how."

"It's instinctive girl," said Jasmine. "You just do it. A look here, a smile there, that's all a man needs. They're pathetically needy, you know."

"So are we, I fear."

"Nonsense. It's our choice. Men only have the illusion of choice whereas we have the real thing. It's one of the facts of life. Always been the same, always will be."

"So how come we're all still single?" Ursula asked.

This gave them too much pause for thought.

"I'll text Kathryn," said Jasmine, and she took out her mobile and texted, 'Need you. Numbers don't match. Men waiting. Jasmine.' She read out what she'd typed and Elena said, "You're not going to send that, are you?"

"Why not?"

"She won't get it. It's too cryptic."

"She's bright. She'll get it," and Jasmine hit the send button. "She'll call, you'll see. And she'll come, if she can. She'd do anything to help us girls out."

"We don't need help," said Elena, at which Ursula broke into another Beatles song and the other two joined in, impervious to the fact that heads were turning. When they'd done, Ursula raised her orange juice and said, "All for one and one for all."

"Three musketeers?" said Elena.

"Bright girl. Only there were four of them."

"Not strictly speaking. D'Artagnan wasn't a musketeer," said Elena.

"What was he, then?" Ursula asked.

"A bit like Kathryn is to us, the leader, only different."

"I thought I was the leader," said Ursula.

"Isn't it me?" Jasmine asked.

"I *should* be," said Elena. "I mean, I have the most responsible job." The others sighed in mock desperation. "But she's the one. She's got The X Factor, right?"

"You're right. Oops. There goes the mobile. Told you."

Jasmine checked her mobile but it wasn't Kathryn. It was her boyfriend and potential lifetime partner Daniel.

"Daniel!" Jasmine squeaked into the phone. "What's up?" The other two listened. "No, she's not here." They kept listening. "No idea, Dan. Hey, give us a man's point of view will you?" Their ears picked up even more. "Are numbers important when you pick up girls..."

"Jasmine!"

"Sorry Dan, it's Elena being prudish. Are they? I mean, when you picked up Kathryn, if she'd been with an odd number of girls, would that have made any difference? What? No, I haven't been drinking. Well, I *am* drinking but it's a sober question, Dan. Just trying to see it from a bloke's point of view. Just wondered if there'd been three of us, would that have meant you and she had never have got talking and the world would have been a different place? Oh ... right." Jasmine started laughing. "See you Daniel," and she ended the call. "That was Daniel," she said.

"No!"

"He wanted to know if Kathryn was here."

"And you asked him a duff question about numbers? Jasmine, you're incorrigible."

They chattered on for a while, enjoying the banter and condemning Kathryn for not answering the text, as if her presence would have brought all the even numbered groups of men swirling around them. They talked rowing, world politics, jobs and economic disaster and the evening vanished in a whirlpool of topics. They were so tired when they got home that they didn't check Kathryn's bedroom, sure she was tucked up in bed, fast asleep.

**4**

Daniel Hart switched off the hands-free headset and focused on the road back to Clapton where he had to make a final call for the day. It was late, but he worked all the hours he could to keep the business growing. He'd phoned Kathryn but she wasn't around which made him anxious, not so much that he couldn't reach her now as that he hadn't been able to reach her for weeks, emotionally rather than physically. Something was wrong and he wanted to help, but she'd been distant and that hurt him. He was, he knew, over-sensitive to rejection. This might well have been his Jewish background kicking in, he wasn't sure, only he didn't feel this was him; this was Kathryn, and because he loved her more than he thought it possible to love anyone and because she loved him just as much, they had to sort this out.

Daniel's orthodox Jewish background weighed on him at moments like this. He felt exposed, open to all kinds of inner insecurities. With her, when they were together, he felt safe; apart, especially since he'd felt this distance arise, he felt in peril. His parents might nod their heads wisely and say 'we told you so; you are a Jew, you can't run away from it, Daniel. The world doesn't want you', but he refused to believe this. Kathryn had convinced him not to believe it and he trusted her. Whatever was causing her distress wasn't him; he wanted to be the cure, not the problem. He would prove his family wrong, despite these anxious moments. His parents didn't understand why he'd done what he'd done, abandoning his heritage like this, and no amount of explanation could satisfy them. They couldn't see why he felt so at ease in the world that was more Babylon than Judah, or if they could, they thought it misguided, but misguided or not, Kathryn was the focal point of all his thoughts, all his feelings and all his actions. No dogma would separate them, ever.

He had to smile; Stamford Hill wasn't exactly Babylon - there were no great wonders of the world here to last millennia. There was a pleasant enough rockery outside the supermarket at the crossroads, but it wasn't a patch on the Hanging Gardens. Oddly, or through some subtle subconscious drive, the orthodox Jewish community was as evident here as anywhere in the country, even more so than Salford where he'd left his family, but he went where there was work and there was work aplenty here.

He liked the energy that simmered in Clapton, and after three years it hadn't dwindled, in fact it was as well-defined as ever. It came, he decided, through the astonishing number of communities living side by side. Whereas their home nations would be tearing each other to shreds, here they were neighbours and got on swimmingly. Synagogues and mosques thrived side by side, Jew and Arab, Turk and Greek, black and white, a whole multitude of united nations muddled through the British system and British weather, never warring, proving something critically important which the wider world was yet to understand, a true multicultural marvel.

Religion, technology and love were as prevalent in his life as faith, hope and charity; a delicate balancing act requiring no small level of skill. As regards the first, he understood why he'd rebelled and he understood the guilt that came with rebellion. History had decreed in its own malicious way that his people had killed the son of God, an idea which never failed to puzzle him. As much as he had turned his back on orthodoxy, he had found the supposedly more rational Christian world full of equal prejudice, and this deeply rooted blaming of his people the most profound of all, and yes, they were still his people. He both loved them for what they were trying to keep alive and resented their influence over him, perverse but unavoidable thinking.

As regards technology, it was his work, and work was what gave life focus. Daniel had started his company three years earlier and it had thrived. He'd decided that two thousand years of studious culture had given his genes a bias towards the more cerebral subjects. Even Maimonides, the great rabbi himself, might have made a super troubleshooter. Attention to detail was the key, which was partly why many Jewish people excelled in areas where the devil was in the small print, figuratively speaking.

He was heading towards a client who had brought a home computer to its knees. Clients weren't bothered whether it was morning, noon or night; if they were in trouble they couldn't wait and Daniel did his best to get to them as quickly as possible. They appreciated this and showed their appreciation by recommendations. Most jobs he could complete quite quickly, but if something looked more complicated he would take the machine either to his Homerton office or the workroom in Hackney Wick. He was still a one man band, but if the work load got out of hand, an agency would send him a techie to ease the pain.

Daniel covered E5, E8 and E9 plus a slice of N16, an intense area where people forged all manner of lifestyles and created all manner of electronic confusion. It never failed to astonish him how people could gum up the un-gummable, wrecking the most stable systems. Sometimes it was human error, but the machines often failed their owners rather than the other way around. The cures, fortunately, were often similar, but Daniel never tired of them - the more similar the cures, the faster he could resolve the faults.

As regards love, he might, a few years earlier, have dismissed it, but now there was Kathryn, and she had changed him - was still changing him. Unfazed by the power of religion or silicon, she loved him to distraction.

"What a mystery you are," she'd said, stroking his head as they lay together, "so full of contradictions."

"And you don't mind them?" he asked.

"Only because you're nice looking," she answered.

She offered what he'd thought was impossible, something pure in a tainted world. When he told her this, she laughed and said, "The world is what we make it, Daniel."

So far, the world had made it a mixture of beauty and horror, but he reckoned that as long as she was with him, he could survive E5, E8 or even E9.

Looking out of the car window as he headed towards this final call, he saw himself in some kind of peculiar time tunnel, an unreal place between belief and an insistent reality. It could almost overthrow him, seeing the modern lights of Hackney alongside the ancient lights of imagination. Did it have any value, this odd civilisation of which he was unexpectedly a temporary resident? From nothing to everything, when he thought of Kath it became the most important place on Earth.

Using the miracle that was satnav, he parked close to the client's house. If only the Israelites had had such technology in the desert, he mused, no pillars of fire, just good old human ingenuity. He checked the job report for the call, sure that he could handle it quickly and get back to Kathryn, sort out whatever it was that had disturbed her and restore the balance which, for some reason he didn't understand, he felt was under threat.

## 5

"Mum! He's here!"

"I know darling. I heard the bell."

"Can I open the door?"

"Just a second, Kylie. Let me check."

Kylie's mother looked through the spy hole in the door and saw the young man standing with his briefcase looking rather tired and cold. She opened the door on its chain and waited for him to introduce himself, which he did with professional ease.

"Mrs Davis? Daniel Hart," said the young man. "Computer saviour."

She opened the door and said, "Nice of you to come out so late. We're in a bit of a pickle."

"No probs," said Daniel. "Here to serve."

He had a light way about him which completely defied the previous heaviness of his thoughts.

"Hello," said Kylie.

"Hello young lady," said Daniel. "Who are you?"

"I'm Kylie."

"And this," said Mrs Davis, "is Frankie. The culprit."

A young boy of about ten had come out to see the visitor. He didn't look happy.

"Not to worry," said Daniel. "I'm sure it wasn't your fault, Frankie. Do you want to show me what happened?"

They led him up to Frankie's bedroom where a sad looking computer sat on a desk piled with stuff – there was no other word for the assortment of odds and ends Frankie had collected around his beloved computer. Daniel had the ability to gauge straight away what kind of job awaited him and he could see this would be awkward, the room being to all intents and purposes the epicentre of some kind of upheaval that had strewn clothes, toys, books and general ten year old bric-a-brac all around. Daniel thought it would be an achievement to get anywhere near the computer, let alone repair it.

"Sorry about the mess, Mr Hart. Frankie, I told you to clean up."

"I did," said Frankie.

"Not very successfully. Come on, make some space so that Mr Hart..."

"Daniel, please."

"...Daniel can sit down. Would you like a drink, Daniel?"

"Tea would be great, thank you ...?"

"Eileen. You sort yourself out and we'll get you fed and watered."

Kylie had been staring at him the whole time, the way children do, intently and intelligently, figuring out if he was friend or foe. He was definitely friend.

"I'll bring you a cake," she said.

"That's very kind! Thank you! I'll get stuck in, then. Frankie, do you want to tell me what happened?"

Eileen Davis disappeared with Kylie for a few minutes whilst Frankie tried to explain what had happened before the computer collapsed. Mother and daughter came back in a few minutes with a mug of tea, a small silver pot of milk and a plate of biscuits. Kylie held a chocolate cupcake out to Daniel.

"All for me? I hope I can solve the problem after such a feast!" said Daniel.

"I'm sure you will," said Eileen. "You come on recommendation, you know."

"Oh yes? Who was the misguided customer?"

"Well, it's a bit of a chain, but my husband's a police officer and he asked around - I phoned him at work earlier today, you see. One of his colleague's had your card, said you'd performed miracles. There we are. Now you're here."

"Right. Well let's see if I can really do miracles," said Daniel, sipping the tea as he waited for the computer to boot up.

"Do you want to be left alone?" asked Eileen.

"I don't mind," said Daniel.

"Can I stay, mum? Please!" pleaded Kylie.

"Best not to," said her mother. "I'm sure Daniel wants to get on and go home, Kylie."

"Please let me! I won't talk," said Kylie. "I'll just watch."

"Honestly, I don't mind," said Daniel. "It might not be that interesting though, Kylie."

Eileen was in two minds. Being a policeman's wife and a sensible woman she didn't think it wise to leave her children alone with the computer man, but he seemed safe enough and it might be good for the children to see him at work, if only for a short time, so she said, "Well, we can all sit and watch for a few minutes, but if Mr Hart....Daniel wants us to go, I'm sure he'll tell us."

She sat down on Frankie's bed with Kylie on her lap and Frankie standing next to Daniel, watching him eagle-eyed.

The computer booted up and then rebooted itself and did this three times.

"Will we need a new computer?" Frankie asked.

"I don't think so. Shall we coax it into action?" he asked, and he slipped a disk into place which did indeed coax the machine into some kind of life. "That's my emergency boot disk," he said. "That was the easy bit, now we have to find out what's wrong with it."

"Is it like going to the doctor?" asked Kylie.

"A bit," said Daniel, getting into second gear and running through some set up tests.

"Looks rather complicated to me," said Eileen. "They say computers are easy to use but that doesn't look easy to me. Matt ... my husband...swears they're bringing the world to rack and ruin."

"He's probably right," said Daniel. "At least they give me something fairly useful to do with my life, though."

Impressively, he was managing to hold a conversation and carry out batteries of tests on the ailing machine. Little Frankie tried to tell Daniel what had happened, and he was surprisingly knowledgeable.

"It's his best friend," said Eileen.

"Have you got a best friend?" Kylie asked. Her mother told her not to be nosey. Daniel looked at Kylie and said, "That's okay. Yes I do."

"What's her name?" Kylie asked.

"Kylie!" her mother said, though she was rather interested herself.

"Her name is Kathryn and she's the very best friend I've ever had, Kylie."

"Are you going to marry her?"

"Kylie! Daniel, I'm so sorry. We'll go and leave you in peace."

"No," said Daniel. "Really, I don't mind. It's quite a challenge to get this machine going and give Kylie here honest answers at the same time."

"Is she nice?" Kylie asked.

"Very nice. I like her a lot."

"What does she do?"

"She's a nurse."

"Mummy!"

"Yes, sweetie, I heard. I'm also a nurse," Eileen explained, "just doing time bringing up the babies." Kylie was going to say something but just looked daggers at her mum instead. "Daniel," Eileen asked, "are you sure you don't mind the interrogation?"

"No," he answered. "I like multi-tasking."

He'd managed to get the computer running from its own operating system but there were more problems and asked Frankie again what he'd done. It appeared, after a few pertinent questions, that Frankie had found out about the registry and tampered with it – clever for a ten year old.

"Is she pretty?" Kylie asked, not wanting to let the subject go.

"Pretty as you," said Daniel.

Eileen gave her daughter a hug and told her that Mr Hart had just paid her a compliment. Throughout the questioning, Frankie had looked askance at his sister as though he wished she'd disappear in a puff of smoke. He was so focused on what Daniel was doing and seemed to be trying to remember everything. There was quiet for a while as Daniel ran various diagnostics and then cleaned up about half a million errors.

"Are you sure it isn't broken?" Eileen asked.

"Mum!" said Frankie in exasperation, "he told you it isn't. I didn't break it, did I Daniel?"

"No you didn't," Daniel said reassuringly. He could have advised him to stay clear of the registry and other delicate areas of the computer's nuts and bolts, but he didn't want to get the boy in trouble with his mother nor to scare him off what was basically a healthy curiosity. The three members of the family watched as Daniel's hands flew faster and faster over the keyboard, apparently performing magic.

"You're very clever," said Kylie.

"Thank you," said Daniel. "I wish I was. I bet you can do things I can't do."

Kylie was delighted, and if Daniel wasn't already taken and she only six years old, she might have married him herself.

"Who does your girlfriend nurse?" she asked, ever more intrigued.

"Children," he said, "like you, although you look fabulously healthy to me."

"Is she at the Homerton?" Eileen asked.

"Yes."

"My husband Matt often goes there. Awful lot of trouble. Hard to believe, really."

"I know. Kath tells me horror stories. Now...Frankie, tell me again which programs you had problems with before the machine gave up the ghost."

Frankie showed him and together they persuaded the machine to do what it had decided not to do. Eileen and Kylie watched in a rather pleasant atmosphere of communal healing. Eileen could see that Daniel knew exactly what he was doing and was only asking Frankie to give the boy confidence and get him involved. No wonder people recommended him, she thought.

"Does your husband work around here?" Daniel asked, attempting to deflect Kylie who was gearing up for some more questions about 'Catreen' as she called her.

"He does, yes, more's the pity. He's based at Stoke Newington."

"Right. I suppose he gets to see a fair amount of ... "

"Rough stuff?" Eileen answered for him. "Yes. A few years ago he policed the murder mile. Bad days, but it's calmed down since then – a little. You're not from around here, are you Daniel?"

"No, I'm from up north," he said in a fake northern accent which made Kylie laugh. "Salford."

"You like it here?" asked Eileen.

"I do, yes. I like the mix of people and the energy."

"Ah, the energy," said Eileen, "yes, it's a busy place. What brought you down here then Daniel?"

"Work. Family. Desperation."

Eileen smiled. He was very sweet, not at all the kind of anorak she'd assumed would turn up. He had a quality about him that was very open and affectionate, and he knew what he was doing, even on automatic pilot. She could see he was only half thinking about the job; it was probably second nature to him and he was doing things he did every day, but it was still impressive.

"Family?" she asked. Eileen was becoming as inquisitive as her daughter.

"Not here. All left behind."

"Oh," said Eileen, and Daniel could tell that she did see, ever so slightly, but she didn't pursue that line of questioning, just said "Families can be trying, can't they?"

"Certainly can."

Kylie disappeared for a moment, coming back with a ragged teddy bear in her hands. She sat down with the bear on her knees, appearing to look intently at Daniel.

"This is Arthur," she said.

"Hello Arthur," said Daniel. "Are you interested in computers then?"

"He's learning," said Kylie.

It was all Daniel could do not to crease up in hysterics. The bear had a peculiar look which almost made Daniel believe it understood the gobbledegook on the screen. Kylie's face was a picture of intensity; she seemed absolutely convinced that Arthur was sentient and a budding computer genius. Frankie shook his head and wished his mother and sister would leave him and Daniel to discuss the finer points of computing. He had got over his initial embarrassment and, unlike Arthur, was doing some serious learning.

The technical resurrection process took about an hour and a half. Kylie and Arthur lasted most of the time and would have lasted the whole time, but were told they had to go to bed, an order which Kylie rebelled against, not wanting to leave Daniel, for whom she had developed a soft spot. When Eileen took Kylie off to bed, Frankie breathed a sigh of relief and started asking Daniel all the questions he'd been unwilling or unable to ask whilst Kylie or his mother had been chatting. When Eileen came down again, the computer was up and running and Frankie had a giant grin on his face having learned a lot and not been blamed. Eileen Davis was relieved, in fact she was delighted.

"You're a lifesaver," she said. "I really thought Frankie had killed it."

"Hard to kill computers," said Daniel. "You can confuse them, but they're quite hardy."

"He's a genius, mum!" said Frankie, enthusiastically.

"Yes," said Daniel with a wry smile on his face, "I know. You're pretty bright yourself, Frankie," at which Frankie beamed even more. "I've left a little remote process," said Daniel. "In case anything else happens, I can help without coming to visit – not that I don't want to, but just in case I'm busy and can't get out. Is that okay, Frankie?"

It was fine. Daniel left behind him a household he'd found under a cloud in an admirable measure of harmony and good cheer.

## 6

"Darling?"

"Eileen. Has the computer buff been?"

Eileen told her husband about the resurrected computer. Matt listened, but his answers were distracted; his mind was elsewhere. He told Eileen he'd see her soon, hung up, then sat back, staring ahead at Lea Bridge Road which stretched out before him, lit by a tailback of ruby lights. His partner, Charlene Okoru, drove, a misnomer for navigating the wagon train of cars moving at less than a snail's pace.

Charlene shook her head and said, "You haven't told her, have you?" Matt didn't answer. "What in God's name is wrong with you, Matt? You've got to end it! In fact, if you don't, I will; I'll tell her myself."

Charlene was furious, not a great emotion to have towards your work partner, but she couldn't help herself. Matt was cheating on Eileen and Charlene wasn't the appeasing type. They'd been working together four years and Matt had hoped to find a sympathetic ear, but instead of sympathy he'd received a torrent of anger and rejection. "What the hell did you think I'd say?" she'd asked. He knew what he'd hoped she'd say, but she hadn't said it. She was stunned, and blasted him with some unexpectedly lively invective. "Matt, you idiot, have you smashed your head? Have you gone over to the dark side? Have you lost your tiny mind? Explain!"

Naturally, he couldn't explain. He'd met Cassie on a case. It was all so predictable, but it was the truth, it had happened. Charlene didn't even know the worst of it. She hadn't asked anything about "the other woman". She wasn't interested. All she wanted to know was when Matt would end the whole thing and got back to being the sound and solid man she'd always believed him to be, although she feared he could never be that man again - he'd gone beyond the pale and it was Eileen who was going to suffer.

He realised his mistake straight away. It was a woman thing, an allegiance he hadn't expected. In his own naïve way he'd thought the loyalty she owed him would be greater than the gender fidelity she'd feel for Eileen, but she didn't owe him anything. Their mutual support went a long way, but he'd owned up to an unforgivable disloyalty and Charlene made him pay a heavy price, spitting fire at every opportunity.

"Listen Matt," she said, "we've worked together four years and I thought we'd work together forever, but now I'm not so sure. In fact, I am sure. I can't. I'm going to ask to change partners."

Matt looked at her in disbelief.

"You wouldn't."

" I would. I will," she said. "We're good police officers, Matt, we're even better together, but I can't take this."

"*You* can't? What about me?"

"You? You? Are you kidding? Do you think you matter in all this?"

Matt knew that whatever he said would have no weight. He was in the wrong and on the back foot. Politician's might be able to wriggle out of tight spots,  but he couldn't, nor did he know how to put things right. Even if he ended the fling with Cassie he had the sinking feeling that he'd done irreparable damage to his partnership with Charlene and to his marriage, whether or not Eileen found out. And yet despite all the logic, he couldn't give Charlene an answer because he couldn't fight the Cassie fire.

"Matt," said Charlene, breaking into his wretched train of thought, "if you give me her number, I'll call her, I'll do it for you."

"Eileen?"

"No, idiot, this other woman, whatever her name is." Matt hadn't told Charlene Cassie's name. He hadn't had a chance. She'd jumped on him as soon as she understood what he was telling her. "I'll be kind," she said. "I won't hurt her more than I have to, but I'll do your job for you if I must. This can't go on. It's going to wreck everything."

"Don't you think you're being a touch over dramatic," he said, which was probably the worst thing he could have said. Charlene looked at him in disdain, as if she'd misunderstood him all these years and he was far less than the man she'd imagined.

"No I don't, Matt! God!" She hesitated a moment, thinking. "Look, you know me, I can be tough when I have to be, but I won't scare her or anything like that. I'll just be firm. I don't know what she's like, for all I know she's an angel, but nothing matters except Eileen and the kids. You don't matter in this, Matt. You're part of a bigger plan and you've got to repair the damage. I'll help you if you're too pathetic to do it yourself."

Matt tried to summon up anger but he couldn't. Charlene had every right to have a go at him.

"I'll think about it, Charley."

"What's there to think about? Just do it. Give me her name and address, I'll go see her. Now."

"No, not now."

"Why not now? You've put this off long enough, Matt."

Matt hoped that by delaying the evil moment the whole sorry situation might somehow solve itself. Charlene knew better. He wished he hadn't told her, but she'd known something was bothering him and he'd blurted it out in his need for understanding and advice. Well, he'd got the advice, but no understanding.

Even the lights around them seemed to illuminate his guilt. Here he was, upholder of law and order in one of the most troubled areas of the country and his moral strength had fallen away. He felt corrupted, caught up in an illicit battle he couldn't and wouldn't win. He should resign, but that was impossible. Policing was his life and he loved it. He was even good at it, and he wasn't, he admitted, good at much else.

Car and city lights hid a multitude of sins, and he and Charlene had witnessed most of them. They knew how to handle the rough, the brutal, the crazy, the sad, the demented, the angry, the manic and the despairing. They were psychologists, arbiters of peace and war, promoters of tolerance, yet here was Charlene threatening everything they'd achieved and could still achieve because of one lousy misdemeanour.

They drove in silence for a while, creeping along, stop, start, stop, start. It was just as well they didn't get a call as there was no way to break through the solid flow of traffic. The atmosphere between them was brittle. Matt wanted to tell her to lighten up, that this was the real world they were living in, that such things happened, like it or not - but he couldn't. The words would have stuck in his teeth and Charlene knew it. Something in her background had brought out the moral soldier in Charlene, not in everything, but definitely now. She liked Matt, but he was playing with fire. This had to stop. She gripped the steering wheel, trying not to pull it out of the dashboard in anger, fighting with herself.

The law was everything, she'd known that from childhood. She'd been blessed, or cursed, with a clear sense of right and wrong and what Matt was doing was dangerously wrong, way beyond the pale. This threatened everything she upheld as a police officer and a woman. You couldn't be strong if you were carrying on like this outside of hours, it just wasn't possible.

"I need time," she heard him say.

"You don't have it," she said.

"Jesus, Charley, ease up on me, will you! I haven't murdered anyone. I'm still one of the good guys."

"Not in my eyes you're not. Not anymore. Not till you put things right."

He shook his head. It was like sitting next to a Harpy. But he'd known this in her before, only it was directed towards the bad guys of Hackney, the thugs, the cruel, the arrogant and brutal, never towards him. He didn't like it and didn't know how to handle it.

"Listen," he said, "we've got to be professional about this."

"I am."

"Okay then, just don't make me feel worse than I already feel."

"I couldn't care how you feel," she said, "it's how Eileen feels. And even if she never finds out, it's what you've done. You've betrayed her and the children. That's just as evil as murder, Matt."

"Come on Charley! That's a bit extreme, even for you."

"Even for me? What's that supposed to mean? You're not going to turn this around and try to make me feel guilty, are you? What, you think I'm too judgemental or something?"

"I do, Charley, yes. This isn't a crime, it's just me being...I don't know, weak, that's all."

She didn't answer as there was little left to say that she hadn't already said. Matt sat glumly, trying and failing to put Cassie out of his head. He had a lovely wife, two great children and a steady job, so why he was putting it all at risk with this madness he didn't understand, but he was, and he felt powerless to change it. Cassie held him in bonds of iron; when he thought of her, everything else dwindled to vanishing point, wife, children, job, all of it. Lights ahead and lights behind, but no light to guide his way, Matt Davis was falling, and all around was darkness.

## 7

Cassie Logan counted the notes.

"All there?" the man asked.

"All there," she said, and started to undress.

"I'll do it," the man said in what was more of a command than a request. Some men were like that, others more passive. It didn't matter, provided they paid. After three years of doing what she was doing she'd learned to handle them all, or almost all. There were a few who unnerved her, but not many. Most were family men needing what family life often destroyed, nothing more. Cassie satisfied the need, and satisfied also something restless and hungry within herself. She had no scruples, no reservation at all; she did what she did and she did it well, at least with those who showed some humanity; with the others she was on automatic pilot and made a point never to see them again. She had no time for those who condemned her. In a world where you simply had to work to your strengths to survive, Cassie worked to hers with an unusual measure of commitment.

The world was awash with hypocrisy and, amidst this sea of lies, she saw herself as a beacon of truth and honesty.

Cassie sensed the client's impatience and knew this would be no more than fifteen minutes; he wasn't a customer to whom she would devote more than a modicum of libido. When he'd gone, she slipped on a nightgown and checked her phone for calls - a few, but none worth answering. She wiped them, took a shower, dressed and made up. Her looks were her livelihood and she took care of them. She was stunning, she knew it and lived it, both the blessing and the curse, with the wisdom to know the difference. Studying her reflection, she saw not just God's gift but a furnace forged inner strength.

The doorbell rang. She slipped on a jacket, picked up her handbag, opened the door and greeted Paula with a kiss on either cheek, leaving behind the lovemaking as if had never happened. They climbed into a waiting taxi, ignoring the driver's furtive glances, directing him to a restaurant, saying nothing on the way. Once they were seated in the restaurant, Cassie said, "Ready?"

"Ready," answered Paula.

Paula didn't have Cassie's looks or charisma, but she had a fierce inner strength which she would have used willingly and limitlessly to protect her friend who spoke in a slow, considered voice. Paula hung on every word.

"The first was Monday," she said, "strong but gentle. Easy manners, experienced. I'd seen him before, just once, I think..."

Paula listened but asked no questions. One by one, Cassie told her of each encounter, conveying sensations with surprising skill. Paula never interrupted. The manager arranged for the food and drink to be served unobtrusively, just as he did each week the two women came, sat in the private area and talked. He had no idea what was going on between them, but he gave them what they wanted as they ate and drank well and paid even better.

"Thursday it was a woman," said Cassie. "Shy, but needy. She was older than me, but inexperienced, I could tell. We..."

Paula listened as if she were being told the meaning of life, glancing at Cassie occasionally, but giving nothing away. When the meal was over, Cassie put down her drink and sat quietly.

"And the policeman?" Paula asked.

"Still there," said Cassie. "Shall I tell you?"

Paula nodded and Cassie stared at her wine, saying. "Matt is strong. If you saw him, you'd know he was powerful. I've never met anyone so responsive. He..." and Paula listened again, sipping wine, transported to some mysterious place only Cassie could take her. When Cassie was done, Paula looked at her friend and they both relaxed into real mode. Neither of them quite remembered when this ritual had begun, or how it had developed, but once a month they met like this, Cassie telling Paula about each client, conveying the sensuality which Paula could only imagine.

"Be careful there Cass," she said. "Thin ice."

"I'll be okay," said Cassie. "He's safe enough."

"He's putting everything on the line for a little excitement with a working girl. He can't be safe."

Cassie didn't seem to care. "He adores me," she seemed to laugh.

Paula looked at her friend with concern. She never scolded Cassie for doing what she did, rather she fed off Cassie's life in a vicarious sensuality, but she was worried; policemen were a high level of risk.

They took a taxi some of the way home, but decided to walk a little, despite the dark and the neighbourhood. This part of Upper Clapton Road was noticeably rough, but still well lit. Cassie held Paula's arm and they walked comfortingly close to each other, looking at the shops and soaking up the East Five ambience.

"Was I okay?" Cassie asked.

"Wonderful," said Paula, "as ever."

There was a pause, then Cassie said, "News, Paula?"

"No news. Same prognosis."

It had been three years since Paula had been diagnosed with a degenerative glandular disease. The doctors had given her two years to live, less without treatment. She'd had both treatment, and Cassie's stories; she swore the latter had been more effective.

"Maybe you're beating it," said Cassie.

Paula just smiled. She wasn't beating it, and she knew it.

They reached the Lea Bridge Road roundabout which separated Upper Clapton from Lower Clapton, a separation of equally troubled but equally colourful neighbourhoods. The roundabout was dominated by Hackney College, formerly a school and before that, so the pupils declared, a lunatic asylum, a rumour which led not only to speculation about ghosts, but also about some of the other pupils, and even a few teachers, who might have slotted smoothly into either institution.

They crossed the recently reworked roundabout which now allowed pedestrians at least a fighting chance of survival.

Lower Clapton was noticeably darker and the ambience less welcoming. There were fewer shops and more odd buildings which were a mixture of sweatshops, factories and flats, all giving a sense of financial struggle, if not penury. The two women turned left a few hundred yards before the beginning of Mare Street, heading towards Chatsworth Road.

As they rounded a corner a man passed them, hands in pockets, staring down, abstracted. He glanced up as he brushed past the two women but quickly looked away and walked on. Paula stopped still, looking after him.

"What?" asked Cassie. "Sixth sense?"

"Sixth sense," said Paula.

Since the diagnosis, Paula's life was in a most esoteric dimension. Her perceptive powers had somehow refined and purified, even to passers-by.

"Sorry, Cass," she said. "Bad vibes."

Cassie held her arm for few moments until the man disappeared from sight, then they turned and walked on. Close to home, Cassie said, "Will you be okay, sweety?"

"I'll be fine. Sorry about that."

"No probs," said Cassie and kissed her friend on the cheek, looking concerned.

"Really take no notice," said Paula. "Can't explain these things. Now go easy on the policeman, Cass," she said.

"I will," said Cassie. "Same time..."

"Same channel," said Paula, and watched in wonder, and not a little love, as Cassie walked away.

# 8

Paula didn't go straight home. She checked her watch, decided it was just about okay to call, and knocked on her neighbour's door.

"Hello beautiful ," she said as the door creaked open and a little head poked out beneath the chain. "Not in bed yet?" From within the heart of the house a gruff male voice called out, "For God's sake, Milly, I told you not to...oh, it's you."

The owner of the voice appeared, a middle-aged, ill-tempered man.

"Hello Ivan," said Paula.

" Margot," Ivan called without acknowledging Paula, " it's our neighbour."

Paula was used to this kind of reception from Ivan the Terrible. Her sixth sense had long ago sussed him out as someone from whom she would never expect a Christmas card, not so much rough diamond as battered granite. A woman emerged looking tired and harassed. She attempted an exhausted smile when she saw Paula and opened the door wider. Her daughter, Milly, held her hand and stared up at Paula.

"Didn't want to come in Margot," said Paula, "just to know what's going on with William."

Margot said, "We saw him today and he was perky enough. Melissa called this evening, told us he was sleeping and that Kathryn would call tomorrow. Nothing much else Paula. They're doing their best. He'll be okay."

"Well, that's good news. If there's anything I can do, just ask."

Margot thanked her, closed the door and headed back to the living room, a shabby place desperately in need of some tender loving care, but the same might have been said of the three occupants, all of whom looked equally shabby, though not completely beyond the redemptive qualities of a basic scrub-up.

Milly sat down beside her mother, staring at the television, her eyes half closed. It was way beyond a reasonable bedtime but no one pressed her so she stayed up to be as adult as her mum and dad allowed.

"What did she want?" growled Ivan, lost in another surly mood.

"To know about Will. You could try being nice to her Ivan, she means well."

Ivan didn't answer but turned the pages of a paper he was half reading, buried in his secret thoughts. Margot didn't think that lecturing him would achieve much. He'd only been home ten minutes from a drinking binge so he wasn't in the most sociable of moods, and the last thing they needed was another family row.

There was a pause as flotsam from the television drifted around the room then Margot checked her watch and tapped it in front of Milly.

"Do I have to?" Milly asked.

"Do what your mum tells you Milly," Ivan said in a stern voice, not looking up from the paper.

Milly slipped off the sofa and upstairs into her bedroom. She undressed, put on her Mickey Mouse pyjamas, brushed her teeth and climbed into bed, trying all the while not to look at the empty bed on the other side of the room. This was more difficult than it should have been and she somehow found herself stealing glances at it all the time. She started to read the book that Nurse Kathryn and Nurse Melissa had given her, then decided, though it was quite late, to phone them, or at least one of them. Both worked in William's ward and had given her their telephone numbers, saying she could call if ever she felt lonely. She felt lonely now so she phoned Nurse Kathryn but there was no answer. Nurse Kathryn had said she would always pick up the call if she saw it was from Milly and she always had done, so far, but not now. Milly scrolled down to Nurse Melissa and pressed the call button.

"Milly! What are you doing up so late?"

"I'm in bed."

"Is everything alright?"

"Yes. Can I talk to William?"

"He's asleep, sweetie pie."

"Is he going to be alright?"

There was no hesitation at all as Melissa answered, "Yes, he will be. The doctors here are very clever. They're doing their best."

"Is Nurse Kathryn there?"

"No she isn't, Milly. Do you want to talk to her? Shall I ask her to call you?"

"I'm going to sleep now."

"Of course you are! I'll tell her to call you tomorrow. Will that be alright?"

"Yes."

"Goodnight Milly. I'm working so I'd better get busy. You sleep well and have beautiful dreams. Promise?"

"I promise."

They said goodbye and Milly put the phone down on the bedside table. She tried to read again but couldn't concentrate, so she got up and rifled through her school satchel looking for her diary. Every day they were supposed to write an entry but she hadn't done today's yet. The diary was marked "Milly Orlich, Miss Ellerman, Class 4E." Considering that her mum and dad didn't have a single book in the house and never read any, Milly was surprisingly keen on them. Her bedroom overlooked Chatsworth Road and she and William often looked out at night when they couldn't sleep or wanted to play games, pointing at people, casting spells or generally just being silly. She looked out now, staring up and down the road at the lights from other homes and shops, some of which stayed open all night. Having stared and thought for a few minutes, Milly took out her pencil and slowly wrote the diary entry which she would read out to Miss Ellerman and the class in the morning:

"Dear Diary, my brother William is still in hospital. He is in Alexandra Ward. Nurse Kathryn and Nurse Melissa are looking after him. He looks very sick. Nurse Melissa said he is going to be alright. Nurse Kathryn gave me a book to read. We are going to see him again tomorrow. He is only five. Nurse Kathryn is my favourite nurse but Nurse Melissa is also nice. The doctors are very kind. I can't think of anything else to say. God bless William and make him better."

Milly was putting the diary back into her satchel when the door opened and her mother stood there staring.

"What are you doing. Milly? You're supposed to be in bed!"

"I was writing my diary."

"You haven't even got your dressing gown on! It's cold, Milly, you'll get sick, silly girl! That's all we need, you ill, too! Come on, into bed, now!"

Milly climbed into bed and Margot stood there, watching and tucking her in.

"Mum?"

"What?" Margot sounded both worried and petulant.

"Doesn't dad love William?"

"What kind of a question is that, Milly? Of course he does! Why?"

"Because he doesn't come to the hospital much and he's always angry. I even saw him angry with the nurses once."

Margot sighed and sat down on the edge of Milly's bed.

"Some men are not very good when people get sick. Your dad's like that, Milly. He hates hospitals and he doesn't know how to deal with William being sick." Milly looked puzzled at this explanation but Margot couldn't explain better. "You'll understand when you grow up Milly," she said in that age old way of fobbing off children. Even Milly had heard it a few times before and had unconsciously stored it in memory for the moment years down the line when she might need it herself.

Margot, like Milly, couldn't help but see the empty bed.

"Do you think he's going to die mummy?" asked Milly.

"No, of course he won't!" said Margot. "He's ill and he'll need looking after, but we can do that, can't we?" Milly nodded. "We'll go and see William tomorrow and you can talk to Nurse Kathryn and Nurse Melissa, Milly, and they'll tell you, promise. Everything will be alright. Now close your eyes and go to sleep."

Margot waited a few minutes, looking out over the exotic panorama of Chatsworth Road and touching William's empty bed before seeing that her daughter was asleep. She tiptoed out and downstairs to her grumpy husband.

"She's asleep," said Margot.

"About time. You're too easy with her."

"She needs company. She's upset." Ivan mumbled something. "Do you want to tell me where you've been, Ivan?"

He looked at her as if she'd asked for his soul.

"No."

"You've to keep out of trouble, Ivan." He didn't answer. "We couldn't cope if you got taken away."

"I'm not getting taken anywhere, Margot. Lay off me."

Margot sniffed.

"You mix with the wrong sort, Ivan."

"You don't know what sort I mix with, Margot, and besides..."

"...it's none of my business."

"Right."

"Just think of William before you do anything stupid."

Ivan screwed up the paper and banged it down onto the table top. He took a deep breath as if he were controlling some deep, seismic anger, but he said and did nothing, just looked daggers at Margot who went into the kitchen to get things in order before the next day landed on them with its fresh trials and tribulations. She heard Ivan slump down in front of the television where someone was blathering on about MPs expenses and corruption. Margot could hardly bear it. If the world wasn't a mad place, what was it? Not everything was fair, she knew that, but sometimes it felt as though absolutely nothing was as it should be, that her life was a travesty and that every sound, sight, smell and sense mocked her, laughed at their poverty, their son's illness, Ivan's temper and her desperation.

She was holding a knife to clean. It would be so easy, ending it all, getting out of the firing line. She found herself unable to do anything else except give way for a while to the depression which hounded her day and night. It was an unstoppable tide, swirling around her, a darkness of despair bringing damning words, condemning her, condemning Ivan, condemning them all. The voices laughed at her, told her how small she was, how useless she was as a wife, as a mother and as a woman. They told her to use the knife, cut herself, get out of everyone's way. They were so loud, so insistent.

But she couldn't.

Whatever she felt, whatever her dumb husband did, the children needed her, and no matter how badly life treated her, she would sell her soul rather than abandon them.

She put the knife in the drawer, closed it and hurried out of the kitchen before it became a graveyard for hope.

## 9

Melissa Cochrane slipped the mobile back into her inside pocket. Nurses weren't supposed to give out numbers, mainly to avoid receiving calls whilst they were on duty, but Milly's need seemed more important than the rules. She wondered why Milly hadn't been able to reach Kathryn, and if she hadn't been so busy she would have called Kathryn to find out, but she had too much to do and didn't think more about it.

She walked over to William's bed. He should have been fast asleep but his eyes were open.

"Hello Will! Not sleeping?" He looked at her with the kind of expression which reminded her just why she'd chosen to go into nursing. "I just spoke to Milly," she said. He looked at her more intently. "She says she's lonely in the room without you. She sends you her love and wants to find out when you're going home."

"I don't know," he whispered.

"Won't be long," said Melissa. "Shall I give you something to help you sleep?"

He nodded and Melissa had a word with the staff nurse.

"Are they coming tomorrow?" Will asked after he'd swallowed the tablet she'd given him.

"Yes, they are. They'll be here every day."

"Will Kathryn be here tomorrow?"

"Yes, she'll be here," said Melissa. "Bright and early. Do you like her more than you like me Will?" she asked with a provocative look. William shook his head, even at five years old and sleepy, aware of saying the wrong thing. Melissa stroked his hair, tucked him in and sat for a while until he was in a deep sleep.

She didn't mind doing nights occasionally, but they upset her sleep pattern more than they did Kathryn's. They preferred to work on the same shifts but the rota and staff availability didn't always allow this, so Melissa was on nights now and Kathryn on the early shift at eight in the morning. Nights had their advantages. They were obviously quieter, but there was still plenty to do, making sure all the children in the ward were comfortable and any problems were sorted quickly. This wasn't so straightforward. Children would often wake at night and be afraid in the unfamiliar surroundings with no one they knew, or had had time to get to know. They started crying quickly and tears could spread if others woke. There was also the contentious problem of finishing what the previous shift hadn't finished, as well as making sure all jobs were done before morning. This was easier in the children's than the adult wards as there was less bickering or infighting, but you had to be on your toes when the rest of the country were tucked up and cosy.

Alexandra Ward was beautifully disguised with posters, paper flowers, pictures, toys and books, but it was still a hospital ward. Parents, friends and teachers always brought in new things, so the staff were never short of material to make it colourful and attractive. Being the artist on the staff, Kathryn had started drawing one or two of the children when she had time, and before long it became a regular feature of the ward with a line of portraits along one wall, affectionately called the Rogue's Gallery.

Melissa had met Kathryn at university. They'd been good friends ever since and Melissa had shared their London life with Kathryn, Ursula and Jasmine until she met Patrick, then she'd moved out, Elena had taken her place and now Melissa and Pat lived in the cosy top flat of a house overlooking Springfield Park. She suspected that it wouldn't be long before Kath moved out, too, with Daniel in tow, but time would tell.

For a borough as badly maligned as Hackney, there were some exceptional green spaces and Springfield Park was one of them. With its rolling landscape and views over the River Lea, it was a marvellous urban green spot complete with an impressive range of trees, shrubs, secret paths, fox holes and protected areas, not to mention tennis courts and a cricket pitch. Patrick was a touch on the lazy side when it came to exercise but Melissa and Kathryn went jogging in and beyond the park whenever time allowed. It was easy to cut over one of the bridges onto the Walthamstow and Hackney Marshes if the energy levels allowed. Once there you could jog till the cows came home, which they rarely did.

During these jogging sessions, Melissa and Kathryn would chat about work, love and the state of the world, at the same time keeping up a remarkably quick pace. Kathryn was usually easy company but she'd changed, dramatically, over the past few weeks. Everyone had noticed, but no one understood, not even Melissa. Kath wouldn't open up to anyone. It was a weird thing, but the world seemed somehow duller and less happy when Kathryn was unhappy, as if her moods touched the soul of the planet, or vice versa. Last Sunday, at the start of what was supposed to be a leisurely run, Kathryn had been unusually agitated and still reluctant to open up.

" Kath?" Melissa had asked, once they were a good distance from home. "Are you going to tell me what's going on?"

"Nothing," said Kathryn.

"Nothing doesn't make you look the way you look, Kath."

Nothing. Melissa did a kind of twenty questions. "Is it to do with Daniel?" No answer. "Is he backing away?"

"No," said Kathryn. "He isn't. He's a good guy, Mel."

Melissa glanced across at Kathryn waiting for more, but nothing more came.

"Is it the commitment thing, Kath? I was just the same with Pat, you know, scared silly of it. Women are changing, more to win, more to lose, more choices. It isn't easy."

"But it isn't that, Mel."

They were skirting around Bomb Crater Pond, a symbolic little spot which seemed to suggest that the better side of humanity could triumph over the darker side, quite appropriate if Melissa had only known. The air was still and their conversation stilted, words slipping out uneasily. Melissa sensed her friend's unusual tension.

"What is it, Kath? I'm sure if you told me you'd feel better."

"Not this time."

"Why not?"

Kathryn hesitated. "I can't bear the thought of hurting Daniel," she said,

"Are you planning to?"

Kathryn didn't answer for a while, then said, "I hope not."

"Hell, Kathryn, you're being really cryptic."

"I love him," said Kathryn. "I don't think anyone could love anyone more."

"Then what's the problem, Kath?"

"Can't say, Mel, believe me, I can't."

Melissa wasn't sure whether to press harder or accept the reticence. They ran for a while without speaking, keeping to the green routes which were surprisingly common in this most perjured of boroughs . They jogged south along the river for a mile or so then across a road bridge which led them onto Hackney Downs, near the site of the once famous, now demolished school. The brief fame of Hackney Downs, formerly Grocers, lasted from the forties to the early sixties when such luminaries as Harold Pinter, Steven Berkoff and Michael Caine attended. It had a wonderful reputation for academic achievement in an otherwise ordinary area, founded and funded as it had been by the Worshipful Company of Grocers a few hundred years earlier. From its glory days post war it sunk rapidly to ignominy, failure and eventual closure. There was nothing left of it for passers-by to see, a whole history wiped out by a subtle but destructive entropy.

They stopped on Hackney Downs for a breather.

"You still doing night runs, Kath?"

"Sometimes."

"Shouldn't, you know, bad idea."

"I'll be okay," said Kathryn. "I like nights. The lights are beautiful and it's peaceful. I don't want to go through life afraid of my own shadow, Mel."

"True, but there's no harm in being wary of shadows, Kath. There are villains about, Miss Innocence."

"I know," she said with a surprisingly deep expression of despair.

"Kath?"

"Give me time, Mel."

"Of course I will," said Melissa. "I hate to see you like this, though, Kathryn. You look so desperate."

"I am," Kathryn replied.

"Tell me why," pleaded Melissa. "A problem shared and all that..."

Kathryn smiled. She had a wonderful smile, so natural and gentle, yet this time it was a mask covering something too horrible to name.

"This is very frustrating, Kath. I want to help, you know."

"I know," said Kathryn. "Let's move again, Mel, I need to run."

They cut back to Lea Bridge Road, heading into the old Waterworks where all that was left of the massive engineering construction were piles of brick and stone. Melissa felt Kath's tension but couldn't read her mind or come anywhere near guessing what was troubling her.

They sat down on one of the broken walls, Kathryn staring at the brickwork as if she were reading its history.

"Marathon today," she said.

"Certainly is" said Melissa. "But Kath, listen to Auntie Melissa. You must open up, even if it isn't to me. This is bad, isn't it? I can tell."

"Yes. Very."

"Is it the job getting to you?"

"No. I love it."

Melissa waited, but Kathryn said nothing, just stared at the ruins and kicked some loose stones. Suddenly she looked up at Melissa with such sad eyes that Melissa couldn't help but hold her and say, "Kath, what is it? You have to tell me."

Kathryn took a deep breath and said, "You won't tell anyone?"

"Not if you don't want me to."

"I don't."

"Then I promise."

Kathryn looked down and whispered, as if to the broken stonework, "I'm pregnant, Mel."

This time it was Melissa who was silent. Her eyes opened a touch wider and her mouth formed a few words without letting any of them through.

"Are you sure?"

"I'm sure."

Melissa hugged her friend and was clearly delighted, if surprised. She was sure the news was going to be bad.

"Kath, that's great news! Really! I'm so pleased for you! Does Daniel know?" she asked. Kathryn shook her head. "No?" Melissa asked, puzzled. "Good God, Kathryn!"

"Why should he?" said Kathryn suddenly and rather too loudly. A couple passing by walking their dog turned and looked.

Melissa stared at her friend as if she were babbling. "What do you mean, 'why should he?'"

"I mean 'why should he'," Kathryn repeated. "He's not the father."

Melissa stared at Kathryn as if she were talking nonsense. She wasn't often stumped for something to say, but she was now.

"Let's go," Kathryn said before Melissa had time to think of a reply. "I can't stay still."

She got to her feet, Melissa staring up at her, rooted to the spot.

"Not the father?" Melissa asked.

"No."

"Who is then, Kath?"

Silence.

The Lea Navigation was quiet and calm beside them but it might have been a roaring torrent because Melissa's head was full of a furious, roaring noise. Kathryn didn't answer but ran along the bank of the navigation. Melissa watched her for a few seconds, then jumped up and ran after her.

"Kath! Stop!"

She didn't stop. There were tears in her eyes but she ran on.

"Does Michael know?" Melissa asked.

"Michael! Of course not!"

Melissa felt the Earth beneath her padding feet shifting as she ran. Nothing seemed substantial.

They reached a bench by the waterside within striking distance of both their homes and paused.

"You must tell me, Kathryn, you really must. This isn't a silly secret."

Kathryn's face was red, due partly to the running, but mainly to the effort and fear of the confession.

"Something happened," said Kathryn.

"I got that far," said Melissa, "and I assume it wasn't immaculate conception?"

"Not immaculate at all."

"Not with Daniel?"

"No."

"Kathryn, this is crazy!"

"I know," said Kathryn. "More crazy than you imagine."

"Tell me all, Kath. You must, no question, or you'll go spare. Tell me now."

This was as much an order as a request, but still something held Kathryn back.

"I can't," she said. "I daren't. You have to believe me."

"Daren't?"

Kathryn looked terrified, as if saying any more would bring about the end of the world.

"No, I daren't."

"Kath, sweetheart, lovely Kathryn! What happened?"

Kathryn looked down, miserable and torn apart. A faint light of understanding reached Melissa. "Kath, did this man, whoever he was, force you?"

Kathryn looked blank. Her eyes were watering and her face was red, both with the exertion of the run and with the effort of holding back a great wave of emotion.

"Yes."

"Oh, poor Kath! Why didn't you say something?"

"There are reasons," she replied. "Good ones, Mel."

"Tell me them, Kath. If you can't tell me, who can you tell?"

"No one. Don't be angry, Mel. Please!"

Melissa took her friend's hand and squeezed it.

"Angry? Kathryn, why on Earth would I be angry? Oh you poor

love!" She hugged her friend who rested her head on Melissa's shoulder but said nothing. "Have you seen him again, this man?"

"No."

"Do I know him?"

"Please don't ask."

"I must ask. The police will ask."

"No! No police!"

"Kath, Kath, calm down! Whatever you say, truly, I won't do anything you don't want me to, but surely you must tell the police?"

"No, never!"

They sat staring at the water in the canal and at the occasional barge and boat slipping by. It was all so weirdly detached, as if they were watching a play. But the situation was horribly real and had to be faced, somehow. Melissa thought she knew her friend, but realised that it was impossible for one person to know another completely. Kathryn had kept this terrible thing quiet for weeks! What strength! What madness!

"Mel, I can't have the baby, but I can't not have it," Kathryn contradicted herself. "Daniel would vanish and my life would be wrecked; it's already wrecked. I can't keep something like this secret, Mel, can I?"

"No, of course you can't."

"But Daniel mustn't know," said Kathryn, "trust me Mel, he mustn't know."

"You think he'd leave you?"

"No I don't. Mel. He's the best man in the world, for me, the only man in the world for me. Oh, I shouldn't have said anything. I wish I hadn't!"

"But you have." Melissa took a deep breath, trying to figure out the best way ahead. Nothing seemed obvious. "We'll sort this out, Kath. You're not on your own. Lots of people love you, and Daniel most of all. God, what monster could do this to you!"

Kathryn looked at her with such an air of supplication it almost broke Melissa's heart, but nothing would budge Kathryn to say more. How she'd managed to pretend for so long, Melissa didn't know. To hide such a thing was beyond belief! Melissa didn't know whether to be astonished or furious, but it was impossible to be furious with Kathryn.

During the following week they'd found a few minutes to talk on the phone, but Kathryn still refused to talk, let alone act. It was now Thursday, the weekend was approaching again and nothing had been decided.

Once the lights were out in the ward there was a deceptive

atmosphere of peace where, in the darkness and quiet, children struggled with their illnesses and fears, all unseen. It seemed to Melissa that life was much like that, an illusion hiding deep and frightening truths. She took a few minutes break around midnight in the hospital cafeteria, looking out over Hackney, a sea of lights hiding as much as revealing human affairs. Her attention was captured by a commotion at the entrance to the hospital, but accidents and emergencies were common, in fact it would have been surprising to see a night shift without some emergency admission, fighting, shouting, anger or other evidence of social and personal turbulence.

Troubled by Kath's cryptic half confession, she turned away and, late as it was, decided to give Patrick a call.

## 10

"Patrick?"

"Mel? Are you okay? It's midnight!"

"Fine. Just taking a break. Wanted to hear your voice."

"Here it is then."

"You're so sweet. You in a bad mood?"

"Vile. What's up?"

"Not a lot. I'm taking a quick break. Did I wake you?"

"No. Haven't been home long."

"Busy day at the newspaper of the year?"

"Haha. Yes, busy. You sound down, love. Are you sure you're okay?"

Melissa hesitated, remembering her promise to Kathryn. She skirted the subject, relieved to hear Patrick's voice. Aware that he needed his beauty sleep, she let him go with a kiss gently blown down the lines. Patrick Connelly hung up but didn't get to bed, he got to work. He might have been tired but there was an article to write and a deadline to meet at nine in the morning. His newspaper was hardly the newspaper of the year, but it was his livelihood and he did what he could to make it interesting. He was their chief crime reporter, a post to which the good people of Hackney furnished him with a wide range of nefarious deeds.

His desk overlooked Springfield Park, at this time of night a shadowy landscape with the lights of Clapton hanging low on the horizon. The room served as a study and lounge, even though it was small, with its limited space even more restricted by a sloped, roof-contoured ceiling. It was cosy, as was the bedroom on the other side of the flat with its panorama of the Lea Valley. What their home lacked in size it made up for in character and outlook.

Patrick had been on the staff for four years and was still yearning to scoop the story of a lifetime. He was, deep down, he believed, and despite the cranky exterior, a man of peace, so it was ironic that he should need brutality of one sort or another as food for his writing, but that was the perverse truth of it. He still had aspirations to write something grand; the unfinished first chapter of a debut novel lying in the bottom drawer of his desk proved this. He was just too busy to tackle it, all his creative juices being sucked dry by the demands of work. He wished he could be like Michael, Kathryn's brother, but they were very different people. He'd been appointed a short while after the murders of the late nineties but the gangs were still in place and the threat was still there. In the years since he'd joined, he'd visited all the known hot spots of Hackney and some that weren't so well known. He was a frequent visitor to the most run down estates, the Hackney and Stoke Newington Police Stations, to families in various states of dysfunction and to the local courts. Sometimes he longed for a features editor post where he could focus on the more positive side of Hackney life.

At times he wondered if he'd made the right move. Coming from Cork, he was only too aware of the blessings of the Emerald Isle in comparison to the difficulties of an urban trouble-spot such as this, but most of the time he enjoyed it in a perverse way, discovering the astonishing variety of lives people led and the ingenuity of their survival tactics. It astonished him how they struggled and how much they had to overcome with so few resources. This had made him even more political and militant than he'd been when he'd arrived in London. Yes, he'd experienced a modicum of trouble in Ireland, but had read about it more than seen it. Here, he wrote about it as much as witnessed it.

He was astutely aware of political hypocrisy, a quality which, he decided, was deeply endemic in the English system. He never hesitated to bring his militant slant into his articles, avoiding the rant but not shirking from the deeply critical view he held of some, not all, UK power brokers. He'd decided that the fault lay in their absolute lack of vision. It was easy to mistake political guile for wisdom or intelligence and the public made it all the time. No one voted into office had the vision to change what so obviously needed to be changed. As Patrick reported on the small time criminals, the thieves, the wife batterers, the home wreckers, the educationally disadvantaged, the chronic prison lovers, the immoral, the amoral, the pimps, the bullies, the downtrodden, the greedy, the disturbed, oppressed, poor and unfortunates of every colour crammed into this area of his concern, he couldn't help but develop a sense that something, somewhere in the corridors of power was amiss and wondered how the buggers who ran the show had ever run a bloody empire. Ruthlessness, that was it, hidden beneath a veneer of civility and caring. But they were being found out, slowly and surely, and Patrick was glad to help find them out in his own small way, and to take a little national revenge at the same time.

He might feel jaded but he never lost heart completely. People read his articles - he knew that by the emails he received, intelligent, furious, despairing and praising as the borough sagged under the weight of its own complexity. If only each political sermon could be morphed into money, materials, direction and purpose, Hackney would be up there with the best of them.

He was often elated, imagining that here in this troubled enclave of London lay not so much the problem as the answer, if only the world would open its eyes and see. Here were a hundred nationalities that should be tearing each other to pieces, trading and mating with apparent ease. There was evidently something in the Hackney air that allowed warring factions to forget their ancient rivalries and live as neighbours, colleagues and even lovers. Patrick couldn't quite figure out the critical factor, whether it was penury, mutual interdependence, a common enemy in the government, mutual economic interest, desperation or just boredom. England, Pat thought, had had its fill of war. It had fought itself close to exhaustion so many times that it had completely lost the appetite to do it again, especially as winning seemed to make no difference to losing, and this jaded attitude to hostility rubbed off on everyone, no matter where they came from. The sole business of the country now was business, and this was nowhere clearer than in the sheer number and variety of shops in Clapton, Stamford Hill, Homerton High Street, Mare Street, Morning Lane and the other thoroughfares of the borough. It was a pot-pourri of business acumen.

The crimes on which he reported weren't always centred around money. The article he had to write that night was about a family rumpus. Family rumpuses were, by a million miles, the main catalyst for violence. He tried as he wrote to weave in some thoughts about civilisation and give the readers something to think about rather than a straightforward account of yet another family dispute, but it wasn't easy. He was under instruction to keep the language, style and content simple. Policemen were 'cops', just as many words and ideas were reduced to their lowest common denominator. It seemed to Patrick that anything in the English language needing more than two syllables to describe it was forcibly shortened for mass consumption. He resented this and thought it patronising, as if people weren't capable of dealing with challenging language or ideas. His editor was firm, though; the paper had a certain audience and Patrick had to bear that in mind or find work elsewhere. This hurt. Words were Patrick's life, and to diminish them in this way diminished him and his readers. There was a self-fulfilling prophecy at work. You didn't satisfy anyone by dumbing down their news, you just limited their imagination and insulted them, even if they didn't know it at the time.

He wrote with ease, because the story wasn't complicated. It was, in its insular way, thoroughly familiar, a feud, fuelling the fires of frustration, leeching out in anger, disrespect and violence, this time a boy punched and hurt in Stamford Hill. The boy, though, was from the orthodox Jewish community, and this always sent the wrong signals and worrying messages, even if the culprits were the same old bully boys.

When he'd done, it was around one in the morning. If it hadn't been so late, he would have phoned his friend Chaim to talk about what was going on. They'd met about a year before when Patrick came to Alexandra Ward to see Melissa. Chaim's son was a patient there and somehow Patrick and Chaim got chatting. It was a weird experience for Patrick as he, like most people, looked on the orthodox Jews of East Five as something of an oddity, but Chaim was bright, witty, thoughtful and well read, and he was genuinely interested in Patrick's political views. They spoke quite often and Patrick had been round to Chaim's home a few times to meet his family. He realised quite soon what a stabilising influence the orthodox Jews were in a volatile area. They'd tried to shift their own community about twenty years before, but it hadn't worked out and they were now well established in Stamford Hill. Rarely indeed did Patrick's crime reporting lead him to their homes. There was a relentlessness about their way of life, rooted in ancient beliefs. They might have lacked the spontaneity and creativity of some, but they had a joie-de-vivre that took Patrick by surprise and, most importantly, they gave the area a balance and stability which would have been badly missed if they'd headed for pastures new.

They were a colourful component of the fabric from which Hackney was woven, and this intrigued Patrick, opening up exciting new ideas and revelations about how humans approached life. Having Chaim as a friend was valuable in itself, but also professionally, and the current mess would be a good time to talk with him. He might also have talked to Daniel, Kathryn's boyfriend, but Daniel carefully avoided religion, ducking and diving quite skilfully around his background and looking distinctly agitated if pressed.

Patrick double checked the article then emailed it to his boss and switched off the word processor. He made and drank a delicious hot chocolate, checked the wonderful Lea Valley from his bedroom window and, feeling an acute tiredness sweep over him, lay down, just before the phone rang, as it was beginning to ring in other Hackney homes.

## 11

A few hours earlier, Mrs Lilly Levinson had done some writing of her own. She wanted to thank the nurses for looking after her youngest son, Jonathan. Lilly Levinson was a loving mother, devastated when the boy had been diagnosed with Gaucher disease a year earlier. Jonathan was doing okay, but that was only because the hospital had been so quick to help and cared for him so well.

Chaim and Lilly Levinson had done as ordered in the Old Testament and gone forth to multiply. Jonathan was the youngest of six boys and three girls. Of the nine children, the middle one, Samuel, sixteen, was, excluding Jonathan, the most cause for concern. He was withdrawn, sometimes sullen and always angry. This was definitely not par for the course. As rigid as any orthodox culture must, by definition, be, the children here were generally contented with their lot, all except Samuel who set himself apart from those already setting themselves apart. By now he should, like three of his brothers have been married with at least two point five children, but he was alone and sulky and a constant worry.

The view of the outside world towards orthodox Jews was simplistic and often totally mistaken. To begin with, there were many sects, not just one ubiquitous group, and even within a single postal district of Hackney there were at least four distinct sects, each firmly convinced that they were right and the others wrong. Some were freer to mix and mingle, yet this would hardly be noticeable to outsiders distracted by sedate black suits. Amongst their own, these vestments were as different as Armani from Versace, but it took familiarity and keen observation to spot the difference. It was an admirable feat in a world that offered so many distractions and diversions that these groups could hold themselves together so well for so long.

Lilly Levinson put down her pen and read the letter. She was trying to thank the nurses for their efforts with Jonathan who had evidently fallen in love with Nurse Kathryn at the tender age of five. This was in contrast to Samuel who hardly looked at her, nor any woman, without appearing extraordinarily severe. They tried and failed to question him and make sure his world was in order, but he stubbornly refused to be questioned, keeping his thoughts and actions s private and secret as a close community allowed.

Lilly had taken so much to Nurse Kathryn that Lilly almost invited her to convert to Judaism so that she might marry Samuel and sort him out, if only he were ten years older or she ten years younger. Kathryn, unfortunately, was taken, but what amazed Lilly was that she had been taken by an ex-Lubavitch. The term 'ex-Lubavitch' was almost a contradiction in terms. It was like being ex-human – an impossibility. Of course, in theory everyone could choose their way of life, but in practise life chose them. To think that the beautiful nurse caring for Jonathan was engaged to one of their own threw Lilly into all manner of confusions. She had learned the astonishing truth from her husband Chaim who in turn had learned it from his journalist friend Mr Patrick Connelly. Lilly couldn't see why anyone would want to opt out, the lives they led were rich, happy and supportive, but apparently this young man had done just that and was attached to the beautiful nurse caring for her son. She was intrigued.

Taking a break from the letter, she started work in the kitchen preparing supper along with Lydia, the eldest daughter, all of twelve years. The other two watched, helped when they could and learned all the time. To the outside world the strict allocation of household tasks might be anathema, but it was not that different to what went on elsewhere. Lilly, like many orthodox mothers, worked because she had to work. Chaim wasn't a wealthy man so Lilly worked three days a week to keep the mighty household together. Kosher food was more expensive than regular food, little of which they were free to buy. The strict laws of keeping kosher forced upon them a certain way of living, shopping and eating, and regardless of whether it was sensible, noble, archaic or admirable, it definitely cost more. The wealthier families even had two kitchens, but Chaim and Lilly had just the one, though it was filled with good food, tasty aromas and willing hands.

They ate together every day because they were a family, and generally the meals were amiable and fight-free. The blue touch paper, as ever, was Samuel who was easily set alight and liable to explode, but his younger sisters managed to defuse him more often than not, especially Lydia. This suggested that despite the harsh exterior, Sam's heart was in the right place. The meals were always preceded by grace and ended with a second, longer grace. Like most rituals, it was a tradition geared towards a humbler approach to life.

After this particular meal, Sam excused himself.

"Where are you going, Sam?" his father asked.

"Out," said Sam.

"Where? Not to ..."

"Just out," said Sam, feebly hiding his impatience to go.

His mother, sensing an argument with Chaim, said, "Sam, if you must go out, post this letter for me please, and be back at a reasonable hour. You know the rules, son."

Chaim didn't want a scene, and didn't want to appear unfair, so he let the moment pass. Sam took the letter and got ready.

They lived close by the River Lea near a timber merchant that, once upon a time, had stretched three times as far and as deep, but which had diminished along with the rivers and canals it had served. That part of the timber yard which had been sold was now a quaint, if pricey, housing development. Lilly and Chaim didn't live in one of these, but in a more traditional, older brick house close by.

Samuel hurried out, kissing Lydia who was asking him a dozen questions about where he was going and whether or not he had a secret girlfriend. He didn't answer.

After posting the letter, Sam crossed the Lea Bridge Road into Lower Clapton and into a Turkish off-licence.

"Watcha, Sam," said a girl of about fifteen serving behind the counter. "He's upstairs."

Samuel cast a sideways look at the girl then hurried upstairs, knocked on the door and went straight in.

The noise was deafening.

"Hi Jemal."

"Sammy! Take a pew."

Samuel sat down and watched as Jemal navigated a Ferrari around the F1 Monaco Circuit. The screen was about fifty inches, mounted on the wall and wired to two giant speakers. The noise and super-fast moving images didn't seem to faze either Jemal or Samuel who watched, involved and attentive.

"Smoke, mate?" Jemal asked. Samuel looked to where Jemal was nodding and picked up a half empty pack of cigarettes with the standard bold, black letters which read 'Smoking Kills'. Samuel took out a cigarette, lit it and focused his attention again on the screen.

"Five thousand points and rising," said Jemal.

"I'll beat that," said Samuel, coolly.

Jemal laughed and drove the Ferrari faster.

On the walls of Jemal's room were numerous pictures of pop stars, barely clothed. Occasionally, Samuel took his eyes off the screen and glanced at the pictures, images which would never in a hundred years have found their way into an orthodox Jewish home. What passed through Samuel's head when he looked was, mercifully, locked away in his own personal and private virus vault.

After five minutes, Jemal stopped and handed the controls to Sam who took them without a word, crushed the cigarette in an ashtray, made himself comfortable in the reclining seat and set about topping Jemal's score, which he did with ease.

"You're a natural, mate," said Jemal, impressed. "Shame you can't enter competitions. You'd win hands down."

"Maybe I will," said Samuel.

"What about mummy and daddy?"

"They don't have to know."

Sam had selected a different car and was racing it through the Monaco streets with the skill and composure of a champion. When the race ended, he hadn't crashed once and the points had risen to ten thousand.

"I dunno mate," said Jemal, shaking his head. "I practice every day and I've never done that. I reckon you really are the chosen people. How are things at home, mate?"

"Same as they've been for a thousand years," said Samuel.

"Right," said Jamal.

There was a knock on the door and the girl from the counter came in. She was provocatively dressed, but totally relaxed.

"Hi weirdo," she said.

Sam looked at her then picked up a magazine and flicked through it.

"Come in, why don't you?" said Jemal to his sister Feriha who was already in and sitting down, making sure Sam could see her legs. Sam seemed surprisingly easy both with the legs and being called weirdo, as if it was a ritual in itself, much like saying grace

"How did you do, Sammy?" Feriha asked.

"He won, of course," said Jemal. "He always wins."

"Not always," said Sam.

"So," Feriha asked, "any women in your life yet, Sam?" He shook his head. "No match-making?" He shook his head. "God, Sammy, we've got to do something about you."

"Like what?"

"Get you hitched. No good being a religious computer geek all your life, you know. Definitely not healthy."

Samuel shrugged. Feriha studied him with a look of concern.

"Still a virgin, then?" she asked. Sam blushed ever so slightly. "Yep, still," said Feriha.

"Nothing before marriage," said Samuel without taking his eyes from the magazine he was pretending to read.

"Or what?" Feriha asked. "You go to hell or something?"

"Jews don't have hell," said Sam. "Christians invented hell."

"That's right," said Jemal. "You don't want to argue with him, Feriha, the boy knows his bible."

"I reckon that's all he knows," said Feriha, spoiling for a friendly argument. "So what happens to Jews when they die?" she asked.

"We join God."

"What, in heaven?"

"Heaven's a Christian idea too," said Samuel.

"So where then?"

"No one knows. Maybe Stamford Hill."

Feriha laughed and patted Samuel on the knee.

"You're a scream," she said. "So what did Jews come up with if it wasn't heaven or hell?"

"God," said Samuel.

"Okay, and what about us Muslims? I mean, if you came up with God and the Christians came up with heaven and hell, what did we come up with?"

"Loads of stuff," said Jemal. "You should read more, sis, then you'd be telling us things instead of asking loads of dumb questions."

"They're not dumb," Sam said, unexpectedly taking Feriha's side. "They're important. People kill each over the differences."

"Stupid, if you ask me," said Feriha. "I mean, who gives a monkey about heaven and hell anyway. And by the way, bighead," she said to Jemal, "I do read."

"Oh yeah? Like what? Bunty?"

"Like proper books, thicko. So, Sammy, d'you fancy me, then, yes or no."

"Maybe."

Feriha laughed.

"Did you hear that, Jemmy, he fancies me."

"He said 'maybe'."

"Maybe means 'yes', doesn't it Sam? We can have an inter-racial marriage, make everyone talk."

"They talk anyway," said Sam, who was showing remarkable coolness in the face of Feriha's friendly provocation. "And they kill each other. It's a tribal thing."

"But you wouldn't kill anyone, would you Sammy? You're too nice."

"He kills me on the racetrack," said Jemal.

Sam seemed more at home with Jemal and Feriha than he did in his actual home, despite the jokes and mild insults. On other occasions, Feriha had asked him about his clothes, why he dressed like someone permanently attending funerals, what the fringe thing was around his neck, why he had to wear a hat all the time (except in their house) and a thousand other questions, but for all of this she was never much the wiser. Everyone was weird, she maintained, even Turks. She herself was the most normal person she knew.

He stayed an hour, helping Jemal hack into some dodgy systems and trying not to look at Feriha who eventually left in a huff when she felt beaten by computers.

"She likes you," said Jemal, but Sam didn't answer. He was deep in some intricate hacking code, although deeper still he registered Jemal's words, and a light flickered in some not-so-dim corner of his mind.

## 12

Feriha watched him leave from her brother's window.

"Shame about the clothes," she said, "he's cool."

Jemal laughed. "I bet 'cool' isn't something he gets called too often," he said.

"Well he could be," Feriha said. "He's good looking."

"You fancy him then, do you?" Jemal asked.

She gave him a disdainful look and went down to the shop where her aunt was chatting to Nilgun, Feriha's mother. Aunt Nurcan was in her early thirties, handsome but severe, even a touch scary. She'd never married and, to Feriha, came across as a cold fish, but that may well have been because Feriha was young and didn't know the infinite ways people devised to hide themselves.

Professionally, Feriha's aunt needed a measure of professional toughness because she ran the Accident and Emergency Department at Homerton Hospital.

"Hello aunty," said Feriha.

Aunt Nurcan nodded at her niece and said with a touch of irony, "Working hard as usual Feriha?"

Feriha kissed her aunt on the cheek, waved to her mother and disappeared through the shop door, a twenty-first century sylph oozing independence.

"She'll be alright," said Nilgun. "She's a good girl."

"That's probably what Mata Hari's mother thought," Nurcan said. "Gets more beautiful by the day, though."

"And she knows it," said Nilgun. "You off to work, Nur?"

"I am," she said, "another night in the madhouse."

"I don't know how you do it," said Nilgun. "It's bad enough during the day, but nights? Can't imagine."

"Some nights are quiet," said Nurcan, "maybe tonight will be one of those. I can do with a quiet few hours."

"And your love life?" asked Nilgun.

Nurcan looked askance at her sister but didn't answer. Nilgun never pressed it, but something about Nurcan upset her, as if she was always in some kind of internal struggle. She wished Nurcan could meet someone – it wasn't natural living alone, but she was wedded to her work. Some people were, especially in this odd country where family often came low down in priority lists. Nurcan walked to the back of the shop where they had a small kitchen area. She made herself an espresso but added a touch of whisky.

"I saw that," said Nilgun.

Nurcan had a long night ahead and needed 'a little something' before driving to the hospital. Nilgun was right, the job was hard. Every unfortunate from the nether reaches of Hackney seemed to find their way to Accident and Emergency. What most people would call minor mishaps, some of the patients who turned up considered life-threatening. They were no doubt there more for the attention than anything else, but whatever the truth of their conditions, Nurcan had to go through the professional motions with all of them. The truly serious cases, however, were always self-evident and Nurcan dealt with them admirably. Security had been improved at the hospital but many dubious characters still made their way there, using it for some kind of masonic social networking.

Nurcan came back into the off-license where her sister was serving a young man half a dozen cans of beer. When he'd gone she said, "You lubricate them, I treat them."

"Life's imperfect, sister," said Nilgun.

"Don't I know it," said Nurcan.

The two of them were close, but not so close that they didn't have secrets, especially Nurcan whose whole life sometimes seemed to Nilgun like a closed book. Nurcan lived in the leafy neighbourhood of Hackney Downs, a slightly upmarket Clapton but still a patchwork of rime and sublime. She was the sole professional in a family where retail was king, although Nilgun had high hopes for her children, even Feriha who was bright despite the revolutionary tendencies.

Nurcan often wondered why she stayed in Hackney. Apart from the one glaring reason which only she knew and which no one else must ever know, it was so different from Nicosia. Hackney was a fragmented place, full of people with whom she had little in common. Her people kept themselves to themselves, just like many communities did, apart from her niece who delighted in the unusual. Maybe it was because of these things, not in spite of them. Maybe she unconsciously enjoyed the variety, the unpredictability and the organised chaos of it all.

She checked her watch and said to Nilgun, "Must go."

"Hope it's a peaceful night, Nur," said Nilgun.

"Miracles happen, so I'm told," said Nurcan.

In the car, she called Melissa. They didn't work in the same department but they'd met and were good friends. When they were both on the same shift, Nurcan gave both Melissa and Kathryn a lift, but Kath wasn't on nights that week so it was just Mel. Nurcan was thoughtful on the way to Melissa's house, more than usual for a number of reasons, not least Kathryn's changed state, but she was quiet enough to be impressed by the lights of the borough - not Byzantium but with their own vitality and character.

It wasn't far from Melissa's house to the hospital but it was good to have company before the shift began, especially before night shifts when the world shifted so much, and even when it was just Mel and her mood was glum.

"Any change?" Nurcan asked. "You're still looking troubled."

"Sorry," said Melissa. "Not sorted yet."

Over the past few weeks, Nurcan had sensed tensions. At first she feared that they'd both sensed something and were telling her in their own way that they didn't want this lift any more, but now she suspected it was nothing to do with her at all. She'd asked Melissa who was either unwilling or unable to talk about it. This upset her but she daren't push too hard, for many reasons, some to do with courtesy, some deeper and very private. For her part, Melissa didn't know quite what to do with Kathryn's secret. She thought she'd be able to handle it alone, but all week it had been plaguing her. She needed advice, and Nurcan was probably the best choice, older, wiser, sensible and totally reliable, but a promise was a promise. Nurcan fought her agitation and her wiser judgement, asking "Have you seen her?" as freely as she could.

"A few days ago."

"But you can't tell me what's happening?"

"I can't Nur, honestly." The way Melissa called her 'Nur' was encouraging – it showed friendliness. "She's got stuff going on at the moment."

"Stuff?"

"Yes."

"I won't press, Mel. The job's hard enough without 'stuff'. If I can help..."

"I know. She'll sort it out. Promise."

"So how's Patrick?" Nurcan asked, trying to lighten the mood.

"Oh bejora, the man's doin' fine, so he is," said Melissa in an accent which always made Nurcan laugh. "Working hard at the Daily Planet by day, saving the world by night."

"Lucky you. What would the world be without men to save it?" Nurcan asked.

"Dull, I should think," said Melissa.

Nurcan was never voluble but she felt excluded and frustrated, knowing at the same time that this was unavoidable if secrets were the order of the day.

They were heading along Morning Lane, a misnomer if there ever was one. Even at night you could see very little of any poetic dawn, primroses, country paths or delicate foliage. Morning Lane was a main thoroughfare which Nurcan only took because she needed to get something from the Supermarket, and yet it was smack in the middle of Hackney, close to the Town Hall which lay on the other side of Mare Street, the backbone of the borough. By night it could at least be considered beautiful by the more imaginative minds, and indeed Michael had penned a few lines about it, but really it was a bit of a shambles, a through route for traffic and a hub of noise and business. Because of its wide, curving arm and its location, it had a certain reputation, but you had to be a lover of urban structures to take a fancy to it.

On the corner of Morning Lane was what once had been the Central Library, an impressive stone building that might have been lifted from ancient Athens. Years before it had closed its doors to books as the Library transferred to a more modern glass block close by and opened them instead to concert goers, but the concert goers never arrived and it was currently in a state of flux, much like many of the residents.

You could, with a little imagination, see a river sweeping around a prehistoric Morning Lane, with tribes camped around either bank. You could also imagine horses and carriages clattering along a curve of roughly gravelled road in the nineteenth century carrying gentry from the city of London to their fancy new homes in the fair borough – Hackney carriages were not so called for nothing. You could imagine a whole host of histories for this central heartbeat of the borough, but it was still easy to be overwhelmed by the noise and underwhelmed by the twenty-first century junction of cars, shops and people, all of whom appeared in a desperate hurry, as if by rushing they might avoid attention and give purpose to life; as with much street geography, it had an Ibsenesque function of illusion.

Nurcan picked up what she wanted from the store whilst Melissa waited, pondering Kathryn's story for the umpteenth time. Was she raped? The thought was immensely disturbing, and if it was true then Kathryn had to tell the police, Daniel or both. Melissa was close to doing so herself, but she needed to wait a little longer, talk to Kathryn again, clarify what had happened. Melissa hated mysteries at the best of times, but this was the worst of mysteries and there was no place for it.

"You really are looking serious, Mel," said Nurcan as she opened the car door. "If ... if you told me, you might feel better."

Melissa put her hand on Nurcan's shoulder, gave it a little squeeze, but said nothing until they reached hospital. In the car park she turned to Melissa and said, "I don't mean to be rude or secretive, Nur, believe me. It isn't my choice. Trust me?"

Nurcan trusted her, but was nevertheless frustrated by the exclusion and worried even more about what was obviously a serious issue amongst people she cared for very much.

Once inside the formidable hospital walls, Nurcan changed into her uniform, psyching herself up for the night ahead. At least it was peaceful for a while, giving her time to settle down and enter nursing mode.

## 13

"Hello Robert, back again?"

Robert was resident of the Salvation Army and a regular visitor to Accident and Emergency. He'd been cared for at the Whitechapel branch for almost thirty years, though he sometimes disappeared for months at a time. He slept there during the colder months but slept rough in London when the weather allowed, and sometimes when it didn't allow. He came to the hospital for warmth and for company, but never stayed long and never caused a fuss.

"Back again miss," he said.

Nurcan smiled at the 'miss'. Robert lived in different worlds and one of them appeared to be rooted in his school days. "How are you miss?" he asked.

"Very well Robert. Have you had a hot drink yet?"

"Not yet miss."

Nurcan told a junior member off staff to get the man a tea and biscuit.

"You're an angel, miss," said Robert.

"Will you be alright getting back home again, Robert?" Nurcan asked him.

"I will miss, yes. But it isn't my home, you know that, don't you?"

"I do, Robert."

"Thanks again miss," said Robert as he watched her disappear into a back room.

Robert sat and drank his tea, dunking the biscuit so long that it crumbled and melted. Around him, slowly but surely, patients arrived, one holding her arm, one young man limping, helped along by a friend. A boy turned up with a cut on his forehead which his mother, if it was his mother, had bandaged so badly that little drops of blood seeped through, dribbling down one cheek. Robert watched impassively, then after a couple of hours he got up and went on his way.

He ambled along Chatsworth Road, not really heading anywhere in particular, wrapping his shabby old coat around him, looking at the pavement rather than ahead. There were few people around this time of night but they all avoided him because he looked like the kind of person they ought to avoid. Psychologists had had a field day trying to piece together his life, but he gave little away. He was surprisingly intelligent and occasionally, just occasionally, snapped into normal mode when a bright, even happy persona emerged, but too quickly it vanished again, hiding in some obscure corner of his troubled mind. He wasn't unusual in that respect. The Salvation Army had known many such characters, intelligent but totally unpredictable, as if their minds had been turned into some kind of maze where the unfortunate owner stumbled along, forgetting what they'd left behind and what lay ahead.

Robert was able to navigate Hackney on automatic pilot. Even staring at the ground he knew by some peculiar sixth sense where he was, and where he wanted to go. Some nights when it wasn't too cold, and this night was surprisingly warm, he could walk miles. Walking was his forte. Staff at the SA though that in his months away he walked the length and breadth of Britain, though they had no idea how he survived.

Despite the tea and biscuits, Robert didn't feel much like sleeping. He still had a lot of energy to burn up and was in the mood to wander for a while before heading back to his bed. Almost like school days! If only it were school days, he'd be more together than he was now. He couldn't quite put his finger on the reason, but something, somewhere, sometime had cut the umbilical cord with life. He was aware of it at moments like this, coloured by little acts of charity. Nurse Nurcan was always kind, and it always restored the connection for a while, but never for very long. He didn't think of himself as stupid, just as a funny old chap who didn't quite fit in. The world was not good to people like him. There were systems in place to keep everyone warm, dry, fed and watered, and if you didn't pull your weight in those systems they would let you go, as they'd let him go. He wasn't lazy. He was walking now, using as much energy as anyone, but he couldn't focus it, that was the problem, he couldn't galvanize himself to be what the world wanted him to be.

The streets of London had become his life's landscape, wandering them endlessly, familiarising himself with all the roads until he knew every single one of them. He could find his way blindfolded, he thought, which was a drawback because he liked to lose himself and never could, not any more. Every street was familiar, and yet nothing in those streets meant anything, not a jot. People and their worldly affairs he simply couldn't handle. It was all noise and confusion and allowed him no respite.

He wandered down to the filter beds along Lea Bridge Road then up Chatsworth again through Millfields and along Daubeney Road, in and out of the side roads.

He saw a woman jogging and for some reason this registered with him. He watched her because he thought it was foolish to be alone at night in these streets. Was she mad? Everyone was a bit mad, he knew that, but still, running around on your own at night was just asking for trouble.

"You shouldn't do that," he shouted, but the woman ignored him. "You shouldn't do that. No! Go home! Go on, go home!"

He could hear his own voice and it shocked him. He sounded crazy. His voice was harsh and loud and the woman looked alarmed. She turned away and ran around a corner, but not before he saw how lovely she was and he felt sad because such loveliness had always been denied him. Despite everything, he was still a man, inside, even if no one bothered about him, he still had a heart.

Another few minutes passed and he was back in Homerton, so he turned towards what the nice nurse had called home, under the alley near the school, and would you believe it, there was the beautiful running lady again with her bright green sweatshirt and matching pants, black woolly hat and white trainers. He shook his head and told himself that no one took any notice of him. Even if he knew for certain that the world was going to end, everyone would laugh at him. They could all go to hell then, and serve them right.

He turned and walked away.

A hundred yards past the alley he heard something, and froze. He heard lots of sounds as he walked the streets, because he listened harder than most people and because that was all he did, even if he tried not to, he saw and heard everything; it was making sense of it all that was hard. But he'd never heard a sound like that before, a series of soft, subtle strokes, slicing the night.

He turned and hid behind a pillar box.

Beneath the alleyway, about two hundred yards away now, he could see the girl kneeling down in a strange position. Near was the slender shadow of a man, standing over her like a guardian angel, except that he held something in his hand. Even at that distance, Robert could see it was a knife. One of the girl's hands was outstretched, the other was holding her neck.

"Bad man!" Robert whispered to himself, then again, "Bad man!"

He couldn't move, but inside he was madly agitated, either not understanding what he was seeing or more likely not wanting to understand. An imaginary part of him rushed towards the scene shouting for help, but the real part watched and fretted.

The girl toppled over but the man did nothing. He seemed to be watching. What had he done to her, Robert asked himself. Oh, it was a bad world and this was a very bad thing.

The man took out a camera. Robert blinked; it was such an odd thing to do. Perhaps this was a film and they were actors? That might explain it. But the girl was very still now and the man just looked on. Both were like statues. The man straightened up and looked directly at Robert who hid, trembling and sweating. Had he been seen? Was the man coming for him? What was happening? He held his breath, listening for footsteps, but he heard nothing.

He waited for what seemed like hours, his heart pounding, his head reeling.

At last he peeked around the pillar box.

The man had gone but the girl was still on the floor.

No one else was around. The girl would get cold and ill. Robert had to do something, but what could he do, useless, useless man!

He started to run towards the alley in a peculiar, loping way, stopped half way and turned back, then turned again and slowed when he saw the blood.

"Oh world! Oh bad world!"

Robert muttered these words and more as he saw the girl, eyes staring blindly at him, lying in a slowly spreading crimson pool.

Robert panicked. He looked around feverishly and shouted "Help!

Help! Oh this is so bad. Please someone help! Where is everyone? Why aren't you here? Someone come!" He raved, gesticulating wildly with his arms and looking everywhere except at the dead girl. "What has he done? Oh, such a bad thing! Such a nice girl! Help! Please help!"

No one came.

Suddenly, an idea popped into his head.

"Nurse Nurcan will know what to do! Nurcan is good. I'll go and find her," and he hurried away saying to the dead girl, "I have to leave you, dear girl. I'm sorry!" He started to run towards the hospital, but he was too unwell to run fast and he had to slow down, ambling all over the pavement like a drunkard.

A couple approached but were wary of him.

"Dead!" he shouted at them. "He killed the girl. I'm going to the hospital to get Nurcan."

"You do that, you loony," said the young man with a look of disdain.

Robert kept going, reaching the hospital in a pitiful state, exhausted and almost unable to speak. He'd past other people on the way but none had listened to his ravings and all of them had been wary of his manic movements.

Nurcan's eyes opened wide when she saw him.

"Robert! What are you doing back. Wh...."

"Girl! Dead! Man! Blood! Bad, bad, thing!"

"Robert?"

"Bad thing! Help! Help!"

A security guard came over to see what was happening; Nurcan told him to back away.

"Sit down, Robert. Sit..."

"No. Must tell. Bad bad thing! You must go nurse, go to help! I will take you."

"Take me where, Robert!"

"I will take you. Come with me! Come...!"

"I can't, Robert. I have to stay here. Have you seen something?"

"Yes. I've seen something. Oh bad world!"

"Shall I call a policeman, Robert?"

"Yes, a policeman. Now. I will take you."

Nurcan called the police station on the hospital hotline. Two officers arrived within minutes, Matt Davis and Charlene Okoru. They tried to calm Robert but he was too agitated, begging them to come with.

"Come with you where?" Charlene asked.

"There! There!" Robert said, pointing wildly. Others in the A&E looked on. This wasn't unusual, attention-seeking people putting on an act, especially at night when they had more of the spotlight. Yet this tall, gangly man looked genuinely agitated, and he wasn't mouthing off about the government, ethnic minorities or the like.

"What is it you've seen, Robert?" Charlene asked.

"Her!" he answered. "She was running. He killed her."

"Who did?"

"A man! I saw him!"

Charlene looked at Matt who was beginning to focus more; he'd been distracted when the call had come, in fact they both had been, but they snapped into operation now.

"What did he do Robert?" Charlene asked. She wasn't sure whether Robert was making all this up or not. In the years she'd been a police officer she'd heard so many lies that she came to expect them of people, from  pillars of the community to poor souls like Robert, but he did something which made Charlene, Matt and Nurcan, who was watching, wince. He dragged his hand across his throat, but he did so with a look of utter terror in his eyes.

"Better show us, Robert," said Charlene. "In the car."

Robert walked in between them, looking back at Nurcan but saying nothing. She smiled to try and reassure him, but she felt nervous herself for some reason.

Robert got in the car, a little quieter, but his eyes were watery and he was still shaking.

"You know where to go?" Charlene asked. Robert nodded and gave them directions, but before they had a chance to start the car, another call came in – report of a body in....Charlene looked at Matt. It was the same location. She gave a peculiar glance at Robert, then the car's blue light flashed, the siren  sounded and they raced the short distance to the alleyway.

A couple were there, the woman holding the man's arm, he holding the mobile phone on which he'd phoned the police. They'd both thought of leaving after they'd made the call, but he, being familiar with the wrong side of the law, knew that wouldn't be a clever thing to do. They stood some way away from the alley. Charlene and Matt left Robert in the car and went to look, but they could already see a body on the floor.

Once they were close enough, the first thing Charlene did was radio in their position and request both heavy backup and an ambulance.

"Jesus!" whispered Matt.

Charlene confirmed the call on the radio. She knelt down by the body and felt the victim's pulse. She knew she would feel nothing. This wasn't a traumatised stillness, this was death. No one could survive that loss of blood. The smell made Charlene want to retch, but she couldn't afford the time or the luxury.

"Get their names," she said to Matt. "And make sure the guy in the car stays put."

Matt led the couple away from the scene. They looked the rough sort but even they were shocked, and the woman was in floods of tears. When they reached the car they saw Robert and the man said, "That's him! He's the bloke we saw! Running away!"

Matt looked at Robert and then at the couple.

"He was a witness," he said. The couple looked dubious. Matt took their names and addresses, checking back to see if Charlene was alright. She was on the radio, reporting every detail, making sure nothing disturbed the scene and that she held herself together in what was going to be a long night. Already she could hear other sirens and in half a minute she saw blue lights, many of them. This was the moment of change, when an act of desecration touched the world and changed it forever. Charlene felt it and fought it, doing all she could to keep professional and do the right thing, but she couldn't help glancing at the young woman's face, so lovely, with eyes that minutes before must have been wonderfully bright, now blind to the insanity around her with the light and noise of a wounded humanity come to bury its dead.

# 3:       Blackout

Within minutes a crime scene ribbon cordoned off the area. Two ambulances and three police cars parked close by. People began to emerge from the woodwork of Hackney, the news of a murder spreading through the mysterious grapevine of human communication with impressive speed. A crowd gathered around, although the body had been covered and a tent was being erected to hide and protect the evidence, such as it was. As immune as people were to broadcast tragedy on the media, to see it live created a peculiar camaraderie, as if it took the witnessing of death to reveal the fragility of life and offer an imaginary measure of protection.

The couple who had found the body sat in another car, separate from Robert who they were sure had committed the murder. The woman was in floods of tears and cried even more when she felt that the audience around her was watching. Her partner had his arm around her in an affectionate, supportive way, also aware that he was being seen and judged by a riveted audience. Robert, on the other hand, only wanted to be away from this nightmare, to be back in his bed, alone with his thoughts and free of all the attention, especially as it didn't seem to be of the most sympathetic kind. He was mumbling to himself and looked every inch the crazy criminal, caught in the act, guilty till proved innocent.

Matt and Charlene spoke to some of the people watching, asking them the usual questions, whether or not any of them thought they might have seen something unusual – none had. Even those who lived close by had seen and heard nothing although many had something to say about the stone passageway, particularly that it should never have been built in the first place and ought to be pulled down without delay.

Matt was doing his best to perform professionally, though he felt in Charlene a certain icy manner towards him. There wasn't room for personal problems at moment like this, but both of them knew that what they'd talked about would have to be talked about again.

Jokes were passed around about CSI Homerton and Hackney Confidential, but the humour was always a defence against the darker side of human nature which had claimed yet another victim.

Leading the investigation was Simon Faraday, mid-forties, sound and thorough. He'd seen a few murders in Hackney but he sensed this was different. He'd developed an intuition at crime scenes, knowing what to look for, what to avoid and who was involved, most often youth gangs playing by dangerous rules. This, he sensed would be a hard nut to crack. It didn't look like a gang crime, it didn't have the feel of anything he'd ever known. It was brutal, but in a frighteningly dispassionate way. There was no evidence of struggle. It might have been a surprise, random attack, but there were no scratches, no torn clothes, no hallmarks of a fight. The woman was out jogging, foolish but not unheard of, so she might have been at the wrong place at the wrong time or she might have been headed there for a reason. There was little evidence, initially, of anything, and all this Simon Faraday sensed in a few momentary glances around the crime scene.

He gave clear instructions to do all that had to be done – mainly preventing any contamination of the area and allowing forensics to do their job. As useless as it might prove to be, they had to search for footprints or possibly fingerprints on the walls, anything close by that might help. Hopefully the body would yield clues, but Faraday sensed that the murderer had taken great care to leave little, if anything, behind. It was almost as if the poor girl had run into a knife which had appeared out of thin air and straight away vanished.

This couldn't be true, of course. Someone had done this and the knowledge motivated those whose task it was to itemise and eventually digitise the scene. Faraday, even in his varied experiences, had never seen so much blood. The girl's body had virtually drained and the ground around it was a crimson lake. Whoever did this was a brute. Faraday, a straightforward family man might have understood the mentality of wayward youths, but this threw him. The brutality of it, and the pitiful state of the victim shook him, but he hid the shock and distress as best he could when he spoke.

There were hints of footprints in the dust, but these had already been smudged. The gravelled ground left little trace of activity, nevertheless forensics were there, checking each millimetre of old tarmac and every brick in the supporting walls. The blood was already drying, but the killer had kept clear of stepping into the macabre little lake around the body. A photographer snapped away, making sure no visual evidence would be lost.

Faraday gave instructions and collated all the information, determined to solve the case, despite the lack of immediate evidence. His strength of purpose and understanding came from his roots, set firmly in this sprawling, varied, wonderful borough. He was a Hackney Boy, finding himself at a murder scene next to, of all places, the site of his old school.

It was all Faraday could do to separate his professional self from his boyhood, traumatic days in an amalgamated school wrought by tremendous social change and turbulence. His memories were not of 'pride-in-the old-school-tie' variety. He'd achieved what he'd achieved in spite of his education, not because of it. He'd seen his schooling mauled by those motivated by anger, ignorance and violence. He'd seen good teachers brought to their knees by a system stacked up against them and watched as authority and respect were dashed away, unwelcome values in a not so brave new world. He had had to fight past every conceivable obstacle to be what he wanted to be and to restore a semblance of order from chaos.

He'd done all this, and yet here he was now, by the site of the long gone school, witnessing yet more spite and wickedness. Sometimes he feared he was losing the battle, that no matter what he did or what anyone did, his beloved borough was in terminal decline. Other times he saw the effort ordinary people made to build lives and bridge supposedly unbridgeable cultural gaps and he found renewed motivation. He was determined as he took in this scene of death and desolation to find the madman who had done this. It wouldn't be easy.

The victim had no papers on her. She was dressed in a track suit and had been out jogging, assuming the prime witness was telling the truth. Why on Earth she'd chosen this isolated spot, Faraday could only guess, but there were often, if not always, reasons for choices. Faraday sensed that this was not a random attack. He could be wrong, such a thing had been known, but he felt something more here than pure bad timing.

If the prime witness was to be believed, there were some odd behaviour before and after the killing.

"Robert?"

"Yes sir?"

He sounded afraid and tired. His night had taken a terrible turn and he feared for the future, doubting he could ever cast the image of the murder from his mind, or worse, never get people to leave him alone again. Like now, all he wanted was to go back to bed and sleep, but here was this policeman asking him questions, questions, questions.

"I'm Detective Inspector Faraday. This lady here will take notes," he said, pointing to a crime scene officer sitting in the front seat. "I know you've had a word with a policeman already but would you mind talking to me, too? It's important."

Robert shook his head. Faraday, sitting beside him in the back seat of the car, wasn't sure if he meant 'No, he didn't mind' or 'No, he wouldn't talk.'

"Tell me what you were doing first of all, Robert."

"I was walking." Faraday didn't press this. He knew enough about those who fell through the sieve of society not to ask Robert why he was out walking late at night. "I'd been to the hospital."

"Really? Were you ill?"

"No. There's a nice lady who give me tea and is kind."

Faraday took a deep breath. Little acts of kindness amidst the horrors made such a bizarre collage of life.

"Okay. Do you know her name?"

"Nurse Nurcan."

"Good. When you left her, where did you go? Straight here?"

"I walked. I like walking."

"Anywhere in particular?" Robert shook his head. "So you came here by chance?"

"Yes."

"What did you see when you came this way, Robert?"

"I saw them. I was over there."

Robert pointed to the spot near the pillar box where he'd hidden.

"Them?"

"The man was waiting."

Faraday listened carefully.

"You're sure?"

"He was waiting. He was leaning against the wall."

"Could you see his face?"

"No.

"But you could make him out?"

"I saw someone waiting."

"But you couldn't describe them?"

"No.".

"And the girl saw him?"

"Yes."

"How do you know?"

"She slowed down."

"Really? And then?"

"She carried on."

"Into the passage?"

"Yes. Then she stopped."

"Did they do anything?"

"No. They just looked at each other."

"They didn't speak?"

"I think so, but I couldn't hear."

"Did they fight?"

"No."

"But something must have happened?"

"She tried to go past him."

"Did she?"

"Yes."

"And?"

"He wouldn't let her. He took out a knife. I saw him."

Robert was getting very agitated and Faraday calmed him down, easing up on the questions for a few moments. When Robert was still again, Faraday asked him to describe exactly what he'd seen, which was all in shadow, like a macabre silhouette. He could give no details. There was a chance Robert was lying, but Faraday didn't think so. He had an instinct for lies and didn't believe Robert was faking. The man was insecure and struggling, but he was probably telling the truth. Faraday pressed him a little further then corroborated the address he gave, asking an officer to phone the Salvation Army hostel. He decided also to bring Robert back to the station. Robert didn't like this.

"Please, I want to go home!"

"We'll take you home later, Robert, but you've seen something very important and we need to make sure it's true."

"It is true!"

"I believe you. Maybe you can help us catch the man that did this."

"Bad man."

"Yes. Very."

Most things Faraday dealt with could be classified as 'bad'. It went with the job. For this particular crime, 'bad' seemed a trifle weak. Everyone at the scene, as accustomed as they were to dealing with brutality of one kind or another, was shaken. Worse, whoever had done this was still 'out there' with knowledge of what he'd done and the capacity to do it again.

Knife crime was hardly news any longer. But this, Faraday saw, was not the 'usual' knife crime. This suggested something deeply disturbed and deeply personal. It was possible to become immune to the waste and cruelty of crime if you saw enough of it, but Faraday had managed never to lose his sense of outrage. This murder outraged him more than most because he sensed a deep seated and callous hatred behind the attack. The girl's neck had been severed with one blow. The blow had been aimed firm and true and executed with strength. Anyone could see that if they had the stomach to look.

Robert wanted to look.

"Why?" asked Faraday.

"When I saw her run, I thought...I thought..."

"What did you think?"

"I don't know. I want to see what he did."

One of countless lessons Faraday had learned was that people were unpredictable. Robert wanted one moment to get away from the scene, the next he wanted to see the body. Faraday led him into the tented area. Robert put his hand to his mouth, but he didn't turn away.

"You okay, Robert?"

He nodded but he evidently wasn't okay at all. Faraday gently led him back to the car, Robert shaking his head, mumbling and anxious,

## 2

There had been no point in taking the body to accident and emergency. It was taken, when all the necessary forensics were done, to the mortuary. Faraday went with Robert and two officers, Okoru and Davis, to Accident and Emergency to speak with the nurse Robert had mentioned and the two officers had seen. Other officers could have gone with him, but Faraday chose these two because he knew something was going on between them. This wasn't guesswork but having his finger on the pulse. No one knew exactly what was going on, but people had noticed a difference in the way they worked together and it wasn't for the best. They were good officers and Faraday wanted to make sure they didn't wreck their careers. He also wanted them focused on this case and not distracted by personal matters. When he had a chance he would challenge them. He just hoped it was a temporary distraction and nothing more. Whatever it was, a case like this had to push it to one side.

They left the scene, still cordoned off and with many officers of one kind or another working there.

"You feeling alright Robert?" Faraday asked.

Robert nodded, but looked troubled. They assumed it was either through what he had seen - or what he had done, if he was lying, which they doubted. To all three of them he seemed more like one of life's victims than aggressors.

They reached the hospital and found Nurcan. Although Okoru and Davis had already confirmed the first part of Robert's story, it had gone a step further with the finding of the body and was about to take a huge step further.

Faraday told Nurcan what they'd found and she listened patiently. It saddened her but there was so much violence around that she knew how to deal emotionally with yet another anonymous murder. She confirmed, as both officers had done, where Robert had been and what he'd said. Faraday thanked Nurcan and they turned to go, but Robert held back.

"Come on chum," said Davis, "time to go."

"I think I see her here," said Robert.

He was staring at his shoes and fiddling with his fingers, deep in thought. The others looked at him, not quite sure what he was saying.

"What's that, Robert?" Nurcan asked.

"I think I see her ... here," he said, "with you."

Nurcan stared at him, wondering if she'd misheard or if Robert was rambling, which he sometimes did.

"With me?" Nurcan asked. Her face had changed; the anonymity of the murder was threatening to become personal.

"Why didn't you tell us back there?" Faraday asked.

"I just remember," said Robert, "when I see Nurse Nurcan. And there...there..." he pointed, because the scene they'd just left was too horrible to describe and the sentence trailed away.

"Do you mean she was a patient, Robert?" Nurcan asked.

"No."

Nurcan felt uneasy and her throat went dry. Hopefully Robert was wrong. She'd seen death at the hospital enough times to know that it altered features, and Robert wasn't the most reliable witness. He must be muddling up his memories.

"Would you ... would you come and see the body?" Faraday asked her, hesitating because he feared this all being too close to home somehow. "I'm sure he's wrong, but if we can identify her, well, you know...."

"Yes, of course," Nurcan said. She was sure, now that she'd had a moment to think, that Robert had made a mistake. The chances of it being someone she knew were remote. She gave instructions to her staff making sure her absence wouldn't throw the system into chaos then gathered herself so that she was psyched up for this unexpected trial.

They made their way to the Pathology department, an odd group of five people each of whom felt the terrible potential of the moment, for each other, for the hospital and for others, all of whom would be in blissful ignorance of how their lives had already changed. Faraday saw it every time there was a murder. The newspapers wrote a brief report and then it was forgotten, but those directly involved, if they had any sensibility at all, would have to reshape their lives – and some simply couldn't. Such sudden losses also triggered unexpected changes in personality and relationships. Faraday had seen all manner of responses, many of them selfish and indulgent, but many heart-breaking. You never quite knew how friends and family would respond – he didn't know himself how he would react if anything happened to his wife or his children. He tried not to think about it, but it wasn't easy. This nurse, Nurcan, seemed a good sort; Faraday hoped she wouldn't know the victim or that it was on a distant, professional level. The sooner they identified the victim the better, but this was all too close to home and unexpectedly sudden.

The body was already in cold storage and they had to get permission from the duty officer to assist with the identification. The duty officer who allowed them into the appropriate room was a friendly woman with gentle eyes, used to looking on the dead as much as the living. She unlocked the compartment and slid out the body which was covered in a white sheet.

The five of them gathered around, Nurcan in front, Robert beside her, the three officers around them.

"Ready?" the duty officer asked.

She gently lifted the sheet allowing Nurcan to see the face.

Even with all the training and experience in the world, there was no way Nurcan could have

seen what she saw without a reaction. Her face paled, her right hand went towards her face and forefinger and thumb pinched the top of her nose. She closed her eyes and held her breath, not willingly, but simply unable to breath. A hand rested on her shoulder, but it wasn't Faraday or Davis or Okoru, it was Robert who, sensing her acute distress, gently reached out to offer comfort.

"Nurcan?" Faraday asked.

She nodded, ashen faced and in a state none of them could remotely imagine. She spoke with a husky voice that was all but breaking.

"Her name is Kathryn Hudson. She's...she was a nurse here, in one of the children's wards - Alexandra. She ... she ..."

Nurcan's voice seized up. She felt feint and they had to lead her away from the body which was gently returned to the freezer. The duty officer took Nurcan to a side office where she sat down, desperately trying to control herself. Robert didn't seem to want to leave her side and remained perfectly still, his heart crying for Nurcan who was always so kind to him, but also for the world which allowed such things as this to happen.

Faraday moved away from them and called his office where a small emergency team had been assembled. He whispered so that Nurcan wouldn't hear, telling them what he'd just learned and giving instructions what to do next.

"How are you?" he said gently when he'd finished the call.

Nurcan was in a state of utter shock. She nodded and said she was okay but she evidently wasn't. No one who knew Kathryn would be. This was the hardest part of Faraday's job, and had to be handled with great sensitivity. He asked her if there was anyone in particular that Kathryn was friendly with in the ward or in the hospital.

"Melissa Cochrane. She's a nurse in Alexandra Ward. She's on now. I know because I gave her a lift in to work this evening. They were friends. We were all ... friends."

"We'll tell her," said Faraday, writing down Nurcan's answers. "Anyone else?"

Nurcan looked at Faraday and he saw something in her eyes which he couldn't explain. He'd seen shock in the eyes of many people, but was still surprised by the intensity of this nurse's reaction.

"Her boyfriend, Daniel Hart," said Nurcan, "and her flatmates. Melissa has all their numbers. Inspector?"

"Yes."

"Kathryn was the kindest, loveliest lady. They'll be torn apart, all of them."

Faraday nodded and, like Robert, put his hand on her shoulder.

"We'll talk to them all," he said softly, knowing how hard this would be and calling on all his professionalism to act rationally rather than emotionally. "Robert," he said, "I'm going to ask some officers to take you to the station." Faraday was expecting an objection but Robert's own distress was secondary to Nurcan's and those who were about to learn of their friend's death, so he said nothing, and this put him in Faraday's good books. "I'm sure you've done nothing," Faraday added, "but we need to speak to you a little longer. You'll be okay at the station, Robert."

Robert kept looking at Nurcan but said nothing. Faraday called for two officers who arrived within minutes. They'd already had instructions about what to do and prepared to take Robert with them. He seemed reluctant to leave, not because he wanted to go to his own dormitory at the Salvation Army but because he felt extraordinary pain for the nurse and didn't want to leave her. It was only when she somehow managed to smile at him and tell him to do whatever the inspector asked that he went, looking crumpled and agitated.

Faraday had a quiet word with Officers Davis and Okoru.

"You two up for this?" he asked. They were. "I'm not unaware that something's going on between you two," he said. Both of them looked shocked. How on Earth did he know, and what exactly did he think? "But this case takes priority over everything. Understood?" They understood. "I want you around me all night. Can you handle that?" They could, though Matt Davis needed to phone home and explain. "Nurcan?" he asked. "Do you want to go home?" She didn't. She definitely didn't. She needed to be there for Daniel, Melissa, all Kath's friends and the hospital teams when they were told.

Faraday got to work. He called the duty registrar, explained briefly what had happened and suggested a meeting with a few key people immediately. This was arranged.

They left the pathology department heading towards the hospital main offices where one of the registrar's rooms had been readied. Some chairs had been brought in and placed around an oak table. People started to arrive – two registrars, Keith Northcote and Daphne Rowe, both in their forties, the staff nurse of Alexandra Ward, Belinda Adams, and Melissa who looked puzzled but not unhappy. Whatever anyone knew, she'd guessed nothing. She'd seen some activity from the window a little earlier when she spoke to Patrick, but there was always activity at Homerton Hospital so she'd thought nothing of it. Belinda, a West Indian woman with a quiet and kind manner also looked perplexed.

When Melissa saw Nurcan, she smiled, but Nurcan didn't know how to respond. She looked away, trying not to betray any emotion, standing next to Charlene Okoru. The two officers and Nurcan preferred to stand. So did Faraday. The registrars, the staff nurse and Melissa sat and waited.

"Thank you for coming," said Faraday. "My name is Detective Inspector Simon Faraday. I won't beat around the bush. I'm afraid I have some bad news."

Melissa listened but couldn't come anywhere near guessing why she'd been called. She thought that a patient might have been hurt or there'd been some damage done to hospital property. She still felt quite detached and safe.

"A little while ago, a member of your staff was attacked."

And still nothing, no connection.

"Who?" asked Belinda.

Faraday took a deep breath and said, in something of a whisper, "Kathryn Hudson."

At last, some recognition. Melissa didn't think but just reacted.

"Kathryn! But...what happened? Where is she?"

Faraday cleared his throat and said, "As I say, she was attacked."

"Attacked?" Melissa asked, puzzled. Was she badly hurt, inspector?"

At this point, Nurcan came over to Melissa and sat down on the empty chair beside. She took Melissa's hand and squeezed it.

"How badly, and where is she?" Melissa asked, an edge of concern in her voice now.

"She's here," said Faraday.

"Where?" asked Melissa. "I want to see her."

"That's not possible."

"Why? Is she in intensive care? Belinda, we can go there, can't we?"

Belinda, less close to Kathryn than Melissa thought she understood, but she still said, "Yes, we can. Inspector?"

"She's not in intensive care," said Faraday. "Look, there's no easy way to say this. The attack was fatal. I'm terribly sorry, Belinda, Melissa, I know this will be hard to understand but Kathryn is dead."

A silence hit the room that was not like any silence Melissa had ever known. It was as if the world had stopped turning for a few moments and everything had been shifted before it would start to turn again. She felt horribly sick and giddy and gripped Nurcan's hand. Nurcan had her arm around Melissa's shoulder and held her gently but firmly. Melissa stared around at the few people in the room, trying to read doubt or error, but all she saw was confirmation.

But of what?

Kathryn dead? Kathryn? She said the name over and over but to link it to death made no sense. There was no one on Earth as full of life and joy and love as Kathryn. It was a contradiction in terms and a breach of reality to say she was dead. Melissa shook her head and said, "I need to see her."

"That's possible," said Inspector Faraday, "in a while. We need you to be strong, Miss Cochrane."

"I am strong. I...I...just don't get it."

No one 'got' death straight away, Faraday thought. How could they? Life was all we knew. We saw people every day, month after month, year after year. We're duped into believing in permanence, but there's no such thing. He could almost see inside Melissa Cochrane's mind, watching images and ideas move like tectonic plates, trying to reform after a massive shift. There was little more he could do to help, except be rational and professional as was expected of him. Melissa's colleagues and friends would rally round, in time. A death such as this was intolerably cruel.

Melissa thought she ought to phone Kathryn, that would sort this mess out, or she could get Belinda to call her in, show everyone that this was all some ghastly mistake. But the people around the table were all sensible and reliable, they wouldn't all be under the same misapprehension.

"Was there an accident?" she asked, more by way of conversation than belief.

"No," said Faraday, "as I said, she was attacked."

"Attacked? Who attacked her? That's ridiculous. Who'd want to hurt Kathryn?"

"We don't know," said Faraday. "There was a witness, but he was far away and it was dark."

Melissa had more questions but she felt too confused to ask them all. "Look," said Faraday, "what we have to do is decide how best to tell people, family, friends, colleagues. Melissa, we'll need your help."

"Help? Yes, of course."

Melissa was in a dream. She gripped Nurcan's hand and tried to hold herself together.

"Right," said Faraday. "Daphne, Keith, you'll handle the hospital side of things." They nodded, both looking shell shocked. "Melissa, Nurcan – Officers Okoru and Davis will help you contact Kathryn's family and friends – if you're willing?" They were, even though both were struggling to come to terms with this new and terrible reality.

"Inspector?" Melissa asked. "Where? And how? I mean..."

Faraday was very gentle. "I won't go into too much detail," he said. "There will be a post mortem..." Something sprang into Melissa's mind and she looked frightened. "Is that alright?" Faraday asked. "Are there religious objections?" Melissa shook her head, but she'd have to deal with this. God! "Well, that will be in the next couple of days," said Faraday. "There'll be an investigation which I'll be leading," he said. "We'll catch the person that did this, and in that respect, Nurcan and Melissa, I will have to ask you questions. They'll seem impertinent and they'll hurt, but we'll need to know."

"Did *what*?" Melissa asked. She needed to know. "Was she shot? What happened? Where?"

Faraday said, "No, she wasn't shot. The killer used a knife."

"Oh Kathryn!" Melissa gasped. The thought of her friend being attacked with a knife sickened her.

"Where?" she whispered.

"Not far from here. Near the old school site."

Melissa couldn't cry. The implications of what was being said was beyond simple tears. How would she tell Daniel? And Michael? She sat still, stunned.

"I want to see her," she said. "Please."

Faraday nodded at Charlene and said quietly, "Okoru, will you have another word with the duty officer? See if it's possible." He then turned to the group and said, "I'm sorry if this is a bit brief. I need to get back to the station and organise the investigation. I want to tell you how involved I am and that I will put all my energies into catching this person. The next few days will be very hard but I'm sure you'll give comfort to each other and to Kathryn's friends. I'm certain she had many, but she might also have had an enemy, so however difficult emotionally it is for you and the people you tell, do remember this is a murder and that the murderer is out there and we don't, of course, want this to happen again. They'll be a hot line set up so you'll be able to get in touch without delay, and if there's any problem, ask for me. I may come back and talk to the whole staff at some point, if that's okay?" Daphne said it would be fine; anything at all to help catch whoever had done this horrific thing.

Any murder was a violation of something sacred, but Faraday had already got the impression, even from the few friends and colleagues he'd just met, that Kathryn Hudson appeared to have been special.

"Would anyone like to ask me anything before I go?" he said.

No one had any questions. All of them were in a state of bewilderment, typical of those in receipt of such news, but also unique because Kathryn had touched them in so many different ways. The news, too, was, as yet, virtually confined to that one room. Beyond it the world turned as before and people who knew Kathryn were either asleep or unaware of what had happened. It felt like the eye of a vicious storm about to break.

Faraday left and Melissa stayed with Nurcan and the two officers.

The first thing she wanted to do was see the body.

"It's her," said Nurcan. "I've ... seen her."

"Please," Melissa said to Charlene, "let me."

The duty officer made allowances because this was an exceptional situation.

They were led again to the mortuary, Melissa walking as if in some devilish nightmare. Nothing seemed real. The very walls of the hospital threatened to melt away.

Her reaction on seeing the body was different to Nurcan who hadn't known who she would see, so was unprepared. Melissa had steeled herself, but nevertheless she was almost broken when she saw her best friend cut down, cold and still as marble. She put her hand to her mouth and closed her eyes, holding on to Nurcan for support.

Charlene and Matt left them for a few minutes, Charlene using the time alone with Matt to whisper, "If this doesn't change you, nothing will."

"What do you mean?" he asked.

"I mean this is life, love and death. It isn't lies and cheating and messing about with some tart and disrespecting your wife and kids!"

"Not now, Charlene. Jesus!"

"Especially now," said Charlene. "This is a lesson, about how to live. Don't you get it? Are you really that stupid?"

"I get it," said Matt, quietly. Whether he got it enough to do what he had to do, Charlene wasn't sure, but either way she'd drop him as a partner. She couldn't believe Faraday thought there was something between them! That was so embarrassing! And everyone talking? What were they all saying? The thought made her angry, as if she were being compromised by her partner's foolishness. That wasn't right. "We've got to keep focused on this case, Charlene. Can't afford to let our argument get in the way."

"It won't," whispered Charlene as Melissa and Nurcan came out. "How are you?" she asked Melissa. Melissa looked white and drawn and she couldn't answer. "We'd better start telling people," said Charlene. "I suppose there are many friends?"

"Quite a few," said Melissa. "I don't really want to tell any of them."

"They have to know," said Charlene. "The best thing would be to call them from here?"

"I don't know," said Melissa. "I'm not sure what to say."

"Why not tell them to come here now," said Nurcan. "Tell them there's been an accident and they need to come to the hospital."

"Look," said Charlene, "if you give us the addresses, we'll go around and pick them up, some of them, anyway."

Arrangements were made for letting people know, Melissa giving out names and addresses in something of a stupor, feeling increasingly sick moment to moment. She wanted to speak to Pat more than anyone else, touch base and make sure he was well. She had this sudden fear that everyone she knew was in danger, that they would all suddenly vanish and she would be left alone and friendless in a dangerous universe. Nurcan held her arm, but it was hard to know who was supporting who. Both women were stunned, not just by the sight of their lost, brutalised colleague and friend, but by secrets which weighed on them heavily, secrets which had been hard enough to keep in life, but in death would be forced out, one way or the other, with consequences that would have to be faced.

## 3

It was Ursula who picked up the phone.

"Hello!"

"Ursula?"

"Melissa?" Ursula sounded hoarse and confused. It's two in the morning! What's going on?"

"I'm at the hospital."

"I know that, Mel, you work there for God's sake. What's wrong?"

"There's been an accident."

"What? Are you hurt?"

"I'm fine. It's Kathryn."

"Kathryn...?" Ursula was going to say that Kathryn was in her room, but they hadn't checked when they got back from the wine bar. "What happened, Mel? Is she alright?"

Pause, then, "Not really."

"What do you mean, 'not really'? Is she badly hurt? What happened? Was it a car accident? Tell me!"

"I'd rather tell you here. Can you come?"

"Jesus, Mel! What's going on?"

"Trust me. Come."

"Shall I get the others?"

"Yes."

"Mel?"

"What?"

"Is Kath alright?" Silence. "Hell! We'll be there, Mel. Where will you be?"

"In the registrar's room. Daphne Rowe. Second floor."

"Have you told Michael? Daniel?"

"They'll be here."

"Mel!"

"I know. See you soon?"

"Are you alone there, Mel?"

"No, Nurcan's with me. A friend."

"Okay. Keep cool, Mel. Won't be long."

Ursula put the phone down and stared at it as if it was something she'd never seen before. Kathryn hurt? Really hurt? Melissa sounded dreadful. Ursula took a deep breath and pushed open Jasmine's door.

"Jas! Wake up girl, now!" Jasmine moaned, turned and was about to shut her eyes again when the light went on and Ursula said in a loud voice. "No more sleep. Trust me. Up!"

"Ursula? What's wrong? Is there a fire?"

"Accident. Kathryn's hurt."

"What?"

"Dressed. Now."

She went into Elena's room and did the same thing, pushing the bed and rousing a very sleepy Elena.

"Hey! What's the time? What's going on?"

"Elly, it's me, Ursula. Up!"

"What?"

"Kathryn's in trouble."

"What kind of trouble?"

"Tell you when you're dressed. Do it quickly."

The three of them, still in something of a stupor, got themselves as together as they could.

"Who told you?" Jasmine asked.

"Mel called."

"What did she say, exactly?" asked Elena.

"That there's been an accident. Kathryn's hurt."

"Badly."

"Hey, would Mel tell us to shift our arses in the middle of the night if Kath had twisted her ankle or something. This is bad, girls. Let's go."

Not too many hours before they'd driven the roads of Hackney in almost adolescent abandon. Now they sat still and anxious, wondering what had happened to their friend and flatmate.

"Shall I call Mel?" Jasmine asked.

"We'll be there soon," said Ursula. "She said she had to make some more calls. She sounded pretty far out."

Elena and Jasmine looked at each other, not knowing what this meant and refusing absolutely to think the unthinkable. Their minds raced, thinking Kathryn had been hit by a car, hurt at work, fallen, something, anything that gave their fears a little shape, but also a little hope.

Melissa phoned Patrick.

"Pat?"

Tired voice. Puzzled voice. She told him half the story just as she'd told Ursula and the others half a story. She couldn't tell him the truth. She felt that if she avoided telling him what had really happened, then she might change things. Reality might shape itself around her hopes and words rather than around this horror.

"I need you to do me a favour."

"You're my girl, Mel. Tell me."

"Go to Daniel's house. Wake him. Bring him here."

Silence.

"Mel?"

"Don't ask, Pat, please. Do it now. Quick. Really quick!"

She gave him the address and said she loved him. Patrick dressed in the same stupor as Kathryn's flatmates. What kind of crazy night was this? Mel wasn't the type to panic over nothing, so this was evidently something.

The air was cold and surprisingly fresh as he headed down the front stairs of his house to the car. The sky was clear and, despite the many street lights, a host of stars glittered in the inky sky, a reflection, he thought, of the lights of this troubled borough and of this troubled world. He'd reported on crime in the area for a while, but it was always with some detachment because he was never part of the melee, just the onlooker. Now he felt himself drawn into something bad, and he wasn't prepared; he wasn't even sure if he could separate the objective journalist from the involved man.

He reached Daniel's house and parked the car, rang the bell and waited. Nothing. He rang again. Still nothing. He took out his mobile and called Daniel. Eventually, a voice.

"Hello?"

"Daniel, it's Patrick. Would you open the door man, I'm freezing."

These weren't the words he'd planned to greet Daniel, but planning had nothing much to do with what was happening right now.

"Patrick? What are you doing here?"

"Just open the door and I'll tell you."

A buzzer sounded and the communal door clicked open. Patrick went upstairs, knowing he shouldn't have shouted, but hell, he couldn't pussy-foot around at this time in the morning.

"Patrick?" Daniel opened the front door and stared at Mel's partner and his friend. "Is this some kind of Irish initiation test?"

"I wish it was mate. You'd better get dressed."

"Mind telling me why."

"I can't, Dan. Sorry. I... " his words trailed away.

Daniel stared at Patrick.

"Patrick, it's two in the morning! What's on your mind?"

Patrick found himself completely unable to deal with the situation, partly because he didn't know what the situation was and partly because, even if he had known, he couldn't function in disaster mode. Life to him was what it was to most people, a kind of game, not to be too deeply felt or analysed. But he clearly had to say something.

"I had a call from Mel. She's at the hospital."

"She works there, Patrick."

"Listen, Dan, she seemed to think something's wrong with Kathryn." Daniel was suddenly wide awake. "Don't know much more than that, Danny, honestly. Might have been some kind of accident."

"What kind?" Daniel was instantaneously business-like and to the point. Something in him had clicked into gear straight away whereas Patrick was floundering with the gear stick stuck in first.

"Really don't know. She sounded serious, mate. We'd better go. She said be quick."

"I'll phone Kath now," Daniel said, but Pat stopped him.

"Better not. I reckon you ought to get dressed and we'll be on our way, eh?"

Patrick sounded weirdly uneasy. This was a weird and uneasy moment and he was struggling to find the right tone. Daniel hurriedly got dressed, not saying a word till he was at the door when he asked, "This is for real, isn't it Patrick?"

"Seems so mate. Let's hope Mel's over reacting, shall we?"

Daniel locked the door and followed Patrick down the internal stairs and into his car. Patrick glanced at him but Daniel was stony faced, staring ahead blankly.

At the same moment, Officers Davis and Okoru were knocking on Michael and Naila's door. They heard scurrying sounds inside. The door opened on a security chain and a young woman looked out, late twenties or early thirties, jet black hair, dark eyes. 'Drop-dead gorgeous' was the expression that came into Matt's head. Charlene didn't react but said, "Sorry to disturb you at this hour. Is Michael Hudson there?"

"He is. What's wrong?"

"Would you mind if we came in? Easier to talk inside."

Charlene held up identification, to confirm they were truly police officers and not two crazies in fancy dress. Naila opened the door, at the same time calling to Michael. The officers saw a young man, also in his early twenties, light haired, not tall, rather fragile, as if his body had been made out of alabaster. Both she and he were in their nightgowns. There was something tremendously powerful about their pairing, stronger than the sum of their parts, even though they were both striking individuals in their own way.

"I'm Michael. I haven't murdered anyone, have I? I mean by

mistake?"

Charlene felt a rush of sadness for this vulnerable young man, something she thought she could never ever do whilst working.

"No, sir."

"Then?"

Charlene pulled herself together as best she could.

"It's about your sister."

Michael's smile vanished and his eyes blazed for a second.

"Kathryn?"

"Yes, sir."

"Is she alright?"

"I'm afraid she's been hurt, sir. She's at the hospital."

Naila stood next to Michael and gripped his hand.

"Is she alright?" she asked.

Charlene ducked the question, saying, "Do you mind if I ask your name?"

"It's Naila. Is she alright?"

"Naila. Michael. You'd both better come with us to the hospital now, if that's alright?"

"How bad?" Michael asked.

"Best not to say now, sir," said Charlene, hoping Michael couldn't read between the lines. "If we go to the hospital right away they can tell you much more than us. I'm PC Okoru, by the way, and this is PC Davis."

"You've been at the hospital?"

"Yes. Kathryn's friend Melissa asked us to call you. She's busy."

"Busy working?" Michael was suddenly hopeful. If Melissa was working, then that meant Kath was okay.

"Yes and no," said Charlene. "Look sir...Michael, Naila, we'd really best go straight away. Quicker the better."

Michael nodded and he and Naila dressed whilst Charlene and Matt waited, looking at the paintings, amazed that such an unobtrusive flat could hold such treasures. Neither were experts, but they felt as if they'd stepped into some rarefied imagination rather than a council home. Charlene was daunted. Michael was so clearly a remarkable young man, but very delicate and she feared how he might react to the news. It was at moments such as these she wished she'd chosen some other line of work. But then again, it might have been such moments which made the job bearable, seeing the other side of the coin, as it were, the love which outweighed the dark side of which she saw so much. In their society of dubious values, Charlene guessed that this murder would reach out further and deeper than most.

"Ready?" she asked in as detached a voice as she could muster, trying not to look at either of them directly.

They were ready, but they were both puzzled and anxious.

"You can't tell us more?" Michael asked.

"No sir. Shall we go?"

The drive to the hospital was surreal for all of them. Davis was struggling to hold his personal life at bay, even in this most demanding of moments. It seemed to him that no matter what demands were made of him, he was caught in a web from which he couldn't extricate himself. Charlene sensed her partner's insistent lack of focus but she had no time for his weakness; she had a good heart and it was hurting for these two people sitting close to each other in the back of the police car, holding hands and looking, as they would, racked by uncertainty. The car moved through the Hackney streets without the siren, but with its blue light flashing, even though the streets were fairly clear. They each felt, in their own way, as though they were not simply moving through somewhere familiar, but through invisible barriers of complete unfamiliarity, into dangerous areas of the unknown, and they each tried to steel themselves for what they'd see when they emerged into what would be a new and altered state.

## 4

A small conference room had been made ready near the registrar's office where someone had laid out simple refreshments on coffee tables around which were a dozen or so chairs. Keith, one of the registrars, was standing by the window looking out onto the Hackney night, talking quietly to Belinda who had been up to the ward but not said anything yet. She would hold a meeting in an hour or so. It was only right that family and friends should know first.

Ursula, Jasmine and Elena arrived first. As Melissa wasn't there, they introduced themselves to Belinda and Keith.

"Is Mel with Kathryn?" Ursula asked.

"Oh, no. No. She'll be along shortly."

"Can we go and see her?"

"Who?"

"Kathryn. Or Mel."

"Not just yet. She'll be here shortly. Please, take a seat and have some tea."

This was all a bit puzzling. The three flatmates sat down looking anxious. Where the devil was Mel?

"Must be busy doing stuff in the ward," said Jasmine.

"Yes, but is this important or not?" Ursula asked. "I don't get it."

Elena had suspicions that she did get it, but she did her best to ignore them. It was just that she'd probably have arranged things in this way, too, if something bad had happened at school.

"Are you all nurses?" asked Keith, trying to make some light conversation. They did their best to chat with him but they could tell he was just trying to kill a little time. Actually, he was pretty good at it and he even had them smiling at one or two anecdotes.

A few minutes later Daniel arrived with Patrick.

"Dan!" Ursula almost screamed. "What's happened? What have they told you?"

Daniel looked around, taking in the scene and the people and the mysterious atmosphere.

"Nothing. I don't know. I really don't."

"Are you Michael?" Keith asked.

Daniel introduced himself and Keith again tried to calm a tense situation, but Daniel was agitated and asked, "Where's Kath? Can we see her? Which ward is she in?"

Keith was about to answer when the door opened and a nurse looked in.

"Is Patrick Connelly here?"

"That's me," said Patrick, trying to be light.

"Would you come with me please?"

Patrick shrugged at the others and left. They stared after him, feeling every moment that they'd entered some parallel universe where nothing made sense any more. They hadn't much time to talk as the door opened again and Michael came in with Naila and the two police officers. Ursula hugged him and then Naila but could offer no news.

Outside, Patrick was hurried along to a small room where he found Melissa sitting with her head in her hands, Daphne standing by her side. It was unusual for a registrar to become so involved, but Daphne could see this was a special case, not only involving the hospital, but many devoted and soon to be devastated people.

"Pat! Thank God!"

Melissa threw her arms around him and cried.

"Mel, Mel, you must tell me, what's going on?"

"Are they here? The others?"

"Yes, all of them."

"God, Pat, I don't know what to do."

At this point, Daphne, who was composed and in as much control as the situation required, said "Melissa. You must tell him. Now. If not, I will."

Melissa looked broken as she said, "She's dead, Pat. Kathryn. She's gone."

Patrick's first odd thought was to wonder why Melissa was telling him and not the others. The fact that Kathryn was dead seemed to take a back seat in his mind, as if he was refusing to consider it for a while.

"She wanted to tell all her friends," said Daphne, "but she couldn't."

"I can't, Pat. I can't look at them and tell them. It's too horrible."

Patrick was taking this all in as best he could. Daphne, however, could see that he was struggling, not just with the news but how to deal with it. Daphne Rowe wasn't a registrar for nothing and she decided that this was the moment to lead.

"We'll go together, now," she said. "The three of us. It isn't fair that her friends wait any longer. Come with me."

She opened the door and led them along the corridor to the conference room. Even in those thirty seconds, Patrick began to comprehend what Melissa had hurriedly told him and held her hand. He hoped he wouldn't let her down.

When they entered the conference room, all eyes focused on Melissa. She held on to Patrick who looked up, then down, then nowhere.

"Hello everyone," said Daphne. "I'm sorry about this waiting. Melissa wanted to talk to you herself but she's a little too upset."

"Where's Kathryn?" a voice asked. At first, no one was sure who'd spoken, because it was such a gentle, almost angelic voice, but it was Michael, who'd stood up and, without hesitation, asked what they all wanted to ask.

"My name is Daphne Rowe. I'm one of the registrars at the hospital. Will you all sit down," she said, "I'm afraid I have some bad news."

"She was in an accident?" Ursula asked.

"No," said Daphne. "She was attacked."

There was a gasp as this horrible word stabbed at them, almost like a secondary attack. Some of them muttered the word as if by doing so they could understand it better. Michael gripped the back of a chair he was standing behind. Despite Daphne's suggestion, none of them were sitting now. They stood and stared, alone and afraid of what was being told.

"How?" someone asked.

"With a knife."

Another gasp. Attack. Knife. Kathryn. The words didn't fit together.

The ideas clashed.

"Where is she? Can we see her?"

Daphne held Melissa's hand and said, "No. I'm so sorry but there is no easy way to tell you all. The attack was fatal. Kathryn is dead."

The scene might well have served an artist as an image of some form of transmutation from one realm to another, from ignorance to knowledge or hope to despair. There was something infinitely sad about the stillness, the shock, the incredulity and the terrible consequence of the news. Deaths were media reported every day to an audience totally anaesthetized; it meant nothing. Animals raged more at the loss of an individual in their pack than humans did in their busy, blinkered struggle for survival. Reported deaths even reached the point of indulgence, focusing attention on those who seemed to revel in it more than affected by it.

Not now. These were the terrible words that all of them had feared, hoping these fears were simply melodramatic. Now, they were proved real. This was Kathryn, lover, brother, friend and colleague, and this was the real world shifting massively and minutely to accommodate a new reality.

Michael stared at Daphne as if she had spoken in tongues. Naila gripped his arm in case he fell. Ursula put her hand to her mouth; Jasmine put her arm around Elena who closed her eyes. Patrick stood close to Melissa and held her hand. The two police officers Okoru and Davis stayed very still at the back of the room, afraid of intruding into something too private. Daphne and Keith exchanged glances but said nothing. Even their professionalism was being tested here. Belinda, the staff nurse of Alexandra Ward, stood on the other side of Melissa, ready to offer help if needed. Only Daniel seemed more alone than anyone else. He looked down, in danger of sinking into some terrible chasm.

"We thought it would be better to tell you together," said Daphne. "I hope we did right."

There was no response because no one knew how to respond. How could this have been tackled in a way that was 'right'. There was no longer right and wrong, just degrees of chaos. It was like placing plaster on decapitation.

The silence lasted an extraordinary time. No one wanted to speak because words were superfluous and intrusive. When, at last, someone said something, it was Ursula and it was a single word.

"Mel?"

Melissa looked at Ursula and nodded.

"I'm so sorry. I didn't know how to tell you all. I couldn't do it on the phone. I couldn't tell you one at a time. Michael, I couldn't tell you at all. Daniel...Daniel?"

"Yes, yes, I'm listening," but Daniel's voice was hoarse and quiet.

"Have you seen her?" This was Michael. Like Daniel, his voice was soft and gentle. He could hardly get the words out. Melissa nodded. "Did she suffer?" Michael asked.

Melissa didn't know how to answer. She would have liked to say no, that death was quick, that Kathryn looked peaceful, but she couldn't. She remembered what she had seen in the pathology department and felt ill. Kathryn's face had had time to settle down, nevertheless there was still that rictus of fear and knowledge, giving every indication that she knew what was happening and had fought to avoid the inevitable. Michael read her expression, as did everyone else. Melissa thought of lying, of saying it had probably happened very quickly, but she couldn't. This was a time of truth, as hard and bitter as it had to be.

"We're not sure," said Daphne, "exactly what happened. The police are investigating this very moment, isn't that right?" She turned to the two officers who nodded their agreement. "An inspector Faraday is in charge of the investigation. He's been here this evening but is already at work to solve the case."

"Solve what?" Ursula asked. "Are we talking murder?"

It might have seemed like a foolish question, but the word hadn't been used yet, and they were all still trying to fix what had happened in some way with a language that was stubbornly banal.

"Yes. It was murder."

"With a knife?"

"Yes."

Ursula swore under her breath. For all of them, the most difficult idea was to associate Kathryn in any way with violence. To all of them she had been the embodiment of gentleness, love and good will. She hadn't had harm in her heart ever. Her life had been pure joy, except when she was made unhappy by others, but she had never had tolerated, understood or used violence. This kind of death was wrong, in every sense and in every interpretation. It made a mockery of morality, a nonsense of a kindly disposed universe, even of a dispassionate universe. How in any system of belief could this vile atrocity be explained?

"Ursula," whispered Jasmine, "I feel sick."

Jasmine started to sway slowly and Belinda, seeing the signs of fainting, took hold of her and  sat her down, letting her sip a glass of water. Elena held her shoulder and sat down beside her. Both girls were white with shock. Ursula could barely handle the torrent of thoughts and fears racing through her mind, putting her hand on Jasmine's shoulder and looking around the room, perplexed.

Naila, desperate for her love and her lover, fearing all manner of consequences, squeezed Michael to her, but he was limp, as if his soul and vitality had been torn away. She let him sit and sat beside him, watching, waiting for some response. Suddenly he looked up and for one horrible moment Naila though she saw bitterness in his eyes, but that couldn't be! He was Kathryn's brother in so many ways, this could never be his reaction, it mustn't be.

"Michael?"

"I'm alright."

"No one's alright, my love."

"No. They're not are they. How's Daniel?"

Naila saw Daniel, still standing alone. He had no one. He wanted no one. All he had ever wanted was Kathryn, and Kathryn had been taken from him. Naila's heart went out to the man.

"Go to him," said Michael. "Don't let him be alone."

Naila didn't want to leave Michael, but she moved towards Daniel who looked up when he felt her approach. They'd never had much contact, and it had always been slightly awkward. There was no understanding nor common ground, a result of the mysterious way humans were put together and functioned. It might well have been a cultural legacy, she being half Iranian, he Jewish, with all the baggage that carried whether they liked it or not, but the fact was that they had always found it hard to make any kind of contact. Now, the circumstances were altered and some effort was needed.

"Daniel?"

"You should stay with Michael," he said.

"He asked me to see you. Come and sit with us."

He joined Michael and sat beside him with Naila sat on the other side. They waited for something to happen, for someone to say something or some logic to explain the inexplicable, but the room remained flooded with confusion.

A figure appeared in front of them. At first Daniel thought it was the hospital chaplain who'd been called in, and indeed she had been called, but it was one of the police officers, a black woman with a strong but compassionate expression.

"Charlene Okoru," she introduced herself. "My partner and I found Kathryn. I know it might not be the time, but if there's anything you want to know, I mean about the police side of things, just ask. We all feel for you."

Daniel didn't hesitate. It was a relief, in a way to ask something practical.

"Do you know who did it?"

"No. Not yet. Inspector Faraday, the officer Daphne mentioned, he'll keep you informed. So will we, if you want us to."

"We do," said Michael.

"Is there a reason?" Naila asked. "Anything at all. It just seems so...so..."

"Random?" Charlene suggested. "We can't say yet. If any of you have anything you think we'd need to know..."

"She had no enemies," said Michael.

"No," said Charlene. "You may be right."

"I am right," said Michael. "How could she? Naila?"

Naila put her arm around him. He looked about to sink with the weight of unhappiness. Daniel was unreadable. This, thought Charlene, was not a five minute grief. The victim had evidently been a deep part of all their lives and she would be utterly missed. In her work, Charlene Okoru came across ranks of selfish souls, but they were still plying their trades whilst this woman who had apparently brought so much joy was gone. She hoped they wouldn't ask her details of what she and Matt had seen, because it would be impossible, and probably wrong, to tell them. She looked at the three of them, Naila cradling Michael and Daniel lost in a blinded world of his own and wished them all she could in getting through the coming days, but she had a horrible intuition that the murder might as easily tear them apart as bring them together.

Melissa joined the three flatmates. Ursula hugged her.

"You did right," she said. "How are you feeling?"

Melissa couldn't answer truthfully. She had seen Kathryn dead and was carrying a heavy secret. She was struggling to say the right thing.

"Lousy," she answered.

The four of them buried their heads together in a huddle, Patrick looking on, a touch embarrassed, ill at ease with the whole sorry mess. Charlene came over to see how they were doing, offering sympathy but also telling them about the investigation and how they could help. Melissa felt for the officer who, despite her evident shock on seeing the mutilated body, was doing her best to be professional in this highly charged situation. For the past few hours Charlene Okoru had been there for her, never putting a foot wrong, and Melissa appreciated it. Should she tell her? She had to tell someone sooner or later, but she couldn't do it, not yet. The moment still didn't seem right.

"Is Kathryn...here?" Elena asked.

"Yes," said Okoru.

"I saw her," said Melissa, and the three waited for her to say more. They hoped she might say Kathryn had looked peaceful, calm or even happy, but she said nothing, unable to hide the horror of what she'd seen.

The two registrars stayed much longer than they would normally have done, partly because Kathryn had been a member of staff but also because the group of people coming to terms with the murder of their friend were so shaken.

"Michael," said Keith, "you're Kathryn's only family, is that right?"

"Here, in Hackney, yes. It's a large family, but not here."

"In London?"

"Some. Mostly spread out here and there."

Naila held on to Michael as he spoke. She loved him for his strength in dealing with these questions, seeing how difficult it was going to be for him to tell his parents. She'd met them a couple of times and knew of their tangled background. They might not have been model parents but they were bound to be devastated by the news.

"Would you like me to tell them?" Keith asked.

Michael answered immediately. "No, thank you. I'll do it. Now might be the right time."

"Shall I come with?" Naila asked.

He shook his head and went with Keith to his office. Naila watched him go, feeling suddenly exposed amongst all these people so much closer to Kathryn than she'd ever been. Daniel, sitting beside her said, "He'll need you."

Naila replied straight away, "I'll be there. And you? Who will be there for you, Daniel?"

Daniel thought for a moment before saying, "Actually, I'm not sure."

Naila felt overwhelmed with the need of these people around her but didn't know what she could offer this man who was so unlike her Michael. She wondered, even at this torrid moment, how people found partners and how anarchic was the whole process of compatibility. She felt the same unease with him as she'd done each time they'd met, as if they were cast from contrasting human material, but nevertheless, Kathryn had loved him and Michael would want her to hold out the hand of friendship.

"You can come and stay with us," she said. "Michael won't mind."

"Thanks Naila, that's kind. I'll see."

"Not good to be alone, Daniel."

Naila knew Daniel's background and he knew hers, which was possibly why they were always awkward with each other, but then again, this was Hackney, the melting pot of nations, an upside down Tower of Babel.

She touched his hand in a show of compassion but he seemed to pull away as if startled.

"Sorry," she said, "I don't know what to do."

"You're doing fine," he said. "Who knows what to do? I'm a bit jumpy."

For a split second Daniel lowered his defences and in that second Naila saw what Kathryn had seen in him, but he quickly closed himself off to her again. She feared she would never be able to help this man who was so distant by nature, culture and now this cruellest of circumstances.

A very down-to-Earth voice interrupted Naila's thoughts.

"How you doing mate?" Patrick asked Daniel.

Naila might have laughed. Despite her well-meaning but awkward efforts, Patrick had just the right tone.

"Bit shell shocked," said Daniel. "Thanks for getting me, Pat. Sorry if I was a bit slow."

Patrick looked embarrassed again. He really wasn't comfortable in the presence of grief, despite the closeness to it in his professional life.

"You were fine. I didn't know what to say Dan," said Patrick. "Still don't," then he turned to Naila and greeted her.

"Hello Patrick."

Naila sometimes wished she could be as down-to-Earth as Patrick and so many others, but she had the blessing and curse of an artistic temperament and, though she wouldn't admit it, artistic talent to match.

"Listen Dan," said Patrick, "if you want to sleep round with us, you can. Melissa won't mind. You don't want to go back to your flat alone, do you?"

Naila might have been hurt if he'd said yes, but Daniel made light of it by saying "So many invites and only one me. Naila just asked, Pat. Can I let you both know? I think I might need some time alone."

"Sure mate," said Patrick. "Whatever you need. Just ask."

Someone else joined them, someone who had kept herself apart with her own thoughts and private passions. Nurcan had been standing alone, uncertain how to offer comfort when she was on the edge of such a steep precipice. She considered leaving the room, but she belonged there, in her own way and for her own reasons. She couldn't bear the thought of going back to work, or even going home.

"Daniel, my name is Nurcan. I worked with Kathryn. We were friends. I'm so sorry."

Daniel thanked her, but no more than that. She didn't know what else he could say or what more she could do. She felt awkward again, an outsider in so many ways. It was as if the reality of life dwarfed the life of feeling and imagination. She felt her spirit shrink to nothing in the face of this real, tangible, broadcast world. She saw Naila look at her and then look away, not nastily, but as if there was nothing to register. This hurt so much.

"Did you work with Kath?" Nurcan heard the question but was so distracted that she didn't see that it was directed towards her. "Nurcan?"

She looked and saw that Naila had asked her the question.

"Oh, yes, and no. I work in Accident and Emergency but I sometimes gave Kath and Melissa a lift to work or home. We were friends."

Naila nodded in acknowledgement but the conversation was forced.

"Nurcan," Daniel asked, "were you with Mel when...did you see Kath?"

"Yes, I was. I did," she answered. "The witness, Robert, said he thought she worked here. It was lucky really," she thought this the wrong word to use, "otherwise we might not have known. I identified her." Naila took Nurcan's hand. For a strong woman, Nurcan seemed suddenly unexpectedly fragile. "I see enough hurt here every day," she said, "but this is ... madness."

Although he tried not to visualize what Nurcan had seen, the image of his beautiful Kathryn, brutally cut and lying in the cold street or the even colder depths of the hospital morgue insinuated itself into his imagination, so disturbing that it threatened to dominate all other thoughts. Naila's voice snapped him out of the nightmare, if only for a moment.

"Were you on duty?" she asked Nurcan.

"Yes, in Accident and Emergency."

Naila was reluctant to talk about what had happened but the others wanted to know and she had no option but to tell them She tried her best to be dispassionate or that any emotion she showed was the natural reaction to such a traumatic night.

"Was it him?" Patrick asked. "I mean this Robert guy, could he have done it and just pretended about what he'd seen?" The journalist in him was coming to the fore.

"I don't think so," said Nurcan, "Robert's a gentle man."

"Was she alive?" Daniel asked with a hoarse voice. He was agitated, trying to piece together the events that had stolen away his love. "When they ... found her...did she say anything?"

"No," said Nurcan. "She wasn't. I'm so sorry."

Patrick shook his head. "Daniel, what the hell was Kathryn doing out jogging so late?"

"You knew her," said Daniel. "She did her own thing in her own way."

To Patrick, immersed in the crime of the borough, this wasn't enough, but it also wasn't the moment to press Daniel. He excused himself from the group for a moment and went to speak with Davis who he knew from a couple of previous cases. Davis looked exhausted and troubled, but Patrick assumed it was just from the events of the night.

"Anything you need?" Davis asked.

"Information," said Patrick. "They're desperate," he said, nodding towards the others.

Davis repeated the registrar's words, that Faraday was in charge and he'd keep them informed. "Inspector Faraday's good," he said. "If anyone can solve it, he can. Just have to wait and see."

Davis was doing his best to be professional, but his private life taunted him, as if he was secretly part of the wicked world he fought so hard to keep under control. Was he already a lost cause? Charlene was right, he had to sort out his life. How could he help these people if he couldn't help himself? He felt out of place in their intimate group, uncomfortable with himself as if his own dishonesty were a visible thing. What angered him most, though, was that despite all the warnings, he was desperate to see Cassie. He couldn't bear the thought of going home without seeing her. He'd witnessed something life changing that evening, just as Charlene had said, and yet inside he was the same man with the same weaknesses. He needed Cassie more than he needed his family, and he didn't understand this. He knew he shouldn't, not if he wanted to do his job and hold his life together, but the desire grew rather than faded as he stood there trying to be what he evidently wasn't any longer, an honest copper.

## 5

There was still a gentle buzz of repressed conversation in the room. People sat and talked or just sat silently with their own thoughts and fears, knowing that everything had altered and not knowing how their own lives would change because of this seismic shift. Naila was looking particularly anxious. Michael had been out of the room quite a while and a fear possessed her of losing him. It was one thing to try and console Daniel who she hardly knew and didn't understand, and losing her love as he had lost his. The thought filled her with trepidation and she was mightily relieved when the door opened and he came in and joined them. Naila immediately took his hand, safe again, but he hardly responded.

"Well?" she said.

"They're coming down. They were pretty cut up."

He spoke with difficulty, as if he were finding it hard to concentrate.

"When will they be here?" Naila asked him.

"In the morning. Early."

"I'll come and see them," said Daniel, "if that's alright with you. I think I ought to."

Michael looked shaken. Naila looked at him as she might have looked at a broken doll when she was a girl, full of compassion, but not knowing how to fix it.

Melissa and Kathryn's flatmates had joined them so that the whole group was together, no one wanting to leave the others alone and no one, not even Daniel, wanting to be alone, even if there was little to say.

The room had taken on a sombre air with no one quite sure what to do or say. They'd each known Kathryn in different ways and the loss would be felt and dealt with in different ways. They understood that something which ought to have been against the laws of nature had happened to their friend, and that couldn't be processed easily. It couldn't, for many of them, be processed at all.

Slowly, they gravitated towards each other. There was a force at work, drawing them together for comfort and understanding, assuming there was any understanding to be had. Melissa had a dreadful fear of how this understand would be rendered truly impossible if she were to tell them what she knew, that Kathryn was pregnant, and not by Daniel. This was awful knowledge, but it would have to be shared at some point. Who with, though? Which of these people should she tell, and why? In the end, they might all know, and she feared the damage a form of Chinese whispers would cause, especially if this leaked into the mainstream news, which it was bound to do. It would turn into a torrent of morbid gossip and all the impact of Kathryn's murder would be lost in a welter of sentiment. Patrick could help, Melissa thought. Maybe he'd have some sway with other journalists, control what they wrote somehow. But no, that wouldn't happen, no matter how much Patrick tried, this whole thing would escalate, Melissa could see that, and her beautiful friend's reputation would be spoiled.

Another thought made Melissa close her eyes and pray to a god she didn't believe in. What if Kathryn had lied, to Daniel, to her, to all of them? What if she was false?

'Let he be good, let her be good, let her be ...' she whispered.

"What's that, Mel?" Patrick was asking.

Melissa had been whispering aloud and the others were looking at her.

"Sorry," she said, blushing with embarrassment and anxiety. "Excuse me."

She moved away, but Patrick followed and caught her before she'd left the room.

"How you doing?" he asked her.

Instead of answering, she clung to him, tears falling on to his shoulder. The others thought it was simply overwhelming emotion, but it was more than that. It was the fear of discovering an awful truth. Melissa could hardly breathe.

"Take it easy love," said Patrick.

"Can I get out, just for a moment Pat," she said.

He led her into the corridor. She left him, pacing up and down, wondering what to do and what to say. Par was sensible, he'd know. She looked at him, standing there at the other end of the corridor, a big man, concern written all over his face, and she loved him so much. She walked up to him and took both his hands.

"I need to ..." she started to say, but the door opened and Ursula looked out.

"You alright, Mel?" she asked.

"Back in a minute," said Melissa.

Ursula closed the door and left them, but in that moment Melissa changed her mind. She couldn't say anything, not now, not here, not yet.

"What is it?" Patrick asked.

She shook her head.

"Later," she said. "I'll tell you later. Let's go back inside."

She knew she was wrong, but there was no clear right and wrong, not then, maybe not ever. She couldn't face revealing something which would hurt so many. She calmed down, gathering herself as best she could, and they rejoined the others.

## 6

"The children will want to know," said Ursula.

She meant the children in Alexandra Ward who often got better as much because of the care of the nurses as the medicines.

"Maybe we can all go and see them," said Elena, "not now, but when they know she's not coming back. We should do something."

They wanted to act, but they had to fight the overwhelming shock of the moment first. It was too early to be creative; they had to absorb the news and adjust first. Doing anything seemed to involve a massive effort of will. Even the idea of leaving that room and going 'home' was anathema. 'Home' had no meaning at that moment. The safety of routine had been disrupted and the thought of going back to the pretence of it all was too much to bear.

The two police officers, Charlene Okoru and Matt Davis said they were leaving but made sure everyone knew they, or other officers, could be contacted at any time. The two registrars also left, but only to their own offices; they would stay the night now and face whatever had to be faced in the morning. Belinda had gone back to the ward.

Elena and Jasmine went into the kitchen which was a small utility room next door where they found themselves crying on each other's shoulder, unable to get to grips with the simple task of making tea and filling a plate of sandwiches and biscuits. The door opened and Daphne looked in.

"You two want some help?"

They did. Daphne quickly got together a decent tray of food and drink.

"She was the best of us," said Jasmine.

"I can see how much she meant to you all," said Daphne. "She did to us too. Better dry your eyes before you go back in."

She handed them the fully loaded tray and Elena took it after doing her best to dry her eyes. When they went back inside, the others were chatting away, almost as if it were a regular social get together. Daniel was standing, looking out of a window at the early morning Hackney lights. Naila and Michael were also standing, a little way away, close together but not speaking.

"Grub," said Jasmine. "Just what we need."

Refreshment was welcome as a heavy tiredness was settling over all the friends. They tucked in with surprising relish, as if food could fight off the devil himself.

"No way," said Ursula. They'd been talking about work the next day. "Not for any of us. Not even you Elena."

"I have to."

"No you don't," said Ursula. "I'll phone, tell them what happened, they'll get a supply easy enough. No work, Elly. If we do anything tomorrow apart from keep each other company it'll be to sleep."

Michael looked as though work was a million miles away from his thoughts, which it was.

"I'll call the college," said Naila. "They'll deal with it."

Daniel just held up his hand as if it didn't matter. He looked as distracted as Michael sounded. It was as if the gesture came from a thousand miles away. Ursula squeezed his shoulder.

"You'll need to sort out the funeral," said Patrick. The words shocked them. It was almost impossible connecting such a thing to their friend Kathryn who was, in their minds and hearts, still so full of life. "But they'll need to do a post mortem," he added. "I mean if you let them, and that will take a few days."

Again there was silence, another idea that hadn't occurred to them. One by one, demands appeared that interrupted both grieving and understanding. Everything was so relentlessly physical, bound to Earthly rules, but being the hack who knew most about the real world Patrick was the one they looked to for the things which had to be done. "Standard procedure," he said, hesitantly. "Sorry Michael...it's..."

"No," said Michael, "that's fine. We have to know."

Melissa heard the phrase post-mortem and thought of the unborn baby. Daniel would be devastated. Melissa imagined it would be more of a death to him than Kathryn's murder. At least now he could keep her memory pure in his heart. This knowledge would infect that memory, one way or the other, and there was no way to avoid it.

"When will this happen?" she asked, trying to hide the anxiety in her voice.

"Soon. Don't know exactly. Maybe we should change the subject," said Patrick, but what subjects could they talk about, if they talked at all? Nothing seemed suitable yet silence was unbearable. It was so difficult to steer a middle ground. Waves of emotion rolled around touching each of them in turn. Oddly, the only one immune to this was Daniel who never shed a tear nor showed any great change of expression. If they hadn't known him and seen him with Kathryn, they might have doubted his grief, but they had seen him with her not to doubt him, but they didn't understand him, none of them.

## 7

It was the arrival of Kathryn's parents which split the group, forcing them to leave the conference room and begin to face the world without their friend.

"Daniel," said Michael. "do you want to come with?"

Daniel, never that comfortable with Kathryn's parents, joined

Michael and Naila.

Patrick took Daniel aside before he left and said, "Come and stay with us if you want, Dan. Here's a key. Save going home alone, eh?"

Accepting the invitation, Daniel took the key and went with Michael and Naila.

It was past four in the morning. They were shattered, but they didn't want to sleep; they doubted they could even get to sleep. For the past few hours the conference room had become an almost sacred place where the terrible news had been told but had also been confined. It was a little world of their own and when they left it they would carry Kathryn's death with them, out into the wider world. All the implications of her death would begin to emerge and their lives would change. It was hard to know anything for sure except that this was a first step to dealing with the murder.

"You can all come back to our house," said Melissa, "if you like. You too Nurcan."

Nurcan had been the most quiet, the least close of the friends, apparently, and the most withdrawn. She declined, wanting to do her own thing.

"That lift to work seems like a long while ago," she said.

"It was," said Melissa. "A lifetime ago."

"Let's all meet tomorrow," said Ursula, "any which way, just to talk."

Elena put her arm around Jasmine. They looked so lost, as if all hope and happiness had been drained away. The whole night seemed like someone else's nightmare, unwillingly shared. There were countless good wishes and temporary goodbyes, then they headed towards the exit. When they eventually separated, it was a real wrench. The news and the manner of sharing had brought them together and forged a bond, a fellowship that was breaking up barely a moment after being formed.

## 8

Michael sat talking with his parents in hushed tones whilst Naila and Daniel stood close by looking ill at ease, Naila anxious about Michael, Daniel unreadable. Mr and Mrs Hudson sat on simple chairs, ashen faced. They knew they hadn't been the greatest parents. As soon as Kathryn was old enough, they'd left her to look after Michael whilst they went on one of their many extended adventures. It was the height of irresponsibility, and a talking point for those that knew them, but all the criticism in the world didn't stop them. They'd travelled the globe and done whatever they pleased whilst Kathryn, along with Mrs Hudson's sister Jenny, helped raise Michael. They still believed they loved their children, and they probably did, but Michael found it hard to empathize when he examined his own sense of abandonment and realized how unaware they both were of this, even now, twenty years later.

He'd tried, when he was younger and suffering from not having them around, to understand why they were missing so much, but didn't understand until he reached his late teens, by which time he found it hard to forgive. Kathryn never said a word against them, although she never made excuses for them either. She told him some life lessons that people rarely did what you expected of them but that this worked both ways and that we probably all disappointed each other in the end, whether we meant to or not. Their parents were just being themselves, she'd said, although she'd said it tight lipped, as if she didn't quite believe in the explanation herself.

"Do they know who did it?" asked Mr Hudson. He spoke in an apologetic manner, as if he was aware of his flawed fatherhood.

"No," said Michael.

"Can we see her?"

"Not right now, Mr Hudson," said Daphne who was still with them, acting as some kind of pacifying arbitrator. "I'm afraid there'll have to be a post mortem, there always is in cases of murder, unless there are religious reasons against it."

"I see."

"Did she suffer?" Mrs Hudson asked. She was in her late forties, still attractive but in deep shock, fighting with her conscience as well the trauma of the moment.

"It's hard to say," said Daphne. "We hope not. It's probably best not to think that she did."

"It was a brutal attack," said Michael with a sudden rush of anger. "It's monstrous to think she didn't suffer. She did." They all looked at him, surprised by his unexpected vehemence. Naila took his hand but he pulled away, which hurt her. "I think it would be wrong," he said, "to soften this. It was the worst way to die," he said. "She was an angel, she was there for me when you weren't," he said to his parents, "and she's gone, horribly. There's no redemption for this, you know, none at all."

Naila wanted to cry for him. She felt his pain, his anger and his turmoil. He was doing wonderfully well to handle it but she was afraid that at some point it would get the better of him. His father looked away but his mother said, with a touch of defiance in her voice, "She was our daughter Michael, whatever you think."

Daphne, having seen similar scenes before, though never one quite so intense, sought to make peace and keep everyone rational. No good would be done by swapping recriminations.

"May I?" she asked, and the argument was nipped in the bud. "It's best to focus on what needs to be done. As I say, there'll be a post mortem. Detective Inspector Faraday is in charge of the police investigation. There's a team here who will be on hand to help if you need help, you know, someone to talk with, a contact point. They will also try to keep the press away from you because the press, you can be sure, will pursue you, and it may well go national. I would suggest you not let anything out that you'll regret, family feuds and the like. The thing is to remember Kathryn. She's the one that's gone, and I know myself what a treasure she was. I doubt that anyone will be able to give you an answer to this, but at least let the world see, if it wants to see, what it's lost."

Mrs Hudson touched Daphne's hand.

"I'm sorry," she said, "you must think we're heartless."

"Not at all. Believe me, I've seen heartless people and you're not, none of you. Kathryn was lucky to have you." Michael looked away but said nothing. "She couldn't have been what she was without good people around her. I may only have known her slightly but I'm a good judge of character. I can see what you've lost. All I can do is assure you that the hospital will be here for you any time, myself, Belinda, the team that supports you, we'll never forget Kathryn and we'll never forget you all."

"You're very kind," said Mr Hudson.

"I'll leave you for a few minutes," said Daphne. "I'll get someone to bring you some tea. Tea is always good."

When she was gone, they each felt awkward in their own way and for their own reasons. Mr and Mrs Hudson might not have been the best of parents, but neither were they the worst and they knew well enough what a treasure they'd lost. Michael didn't bother fighting the resentment towards his parents, it was too deep to battle, but he couldn't put into words or even thoughts his feelings towards Kathryn. She'd been his sister, his surrogate mother, his muse and his conscience. She'd been his reference point for life all the years of his growing up. If he had any love in him now that he was a man, it was because of her, and if there was anger in him it was because of them and now something worse than anger because she was gone.

Naila stood by his side feeling powerless. She wanted to do so much, yet she feared Michael wouldn't let her do anything. She sensed that his parents didn't care for her, but that didn't bother her; what bothered her was a terrible apprehension that Michael might drift away. She loved him to distraction and wanted to believe that love conquered all, but she had doubts. She saw that the deepest foundation in him had been taken away and that he was unsteady. She wanted to rebuild his trust and confidence, be everything that he needed to grow and be the man she saw he could be, but these were critical times and she feared disaster.

As for Daniel, he had no point of contact here, no obvious point of contact anywhere. Like Naila, he'd not felt close to Kathryn's parents and his own family were not just many miles away, but an emotional distance away too. His single point of contact with anything at all meaningful had been taken away and he didn't believe there was a single kindred spirit alive who could touch him as Kathryn had touched him, and even if there was, the sheer cruelty, barbarism and inexplicable injustice of this murder defied any explanation of any kind. It was sheer chaos, and he felt his soul falling into an abyss of confusion.

"We told Jenny," said Mrs Hudson. "She and Trevor will sort out whatever has to be sorted out."

Michael thought 'Always the same, always hand over to someone else.' He felt so dejected but he heeded Daphne's words and said nothing. "I've called them," his mother went on, "and they'll come down soon. I'm sure you want to see your aunt, Michael?"

He didn't answer. He hated this time together, wanted so much to be alone with his thoughts, even, he admitted to himself, away from Naila.

"Daniel," said Mrs Hudson, trying to steer the conversation away from dangerous ground, "how are you?"

Daniel looked up, surprised. He'd been listening but not particularly involved. How did you answer a question like that at a moment like this?

"I'm okay."

"She loved you very much, Daniel. She told us, many times."

Daniel should have been pleased to hear this, but it agitated him. He'd never been easy with their relationship discussed by others, and the idea that Kathryn had spoken of him to her family upset his enhanced sense of privacy. If he'd been more assured of who he was and what he and Kathryn had together, this might not have bothered him so much, but he didn't, and it did. He couldn't say anything that would sound remotely sensible or honest. Michelle Hudson then did something most unexpected. She put her right hand gently on his left cheek and said, "We'll all have to be strong, Daniel. It's a horrendous thing to happen. We'll need each other."

Daniel was, to say the least, a little taken aback. It was the sudden show of affection from someone who'd denied it to her own children which puzzled him. He was also wary of these people intruding too much into his life because, sadly, they meant so little to him. They hadn't cared much, or shown much care when Kathryn was alive, and now she was gone he found it hard to find comfort in them. He wondered where on this Godforsaken planet, one which allowed such horrors to happen, he'd ever find comfort again. At that moment he wanted, like Michael, to get away, to run, fly, vanish, just be alone, more than anything else, be by himself and let his feelings settle down. It was all he could do to remember that there were rules of behaviour which took priority over needs of the self, and he'd better follow them; he didn't think Kathryn's family, as vulnerable as they were, would forgive him if he let them down, not now of all times.

Michelle Hudson then turned to her son and said, "Don't hate me, or daddy, Michael. Kathryn wouldn't have wanted you to."

"You don't know what Kathryn wanted or what I want. I don't hate you, mummy, I just need time. We all do."

Naila opened her eyes wide when she heard Michael calling Michelle 'mummy'. It was like some quaint English custom, but it suited him because, in so many good ways, he was still a boy.

"We told her not to come here," said Mr Hudson. "You too, Michael. I wish you'd both listened to us."

Michael held himself in check. Yes, his parents had told them not to come to Hackney. They'd never seen the borough but they thought of it as a den of iniquity, and now they were evidently proved right. Kathryn had laughed it off, but though she never argued with her parents, she was very firm about what she wanted to do. Both she and Michael had thrived in Hackney, and he said so.

"This could have happened anywhere," he said. "She was in the wrong place at the wrong time."

"This is always the wrong place," said Mr Hudson.

"Daddy, I'm not going to argue with you, not now, but Kathryn was fine here. I suppose you're going to blame me now because she wanted to be where I was."

"You wanted to be where she was," said Mr Hudson, "but no, I'm not blaming you Michael, of course I'm not! Don't say that. I just wish you both hadn't lived here. It's dangerous, everyone knows that. And what the devil was she doing out running so late at night? That's madness."

"She was independent, you know that," said Michael, but he couldn't say it with any degree of certainty because it was truly an odd thing to do, even for his sister, but though he agreed with his father, he wouldn't admit it. He'd never question Kathryn, especially now.

Mr Hudson looked agitated. "Don't they have a clue?" he asked. "Was this really just a random thing? It's so hard to accept."

"Would it be better if we discovered there was a reason, darling?" Michelle asked. "It might be worse."

"There couldn't be a reason," said Gordon Hudson. "We all knew Kathryn. What possible reason could there be? And yet a random killing is just too awful..."

He put his head in his hands and his wife put her arm around his shoulders.

"We'll find out soon enough," she said. "The main thing is that we do the right thing now for Kathryn."

Michael wondered what the right thing was. He assumed it meant getting the funeral organised properly and making sure, as the registrar had told them, that they didn't let the media hijack their lives. His heart was full, his mind was full and he was desperately tired, yet he was also brimming with an unusual energy. Naila could sense it even though he wouldn't let her even hold his hand.

"Daniel," said Michelle, "you'll help with the arrangements for the funeral?"

Daniel had drifted away again but looked up and nodded. He'd listened to the seeds of argument between Michael and his parents and sensed the same thing between himself and his own parents. He'd have to tell them, but he dreaded it. Just the thought of diminishing this horror with words filled him with dread.

"Anything," he said.

"I'll help too," said Naila. "Just ask."

Michelle smiled at her but said nothing. Naila felt that distrust again, as if they still didn't know what to make of her - beauty, brains and love notwithstanding.

They tried to talk about the funeral, where it should be held and how to arrange it, but it all felt surreal, as if they were planning it for someone they didn't know. It couldn't be for Kathryn! She'd walk in any moment and all would be well, or she'd phone and say there'd been a ghastly mistake and it was some other poor soul who'd been killed and not to worry, life was going to go on as usual. The reality weighed down on them, a terrible weight that wouldn't be contradicted by foolish dreams.

Gordon Hudson stood up and walked to the window. Michael's father looked much older than his years. His head sunk and his arms trembled on the window sill. Michelle joined him and they shared a muted conversation. The sight of the two of them there reminded Naila of how she'd stood with Michael at the window in their home not too many hours before when life was impossibly different. She felt that fate was playing some extraordinarily tasteless game with them.

Daniel, more alone of the five than the others, stood up, wanting to go, but Mr Hudson, without seeing him, said to the reflection in the window.

"Michael, were we really bad parents?"

"You weren't there for us," said Michael, "you know that, but there's no point in going over old ground, is there, and I'm sure the others don't want to hear it, not now."

Gordon Hudson turned around and said to Naila, Daniel and the patient Daphne, "Forgive me. Families can be trying."

'Don't I know,' Daniel thought.

A few awkward moment's passed before Michelle said, "We ought to leave, Michael. You must be exhausted – you all must be. Daniel, what are you going to do?"

For a second, Daniel thought she meant what was he going do the rest of his life, and he had no answer. The rest of his life was unexpectedly irrelevant.

"I'll go home," he said.

Naila was about to repeat the offer that he could stay with them, but in all honesty she wasn't sure she wanted Daniel there. He disturbed her still, even at this time when they should all be supporting each other. She hated herself for it, but it was the truth. Daniel may or may not have noticed her hesitation, but he didn't react. He waited without purpose, feeling as though he were watching some weird dream sequence, or was part of a film the director ought to have left on the cutting room floor.

They made arrangements to talk after they'd rested, although they knew they wouldn't rest, any of them. It was already Friday and the world was beginning to stir, only it wasn't the same world they'd seen out the day before. Then, Kathryn was a part of it, and for some of them she'd been the hub around which their lives had revolved. Now she was gone and they felt themselves in danger of spinning off into space.

"Will you be alright driving, Daniel?" Naila asked, trying to be considerate.

"I'll get a taxi," he said, feeling the same awkwardness and lack of common ground. "Patrick brought me. No problem."

"No," said Michael, "we'll take you. Mum and dad can squeeze you in."

It was the last thing Daniel wanted. He'd prefer to take a taxi alone and just be free of people, but he hadn't the energy to argue. They thanked Daphne for helping; she'd kept the peace, such as it was, but nevertheless watched them go with guilty relief, puzzled that even a beautiful soul such as Kathryn could leave behind a measure of discord, even if it was no fault of hers.

## 9

The lift home for Daniel was an uncomfortable, if brief one, in every way. They left him at his doorstep with good wishes, too many to handle, and he watched them drive away, unsure whether he wanted to go inside yet.

He gazed into the night of this strange borough, but it was as if a pall of despair had smothered all the lights and the hope. He really didn't want to go inside. Instead, he walked the short distance to his office and settled at his desk. A few hours before, he'd been on call and everything was ticking over nicely. He'd made a friend for life in little Frankie Davis, registering another satisfied customer. All was well. Now all was not well, nor ever would be. Nothing in the office felt substantial and he wanted no more to do with it. It made him dizzy, this evidence of things still existing when Kathryn was gone.

He started writing a note addressed to the temp who was due in the next morning. When the workload was high, as it was, he called a local agency for help, if not here, then in the Wick workshop. He told him what had happened and left a list of jobs. As futile as it all seemed, life was work and he had enough sense of responsibility to make sure it would operate without him for a while.

Daniel had a clear work ethic. Indeed, many Jewish people had the same drive, developed over two thousand years employed in foreign lands. He even thought he might be able to work off the grief, but it wasn't grief he felt, not yet. He stood at the edge of a deep chasm with either madness or death at the bottom. If he worked hard, he could avoid the fall, avoid everything, just endure, which was the watchword of Judaism.

Endure.

No matter what. No matter who hated you, who tormented you, who beat you, who humiliated you, who enslaved you – always endure.

How, though, was he to understand, let alone endure this crime? Was it his loving but powerless God with reasons unfathomable to the human heart? More likely, he feared, it was nothing at all, simply the existence of random malice in a universe devoid of morality. He felt the age-old sense of persecution and with it the age-old guilt. It was the fate of his people always to be the focus of perversity both in thought and deed. There was no explanation and no understanding, it was simply the way things were.

Memories flooded back, so many of them, when they'd first met, their first date, the excitement, the hope, the unexpectedness of it all.

"Can't you tell when a woman makes a pass at you?" she'd asked.

Had she made a pass at him? He couldn't tell, and this made her laugh.

Oh, that laugh, it filled him with such delight! Everything about her filled him with delight. He saw the dainty green beret she wore and the little woollen scarf, the smart leather jacket and the white trouser suit.

"You have style," he told her once.

"So do you."

"No, I'm a style-free zone."

She took him shopping, made him look as near to cool as was possible.

In his mind's eye he saw her move, so assured, so strong. He could have watched her all day, the ease with which she walked the Earth, and the strength she carried with her, everywhere. It was uncanny.

"It's an act," she said.

"Don't believe it," he answered.

He saw the look in her eyes, not just one look but so many, moods of all colours, shades and moments, emotions and mysteries he would never see again.

He shouted something aloud and stood up suddenly, desperately sad.

He really doubted he could work this thing out of him. How could he ever be anywhere Kathryn had been, his home, this office, anywhere she had touched with her loveliness? It was impossible.

He closed his eyes and tried to feel her presence there now. He wanted so much to see her, feel her, smell her. The physicality was so strong, it surely had to be real, but he opened his eyes and saw no signs of her. He would only ever feel her absence, a vanishing spirit, disappearing into his past, the past of the world and into nothingness. He couldn't let this happen, yet he couldn't stop it.

He lifted the blinds of a window and looked out. This polyglot cauldron of a borough had brought him and Kathryn together, spirits from two different worlds, and now it had separated them. Someone out there, perhaps considering their night's work that very moment, or worse, not considering it at all, had committed this cruellest of crimes, an act of such brutality it defied belief; but it had happened, undeniably.

Daniel gripped the window sill. What would he do if he ever faced the monster that had committed this atrocity? Would he feel anything at all? Maybe he was so lost in thought that he would do nothing. What was done couldn't be undone and no act of retribution would bring Kathryn back. There was little to be gained by hating.

And he didn't hate. He was too lost and beaten to hate. Annoyingly, his heart was full of love, as if Kathryn's spirit wouldn't let him feel anything else.

He finished the note and put it in an envelope, marked it 'Urgent' and propped it up on his desk. He then tried to formulate a plan of action, but his head was aching and his thoughts fuzzy. He wanted to do nothing but get away, from Hackney, from people, from everything, even if it meant ... but no, that would be such an admission of defeat.

He took a lingering look at the office. He wondered if he would see it again. That same feeling of unreality overwhelmed him and he felt dizzy with it, almost unable to stand. He had to leave, go home, face whatever had to be faced, be his usual stoical self. He shook his head at the frustration and madness of it all.

He picked up a photograph of Kathryn which sat on his desk. What yesterday had been the focus of his life was now an empty ornament. He didn't know whether to smash it or caress it. He looked at it with a puzzled expression, his eyes haunted and pained. What was he to make of this picture, so full of adoration, hope, beauty and love which now spoke of a world way beyond sadness?

He wanted to shed tears but they wouldn't come. Was he stony hearted? Was he tainted by evil as the world wanted him to believe? He felt guilty in ways he didn't understand that this had happened because of what he was, not who he was. If he'd been anyone other than a Jew in hiding, Kathryn might have been alive! Could that be the truth?

Well, damn them all and damn me too! He spoke the words aloud, shocked by the venom in his voice and the breaking of the silence.

He put the photograph back carefully.

What mattered, and what would always matter, was Kathryn, her love, her faith in him, her belief and her kindness, beauty and devotion. Nothing could touch that, not now, not ever.

He tried to gather himself, to sort out his thoughts and his heart, but it was so hard.

He sat down again with his head in his hands. He would wait there, like that, till morning.

He didn't know what else he could do except what Kathryn had tried to teach him, to be happy, be confident, be at peace and enjoy the better side of his nature.

When he raised his head after a brief time in the darkness of his thoughts, he found his hands wet with tears.

Decidedly shaky but also determined to endure this, whatever it took, he left the place and walked home.

## 10

Nurcan returned alone, but not to her home. She couldn't bear the thought of going back alone. Not for the first time in her life, she regretted not having a family, something rare in her culture, but she had her sister, and it was to her sister that she returned.

"Nurcan! What's wrong?"

Nilgun had looked through the spy hole of the front door, seen her sister and opened at once.

"Can I come in?"

No sooner had Nilgun let her sister in than she put her arms around Nilgun's neck and started crying, repressed, unstoppable tears.

"Nurcan! Tell me!"

"Let me go inside," Nurcan whispered.

Nilgun took her into the living room where she switched on the light and heating, wrapping her own dressing gown around herself to keep warm and a blanket around Nurcan who was shivering. The room was a wonderful example of East meeting West, sometimes colliding but everywhere a love of life. There were footsteps on the staircase and then Feriha poked her head inside.

"Hello aunty!" she said. "Are you alright?"

Nurcan nodded but didn't say anything.

"Feriha," her mother whispered, "better go back to bed."

"I'm not a kid, mum," said Feriha.

There were more footsteps and Nilgun's husband Orhan came down, followed by Jemal.

"What's up, mum?" asked Jemal.

Orhan, a big, stern but not unkind man, stood waiting, unsure of what this was all about.

"Nur?" he asked. "You want something?"

She shook her head and said, "I'm sorry. I didn't mean to wake you all up."

"No problem," said Jemal, who, like Feriha, had no sense of minding his own business. His mother often told him he had no sense at all, except for computer games. He registered that "something was up" and decided that if Feri was there, he ought to be, too.

Orhan sat down and listened. They all did. Nurcan had no choice now but to speak.

"There was a murder," she said, "a nurse ... my ... friend."

There was a gasp. Feriha put her hand in front of her mouth. Jemal swore under his breath. Orhan shook his head.

"Melissa?" Nilgun asked, shocked.

"No," said Nurcan. "A mutual friend. The one I give a lift to. Kathryn Hudson."

"Oh no!"

Feriha kept her hand in front of her mouth but she couldn't stop the words slipping out. Her family looked at her thinking she was reacting to Nurcan's shock, but she wasn't. She knew Kathryn. This was one of the nurses treating Sam's little brother Jonathan. She'd been to the ward with him, seen her badge, spoken to her. Sam was fond of her, had a crush on her, Feriha thought.

"What happened?" asked Nilgun.

Nurcan told them, a knife attack, no reason, at least not obvious, and the attacker was still out there.

"I saw her," said Nurcan, "poor Kathryn! I can't get it out of my mind, Nilgy!"

She put her head in her hands. Nilgun squeezed them and put her arm around Nurcan.

"Mum," said Feriha quietly. "I knew her."

"*We* knew her," Jemal corrected her.

Nurcan looked up, inquisitively. Nilgun waited for Feriha to explain.

"Kathryn. She's the nurse that Sammy likes, you know, the Jewish boy..."

"My friend," said Jemal, "the computer nut. His little brother's in hospital and she's a nurse there."

"That's right," said Nurcan. "Alexandra Ward."

"Yeh, there," said Jemal. "Jesus!"

His mother gave him a warning look but said nothing.

"She was beautiful," said Nurcan. "Special. The children loved her. What a place, Nilgy, really, what a place!"

"Flip, murdered!" said Jemal in the kind of way any teenager would say the word, as if it was all excitingly newsworthy. He felt a strong hand on his shoulder. His father was telling him to listen and hold his tongue. Just look and learn, he was saying. Jemal looked at his aunty and saw how upset and scared she was. Aunt Nurcan was always strong - he'd never seen her like this, all broken up.

Feriha sat on the other side of her aunt, holding her hand. Though a teenager like her brother, and able to do dumb things along with the best of them, she had the gift of warmth and understanding and she felt for her aunt who was a good lady in a lot of distress.

"Where?" Nilgun asked. "Near here?"

"Not far."

"Poor girl!" said Nilgun. "Have they told her family?"

"Yes, they came. Her parents, her brother, and her boyfriend, a Jewish boy."

Feriha looked up. She wondered if she'd heard right. Not that her mum or dad knew she had a crush on Sam, but it might help, although she decided that was a weird thing to think at a time like this and definitely too weird to talk about. Jemal gave her a quick look.

"Was he a real Jewish boy?" she asked.

Nilgun said, "That's a strange question to ask, Feriha, even for you."

"Actually," said Nurcan, "he was wonderful. His name is Daniel and he's a good guy, Feriha. Very intense, but good."

That didn't surprise Feriha. Samuel was about as intense as they came. He'd make a black hole look sloppy.

Orhan shook his head and said, "Wicked people, the Jews. He probably did it."

"Daddy!" shouted Feriha. "That's really dumb, even for you!"

Now this was a dangerous thing to say to a man like Orhan with a quick temper and strong opinions on everything, but at a moment like this he wouldn't react, and besides, his wife supported Feriha.

"How can you say such a thing, husband?" she said, furious for a moment. "Is this the nonsense you share with your brainless friends?"

"He's a lovely man," said Nurcan, looking at Orhan who really could be a cauldron of prejudices. "He was devastated, Nilgun, we all were. My god! It's so ... I don't know what words to use."

Feriha felt sorry for this Daniel, even though she'd never met him. It must be horrible to lose someone you love, and it sounded as though he loved her very much. She sighed.

Jemal asked, "Was she out by herself, auntie?"

They looked at him as if he'd asked the strangest question, but Jemal had a logical mind and was trying to visualize what had happened. Nurcan said yes, she'd been out jogging.

"What, at midnight!" Jemal exclaimed.

Nurcan hadn't thought much about the whodunnit side of things. She was, like most of those at the hospital that night, trying to come to terms with what had happened and with her own involvement, so private, despite the willingness of her family to listen. Jemal was more interested in the reasons. His father agreed with him but was afraid to say more in case he upset his wife again. He'd always been a little afraid of both women, especially Nurcan who was usually so severe, but here she was in floods of tears. He didn't understand her and was increasingly nervous, unable to deal with this show of distress.

"Well," said Nilgun, "the police will find out in the end, but it sounds strange, Jemal, yes, I suppose so."

"She was a good girl," said Nurcan. "The best."

Nurcan could hardly speak these words. It was as if she wanted to say more but daren't. Jemal wouldn't argue, not now, but to be out jogging by yourself in the dark in Hackney was a sign of madness or mystery. He'd bet she'd been up to something.

"She was alright, in the head I mean?" Feriha asked. "She seemed okay when I met her."

If she hadn't known her niece, Nurcan might have been offended, but Feriha was a golden hearted teenager with a lot to learn about tact.

"More than alright," said Nurcan. "She was funny and kind and all the right things. God, Nilgun!" and the tears started falling again.

Jemal and Feriha would normally have turned their eyes to heaven at this kind of thing, it was so much like a TV drama, but they respected their Aunt Nurcan and both realised this was something they hadn't had to deal with before, that she was feeling something they didn't understand and they'd better not say or do anything daft. Feriha in particular was very attentive to her aunt, holding her hand and stroking her jet black hair.

"Orhi," whispered Nilgun to her husband, "maybe it's best to leave us two here. You go back to bed."

Orhan was relieved as he was uncomfortable and didn't have much to offer. Jemal wouldn't have minded staying because he wanted to question her about what she thought had really happened but this would have been suicidal, so he left, not forgetting to take some biscuits first. He looked at Feriha sending her a telepathic message to leave too, but she either wasn't receiving or ignored him.

Feriha was in fact determined to stay. She was wide awake now and wanted to be grown up like her mum and her aunt. The more grown up they thought she was, the more she could get away with.

"Shall I make you some more hot tea, aunty?" she asked.

Nurcan said she was alright.

"You're shocked," she said, as if revealing something new. "I'd be shocked too. It's horrible. And to think that I've been there, to that ward mum!"

"This isn't about you, Feriha," Nilgun said quietly, "it's about your auntie."

Feriha felt so small and rather annoyed with herself.

"Sorry auntie," she said, but Nurcan, instead of saying anything, just put her arms around Feriha and hugged her.

"You have to take care of yourself, Feri," said Nurcan, "we all do. There are such bad people in the world!"

"This could happen anywhere," said Nilgun. "I hope Orhan doesn't use it as another excuse for leaving. Anyway, how are you doing, sis?" she asked, squeezing Nurcan's shoulder. "You must be bad to leave work. I've never known you do that before."

"I identified her," said Nurcan, and she told them in more detail what had happened.

"Oh aunty!" said Feriha. "I bet you'll never forget that!"

Nilgun was patient with her daughter, but sometimes Feriha was just a child in teenage clothes. She gave her daughter a look and Feriha promised herself again to listen and keep shtum, a word Sammy had taught her.

"No, I won't forget," said Nurcan. "I'm used to seeing so many things at the hospital, Nilgun, but not this, not her, of all people, not like that!"

Feriha wanted to ask what "not like that" meant but this time she really did hold her tongue, although the gruesome nature of what had happened fascinated her, just as death did, because it was still so unreal. Feriha had never felt so grown up, and also so feminine. The men had vanished, unable to help, but here she was learning what it meant to deal with some of the rougher stuff life had to offer.

Nurcan was, on the surface, the strongest of three sisters and two brothers, but she was struggling hard to hold herself together here. Nilgun suspected there was more that her sister wanted to say, but she wouldn't press.

"Best thing is to stay the night, Nurcan," said Nilgun.

"You can have my room, auntie," said Feriha. "I'll sleep down here. I don't mind."

Nurcan stroked her niece's face and said, "That's very kind of you," but the thought of her niece being kind set her off again and she buried her head in her hands. Nilgun looked at Feriha who was about to say something and the words evaporated, fortunately.

Feriha decided she had to see Sam the next day. His little brother was involved in this murder, even in a small way, and Feriha wanted to offer her support to him just as Nilgun was doing to Nurcan. Sam would need support, she thought. Maybe this was the time to see if she could make him kiss her, just a friendly one, but it was definitely a good opportunity. His defences would be a bit weak. She made a mental note to see him, even if Jemal had to help. At the same time she was thinking these bizarre thoughts she put her hand on her aunt's shoulder and felt a pulse of energy that surprised her. Nurcan's body was taut and tense, as if something inside were struggling to be free, something adult and powerful that Feriha wanted herself. She didn't know what it was, but she sensed that it was there, inside her too, just waiting for the right moment to be born.

"Feriha?"

Feriha looked up, surprised. She was so lost in her planned seduction of Sam that she hadn't heard her mother calling. "Time for you to leave," said Nilgun.

"But mum!"

"Just go," said Nilgun, "you've been very kind, Feri, but your aunt and I need to talk alone."

So, just as she was starting to feel grown-up, her mother made her feel like a girl again.

"Alright, mum," she said. "Goodnight aunty, I hope you feel better tomorrow – well, today."

Nurcan kissed Feriha who hurried off to bed, her head full of love and murder.

When they were alone, Nilgun squeezed her sister's hand, looked at her and said, "Okay, Nurcan, they're gone. Just us now. Time to tell the truth."

And she did.

## 11

The three flatmates had driven back together in silence. It was only when they neared home that Ursula said, "I really don't want to go back, not yet."

"Park at the marina, Ursula," said Jasmine. "We can sit by the river."

Her voice was flat and tired, but Elena said it was a good idea so Ursula drove down Spring Hill and parked near the marina where they went rowing. At this early hour it was dark and deserted. It occurred to them that whoever had attacked Kathryn was still out there, not far away, but this seemed like an important and necessary thing to do, so they ignored their fears.

Wooden benches were permanently in place outside the cafe which served the Lea River rowers. In summer it was heaving, not just with rowers but visitors walking along the bank, either south towards the Thames or north towards Tottenham. They'd never been there at this hour, though they'd done night rows in warmer weather.

They sat on a bench facing the water. If they hadn't been weighed down by an awful sadness they would have revelled in the beauty that was this part of Hackney by night. Humans had a bad habit of working against nature rather than with it, and in Hackney they'd managed more than their fair share of spoiling, but a few had also managed, with surprising care, green and pleasant places, and this was one of them. At night it was even more beautiful, allowing nature a measure of freedom, as if humans were just passing through and that it was simply biding its time till they departed and it could once again have the world to itself.

The Lea navigation channelled the River Lea along a deep, long but narrow cut through much of Clapton. In both directions it joined with other waterways built centuries earlier and only now being appreciated for what they had to offer. There were occasional buildings dotted along the river, but very few, with the Walthamstow and Hackney Marshes bordering the Eastern bank for some miles.

There was no discernible green at that hour, just a silver shadow over trees, marshes and water. The navigation itself was still and spectacularly tranquil, a line of darker silver running past Springfield Park and on into the distance. Across the water from where they sat, the house of the warden of the marina hid in shadow and around it, moored fast, were dozens of boats, almost like a sleepy fishing village. They came in all sizes, barges as well as boats, some battered, some beautiful. Even though the night was still, the boats sometimes knocked into each other and made light tapping sounds above the occasional lap of water. Above, the sky was surprisingly clear. A crescent moon shone down, reflected in the navigation, and around it a host of stars, just beginning to fade under the approaching dawn.

The three girls put their arms around each other and rested their heads on each other's shoulders. No amount of beauty could make up for what they felt nor any amount of tranquillity for the unease threatening to overwhelm them. They held on to each other tightly, as if some evil force were threatening to pull them apart or some lapse in gravity would fling them from the world's orbit.

They weren't sure what to say. Words seemed inappropriate, powerless against the massive shock which had hit them with such force. So close to home now, the minutes passed like a ticking time bomb of despair. They were too young to be experienced with loss, but too old to be mawkish about it; they were clever enough to understand what had happened and sensitive enough to fear the consequences – a wrong word, a wrong thought and the fragility of life would be exposed. They felt, in brief, terribly vulnerable.

"What are we going to do girls?" Ursula asked, and it was probably the best and only question to ask. She didn't mean just that moment, she meant, as they knew, what were they going to do. Life had taken a different turn. The idea of staying in the same house without Kathryn was impossible to imagine. Her vitality and joy and good nature had held them all together; now and forever after there would be just the memory, nothing more. None of them could bear the thought. They couldn't bear the idea of returning to the house at all, not even for a moment, let alone soldiering on.

They weren't naïve and knew what went on in the world. They heard of killings and loss every day, yet the world kept turning. But to be involved was different; it was abhorrent. Fear upon fear threatened them and they wondered whether they were strong enough as individuals and as friends to withstand whatever lay ahead.

"I guess the funeral is first," said Elena. "We'd better get our heads round that."

Jasmine breathed out and shook her head. She couldn't match the idea of a funeral with a vibrant, delightful Kathryn.

"We're her friends," said Ursula. "We loved her and we'll do whatever we have to do. We're strong enough. Think of Michael and Daniel, they'll need us."

"You think Daniel's still at the hospital?" Elena asked. "I mean, if he's home alone we could go and cheer...I mean go and keep him company. I hate the thought of him being there by himself."

"We'll see him later," said Ursula. "We can ask him then. You okay, Jaz?"

Jasmine had tears streaming down her face as she stared at the river.

"Not really. This is going to be a bit tough, isn't it?"

"Yes," said Ursula, "but we are tough. We have to be."

"What the heck was she doing," said Elena, "out by herself at that time? Even for Kathryn that was a bit reckless. I don't know, it's just not right. It doesn't fit!"

"It doesn't," Ursula agreed. "I know. You reckon the inspector...what was his name...?"

"Faraday."

"Yeh. You think he's on the ball?"

"I hope so," said Elena, "but..."

"But what?"

"Well," she hesitated, "I might have been reading too many detective stories, but if she wasn't just being reckless, if she knew what was going on, then..."

"Then it was someone she knew?"

"And someone we know?"

Silence.

"Impossible," said Jasmine, drying her eyes. "That's crazy."

"Why?" Elena asked. "Most murders are domestic."

"You mean Daniel killed her?"

"No, I don't think he could kill a fly, but we didn't know everything about Kath. She had a secret side. We all do."

"I don't," said Elena.

"Nor me," said Jasmine. "Besides, she loved Daniel. It was the real thing, don't you think?"

"They didn't live together."

"They would have done, soon enough."

This would never happen now. So much else that might have happened would also never happen now. Time had turned on a moment.

"But you don't really believe that someone we know could do this, do you El?" Jasmine asked.

"Someone she knew," she answered. "Maybe not someone we know. It's possible."

Ursula and Jasmine exchanged glances.

"Scary world," said Ursula.

"Sick world," said Jasmine.

"It shouldn't be," said Elena. "Look at this." She gestured at the astonishingly lovely scene in front of them. "Doesn't make sense, does it?"

It was her turn to cry now, unable to stop the almost subconscious rotation of tears, as if it were too much for all three to weep together. But they were desperately honest tears. Kathryn's death was a mystery in every sense of the word and something that simply should not have happened. There seemed, in the eyes and understanding of the three friends, to be no providence at all, let alone the fall of a sparrow. You couldn't be ready for a thing like this and you couldn't operate in a world where such wicked, unseen forces pulled the rug from beneath faith, hope and love.

"We'll always have great memories of her," said Ursula. "Nothing can take that away."

"That's true," said Jasmine. "It doesn't make me feel any better though."

"Nothing will," said Elena trying to dry her eyes and talk at the same time. "Not yet. I mean, what can?"

"Time might," said Ursula. "Kath wouldn't want us to be in floods of tears for the rest of our lives, would she?"

"Doesn't matter what she wanted anymore," said Jasmine.

"Yes it does Jaz!" said Ursula. "You know it does! It matters more than anything!"

It was really hard for them to see why anything should matter when the devil could play havoc with them in this way. They each felt so shaken, not just for the loss of Kathryn but for the blow to faith in how the Earth and heavens operated. There were some pretty fundamental questions they had to answer and deep wounds to their souls which might never heal.

Ursula moved away slightly, brought her knees up to her chin and hugged her shins, resting her chin on her knees. She stared out over the river, thinking.

"Urse?"

"I'm okay...no I'm not."

Jasmine stood up, her eyes visibly red even in the very early dawn.

"I think I know what we should do," she said. They waited for more. "Ursula, you've got a key," she said, and motioned towards the boat house.

Ursula tapped one of her pockets.

"Sure - you're not - are you?"

"I am."

Elena said, "I think she's right Ursula. Great idea, Jaz. Kath would approve."

They walked over to the boat house. It was a substantial building, large enough to house numerous boats of various sizes, including the eight man sculls. Ursula took a bunch of keys from her pocket and searched for the one that fitted the padlocks on the double doors. She turned the key and removed the locks. The three of them pulled open one of the doors, the one behind which rested their usual four-seater scull.

They knew what to do, even without the fourth member of the team, who, they felt, was there in spirit, more than at any time in the past few hours.

Boats were racked in neat lines. All were well cared for, including their own scull, which was situated on the left, one from the bottom row.

They took their places and carefully lifted it out, avoiding all the other obstacles, and brought it over to the bank of the river.

They gently lowered it to the ground, prepared the oars, and lowered it into the river.

As ever, Ursula climbed in first, then Jasmine, then Elena. They almost waited for Kathryn to climb in last, which she liked to do, and they felt the boat rock slightly as if a ghost might have lightly stepped on board.

When they were in position, they pushed away from the navigation's stone walls and drifted into the centre of the river, gently prodding the water to stay parallel with the wall. It took a few moments for the boat to settle in position. Another crew might have struggled, but these three were experts. They gently manoeuvred the scull into the centre of the river and began rowing in perfect harmony, three silent figures who knew exactly what they were doing.

The empty fourth seat haunted them. They couldn't help but look at it, but this didn't matter; it was what they wanted. They needed to feel Kath's loss in the most direct way, but also to feel her presence, and this was the way. She was there with them, in spirit or in memory, keeping up the stroke, holding the boat steady. They could read each other's minds, following Ursula's rhythm, hardly causing a ripple in the dark water around them.

They headed east towards the centre of an almost forgotten Hackney, lost by the water's edge. They passed the old waterworks where Melissa and Kathryn had spoken the week before, the old matchbox factory where wonderful toys had been made for decades; they slipped past moored boats and moor hens, shrubbery and marsh; they passed tow-paths and drifted under bridges, never saying a word. A few birds flapped away, disturbed by the sound of the passing scull, minimal though it was. There were very few lights to be seen, and only in the distance. Hackney was blacked out, as were the hearts of the three rowers.

They stopped shortly before the first lock a mile or so from the marina. A willow overhung the water and they drifted beneath it. Ursula lifted her oar and let it rest in the boat, Jasmine and Elena did the same. Then they bowed their heads onto their tucked up knees and gave way to reflection.

An artist might have made a masterpiece of the scene because it had within it so much of what made life worth a visit. Whether they were the closest to Kathryn didn't matter; what mattered was that she was a vital and good part of their lives and she had gone; what mattered was that they were young and the great panorama of the future which, the day before, had been full of hope and belief was suddenly ruptured, their emotional landscape blown apart. They were each faced with something they didn't understand, something which even people who had lived long lives didn't understand, the sheer uncertainty of time, the second by second volatility of it all. But mostly they faced never seeing their friend again, hearing her laugh, seeing her smile, feeling her generous nature and knowing that, whatever happened elsewhere, she was a safe harbour for all things good.

It was only reluctantly, shortly after the sun had risen, that they turned the scull around and headed back to the boat house, still unsure how to face the new day.

## 12

When Matt Davis had parted company with Charlene Okoru that evening, he'd promised to do what she'd asked, or more accurately what she'd told him to do. They were both exhausted. Their shift had been extended by hours and had been by some measure the hardest one they'd ever known. They barely spoke as they left the hospital and when Faraday told them they'd better go home and get some rest, that was exactly what both of them intended to do, so it was a mystery to Matt that he found himself at Cassie Logan's door.

"Matt?"

"Yes."

"Are you arresting me?"

"No. I need to see you, Cass."

Silence, then, "It's four in the morning!"

"Let me in Cassie, please."

She opened the door and he came in, not in uniform and looking as though he were about to flake out. Cassie said, "This isn't good, Matt."

"No, it isn't is it."

"Did something happen?"

"Yes."

"Well, tell me. Sit."

He pulled up a chair in Cassie's small living area, struggling to find the words. She sat opposite him, waiting.

He didn't particularly want to talk; he wanted to touch her, hold her, aware that his life was hanging by a thread and that Cassie could cut him adrift with a single wrong word, but this had to be said.

"I need ... we need to stop seeing each other, Cass."

Cassie looked at him, baffled.

"You came here at four in the morning to tell me that?" Matt looked down. "And we don't see each other, you see me. But this isn't why you wanted to visit, is it Matt? There's something else," she said, "isn't there?"

How she did it he didn't know, partly her voice, her manner, just being the siren that she was, but he felt so hopelessly weak when he was with her. Charlene would never understand. He kept talking, afraid of himself and what was probably inevitable.

"There was a murder."

"Another one?"

"It isn't sin city, Cass. A young woman was killed. Knifed. Charlene and I got called in first. It was rough." Cassie didn't speak, just waited. "It put things in perspective for me."

"Seeing a murder did that?"

"Yes."

"The kind of perspective that makes you want to call on me at four in the morning to say goodbye?"

"Yes."

"Not for any other reason?"

He glanced at her, but he daren't look for too long. Those green eyes tore into him, that skin, even in the direst tiredness, tortured him.

"No."

She sighed and uncrossed her legs, slowly and deliberately, knowing her power.

"Wait," she said, standing and touching him on the shoulder. Her touch set his body on fire, drove out the tiredness and utterly wrecked him. She took two small glasses from a cupboard, each movement overwhelmingly graceful. She poured a little whisky into each. "Here," she said, and as she gave it to him she touched his hand. He knew what she was trying to do, little touch after little touch, arouse him, don't push, just be patient. He understood, but he was too needy to fight it. "Early morning pick-me-up," she whispered. She sipped her drink and watched as he sipped his. "Poor boy," she said. "You must be in a state to come here at this time."

"I am," he said.

"Tell me then," Cassie said, and the surprising thing was she listened, attentive, waiting to hear more.

"This was different," he said, "just a woman, younger than you. Beautiful," he added. "There was something about her. She must have been lovely."

"And?"

"Someone cut her throat."

Cassie made a slight movement that might have been one of

repulsion; it was difficult to say. She moved back an inch or two, blinked and breathed more deeply.

"You know who, or why?"

He shook his head.

"We'll find out. Charlene and I were first on the scene. Found it hard to hold myself together, Cass."

Cassie moved gently, re-crossing her legs. Her blue dressing gown slipped past a knee and she pulled it back up, aware that he was looking.

"Matt?" she asked. He waited. "Why are you telling me this, I mean now, this moment? You know who you should be telling, don't you?"

"Of course I do."

"So?"

He tried to find the right words.

"Can't seem to help myself, can I?"

She didn't smile. She knew the effect she had on him, knew the effect she had on most men, and not a few women. You got used to it after a while, made use of it where possible, ignored it where it didn't matter.

"Go on, Matt." Her voice was low, husky with tiredness, but interested.

He tried not to look at her as he went on.

"She was a nurse, at the hospital. Out alone…"

"Silly girl."

"Jogging."

"Really silly girl."

"Lived local. Her friends came, and a brother, and her boyfriend. Not the usual type."

"Is there a usual type, Matt?"

He thought and said, "Yes. Is that rude?"

"Probably."

"They were good people, all of them. I like them. It'll wreck their lives, Cassie."

"People are stronger than you think," she said. "Even you. You have your weaknesses, Matt…" He glanced at her but said nothing, "but you have a strong side. That's why I took up with you. I don't like feeble people."

"I feel feeble," he said, "when I'm with you."

"I know," Cassie answered, honestly, "but you're not. Sex is a powerful drive." He almost laughed, but this wasn't the moment. "Go on," she said, "tell me about the friends."

He told her about each of them and how they'd touched him,

especially the brother and the boyfriend. "Intense," he said, "both of them, but in different ways."

She asked him to describe them, visualizing them, not just passing time. This was the peculiar, enigmatic thing about her, he thought, how, despite what she did for a living, she gave him time and attention.

"So sad," she said, "and scary. The killer is still out there, then?"

"Yes, but we'll find him."

"You're sure about that? Doesn't sound as though he gave away too many clues."

"No, he didn't. Hardly any. But we'll dig around. He'll give himself away."

Cassie studied him for a few moments then moved her chair closer and stroked his face.

"You look shattered," she said.

"I am."

"Has it changed you, then, this killing?" she asked.

Yes, he feared it had changed him, and this was, he thought, why he'd come to see her, to find out how. Somehow he had more faith in Cassie seeing the answer than Eileen who was so trusting in the here and now, so full of the business of life that she'd lost sight of him.

"It would change anyone," he said. "You can't see a thing like that and stay the same."

She stood so close to him. He could smell her, feel her, touch the blue fleece gown wrapped around her. All he wanted was to open the gown and see her. He couldn't bear the thought of going back to real life without making love to Cassie once more, just the once, then goodbye forever.

"Poor Matt!" she whispered.

He looked up at her like a sad little puppy.

"Why?" he asked.

She stroked his hair, ran her hand down his neck.

"You're in danger," she said.

"How," he asked.

"You come to see me at four in the morning and you ask why you're in danger?"

"I can't help myself."

She didn't smile. She was giving so little away, just quietly revelling in the power she had over him, yet not cruelly. Cassie Logan was not a cruel person.

"You have to," she said, "or you'll go under."

"Will I?"

"Of course. You can't do this – see me, I mean – and carry on as if nothing was happening. It'll do you harm. It'll harm your wife and your children."

Matt tried to think of Eileen, Frankie and Kylie, yet Cassie's close presence overwhelmed him. He could be in mortal danger but desire for this beautiful woman would kill him first. He tried to think of his work, he was a police officer for heaven's sake! This was the last thing an officer of the law should be doing! What possessed him? A devil, for sure. He needed her so much, more than ever before. He'd seen death that night and he'd seen love in shock and mourning. What was he supposed to do? Could he really go straight home, make himself a tea, greet his wife and kids and go to bed as if all was well? Was that being professional?

There was silence between them for what seemed to Matt like forever. She looked at him with her still, green eyes, totally unselfconscious. He looked back, watching for hints of contempt, but he couldn't see any. She was an enigma with an even greater enigmatic hold over him. He didn't understand it and couldn't fight it. For a few moments he feared she was going to reject him, send him home without satisfaction, but Cassie was not foolish. She knew when to withhold and when to give. If she'd denied her policeman then, he might have found the strength truly not to see her again, but to give him what he was so obviously crying out for, despite the murder and the tiredness and the talk of change, that would bind him to her tighter, ruin him a little further.

She sat astride his knees, lifted his face to hers and kissed him. He let her, lost in her warmth and the reckless abandonment of sense and order.

"You're a bad policeman," she whispered.

He felt horror at his weakness. He was a good policeman, one of the best. This was excusable, it had to be or guilt would suffocate him, but he didn't answer. He couldn't speak. He felt her body working into his and couldn't stop it responding, moving in gentle rhythm with hers, finding that elemental beat which never failed them. Was she like this with everyone, he asked himself? Was she that skilled that she could dupe him over and over again or did she have that weakness for him which his vanity suggested.

The thoughts waved and faded as she led him to the bed, laid him down and massaged his neck, his back, his legs, slowly moving towards him, sensing his need and his response as if she were already inside him.

He turned and pulled her down, kissing her again, for so long that he thought the world would melt away and this kiss would be all that was left. He never wanted life to return, to have Charlene berate him or to feel tortured with Eileen and the children.

His mind was a fury, a battleground between what should be and what was. He loved his family, he knew he did. The faces of his children kept peering at him from a distance, and Eileen's voice called to him, but Cassie's power sucked him deeper. He loved the lovemaking more than he loved love, that was undeniable despite his feeble rebellion. She touched every nerve and brought his body into a state of bewildered joy that he'd never experienced before. It was truly like sinking into a dark sea of forgetfulness, which was what he desperately needed, only he feared the light when rationality returned. It should return now, there was still a hint of it, but Cassie worked on him so well, turning him as he turned her, feeling him as he felt her, bending and flowing with him wondrously. The traumas of the night were gently squeezed away, the horror of such violence replaced by the mystery of an embrace from this clever woman. She seemed to know where to touch just when touch was most needed, to kiss when kissing was most desired and to relax when a climax was too close. She wrapped herself around him physically and emotionally until there was no room for thought of any kind nor guilt nor regret. He grew into her and she squeezed him gently, firmly, knowing just how far to hold him, to release him, to tie him to her. And she knew the very moment to make it all end, to bring the long, long embrace to a conclusion that pressed all the nightmare, revulsion, fear and dread from him as if a deadly poison had been nullified after a monumental battle.

He shouted and she put her hand over his mouth.

"Neighbours!" she whispered.

He laughed, then cried, fell into her with a mad mixture of joy and despair.

He couldn't let her go. Her softness tormented him. Her hair fell on him like strands of living darkness.

"Cassie," he whispered. She was still. "I love you."

She sat up, looked at him, gently pulled away.

"This isn't love, Matt," she said. "It's work."

He understood and wasn't offended, just amazed at how he could accept these two so different colliding worlds.

"I shouldn't have said it," he answered.

"No, but I appreciate the sentiment. You enjoyed it, Matt?"

"You know I did, but I don't think 'enjoy' is the right word, Cassie."

She gave him one of her enigmatic looks. "Do you feel better Matt, at least?"

He wasn't sure. A tension had been released but it would be back with a vengeance, he feared. And how could he "feel better" after such a night? She saw this and said he was a good man but a bad policeman. This hurt.

"Explain," he said.

"I don't have to," said Cassie. "It isn't possible to mix your work and me, Matt. You might think you can, but it will all unravel. Trust me on this. You said so yourself."

"So what should I do?"

"I can't answer that, only you can, and what you 'should do' is not necessarily what you can do or will do. I'm sorry for you, Matt, really."

"Yet you still see me."

Cassie did what he knew she had to do and held out her hand. He leaned over the edge of the bed, picked up his trousers, took out his wallet and gave her a wad of notes. She didn't check them; she trusted him. It was a travesty of love, he knew this, yet he was caught in the madness of desire. He watched her put the money in a drawer, her face impassive. Watching her, he felt the need arise again, so unexpectedly soon. There was no end to it, that was obvious, and she was right, that was also obvious. He couldn't mix upholding the law and this secret vice, it was tearing him apart. If Charlene knew what Cassie did for a living she would cut Matt off forever, he had no doubt. She was angry enough as it was, but if she knew everything she would hate him. Charlene was tolerant only up to a certain point which was not particularly far along the line of human frailty.

"I'd better go," he said.

Cassie stood and wrapped her dressing gown around her, then helped him to dress. It was such a gentle gesture. Again, he felt his blood rise and his passion begin to get the better of him. Was there any redemption from this mire? How could he pay this woman for the astonishing pleasure she offered then hide in the lie that was his family and his work? Which, indeed, was the lie? He loved his family, he was good at his work, he couldn't imagine living without them; but neither could he imagine giving up Cassie.

A thought occurred to him. He needed redemption and that would only come by focusing his mind. And wonder of wonders, Cassie read his thoughts.

"You'll catch the bastard," she said. He looked at her as if she were the Delphic Oracle. "That *is* what you're thinking about, isn't it?" she asked.

"How...?"

"I just know," Cassie said.

"Yes, I want to help catch the bastard. Who wouldn't?"

"You've seen death and love and lust all in one night, Matt. I guess you're head is a bit of a mess. Go home and get some rest. Then catch him and string him up. I hate him, whoever he is."

He caught a glimpse in her eyes of real hatred ... and real fear. Here was yet another paradox, that this woman who was ruining his soul needed him to protect her body. And he would. Despite all the nightmare of this desperate liaison, he'd do whatever it took to catch the killer; that purpose would keep him sane, at least for a while longer.

## 13

"You going to be alright, Mel?" Melissa held on to Patrick's hand as they sat in the car at the hospital car park. She wouldn't let him start the car to take them home. "You want to talk?" he asked her. She sat there dazed, even after all those hours together in the hospital she couldn't take in what had happened, let alone tell others what only she knew.

"We can't go home yet, Pat," she said.

"Okay. You know I'll do whatever you want, Mel. But we can't sit here, it's cold and it isn't good. Where do you want to go?"

Melissa wondered where Kathryn's flatmates had gone, what Michael would do and where Daniel would go. She felt for them, so lost in this sudden storm. Her head span and her heart was heavier than she thought possible, and the worst might be yet to come.

"Just sit, Pat, for a few minutes, then we'll decide."

Patrick knew something was on her mind but assumed she was struggling with the killing. She squeezed his hand but didn't look at him, staring out of the car window at the other parked cars and the Homerton skyline. It was all so familiar and she felt terribly small, as if this horrendous loss was nothing to the vast world which would soon wake and begin another day as if nothing had changed, and yet everything had changed. It couldn't lose someone as beautiful as Kathryn and not register it in some way, that made no sense. Alexandra Ward was probably being told at that moment. All their friends would be devastated but would work on through the night. There was a momentum to time which nothing could touch.

"Pat?"

"Hmm?"

"I have to tell you something."

"Of course, sweetheart, anything, you know that."

"Something I don't understand," said Melissa.

"Okay. Maybe I can help?"

"I doubt it."

"Is it to do with Kathryn?"

"Yes."

"Tell me then, Mel, what is it?"

Melissa found the words hard to utter. She wondered whether her memory of what had been said was wrong because it was so unreal and unwanted. She searched for reasons to doubt them, but couldn't find one that rang true. It was real and couldn't be hidden. She would make things a hundred times worse if she held her tongue. She turned to Patrick and looked him full in the face.

"Kathryn was pregnant," she said.

He took in the sentence as she knew he would, assuming that Daniel was the father and that the tragedy was twice as cruel as it had been moments before.

"Oh, love, poor girl! Poor Daniel!"

"Yes," said Melissa. "Poor Daniel."

She said this in a peculiar way, Patrick thought, but he couldn't work out what she meant.

"He doesn't know, does he?" Patrick asked. Melissa shook her head. "He would have said," Patrick observed. "Why didn't she tell him?" he asked.

"Guess," said Melissa, wanting to hide the truth as long as possible.

"She didn't have time? She wanted to make sure? She was scared?"

"She did have time, she was sure and yes, she was scared – of something."

"Of what, Mel?"

"Can't you reason it out, Pat?"

He got fidgety, as if she was accusing him of being dense. Another time, another place, another situation, he would have had a go at her, but not now. He tried hard to see what she was getting at but he couldn't. Sometimes the obvious is remarkably evasive.

"I really can't, Mel."

She sighed, summoned up the courage to say the words that would alter Pat's and everyone else's view of Kathryn and said, "Daniel wasn't the father."

"What?"

"He wasn't the father. Kath told me, last week. We were out running. She was petrified."

"Jesus!" Patrick could make as little sense of this as Melissa.

Kathryn and Daniel were about as close as two people could be without merging into a single soul. Kathryn loved him to distraction and Daniel, for all his intensity, was in a constant state of adoration. To suggest that someone else had fathered Kathryn's child was to defy the laws of nature. "You know this for sure, Mel?"

"I wouldn't make it up, would I?"

He shook his head. He could get his head around most things, but this evaded him completely.

"Who then?" he asked. "Who's the father, Mel? Did she tell you that?"

"She didn't," Mel answered. "I asked her, but she wouldn't say."

"Or couldn't say?"

"Maybe."

Patrick sat back in the driver's seat of the car, still holding Mel's hand, but his mind was buzzing away at a hundred miles an hour. Hackney had never made much sense to him. It was the biggest melting pot in the universe and at times he wondered at how well it worked whilst at other times he shook his head at how it all seemed to be falling apart. As he wrote about the dark side, his perceptions were coloured by the seedier elements of the borough, of which he'd witnessed many, but this was different. He thought he understood motives pretty well having witnessed all manner of crimes, but this stumped him. His mind whirled with possibilities, all of them nasty, brutish and disastrous. Was Kathryn a liar? Had she deceived Daniel? Was this a crime of passion and not a random attack after all? "Jesus!" he whispered again.

Outside the car, in the last hours of night, there was a deceptive peace. There always was. Night gave nothing away, even though the wickedness was ever present, no matter how tranquil or beautiful it all appeared from a distance. Tonight the tranquillity was more of an illusion than ever because a monster roamed the streets, someone who could kill an angel.

An angel? Truly? He'd lost so many illusions, everyone did - it was the way of the world - but some had to be true, surely. If someone like Kathryn was a cheat and a fake, then what hope was there for any of them? Was everything a tissue of lies? The whole emerging nightmare was like some formula that didn't add up, a discovery which threw into question everything you knew about the laws of nature. There had to be an explanation, and one that wouldn't incriminate innocence.

"She was raped," he said suddenly as the thought popped into his mind and out of his mouth without a censoring moment in between.

Melissa turned to him, her eyes red raw with tiredness and distress, but also grateful that Pat had understood.

"I think so too," she said, "but she wouldn't say."

"No, she wouldn't, would she? Mel?" She waited. "We've got to tell Faraday."

"I know."

"Now."

"It's just ..." she hesitated, then stopped, and he knew why. Once Faraday knew, it would be part of the investigation and everyone would know. There would be doubt and rumour and everything good would be tainted forever. It would be horrible and messy, yet they had no choice.

When Melissa was about as composed as she could be, Patrick let go of her hand and started the car.

Stoke Newington Police Station was a relatively new glass monolith replacing a Dixon of Dock Green structure some twenty years earlier. It had a counterpart in Lower Clapton, an original classical masterpiece that might just as easily have been an art gallery as a police station but definitely not suited for twenty-first century policing. Faraday was based, unsurprisingly, at the newer building.

Melissa and Patrick didn't say a word as they drove there. It was a brief drive, and they were familiar with the route, but nothing appeared familiar. Streets felt strange; buildings they'd seen a thousand times looked insubstantial; the very geography of the neighbourhood looked alien. Hackney had a lived-in quality, a robust but neighbourly grubbiness; now, though, it looked far from neighbourly - it felt hostile, a landscape that had witnessed a terrible killing, was possibly keeping an even worse secret, and done nothing to stop it.

They parked near the station and walked to the entrance. A few dodgy looking people were hanging around in the waiting area as they did every night, each of them troubled in their own intense and unredeemable way. A woman sat with a young boy and girl in tow; a couple of young roughnecks sat talking aggressively to each other; another young man sat stony-faced staring at nothing; a girl of about fifteen sat with a boy of about sixteen, holding hands and looking miserable as sin. Heaven knew what brought these citizens out at such a time, but they and many more like them were always out, at each of the four police stations and in the hospitals, assuring any casual observer that the volatile lifeblood of the borough was in a healthy state.

"We've come to see Inspector Faraday," said Patrick to the receptionist, a tough looking black woman who quizzed them firmly but kindly then called through on some secret hotline. Two minutes later, no more, a door opened and a fresh-faced officer called them in. The others in the waiting area wondered why these two might be getting preferential treatment, but as rough as they were, they knew better than to kick up a stink.

Faraday was waiting for them on the second floor. They guessed he hadn't gone home and they were right. He'd already assembled a team of about half a dozen officers working away in a room set aside for the case. He looked tired but determined and smiled in surprise when he saw them.

"Come in Melissa. Come in Patrick. I'm taken aback a little to see you. Is something wrong?"

Melissa looked at Patrick but said nothing. Faraday took them through to a small office close by where they sat on two tub chairs. He leaned lightly on a wooden desk and waited. He spent much of his working life waiting and watching, taking in everything that needed to be taken in before he took action himself.

"We've got something to tell you," said Melissa. "I should have told you before but I wasn't sure what to do."

"That's fine," said Faraday, "you were all marvellous at the hospital. I'd excuse you anything. What is it?"

"It's about Kath," said Melissa. Faraday nodded. "We went jogging last Sunday," Melissa continued, "she was upset about something."

She paused.

"Did she say what?"

"Yes, she did, eventually, but it was hard for her to tell me."

"Something personal?"

"Very."

There was quiet. Faraday didn't press. This wasn't an interrogation. They'd come here and were obviously under stress to say what had to be said. He had absolutely no idea what was coming.

"Is this confidential?" Melissa asked.

"Depends," said Faraday. "I doubt you'd want to tell me something that had no bearing on the case, so it probably won't be, no, but anything you say will be treated with respect, you know that."

Melissa nodded.

"She was pregnant, inspector."

Faraday looked puzzled.

"She told you this for certain?"

"Yes."

Faraday thought just what Patrick had thought, poor Daniel. He also thought that had he known, they might have saved the baby, but he would never tell these two such a thing; they'd live their lives regretting it...unless...

"I'm assuming it was Daniel's?"

It was something in the way they looked at him which told him that such an assumption was wrong. Patrick confirmed it when Melissa couldn't talk for tears.

"No, sir, it wasn't, apparently."

"Apparently? Melissa?"

Melissa composed herself again and told Faraday what Kathryn had told her that day which now seemed like a lifetime ago, something that had happened in a parallel universe, not here, not in their stable, happy, safe little world.

"I think," she said, "that Kathryn might have been..."

She couldn't say the word.

"Raped?" said Faraday. Melissa nodded. The idea filled her with horror, as much as it had done when she and Kathryn spoke about it last week. "She didn't report this...attack?" Faraday asked.

"She could barely talk about what happened," said Melissa. "I really don't know much more than this. I wish I did."

Faraday sat still, hardly moving.

"No idea at all who might have been responsible?"

"None," said Melissa.

"Someone she knew?"

"Possibly."

"It's important, Melissa. What did Kathryn say to you, exactly?"

Melissa thought back to their marathon run last Sunday.

"Only what I've told you. She was desperate, but this had happened weeks before. I mean it had to, hadn't it? She was pregnant."

Faraday stood up and walked around the table, looking out of the window at a dark Stoke Newington. This was going to be one hell of a case. He hoped, beyond his expectations of the world, that this Kathryn was a good woman. He sensed that she was. She needed to be for the wellbeing of all these people who so obviously loved her. But truth was truth. It had its own laws and Faraday's job in life was to discover the truth, however shameful it might be.

"You believed her?" he asked.

"Sorry?"

"You believed her?" he repeated. "You didn't think that she was making this up to hide an ... indiscretion? I have to ask," said Faraday. "I will have to ask even more hurtful questions in the next few days."

"No," said Melissa. "Kathryn couldn't lie. Whatever you ask about her is fine. She had integrity, inspector, I'd stake my life on it. That was who she was. An angel."

"Angels are heavenly creatures, Melissa," said Faraday. "This is Earth."

"Melissa is right, though, inspector," said Patrick. "Kathryn was put together differently. If you'd seen her you'd know. If Mel says it wasn't an indiscretion then it wasn't."

Faraday had seen Kathryn in death, not life, yet he had the feeling that what these friends of hers said was true. He'd seen many things in his time, and he'd see many more if he could stay the course, but he doubted anything would come as close to defeating him as seeing the brutalised body of Kathryn Hudson. All night, as he'd got together his team and set about a plan of action, her features had been nagging away at him, as if the dead girl was trying to communicate somehow, to tell him something. As a good officer, he was trained not to get involved or react emotionally, but it was hard to see innocence murdered and feel nothing. He determined to channel the horror into catching the miserable murderer who had done this.

"Then she was raped?"

"Yes."

"And she never spoke of it?"

"No."

"Till she spoke to you?"

"Yes."

"And you don't know what suddenly made her talk of it?"

"I guess it had been building up inside her. She only found out she was pregnant a few days before."

"Right. But no names?"

"None. She was scared."

"Scared?"

"Yes. Terrified."

"Of what? Of it happening again?"

"I don't know. Maybe. I would be."

"Yes, of course. Many women don't want to tell when such things happen. You think Kathryn was ashamed?"

"Yes. But..."

"Mmm?"

"There was something else."

"What?"

"Hard to say. She was just so desperate for me to keep it quiet."

"She was afraid of losing ... Daniel?"

"She said no."

"Really?"

"She thought, if he knew the truth, he wouldn't leave her."

"Interesting. Any ideas why she was so adamant not to tell anyone? I mean, if she thought Daniel would stay with her, what was she afraid of?"

"I can't guess, inspector. All I know is that she was desperate and I wouldn't have told anyone behind her back. I didn't even tell Patrick."

"No," said Patrick, "she didn't. Only tonight. Just now. I was gobsmacked, inspector. Doesn't make sense, does it?"

Faraday came back from the window and pulled up a chair near them.

"It will," he said. "Truth has a way of surfacing, eventually. There'll be the DNA, if her family agree." Melissa and Patrick looked blank. "Of the foetus," said Faraday.

Melissa out her hand to her mouth. The baby had been somehow outside this whole story, a peripheral fact, but now it took centre stage.

"We'll take DNA from the baby," Faraday said. "It will all but tell us who did this."

It made sense, of course, but it was also heart-breaking that the sole purpose of this little unborn creature would be to reveal its father as the murderer of its mother.

"Nevertheless," Faraday went on, "we can't forcibly take samples from everyone that ever knew Kathryn. We need to do follow standard procedures and that will be painful."

"How do you mean?" Melissa asked, but it was Patrick who answered.

"Emotionally," he said. "They'll be tricky questions, love. They'll hurt."

"He's right," said Faraday, "but what you've told me is enormously important. I realise how difficult this will be once the news gets out. People will talk, they always do, and the papers will have a field day."

"Not if I can help it," said Patrick.

"I doubt you'll be able to do much, Patrick," said Faraday, "though it's right that you try. From our point of view, the police that is, there's no certainty, despite what I just said, that there's a connection. I mean the murder might still have been random, but something happened in Kathryn's life which we have to discover, whether or not it will help the case. You can't discount any possibility at this stage."

"She had no enemies," said Melissa. "It doesn't make sense that someone who she knew – that we knew – killed her. She was loved, not hated."

Faraday looked away, remembering other cases where good people had fallen victim to spite and malevolence. He could no longer believe that goodness was untouchable, if he ever believed it at all. He was a good person himself, but his schooldays at Homerton had been fraught with bullying, aggression, injustice and chaos. It was a wonder he'd retained any sense of moral purpose, let alone dedicated his life to setting wrong things to right.

"That may be, but unless this was either random or mistaken identity..."

"You think that's possible?"

"Anything is possible right now. As I say, we'll follow up all leads. I wasn't going to ask you this until tomorrow - I would have wanted you to rest first - but as you're here, maybe we should start with a few questions?"

Melissa said that would be okay, even though her head was spinning and she felt battered. Faraday called in a couple of members of his team and introduced them to Melissa and Patrick, then he began to ask them the kind of uncomfortable questions which dug deep into Kathryn's and all their lives. It was as if Melissa was suddenly seeing her life and the lives of all Kathryn's friends from a totally new perspective. It made her think about who they really were and what might be going on beneath the surface of civility, but at the same time, she never felt she was uncovering anything suspicious. It might all be made to sound suspicious, if you had a twisted mind or malicious purpose, but even so, this would be difficult. They were regular people leading the best lives they could and Kathryn had been a super lady.

When Melissa and Patrick had to give details of where they were at the time of the murder it made Melissa realise they were all suspects, that Faraday's warning had been real – this really was uncomfortable. Faraday did his best to relax them, he didn't suspect them in any way, and yet the rigours of his work forced him not to discount anyone until the case was proved beyond doubt.

They spoke to him about Daniel, about Michael and about her flatmates. This was awful, but at the same time Melissa saw that it had to be done and that there might well be clues hidden away which only Faraday or someone in his team might see. They were objective, not hampered by emotion, affection or prejudice, but she would still have been astonished if anyone she mentioned had been implicated – even in a world that made little sense, such a thing was unbelievable.

"Was there anyone at any time who upset her, who made her feel ill at ease?" Faraday asked.

Melissa thought hard but she couldn't remember a single likely person. Not that Kathryn had walked the Earth with her head in the clouds, she was well aware of human frailties and of people to avoid, but in their circle there was no one.

Except...

Faraday looked up.

Melissa recalled something Kathryn had said a while back.

"She visits – visited an old lady," said Melissa, "close by. Marge – Mary – I'm not sure. You'll find it in Kath's address book. She went round there occasionally. Kath was fond of her. She helps – helped her do stuff in her house. She's really old. Over ninety. They were putting together a history, a kind of project, about the woman's life. I think she'd lived in the same house forever."

"And?" Faraday asked.

"Kath told me that she'd been round there one evening and the woman's grandson, or great grandson, I don't remember exactly, was there. He took a shine to her, she said, but Kath didn't like him. There weren't many people she didn't like, hardly any, so that stuck in my mind – for a while. Sorry, I should have said something before."

"No problems," said Faraday. "I don't suppose you remember his name?"

"No, but Mary – Madge – the lady will tell you."

"What didn't Kathryn like about him, Melissa?"

" Kath called him a space invader."

"How's that?"

"Got too close," Melissa explained. "He must have been a bit weird for Kath to feel that way, and I think she was surprised. It put her off going for a while. Kath said that she told her he only came to see if she was still alive and to make sure she'd remember him in the will."

"Ah," said Faraday, "not particularly unusual. Wills keep lawyers in business. We'll follow it up."

"Actually," said Melissa, "the girls were talking about her in the hospital tonight."

"The girls?"

"Ursula, Elena and Jasmine. She called them. Tonight."

"This lady?"

"Yes. She was worried."

"Why was that?"

"Because she wanted to speak with Kathryn and she couldn't reach her."

"What time was this?"

"Not sure. They'll tell you."

"Was there a reason she was worried, do you know?"

"I really don't. But I guess when I get to ninety I'll be worried too, about everything."

Faraday smiled and apologised.

"Silly question," he said. "Anything else?"

There wasn't, not that Melissa or Patrick could think of.

"Listen," said Faraday, "I appreciate you coming here to tell me this. You did right. I doubt anything could have saved the baby, so don't think along those lines. The best thing you can do is get a few hours sleep, if possible. I've got your details in case I need to contact you."

"Inspector?"

"I know what you're going to ask me," he said. "Is there any way we can keep this quiet, about the baby, am I right?" He was right. "I doubt it," he said. "There'll be a court case at some point and I suspect Kathryn's family and good friends won't want to find out such a thing in the public arena. It may be best coming from you – or me, I don't mind."

"I think I'd like to tell Daniel now," said Melissa. "He might be angry if he thinks I didn't tell him sooner. Is that okay?"

"On one condition," said Faraday. Melissa was taken aback. Why would he set a condition? "I want to see his reaction," Faraday explained. Melissa realised that Faraday really didn't know Daniel. He didn't know any of them, and once again she saw that they were all culpable. "You really want to do this now?"

She did. Instinctively, she felt that Daniel ought to know right away.

## 14

Daniel wasn't asleep. He wasn't even resting. He was sitting in the kitchenette, drinking a steaming hot liquid, staring at the table top, lost in thoughts so bleak they filled the air around him. Faraday, his supporting officer, Inspector Vivian Fowler, Melissa and Patrick were unexpected but not unwelcome visitors.

"Are you alright on your own, Dan?" Melissa asked, touching him gently on the arm.

"Not particularly. Hard to know what to do, isn't it?"

"What are you drinking?" Melissa asked.

"Nothing alcoholic, just cocoa. Has something happened? You haven't caught someone already, have you?"

Faraday never spoke to anyone on a case without taking in everything about them. Daniel's home was small, tidy and friendly.

There was nothing in the layout or feel of the place that suggested a warped life, or in Daniel himself. Just as in the hospital he was intense and composed, but not in an arrogant way. You could never be absolutely certain what anyone was thinking, but Daniel gave a pretty good impression of someone in a state of deepest anxiety and control. His eyes were darker than usual and his skin pale, taught with tensions.

A photograph of Kathryn rested on a small upright piano. It lit up the room.

"No," said Faraday, "but we do have something to tell you. Miss Cochrane wanted to tell you herself but I felt I ought to come, on a professional basis. It isn't easy news."

Daniel led them into the lounge area where they tried to find comfortable places to stand or sit in an uncomfortable situation.

"Couldn't be much worse," said Daniel, "could it? I really can't imagine what."

Faraday felt an unprofessional sympathy for Daniel. The man was almost naively innocent, albeit distractingly deep and definitely not wysiwyg. Some people were clear cut, what you saw was what you got, but this oddball lover of the dead girl was a knot of anxieties. He was a difficult man to understand but he wasn't a difficult man to like – he had a certain charm and cuddliness which transcended his thoughtfulness.

"Oh, Dan!" whispered Melissa.

Daniel looked at her with a puzzled expression. He tried to steel himself but he was already so battered that he had no idea what to steel himself against.

"Dan," said Melissa, "there isn't a good way of telling you this, there really isn't." Patrick held her hand as she spoke. "But I wanted you to know first, well, first amongst us." Daniel waited, his expression a mask of apprehension. "She was pregnant, Dan. She was going to have a baby."

Daniel absorbed this news with the same enigmatic process he had accepted the news of her death. None of those present were mind readers, but they each sensed his sudden fleeting vision of a lost fatherhood, then the realisation that this was not his baby. Only Daniel knew what had passed between Kathryn and him, but though the world took for granted that sex before marriage was no longer a moral issue, the world wasn't always right. An almost imperceptible look of desolation passed across his handsome features. An internal force appeared to be tearing him apart though he was doing all he could to hold it in check.

"Oh," he said, very quietly, "that's hard to take."

'And so was that', Faraday thought, but he said nothing. He was used to outbursts of emoting by people wanting to shine for a few minutes in the blooded light of killings, but Daniel seemed to vanish, rather, down a tunnel of absolute darkness.

"You've done a post mortem already?" Daniel asked with another show of rationality over emotion.

"No," said Faraday.

"Then..."

"She told me," said Melissa, "last week, while we were out jogging. She told me it wasn't you." Daniel flushed with humiliation as much as anger. "She was devastated, Dan. It was killing her... I mean..."

Faraday came to Melissa's rescue. "We think this might be a case of rape Daniel."

"You think?" Daniel asked. "You can't be sure?"

"If what she said to Melissa is true, then yes, it was rape."

"*If* it was true?" Daniel said. "You doubt her?

"It's my job to investigate, Daniel, not to take anything for granted."

"No. Melissa, you believed her?"

"On my life, Dan!" She held his hand and looked into his face, trying to offer him some comfort. "She was in torment."

"But she told you, not me."

"Be wise, Dan," said Melissa, "would she really tell you?"

"She told me everything. I told her everything. There were no secrets."

"Oh Daniel," said Melissa, so sorry for him and for Kathryn and for what she had to say, "this was beyond all that. She was raped!"

Melissa's words drifted through to Daniel from a distance and bore no resemblance to his life or Kathryn's. They were too cruel and too irrelevant to elicit any reactions. How was he supposed to react? He lowered his head and dug his hands into his dark hair, as if he were trying to keep his mind from exploding.

"Danny, mate," whispered Patrick, "are you alright?"

After a minute or so, Daniel looked up, surprised that people were still there as his world crumbled and the devil mocked him. He glanced at Patrick but didn't answer. Instead he turned to the inspector and said, "Forgive me if I'm not that communicative, inspector. I'll try. It's just..." He paused. Faraday wondered whether Daniel would be able to handle the kind of truth that didn't just hurt, it killed - faith, hope, everything. " ... just ... no, it doesn't matter."

He sat back and looked at Melissa and Patrick as though they were strangers.

"Shall I make you something to drink, Dan," Melissa asked, her heart reaching out to him but resorting to the banal for comfort, "or something to eat?"

He stared at her as though she was talking in riddles, but then gave her an unexpected smile and said either would be good.

Melissa found her way around Daniel's kitchenette in something of a daze, distraught in case Daniel should lose himself in this cruel truth. He was on the edge of a dizzying drop and she didn't know what could be said to keep him safe. She could barely imagine what he was feeling. It was a surprise when she heard him speak to the inspector.

"You will find the person that did this?" he asked.

"I'm hopeful," said Faraday. "I know you're shocked, Daniel, but might I ask a couple of questions now?"

Melissa had to admire the inspector's stamina and perseverance. She thought he would have let Daniel recover, but he evidently had more faith in him than she did. His sole concern was solving this case as quickly as possible. There was a monster out in the streets of Hackney and Faraday was very aware of this; it took priority over all feelings and reactions. He might also have wanted to divert Daniel away from Melissa's revelation.

"This is an awkward question Daniel, but I need to know where you were this evening," Faraday said. Inspector Fowler held a notebook with a pencil poised. Daniel grimaced, took a deep breath, aware that neither he nor anyone Kath knew was exempt from suspicion.

"On various call outs," he said, his voice rough and tired. "I have the details."

"May I see them?" Faraday asked.

Daniel brought over his briefcase and opened it. He took out a leather binder with a stack of papers clipped inside. He skimmed through them and held them out to Faraday.

"These were my call-outs," Daniel said.

Faraday was flicking through them as Melissa came in carrying a tray of refreshments. She put it on a coffee table and passed teas around. Daniel held his with both hands, staring at the mug as though it held the secrets of life and death.

After a few moments Faraday raised his eyebrows and said, "Small world, Daniel." Daniel looked puzzled. "Your last call – Eileen Davis?" Daniel remembered her, Kylie and Frankie. They seemed to be part of a distant world, one that he'd visited in a previous life. "I know them," said Faraday. They all looked at him, uncertain what he was about to say. "The officer at the hospital? PC Davis?" They all remembered.

"He's Eileen's husband."

Daniel saw that Faraday was not only trying to do his job, but also to distract him. He didn't know whether he appreciated it or not. All he wanted was to be away from Hackney, from people, from everything he knew, to lose himself and escape reality, but the world imposed itself upon him relentlessly.

"Yes," he said, "I remember her saying that her husband was in the police force. Nice family."

"Daniel," said Faraday, " I need to ask you a couple more things."

There were no objections, though Daniel looked so distracted, almost as though he would struggle to remember his own name.

"Did Kathryn talk to you at all about anyone, in any way, that made you think she was afraid?"

There wasn't.

"Anyone she disliked?"

Nobody.

"Not this grandson from the lady she was helping?"

Oh, yes, she did mention him, but nothing serious.

"When did she first mention him?"

About two months ago.

"Had she been behaving oddly since then?"

Yes, but Daniel didn't think the two things were connected.

"Why?"

He just didn't. Kath hadn't given him any reason to believe it.

"But she was different?"

Yes. And he knew why now.

"She hid this from you completely?"

She had. She'd said she was unhappy about something.

"But you didn't ask her what?"

Of course he did, but she didn't want to talk.

"No one else?"

There was no one else. Kath had no enemies, at least none that she knew.

Faraday looked as though he'd finished asking questions and relaxed a little.

"Inspector," Daniel said, "you know I'm Jewish?"

"I do. Is it important? I mean to the case?"

"I hope not, but you ought to know. I don't want to hide anything from you." Faraday appreciated this. "Kath understood me, inspector, every thought, everything that makes me, me. I would never have hurt her. Do you believe me?"

"I do, Daniel, but I have..."

"I know. It's just that if I'm diffident and awkward, please put it down to a religion that is diffident and awkward in the sight of the rest of the world, for whatever reasons, not because I've got anything to hide."

"I believe you, Daniel. I'm very sorry for what's happened. Very sorry."

Faraday wasn't acting. He felt for Daniel, a good guy in some danger of going over the edge. He checked his watch and told them all that he and Inspector Fowler had nothing more to ask for the time being and would leave them alone now, apologising again for having to ask such difficult questions.

After they'd gone, there was an awkward silence until Melissa asked, "Can we stay, Daniel, or you come to us? I don't want you to be alone here."

Daniel raised his head slowly, his thoughts weighing heavily, and said, "I'll be alright, whatever that means on a night like this. You've been great, Mel, and you too Pat. I need a little time alone."

"No probs, Daniel," said Patrick. "You call us whenever you want, any time, night or day. Right Mel?"

Melissa put her arms around Daniel and squeezed him. He didn't respond, except for a gentle return of her affection.

"We all love you, Dan, you know that?"

He didn't answer but tried to force a smile which was all the more moving for the effort he made.

"Pat," he said, "I don't know if you'll be handling this..."

"Doubt it mate," Patrick said.

"But just in case you do, or you have any influence, treat her gently, will you?"

For a moment Patrick wondered what Daniel meant, but when the penny dropped he said, "No other way, Dan, not from me or mine, I promise. National stuff I don't know. If they get hold of it they won't listen to a hack like me."

"No," said Daniel. "I suppose it doesn't matter, though, does it? We know who she was, right?"

They did, but they also knew there was often smoke without fire - even without any heat at all. Daniel feared what might be said about Kathryn now this news hung in the air. It was a heaven-story for the media if they took it up. It could be warped in so many ways and Daniel hated the thought of Kathryn's name being bandied around in the name of gossip. He couldn't care about himself, they could say what they wanted. He hated the very thought of existence without Kathryn, but more, he couldn't bear the thought of what she'd gone through. He was sure of her, he told himself, she'd never have betrayed him. The world would stop spinning and turn the other way if she'd been untrue.

Nevertheless, the thought had taken seed and was as bad as the idea of rape, immeasurable horrors, in their own way.

"Kath," he whispered into the air, "why didn't you tell me, you foolish, lovely girl!"

He tightened his fist, gripped thin air and squeezed until his knuckles hurt, trying to rid his soul of hurt and anger, but it was impossible. Both possibilities tormented him, and no matter how he paced the room, pounded one hand into the other or squeezed his fist, neither thought would let him be, and he doubted if they would ever let him be again.

### 15

Faraday decided not to go to the station but back to the scene of the murder, dropping Fowler off at Stoke Newington first.

It was early morning but forensics were still in top gear. A tent had been rigged around the murder spot in the alley and ribbons secured a sizeable area around. He spoke to some of the team, asking them how they were doing and mentally trying to piece together some logic to the crime. Faraday was a logical man, but he felt moved as much by emotion as by pride in his work to solve this particular killing. He managed to stay detached as a rule, but not tonight. He'd felt more and more drawn in to the friends of the lost girl, and having seen her, if only in death, he understood their affection and Daniel's desolation. Nevertheless, he was sufficiently trained that part of his mind worked on automatic pilot, figuring out all manner of possibilities.

It was early days, but he could see that the girl, as innocent, beautiful and special as she might have been, elicited passionate reactions in others. He'd rarely seen a group so devastated and so selflessly mourning. The girl had touched them all in positive ways, but evidently she'd touched someone else in a disastrously negative way, intentionally or otherwise. The case wreaked of light and dark. Faraday doubted, with the accumulated years of experience feeding intuition, that this was a random attack, 'wrong place, wrong time' kind of killing. It didn't add up. So amongst those he'd seen that evening, or amongst their friends and the circle of people Kathryn knew, there was a monster, still at large.

What state of mind was he in? Was he fearful, gloating or detached from what he'd done? Perhaps he was simply demented. There were those out there, and not just a few; Faraday had met them. The type he feared most were those who didn't care, who played twisted psychological games without batting an eyelid, those who could kill without conscience or a shred of guilt. He'd met all types, but the conscience-free mutants were the most dangerous and the trickiest to catch, people easily disposed to murder and as easily disposed to forgetting their crimes, as if they had absolutely no on-board moral compass.

Faraday's main concern was that whoever had done this, whatever their state of mind or warped morality, was free to do the same thing again, and probably would, in a day, a week, a month or whenever, and whilst they were out there, he couldn't rest. His sole purpose for joining the police force, and sometimes he thought his sole purpose of living, was to repair the damage done by criminal actions. Any crime was an affront to law and Faraday had the kind of tenacious mind-set to pursue a cause until justice had been meted out and equilibrium restored. He couldn't bring back the dead, he couldn't even make amends for some of the terrible crimes he'd seen, but he could bring about some measure of retribution and hope that redemption might follow, if not for the murderer then for those touched by his malice.

The feedback from the forensics team was not, unfortunately but not unexpectedly, hopeful. The killer had left few traces of his presence. Faraday hadn't thought they would find much on site, but he now knew that, in all probability, the killer had left something much more incriminating – DNA. As tough as he was, Faraday fought a deep sense of sadness that the sole purpose of the unborn child would be to identify its father. This was about as sad a business as he'd known, and once again he found himself wondering whether or not he was up to the job.

It was, after all, supposed to be just a job, but he'd already become entangled. It was a prime requisite to stay detached and he'd always felt that he could handle anything dispassionately, but he wasn't dispassionate now. It was getting to him and he didn't like it. He was just tired, after all, he'd been up all night, but he didn't feel like going back home and instead walked around the scene of the crime and the area close by, close to the site of his old school, scenes of less offensive but still remembered crimes.

They were rough days. It wasn't that he'd been put upon much himself because he was a tough customer when he needed to be, but he saw others suffer and was acutely aware of flaws in the system. He'd done what he could to put things right, but it was heavy going then and it was even more so now. In those distant school days he'd seen in embryo what he'd seen since in more mature forms - the cruel, the malicious, the vicious, the nasty and the pathological nutcases. They were all there, in his school days, rehearsing their later roles in life. He wondered if he would have chosen the same career path if he hadn't seen the kind of things he'd seen at school, good kids bullied and a system warped by rampant egos. You never really know how your life would have turned out if your school days had been different, but Faraday suspected he might not have been so uptight about the law if he hadn't seen it so frequently undermined by thugs.

He never thought he'd run out of steam, but he had a growing desire to give the whole thing up after this case, to let someone else solve the murders and bring retribution down on the guilty, so many of whom were given futile punishments. He wasn't so much tired as exhausted, sick of the endless waste of life and chronic misdirection of human potential. It was the nature of his work to see the dark side, but he tried to see the light whenever possible.

This time he was struggling.

Kathryn Hudson's death was a shock to something so deep in him and in those who cared for her that it rattled some pretty important foundations of faith. He was beginning to think that he couldn't take much more of the madness, that he'd done his bit to redeem the lost world but that the tidal wave of insanity would just keep rolling in and that if he didn't retire to the hills soon he'd be swept away and lost forever.

The school was no longer there. It had been knocked down some time before, but the site was rich with ghosts. Faraday thought it would be fitting if this murder, which had happened so close to the old entrance, should be his last. He had formulated his anger and his determination there, had chiselled out a course to follow in life and now, full circle, once the killer had been caught, he could rest easy and let others fight the good fight.

"Sir?"

His radio came to life.

"Faraday here."

"Sir, we have a call for you from a Miss Shahidi."

"Don't know any...say again?"

"Shahidi. Naila Shahidi?"

"Oh, yes. Naila. Is she there?"

"Yes. She's very distressed."

"Put her on."

Naila's voice was more than distressed, it was anguished.

"Inspector Faraday?"

"Yes."

"This is Naila. It's about Michael."

Oh no, thought Faraday, not him, not now.

"What's happened, Naila? Is he alright?"

"I don't know," said Naila, almost shrieking into the phone. "He's gone!"

## 16

Faraday arrived at Naila and Michael's flat in fifteen minutes. He would have been impressed by the paintings and bohemian style of the apartment if Naila hadn't been beside herself with worry.

"Melissa called," she said, wringing her hands, "she told us what happened –about Kathryn being raped, I mean. Michael seemed to fall apart, inspector, I can't describe it - he just changed, right in front of me. I tried to comfort him but he wouldn't let me. He said he needed some air and left. I tried to follow but he said he didn't want me with him. He's never said that before, inspector, never. And I'm afraid for him. He'll hurt himself, I know it. You must find him! You must!"

She wouldn't be calmed. Faraday asked her for a photo of Michael and she took out a tin of about a hundred. He didn't ask because he knew - Naila loved him so much she'd taken these pictures out of sheer adoration. Faraday took one and said, "I'm sure he's fine Naila. We normally don't go looking for people when they've been missing such a short time, but in the circumstances I'll get a team onto it."

"Yes," she said, "do. Thank you. I couldn't bear it if anything happened to him!"

Faraday believed her. He felt the panic in her voice and realized just how much she loved Michael.

"Would you like me to ask an officer to come and sit with you for a while," he said. "I'm sure I could find someone. I feel uncomfortable leaving you here alone."

"I'll be alright," she said with such anxiety that he doubted she would ever be alright again. "Just call me when you find him. Please?"

"Of course," he said.

He took the picture and left.

Naila watched him go from the same window where she and Michael had been standing a few hours earlier. How unbelievable that in barely a few degrees of turning life could change so much.

It was dawn now, and within its dusty boundaries Hackney lost the shadows of night as the familiar, cluttered cityscape eased into view.

Naila stood upright and stiff, her knuckles pressed to her mouth, her eyes red raw and her heart a torment. This was neither just nor fair. It couldn't and shouldn't have happened, yet here it was before her, cruelly undeniable, murder and confusion. If Michael had harmed himself, as she feared he might, she would follow him. She knew she could. Her life only had value through him; without him there was unbearable emptiness. She felt herself sucked into a whirlpool of despair. She wrenched herself away from the window, stumbled into the kitchen and poured herself a little water, the room swimming around her.

Michael would be back. He would find the strength to face his sister's destruction and come back to her, his only hope of salvation. He had to return. He wouldn't take his own life and leave her! It would make a mockery of tragedy and turn hers and all their lives into a farce of loss. No, he daren't do that! 'Poor boy', she whispered, 'don't suffer alone. Come home, come back!'

She tried to reach her bedroom but everything was spinning. Nothing remained where it was, or appeared where it ought to be. She reached for a chair but it moved away, for a table top which slipped beneath her grasp. She sensed the floor coming towards her and tried to hold on to something before an irresistible blackness swept over her and she crashed down, oblivious to the unfolding misery.

## 17

Michael walked the dawn streets in a daze. He'd always felt ill at ease in the world, as if his head was wired differently, yet people never saw him in this way, never aware in any way, shape or form of his struggling psyche. Nor was he aware of them. He saw projections of people but had no sense of their true selves, so how could he expect them to see him?

Except Naila.

But Naila had an untamed heart and untainted vision. This was why she loved him and why he needed her so much – almost as much as he needed Kathryn. This was the rub, of course. He'd always known it, ever since Kathryn had taken over the reins of his life when their parents had vanished. 'Just you and me for a while, Michael,' he remembered her saying. 'Maybe that's the way it's supposed to be.'

Yes, he thought then as he thought now, maybe that was indeed the way it was supposed to be. He was only six, just getting some kind of handle on the world. Their parents were in and out of their lives like a jack-in-the-box, and now they'd popped up and out and away. He remembered the moment, sitting on his bed with Kathryn, not much older but worlds wiser, holding his hand and telling him all kinds of things about how they'd get by.

"They should be here!" he insisted. "They shouldn't keep running away. I don't want to go to Aunt Jenny again! I don't! I want to stay here with you, Katree."

She adored the way he said her name and cuddled him tightly.

"It won't be for long," she assured him. "They'll be back soon. They always come back, Little M."

She looked around at his funny bedroom replete with bears, bunnies, books and puddles of toys. It was a cute room and he was a cute boy, very handsome but very shy. He buried himself in his books even at that young age and rarely touched the toys his parents brought back from their amblings around the world. He didn't mind the soft ones, the ones that had friendly eyes, but he never cared much for the others. He would have much preferred it if his parents had been there all the time and he had nothing, but it didn't seem to matter what he wanted. He was already learning that no matter how hard he cried, he couldn't always shape the world to his needs, but where the gaps were, Kathryn filled them with her kindness.

"Maybe they won't come back this time," he said.

"Oh, they'll be back Little M, in a few weeks or a few months. They're not bad people, just a bit immature."

An adult listening to a nine year old girl talking in that way would have been touched both by sadness and delight; it was such an image of generosity in a selfish world.

"They're wicked," said Michael. "Only wicked parents leave their children."

"No, Little M, they're not, really. There are lots of truly wicked people and if you or I ever met one we'd know it."

"How?" asked Michael. "What do they look like?"

"Oh, you can tell wicked people a mile off," said Kathryn. "Even with your eyes closed."

"No!" said Michael. "That's impossible! You can't see anything with your eyes closed!"

"You can see wickedness," said Kathryn. "You can see that anywhere. That's how I know mum and dad aren't wicked."

"What are they then?" Michael asked. "Im...im..."

"Immature. Yes, that's what they are, not grown up like you or me."

Michael almost laughed. It was so funny to think that he and Kathryn were older than their parents.

"Katree?"

"Yes Little M, what's up?"

"What are we for, Katree?"

Michael stood still in his blind wanderings through the streets of Hackney, remembering the words so clearly, almost saying them aloud again. "What are we for? What are we for?"

"What a funny question, Little M!"

"No it isn't. If mummy and daddy wanted us they wouldn't leave us all the time. So why did they have us?"

He remembered Kathryn's face, her look of amusement, wonder and curiosity. She never gave him bland answers, never lost patience with him. She always thought through what she said and fed him the best and wisest ideas.

"They love us, silly. They just don't know how to love properly."

"Do you?" he asked.

"I don't know," she answered. "I can't say. You'll have to tell me that, Little M."

"I love you more than mummy and daddy together," he said. "I always will."

And he always did, not in the same way he felt for Naila but something profoundly part of him, as if Kathryn had given him that vital foundation when he was a child which was supposed to hold him together now he was adult. A world without Kathryn made no sense to Michael, not in a temporary way that he would learn to overcome, but in a way that shattered perspective totally. Even then, he felt he might just have found a way to overcome confusion, but the idea she had been raped wrecked any semblance of belief in a just and ordered world.

"It isn't fair!" he heard himself saying to Kathryn when they were with their Aunt Jenny and Uncle Trevor. "I don't want to stay here! This isn't home!"

"No," she'd said, "it isn't fair, but we're not going to scream and shout about it, are we Michael?"

He saw her being so earnest with him again, her lovely eyes full of adoration for her baby brother, her instinct to care for him and show him the way when their parents had all but abandoned them. He remembered how he felt as he lay in bed, unable to sleep, full of anxieties and bad dreams. She sat with him every night, held his hand, stroked his hair, read him story after story, reassured him that the world was not too bad, that their mum and dad might not be the best  but that he would always have her to light the way.

She never ever let him down, never shouted at him, never told him off, always understood and comforted his loneliness and never condemned him for being different, because different he most certainly was. He knew that. He sensed it at five, knew it at six.

"You, Little M," said Kathryn, "are special!"

"Am I?"

"Yes you definitely are. You're more precious than gold, Little M."

"Am I?"

"Yes you are. You're an angel."

"A real one?"

"Yes. From heaven. That's what you are."

He remembered the funny little conversation they had, not just that once but many times, when she made him feel that though their parents might not want them, she needed him more than anything in the world.

"Anything?"

"Yes. Anything."

"More than a television?"

"Much more than a silly television."

"More than all your clothes?"

"Much more than all my clothes."

"More than your bed?"

"I told you, Little M, more than everything. Do you believe me?"

He wasn't sure. He'd always felt quiet and alone, but he hadn't minded it until he realised his mother and father were happy to leave him behind, then he began to worry, to wet his bed, to get sick and cry a lot. There wasn't a single time that Kathryn hadn't been there for him, always filling in the void, catching him before he fell or before he hit the ground.

He passed St. John's Church near the Narrow Way, turned into the grass square, his mind engrossed in memories of childhood, fighting the insistent thoughts of what had happened to his sister. He couldn't do it. The images and implications grew, inexorably, like some kind of disease infesting all parts of his mind.

A police car drove by, past the gates of the church towards Mare Street. Michael took little notice, entertaining a faint hope that they'd found the killer, but it wasn't particularly important. He might even have passed the murderer on the street. Would anything have passed between them? Amazingly no, nothing. They were all such small, lonely, isolated beings.

"Are you frightened, Little M?" she asked.

Kathryn slept in the same room – Aunt Jenny and Uncle Trevor only had one spare room.

"Yes. I had a bad dream."

She came over. She was never too tired, never told him to go back to sleep, always took his worries to heart.

"Poor Michael!" she said. "I hate bad dreams too. What was it about?" He told her how he was running away from somebody – or something – but the faster he tried to run the slower he seemed to go. "You know, Little M," she said, "I've had one of those too. Looks like we have the same dreams. What shall we do about it?" Michael shook his head but was very attentive; Kathryn was always so wise in her answers. "I think we'll just have to wait for them to go away," she said. "It's probably because we're worried. Are you worried, Michael?" He nodded and looked at her with his wonderful eyes full of adoration. "Suppose I do all the worrying for you, will that help?" she asked.

"Don't know."

"Well, we'll try it. Dreams are just dreams, Little M, they can't hurt you."

"I was afraid."

"Yes, poor boy, I know. So was I. But they really are silly things. Tell you what, if you have a bad one, I'll come and hold your hand, and if I have a bad one, you come and hold mine, that way the dreams won't know where to go and they'll just disappear. How about that?"

"Alright."

"Do you want to try and go to sleep now?"

He did, if she stayed with him.

He remembered her so clearly, night after night, being there for him like no one else ever was. He stopped walking for a moment, lost in thought. Her presence was so strong, as if the power of the memories might make her real again. The realization that he would never see her again made him stumble. He grabbed hold of the railings by the side of the church to stop himself falling. Never see Kathryn again? How was he to accept such a thing? The truth of it lodged in his chest so that he could hardly breathe.

"Mikey?" He was seven and he'd fallen off a swing in the park and hit his head. "Mikey?" He saw her face in front of his, wavering a little, floating like a balloon. "Can you hear me Mikey?" He could, just about. His arm hurt badly. It lay at a peculiar angle beside him and when he tried to move it he cried out with pain. "Don't move Mikey. We've called an ambulance; they'll be here in a minute."

"Am I going to die?"

"No, silly boy, of course not! I wouldn't let you die, and you won't let me die either, will you? Just like our nightmares, remember? We'll look after each other."

"My arm hurts"

"I know, brave boy. I think you've broken it. What a silly thing to do, eh Little M?"

Michael remembered the ambulance ride with Kathryn sitting by his side the whole time. She kept him company in the hospital, making sure he was never alone. They went back to Aunt Jenny and Uncle Trevor with him all strapped up like an Egyptian mummy. He was tired but also excited. He'd come through a tough day with flying colours feeling very proud of himself.

"Kathryn!" he called aloud.

A couple of early morning passers-by stared at him as if he were mad, and he was. He sensed the madness as surely as if it had announced itself before reducing him to tears.

He stumbled on with a growing idea of where he wanted to go, but he would have to keep it a secret, then they'd leave him alone, let him reach there in peace.

"Kathryn?"

"What's up, Michael?"

He was twelve, she was seventeen, beautiful and as loyal as ever. Their parents were off again, but he'd got used to it. They didn't have to go to Aunt Jenny any more but looked after themselves. He amused himself by writing, all kinds of stuff but especially poems.

"Read something?"

She always read whatever he wrote with touching attention and he knew immediately by her expressions whether or not it had any value. When she gave her verdict and made suggestions he would invariably listen and make changes.

"I think you'll be an artist, Michael," she said.

"But I can't paint."

"Not that kind of artist," she laughed. "You've got an artist's soul, Little M."

He laughed out loud and she did too, not really sure why, but they found the way she'd said it funny.

When the laughter ended, they curled up next to each other on the bed, staring at the ceiling, discussing something serious - what Michael would do when Kathryn went to university.

"We'll work something out," she said, but this time they couldn't. She went off to study but he stayed behind, cared for in the same haphazard way by his here-today-gone-tomorrow parents and long suffering aunt and uncle. That was the first time he felt grown up, when she went away and he had to cope by himself, alone with his funny artistic soul.

Five years passed. University ended for her, began for him. She was still in Bristol, he in London.

"Michael?"

"Hello big sister."

"All okay?"

"I'm fine. No need to worry Kath, really."

They talked on the phone every few days. She called him, anxious in case he was in one of his bleak moods.

"I do worry, Michael. I can't help it. How's the artist doing?"

"Oh, getting along," he said, "struggling to find a voice."

She laughed and said, "It'll turn up one day Michael. Someone will help you find it."

He wasn't sure about this. He didn't seem to be on the same wavelength as anyone, boys or girls, whereas Kathryn had boyfriend after boyfriend. Every one of them she introduced to Michael, and if they were rude or patronising she would dump them straight away. Even the ones who liked him she dumped after a while. Michael was puzzled by his big sister. She seemed so together and wise, but she got through boys at a rate of knots, whereas he could barely open his mouth in front of girls without getting tongue tied. He asked her about this once during a phone call. She seemed reluctant to talk about it, possibly because she didn't understand.

"There is one guy," she said. "He was visiting a friend here. I might hook up with him for a while."

"A while? Like a week, maybe two?"

"Whatever. He's different. I like 'different'."

"How different is he? Two heads? Scales?"

"No. He's handsome."

"What's his name?"

"Daniel."

"Nice name. You going to break his heart too, Kath?"

"I've never broken anyone's heart, Little M." She still called him that when they were jousting. "No one I've met yet had a heart to break. He does. Like you."

"Do I have a heart, Kath?"

"You know you do. We both do. Have faith."

"In what?"

"In yourself, silly, what else?"

When Michael first met this Daniel, he wasn't sure he liked him. For some reason he'd always believed that Kathryn would choose someone like him, Michael, but Daniel was nothing like him. They were light and dark, opposites in so many ways, but Michael could see that Daniel was definitely different. He just couldn't say why. Daniel wasn't an artist, a writer, a painter or anything like that. He seemed a heavy sort of guy for his ethereal sister. They didn't dislike each other, but they couldn't find common ground.

At least this Daniel wasn't jealous. Some of Kathryn's boyfriends had clearly been jealous of him. They saw how close she was to him and didn't like it, but Daniel seemed unfazed by them.

As he wandered the streets of Hackney, heading towards his final destination, Michael tried to think of Daniel and all Kath's friends. They would need to support each other, and yet he doubted he could offer any of them what they needed. They may have loved her in their way, even Daniel, but it was different between him and his sister. There was something too deep to be unearthed and too connected to be severed. He'd never really liked sharing her, even after he'd met Naila, and he certainly hadn't liked sharing his grief with them at the hospital. Naila would want to help him, she would put her heart and soul into comforting him, but the truth of the matter was that there was no comfort to be had, not for her, not for Kathryn and certainly not for him.

He reached the Latham Timber Yard by the river and looked at the once familiar landscape as if this was the first time he'd seen it. He'd walked here at one time or another both with Kathryn and Naila. Now it was as if he'd never laid eyes on it before. The yard, the water, the marshes beyond, all seemed insubstantial, especially with the very early morning mist obscuring the horizon.

He found a wooden bench damp with morning dew, but he sat, ignoring the cold. If Naila truly loved him she would know he was there and come for him. Abandoned and miserable, she would find a way to reach him if she truly felt his presence as she always said she did.

Nothing happened and no one came for him.

All was peace and beauty on a Spring morning. People were beginning their day and the working world was on the move again. It all seemed the same, and for many it was the same. The ripples from Kathryn's death might already have begun to spread, but the world was so vast and the affairs of man so noisy that they would make no difference, except in his own heart which they tore to shreds.

*Go back*, he told himself. *Go to Naila. She's your gift. She loves you and will help you understand.*

But he couldn't, he decided, not with all the comfort in the universe.

This was beyond comfort. There was no tract in any religion that could explain this nor any philosophy that could appease him. It was the way an unwatched universe operated, pure and simple. There was no answer to it.

Except one.

It made perfect sense and he could see no other option. The idea of him going about his life on this busy, busy planet without his darling sister there was anathema. He could never make love to Naila again, never share what he'd shared just a few hours earlier. That was another self in another existence. These hours had changed him. They had sucked hope from him in a ruthless asphyxiation. He felt as if he no longer belonged here, as if he were already part of some other realm where Kathryn waited and all would be healed.

*You can do it,* said an inner voice. *You must! It's the only way to peace!*

His head was a ferocious storm of conflicting emotions. He felt as if he hadn't the strength to stand, but he did, stumbling towards the bank the navigation.

Someone would see him. There were houses close by and someone would surely look out and rush to save him.

Still no one came. It was as if he was being granted this time because it was the right thing to do.

He was so alone, not the loneliness of his childhood when Kathryn was there to stave off the fears, but a physical and metaphysical isolation.

*"Little M?"*

He heard the voice, as ever. It never failed him.

He took a step closer to the navigation. The water was calm, hardly running, after what must have been a still and quiet night, but his thoughts swirled in a storm of conflicting pressures.

*Don't do it Michael,* he heard.

Was that Kathryn calling?

*Yes, do it, Little M, come to me! I don't want to be here alone!*

Michael lurched closer to the edge of the navigation.

A few boats moored close by rocked in the gentle lap of water. He was aware of them, as he was aware of a few birds circling overhead. He could even see water boatmen hovering over the surface of the water. Life was relentless, and it would persist regardless of this act. It meant nothing - it meant less than nothing. He'd been a fool to think that people like he and Kath could survive.

*We can't, Little M,* he heard her say.

His heart was bleeding for her, so long and so painfully that he could barely breath. He didn't want to breathe. He was desperate for release from the shackles of consciousness.

*Forgive me, Kath!*

He tried to speak the words but his voice sounded oddly gruff.

*I can't be here without you, Kath. I can't accept what's been done to you, lovely girl. Don't be angry with me!*

He teetered on the edge of the navigation, on the edge of dimensions, light on one side, a new day just dawning with a bright sun emerging over the Leytonstone skyline. The others would have to deal with their grief, Naila included. The love she offered him was wonderful, but it dwindled to nothing set against this revelation of being.

He caught the reflection of his face in the water. It was surprisingly calm, nothing of the eruption inside him visible. Nothing of anything showed. All was hidden, a mystery cloaked by a deep, overwhelmingly vast void, obscured by the brutal ways of men.

The face came suddenly closer, staring at him for a fraction of a second, then broke apart.

Just a little splash, a little fear, and all, once again, was well.

# 4:     **Fallout**

"It wasn't you Sam, was it?"

"Feri! Are you nuts? What kind of dumb question is that?"

"Just asking! Blimey! You didn't, Sam, did you?"

Samuel looked at Feriha and said, "Yes, now you ask me, I did."

They were sitting in a fast food restaurant, home from home for Feriha and Jemal, but the depths of hell for Samuel. If anyone he knew saw him, there'd be some serious questions to answer. He wasn't eating, that would be totally beyond the pale, but he shouldn't have been in there at all, only Sam liked bending the rules to breaking point. He sat still, eyeballing anyone who dared look his way.

"You're weird," said Feriha, hardly able to take her eyes off him. It was a match made in some secret recess of heaven where two angels were either having a wager or simply intrigued by the notion of putting humans to the test again.

"You keep saying that about him," said Jemal, "but you keep seeing him too." Feriha took a sip of her chocolate and nibbled some chips. "You'll have to forgive her, Sam."

"Do I?"

"Sure," said Jemal. "She's ... you know," and he pointed to his head. "Anyway, are you alright? You kind of liked her, didn't you?"

Sam played with his tumbler of water and said, "She was good to my little brother."

"Our aunt was in a state," said Feriha. "I've never seen her like that. She turns up in the middle of the night in tears! I never thought she could cry."

"You just don't think, do you?"

"I do," said Feriha. "You can't tell me you weren't just a little bit surprised, can you? Sam, she's a hard nut is our aunt, but she was weepy like a flipping waterfall."

"They were friends, dummy, " said Jemal, "how d'you think she'd feel? You sure you're alright, Sam?"

"What did your aunt say?" Samuel asked, ignoring Jemal's question.

"Everything. That she .. the nurse ... had been knifed, near here. This place is the crime centre of the universe, Sam."

"Do they know who did it?" Sam asked.

"I wouldn't have asked you if they did, would I?" said Feriha. "You know I didn't mean it, don't you?" Sam looked at her but he didn't smile. "It's just..."

"Just what?" said Jemal.

"Just that, you know, Jews are supposed to drink babies blood and all that."

"Yuch, Feriha, who told you that?"

"I just heard it. It isn't true, is it Sam?"

Sam had a strangely blank expression as he said, "That's true too. It's quite nice of a night instead of hot chocolate."

Jemal laughed out loud and said, "Feri, you say he's weird, but you're weirder. Where d'you get these stories from?"

"They're not stories. Everyone's heard them."

"Everyone's dumb then," said Jemal. "Isn't that right Sam?"

"If you say so."

He looked even more thoughtful than usual. Feriha was only joking when she'd asked him if he'd done it, but she didn't understand Jews. They were mysterious, distant, in a world of their own. Sam intrigued her, and she fancied him terribly, but she tried to hide it, though not very successfully. How she'd managed to get Sam into the fast food place was a miracle worthy of the bible, though not one Sam would want told. This was bad karma for him, but Feriha didn't want him to leave, even if it meant his soul would burn in hell for eternity.

"She was a mensch," said Sam.

"A what?"

"A mensch. It's Yiddish. She was good," he said. "She was beautiful."

'I'm good and beautiful, too, aren't I?' Feriha wanted to ask. She had the idea in her head when Aunt Nurcan turned up that she might be able to use the murder to draw Sam in a bit further. It wasn't a thought she was proud of, but all was fair in love and war. She wanted him to notice her, which he did. Most people did. It was hard not to notice her, even if she didn't open her mouth. She had striking looks and dressed to kill. A dozen and one Turkish boys wanted to date her, but they didn't interest her. She was drawn to Sam, an irritating attraction as she had to prise him away from a rock solid community, but this was a start. Anyway, she didn't ask what she wanted to ask, but said instead, "It's rotten luck, I mean being killed like that."

"It's rotten luck being killed full stop," said Jemal. "Do you know where she was, Feri?"

"Just down the road, near the old school, in that miserable passageway."

"What the heck was she doing there?" Jemal asked. "I mean, it's spooky enough during the day, what was she doing there at that time of night?"

"Jogging," said Feriha.

Sam looked up, puzzled. He wanted to know more, but didn't want to give out that he wanted to know more. He was actually shaken up inside quite badly. She'd been a sweet nurse to Jonathan and to his family. They all were, but she was different, though he wasn't sure why.

"That just goes to show," said Jemal, "jogging! At that time of night! Was she nuts or what?"

"No," said Sam, "she wasn't."

"Told you he liked her," said Jemal.

"What's that word you use," asked Feriha, "for someone who's nuts? You told me it once..."

"Meshigga," said Sam.

"Yeh, that's right," said Feriha. "Machega! I like these words you teach me, Sam. Pretty soon I'll be able to speak Jewish just like you..."

"Not Jewish, Yiddish."

"Right, then you can learn Turkish."

"Not a chance," said Jemal, "is there, Sam?"

Sam was miles away. He was the closest person Jemal had ever met, deeper than the Pacific Ocean, but they got on well, not just because of computers, but for some inexplicable reason that makes one person like another.

Feriha turned to Jemal and said, "Everyone's cut up ... I mean upset. That's what Aunt Nurcan said. Especially her boyfriend. He's one of you," said Feriha, knowing this would interest Sam, and Sam indeed looked up.

"One of me what?"

"Jewish."

"She had a Jewish boyfriend?"

"That's what aunty said."

"She was wrong."

"No. Why do you say that? Wouldn't you ever have a Turk ... I mean an un-Jewish girlfriend?"

"Non-Jewish," Jemal said, "not un-Jewish. That makes him sound like the un-dead, Feri."

Sam didn't answer, instead he asked another question. Feriha noticed this about him, he often answered questions with more questions.

"Was he like me?"

"You mean weird?" said Feriha. "No, he was normal, I think. I reckon he must be broken hearted this morning."

"I wouldn't be if it was you," said Jemal. "I'd get over it pretty quick."

Feriha pinched her brother then looked at Sam and asked, "Would you go out with someone who wasn't Jewish, Sam?"

Sam looked at Feriha and, even if he knew what she was getting at, ignored the suggestion. This was serious stuff for him.

"Don't push the man, Feri. You know the rules."

That was the thing, Feriha didn't know the rules, or if she did, she ignored them.

"I'm not pushing him. Am I pushing you, Sam?"

"I don't know what you're doing, Feriha."

"Oh, look, he speaks to me!" said Feriha.

"Come on Sam," said Jemal, ignoring his sister, "you're brainy. Who do you think did it?"

"A rival," said Sam, without a moment's hesitation.

"A what?" asked Feriha, impressed by Sam's vocabulary, as well as by his unexpected speed of thought.

"A rival," Jemal translated, as if repeating the word might help it sink in. "You mean a love rival, Sam?"

"Probably; that's what most murders are about."

"But she was out all by herself at night," said Feriha. "Don't you reckon it could just have been bad luck?"

"No," said Sam, surprisingly sure of himself, despite knowing absolutely nothing about the case, "unless it was a serial killer."

"Like the Yorkshire Ripper?" said Jemal.

"But this isn't Yorkshire," said Feriha.

Jemal and Sam looked at her as though she were, in Sam's words, Meshigga, but she stared at them, defiantly.

"It's Hackney," said Jemal. "This could be the Hackney Ripper."

"God!" exclaimed Feriha. "I could be next! You're probably safe because you're men – well, boys."

"Men," said Jemal. "You're right though. Serial killers don't go for men."

"That's because they're cowards," said Sam.

"But you reckon the killer was a rival, then?" said Jemal. Feriha listened carefully. A passionate love triangle was fascinating.

"What else?" said Sam doing his question–question thing.

"Like Romeo and Juliet?" Feriha asked.

"Never read it," said Sam.

"What! And you seventeen going on eleven? Don't you do Shakespeare at school?"

"Not if I can help it," said Sam.

"But you reckon this was a love killing?"

"What do you think?" Sam asked, and he looked directly at Feriha.

"Love sounds like a good idea to me. Shame, though."

"What d'you mean, shame?" Jemal asked.

"Shame love always leads to people killing each other."

"Not always," said Jemal. "Our mum and dad haven't done each other in, have they"

"Not yet," said Feriha, "but there's still time. Your mum and dad get on then, Sam?"

"Feri!" said Jemal. "You don't half ask embarrassing questions."

"They're okay," said Sam.

"Okay!" exclaimed Feriha. "Love is supposed to be more than okay!"

"You mean like passionate," said Jemal, kissing his fingers with loud slurpy noises. "Not much point in passion if you end up killing each other. Jews don't do that, do they?" he asked Sam. "I mean, passionate killing for love and all that?"

"Do Turks?" he asked.

"You see?" said Feriha, "he does that all the time. I reckon when he gets married the priest will say "Do you take this woman to be your lawful wedded wife and he'll say, 'Would you?'"

This creased Jemal up and even Sam laughed, though he said, "Doubt it will be a priest. You mean Rabbi."

"Not if you marry me," she said without thinking, then turned red. Sam turned a bright shade of pink. "Or someone," she added, "not Jewish."

There was a brief pause as they watched the customers in the restaurant gobble down their burgers and chips. Sam didn't like it in there, but he had to admit, he liked the company. Feriha excited him. She was interesting, different from the girls he was expected to mix with, although that wasn't many or often. He knew he was dicing with disaster, at least from his parents point of view, but he was on a quest to find himself and to find out what made the world tick.

"What did you say about her boyfriend?" he asked.

"Who? Oh...right...yeh. He's Jewish. Nice guy, aunty said. She was with them at the hospital till late. All of them."

"All who?" Jemal asked.

"Family and friends," she said. "Auntie said it was very sad."

This was another thing about Feriha that intrigued Sam – she was a grown up woman one minute, a little girl the next. She said 'auntie' like she was a girl, but Sam liked it.

"What was his name?" he asked.

"I didn't ask," said Feriha. "Why should I?"

"No reason. Maybe I know him."

"What, like you know all the Jews in the world?"

"Most of them, yeh," said Sam. "We share buckets of babies blood together on a Friday night..."

"God!" said Feriha, trying not to laugh, "he's really sick!"

"...and taking over the world by stealing all the money," Sam added.

Jemal picked up a knife from the table and spun it in his hands.

"You really think she knew the killer, Sam," he said. "You don't reckon it was bad luck, you know, wrong place at the wrong time."

"He's only guessing," said Feriha, "he doesn't know, do you, Sammy?"

"'*Sam*'," he told her, even though he knew she was teasing. "You have to think about it logically. It's the only answer."

"Sam's good at logic," said Jemal, "they talk logically about the 'Toyrah' till the cows come home, isn't that right, Sam?" Sam said it was right, that they discussed the finer points of law all the time.

"Why's that, then?" asked Feriha who couldn't think of anything more boring.

"Keeps our minds busy," he said, "stops us turning to crime."

Feriha didn't know if he was joking and started tapping her fingers on the table. Every time she met Sam she wondered just how far beyond the pale he was prepared to stray. Maybe he was only playing with them and would run back to his mummy and daddy when push came to shove, but then she might do the same thing. It was hard breaking away from your roots.

"So you don't reckon the killer is Jewish?" she asked. Sam asked why she said that. "Because you're all so busy talking about the law all the time."

"Could be anyone," said Sam. "Could be Turkish."

"Nah," said Jemal, "no way."

"What they'll have to find," said Feriha wisely, "is motive. Isn't that right Sammy, like you said, a love rival or someone with a grudge?"

Sam looked at Feriha, trying to work her out as she tried to work him out. They really liked each other, but were creatures from different worlds, and though they spoke the same language their brains were wired in totally different ways. It was fun trying to tune in to each other.

"Probably," said Sam. "You should be a detective," he said to Feriha.

"I'll think about it," said Feriha. "Better than working in the shop for the rest of my life. Sam?" He waited. "Are you going to the hospital today, to see your brother I mean?"

"We go every day."

"Oh, 'we'," she said. "I just wondered..."

"She wants to go with you," said Jemal.

Sam looked horrified, but at the same time a part of him said '*why not*?

"Another time," he said gently, and it was the gentle side of him that always excited Feriha. She didn't come across it too much but she saw it in Sam, despite his sometimes aggressive stance against the rest of the world.

"That's alright," she said, and she meant it. "I thought you might like some moral support. It will be sad there, and Jonathan'll be upset."

Sam felt a peculiar something when Feriha said this. He wasn't sure what it was, but he liked it. He was also impressed that she'd remembered his little brother's name. She surprised him as much as he surprised her. "And anyway, it's Friday night tonight," he said, "our Sabbath. We all get together..."

"..and play computer games?" suggested Jemal.

"Not quite. No, it's a family thing. Everyone has them."

Jemal wasn't sure about that. His family was together all the time in the shop, but not for anything involving God. He knew it was a waste of time trying to get Sam to play computer games on a Friday or Saturday. It was set in stone to keep the day special, and not even Sam had the umph to do otherwise.

"Better get going," said Jemal, checking his watch. He got up and so did Feriha, but Sam stayed sitting, lost in thought. "Are you alright Sam?" Jemal asked.

"Yeh," said Sam, standing up and looking at Feriha in an odd way. "I might be wrong," he said.

"About what?"

"About motive."

"Oh, right."

"And if I am," Sam went on, "there's a nutter out there who might have a go at someone else. So you shouldn't go out alone," he said to Feriha.

Feriha and Jemal stared at Sam, touched, surprised, embarrassed.

"I won't," said Feriha simply. It wasn't often that anyone thought of anyone else, not in her limited experience, and for someone like Sam who inhabited a peculiar world of his own, his sudden concern moved her. "But if I do," she added, "and someone has a go at me, I'm sure you'll be my knight in shining armour ."

## 2

When Faraday left Naila, after arranging for a description to be distributed, he decided, as early as it was, that he ought to see Margaret Hargreaves. He could be gentle when he needed to be and the last thing he wanted was to alarm the old lady, but the investigation came first.

It was six in the morning when he first rang the doorbell - it was four minutes past and he was about to leave when he heard footsteps and then a voice.

"Who is it?"

"Police, Mrs Hargreaves. Sorry to bother you."

He held up his identification to the spyhole in the door.

"What do you want?" she asked.

"I need to talk to you. I apologise, it's early in the morning, but it's important."

"What do you want to talk about?"

"About Kathryn Hudson."

Silence, then, "Is she alright?"

"It's difficult to talk through the door, Mrs Hargreaves."

The door opened on a safety latch and Maggie Hargreaves peeped out at Faraday who held up his identification again. Maggie peered at it, then at Faraday, and said, "It's very early."

"I know, Mrs Hargreaves, but it's important."

Maggie thought for a moment, studied the card and Faraday's face again then undid the safety catch.

She was wrapped in an old pink gown and wearing little pink slippers. Her thin white hair was ruffled from sleep but she looked quite alert and led Faraday into the lounge.

"Shall I make you a cup of tea Mr Faraway?" she asked.

"Faraday," Faraday said. "No thank you Mrs Hargreaves, I'm fine. Shall we sit down?"

Maggie settled into a faded armchair and Faraday sat opposite. Now that he was here, he wondered if he'd done the right thing. There were probably far more important leads to follow up and he really didn't want to alarm the little old lady who sat staring at him with her distant, ancient gaze.

"I'm afraid I have some sad news," he said.

"About Kathryn?"

"Yes."

"Oh, dear! Has something happened?"

"I'm afraid so."

Maggie gave a tiny choke and put her hand to her mouth. Faraday felt terribly sorry for her. At least Kathryn's friends had each other; this old lady had no one and would have to bear the shock of the murder alone.

"What?" she asked.

"I won't beat around the bush," said Faraday, "but it is very sad news."

"You wouldn't come here at this time in the morning to bring me good news, would you inspector?" said Maggie, which surprised Faraday, but he could see she was sharp and together, despite her age.

"No," he said, "I wouldn't. There was an attack late last night."

"An attack?"

"A murder."

"Oh dearie me!" Maggie had already seen what was coming and had clasped both hands together. "Nell?"

"Sorry?"

"I called her that, my Nell. Kathryn?"

"Yes."

Maggie said nothing for a few moments, just took in the news by staring at her hands, then at the floor, then at Faraday. "This is such a brute of a world, isn't it inspector?"

"It can be, yes."

"And it was definitely Kathryn?"

"It was, no doubt."

"Oh, the poor girl, she was a real sweetie! Who would do such a thing?"

Faraday looked a little uncomfortable and shifted in his chair, not sure whether Maggie was expecting an answer or was in a state of shock and asking the question rhetorically. When there was an awkward silence, he said, "That's partly why I've come to see you, Mrs Hargreaves." Maggie looked at him, puzzled. "It's about your grandson."

"My grandson?"

"Yes. Jerome? Is that right?"

Maggie was trying to make a connection.

"That's the boy's name, yes, but he isn't my grandson. What's he got to do with it?"

"Hopefully nothing," said Faraday, "but at this stage we have to follow up all leads, and rather quickly, which is why I'm here so early. Some of Kathryn's housemates said she received some nuisance calls from him."

"Nuisance calls? From Jerome? I knew he'd find her number! Oh, the little shit!" If it wasn't such a delicate and sad situation, Faraday would have smiled. "And you think he did this?"

"I have no idea, Maggie. May I call you Maggie? As I say, I'm just trying to piece together information at present."

Maggie sat upright, her eyes shining.

"You're wrong," she said, "if you think he could have done this. He can be a fool, but he isn't a murderer."

"I hope not. But you say he isn't your grandson?"

"No, a relative maybe. At least he says he is."

"Can you tell me where he lives, Maggie?"

"I can," she said, "but he's away a lot."

Maggie felt partly protective and slightly angry at her mysterious relative. She'd taken his word that he was who he said he was, because he could be charming and had been nice company for a while, but if he'd hurt Nell or even bothered her, she'd wrap his balls around his neck and hang him up to dry.

"What a thought, inspector!"

"I know, and it will probably come to nothing. Can you tell me what happened when they met?" he asked, and added, "It would help me understand a little."

Maggie told him what she remembered, that he'd liked her and asked Maggie to give him her telephone number. She hadn't, but the rascal had probably dipped into her purse and found it.

"He's a forceful young man," said Maggie, "but I suppose you have to be in this day and age. Oh my, poor Nell! I'm sorry inspector. She was such a darling!" Maggie wiped her eyes, and Faraday couldn't help but wonder what it must be like to have seen so much of the world over so many years yet still be shocked by its cruelties. "Did they tell you what she did for me?" she asked, composing herself and looking very strong all of a sudden. The flatmates had spoken to him a little at the hospital, but he knew very little. "She rescued me from the hands of thieves," said Maggie, "and from the disinterest of the world. She was helping me with my life story," Maggie went on, "which will never get finished now. Doesn't matter, though, does it, little thing like that compared to this news. I'm upset, inspector."

"I understand," said Faraday. "If you like I could call a colleague who'd sit with you for a while."

"No thank you," said Maggie. "Believe me inspector, I'm not being rude. I don't need company, especially now. Kathryn was sent by the angels and now they've have taken her back. She took an interest when no one else did. And to think that Jerome upset her!"

"Yes," said Faraday, "about Jerome. Do you have his address Maggie?"

"Address? Oh, yes," she said, "but are you sure about this? Do you think he fooled me?"

"We can look into it," he said. "I hope he didn't fool you and that he had nothing to do with this, but we have to investigate. I'm sure you understand."

Faraday couldn't pretend to be a man of the world in front of this lady almost twice his age, but he had heard the same thing many times. No one really knew anyone else, and everyone was capable of violence given the provocation, or even lack of provocation.

Maggie sighed, stood up, rather more shakily than when she'd sat down, and fetched her handbag. She rummaged around inside for her address book, took it out and sat down again, turning the pages slowly, then read out Jerome's address in Richmond Road, not far away. Faraday wrote it down carefully, together with the telephone number.

"Is he likely to be there now?" he asked.

"Not a clue," said Maggie, "he travels a lot."

"Doing what?"

"No idea," she said. "If he told me, I've forgotten ... Inspector?"

"Yes?"

"I don't think I could forgive myself if he was guilty."

"Why?"

"Because they met in my house. He must have found her number in my address book."

"That doesn't make it your fault," he said.

Maggie looked doubtful.

"I'd still feel guilty," she said. Faraday thought she already looked too uncomfortable, as if a deeper memory was haunting her. "We're all capable of killing, aren't we, inspector?"

This took him by surprise.

"Are we? I don't know."

"But not her, not her!" said Maggie. "Who would do such a thing?"

"Very hard to say, Maggie. It might have been bad luck, you know, wrong place, wrong time, or it might have been planned. We'll let you know, if you want to know."

Maggie rubbed her legs as if she were cold and said, "Oh I want to know alright, inspector. Awful, awful!" She waited a moment, then asked, "What about her boyfriend, what's his name... Donald, David or something, isn't it?"

"Daniel. He's distressed, as you can imagine. Did she talk about him to you?"

"Only all the time," said Maggie. "Loved him to bits. Except..."

"Yes?"

"Except the last few weeks she was a bit anxious about something. Don't know what, but she hadn't been the same Nell I knew before. I asked her if something was troubling her but she wouldn't say. Do you know?"

Faraday paused before saying, "Yes, there was something, but I'm not at liberty to say right now, Maggie. Sorry."

"That's alright," she answered, "don't want to be a nosey old bat. Just being old and a bat is bad enough." Faraday stood up but Maggie stayed sitting. "I don't suppose you'd like a cup of tea," she said. He said he couldn't; he had to move on. "I think I might change my mind about something," she said. Faraday asked what it was. "Company," said Maggie. "I'm not sure I want to be left alone right now. Thought I would be alright but I feel a little peculiar."

Faraday didn't think twice. He called the station, explained in a quiet voice what was going on then sat down again and said, "Someone will be along shortly. A lady officer. Very kind. She'll sit with you until you're ready."

"Do you know, inspector," said Maggie, "I'm not sure I'll ever be ready, except to bugger off." Faraday didn't know which way to look. Maggie shook her head and said, "It isn't right, is it inspector?"

"No," said Faraday in a gentle voice, "it isn't right."

Maggie's strength seemed to ebb away in front of him and she started crying, looking for all the world like a little girl who might have fallen over and hurt herself. Faraday hesitated to imagine what she'd seen in her many days, only to landed with this at the very end of them.

"If he did do it," Maggie said, "I'll ..."

She stopped and looked at Faraday, and for a moment he was shocked, as if he saw in her eyes a spark of something not quite in keeping with her 'little-old-lady' persona.

"We'll let you know," said Faraday.

A community officer arrived shortly. She had an engaging smile and shook hands with Maggie. At the same moment a call came through for him. He listened and said, "Now?"

"Now," was the reply.

Faraday hurried away, trying to be polite, but aware that things were falling apart on his watch. He wished Maggie well, hoping that he wouldn't have to bring her more bad news. Truth, though, was a dispassionate master; the call had been from his office – a body had been found in the river and they needed him there straight away.

## 3

When Faraday arrived at the scene by the navigation, he had tried to prepare himself, but there really was no preparing for this kind of fallout. A tent had been erected, the second Faraday had seen in twenty-four hours. Inside lay the body of Kathryn's brother Michael. A small crowd had gather around from the bank-side homes to see what was happening, but rumours had already spread about a suicide. A young man out walking his dog had spotted the body floating face down in the waters of the Lea Navigation. He'd called the police and was still there now, giving evidence, his dog sitting beside him, desperate to get going again but aware that something was amiss, watching the comings and goings with wide-eyed interest.

"Yes," said Faraday, "that's him."

Michael had had some identification on him, but no one had made any attempt to confirm identification until Faraday arrived. One of the officers on the scene was Charlene Okoru, back after just a few hours rest. She looked a wreck and the first thing Faraday asked her was whether she wanted a break.

"No sir," she said. "This is our patch. I want to be involved as much as possible. Catch the bugger."

"I understand," said Faraday, "but if you feel it's too much, let me know. It's a daunting situation for all of us."

He looked thoroughly exhausted himself. The job was often demanding, but a night like this was unique, impossible to classify.

It was now half-past seven in the morning. There was a little activity on the river, along its banks and in the homes close by. The morning was fresh with a sharp chill, even though Spring was supposed to have arrived. Across the navigation, the Walthamstow Marshes were more impressive than ever, bathed in a light mist with dew drops hanging from every blade of grass and every leaf of every shrub and tree. It was astonishing that this mystical sight was in London, and not just in London but covering a great swathe of inner city land from Leytonstone through Hackney to Tottenham and beyond. The tranquillity, however, was a reminder that nature witnessed everything but objected to nothing. The most beautiful lived alongside the most terrible with no moral acknowledgement of either.

Faraday made sure that everything was done correctly. Some of the forensics team from the first case had been called but new officers were also drafted in from other forces, they were so stretched now. It was apparent to everyone, especially once they knew the victim's story, that he had taken his own life. There was no evidence of struggle, nothing at all suggesting foul play. Faraday knew from the little time he'd spoken to Michael that he was struggling with his sister's death and that they had been particularly close. Michael had seemed to Faraday a vulnerable soul, strong in some respects, but with a mightily thin skin.

Nevertheless, Faraday hadn't expected this. He should have done, but he knew how wonderful a thing was hindsight. The bond between brother and sister must have been soul deep. Faraday couldn't imagine Michael's pain and it was all he could do to separate himself from the emotions of this tragedy.

And then there was Naila. He knew he had to tell her, but dreaded it. He had a fleeting vision of her taking her own life and feared this cascade of despair.

"Sir?"

It was one of the members of the forensic team from Kathryn's site come to help out.

"News?" he asked.

"Some fibres on the wall, vague prints in the dust, all very messy. We'll keep looking, but there's also this, sir."

She showed him some papers and photographs from the scene of Kathryn's murder. She said that they'd noticed something but were wary of being a touch dramatic. She showed Faraday some photographs of Kathryn's body. One hand was behind her, but the other was curled up in front, lying in a thick pool of blood.

"Her forefinger," the woman said, pointing at Kathryn's hand.

There were five images altogether a couple at a distance and three close-up, each of the three zooming in at a slightly different angle. Faraday peered at each in turn, shifting them one beneath the other.

"It might just be a nervous response," he said.

"Possible."

"What do you think sir?"

"Interesting," he said.

"We thought we'd better tell you."

"You did right. Thank you."

She left him to consider what he'd seen. There was doubt, but it looked as though Kathryn had been trying to write something in her own blood, and for all the world it looked like the letter 'J'.

## 4

Naila Shahidi had a fiercely independent spirit, an even fiercer artistic temperament, a volatile character and a soul full of compassion. In loving Michael she'd drawn on all these; in losing him she lost everything. Love was what made her who she was, and in losing it she lost herself.

Michael had been all she'd ever wanted in a man. That there were such men in the world had astonished her, so used to a different species of male; that she could find one to adore, and be adored in return, was a gift from the gods. Now the gods had taken back their gift, leaving her worse than had they never offered her sight of him. It was as if all the tricks she'd learned to hold her passions at bay had been forgotten and she was left vulnerable and exposed in a harsh, brutal world.

When she learned what had happened, those who told her dwindled to distant shadows, disembodied voices in the darkness. She was aware of being carried, of leaving her home, of lying in a bed and feeling almost pleasantly drowsy, but she was also aware of screams and hysteria, probably her own. When the screams died, she thought she might like to die with them, but instead she was persecuted by relentless, destabilizing thoughts. Death would have been a welcome oblivion but it wouldn't take her. All manner of devils invaded her inner quiet, and an emotional storm brewed, as if her soul rebelled vainly against life, perversely punished for its innocence.

As a girl she'd been bad tempered, angry without reason, stubbornly opposed to authority. She remembered hiding under tables and banging the floor in anger. She had always been aware of an emptiness, a vacuum which nothing satisfied until she'd met Michael. She had a large family, but they exacerbated her isolation. She had never been abused, never been hurt, never been demeaned because she was a girl in a man's world, she was just put together wildly, with passions that threatened to rule her. She feared madness, but love gave her direction, strength and hope.

This insane night had banished all of them and she lay in a troubled state, part life, part dream.

"I'll sit with her, sir," said Charlene. "I know I'm not a friend, but

I'd like to stay for a while."

"We'll both sit with her," said Ursula.

Faraday left them. He was still shaken by Naila's reaction to the news, complete mental and physical collapse, but he was also buoyed by the resilience of these people who showed their best qualities under stress.

Charlene sat on one side of Naila, Ursula on the other, holding her hand. A drip feed kept Naila drowsy and the wild reactions at bay.

"I'm not officially on duty yet," Charlene said, "but Simon ... Inspector Faraday ... thought it might be good to have a familiar face around in case I'm needed.

They were in a small ward at the Homerton, closed in by white curtains. It was a strange threesome, but the events of the night were throwing people together in strange ways. Faraday felt that Charlene was emotionally tuned in to the case and wanted her to be with Naila when the news was broken. Naila had known what they were going to say as soon as she saw them, but there was no easy way of telling her. She didn't scream or shout, she just seemed to drain away, as if her soul had suddenly fled and left behind a vacuum.

Then the fit began, sudden, visceral and frightening in its intensity.

They called an ambulance and she was taken to hospital.

When Ursula told Jasmine and Elena, they wanted to come too, but decided it was best to take turns.

Michael's death didn't seem to register. How could it? It stretched human emotions too far and had to be handled on reserves of strength and rationality. They had no techniques, no learned responses, nothing to deal with this, but they found a way through with surprising fortitude. Elena remembered what someone had told her about the children in her class, that you could always tell when they were really tired or when they were struggling because they went quiet – at all other times they complained relentlessly.

"Do you know her well?" Charlene asked.

"Naila? Not that well," said Ursula. "She and Michael were very close and kept themselves to themselves. But we'd met. I was a bit scared of her."

Naila lay between them like a wonderful sculpture, her brown skin almost halfway between Charlene's black and Ursula's white. An artist might have made much of the threesome, the bringing together of cultures and the terrible intensity of the event that made them share the same space for a brief while.

"Scared?"

"A little, yes, but Michael calmed her down, and Kathryn calmed Michael down. That's the way it seemed to work. Not sure how it will work now. Nothing much left to work anymore, is there?"

Charlene saw that. She asked about Kathryn and Michael.

"Michael was her baby brother and proud of him. She virtually brought him up," said Ursula. "I think Kath was Michael's guardian angel."

"And Naila?"

"Hard to understand, isn't it?" said Ursula. "They were so different, fire and water, but they were perfect together. He really shouldn't have done this!"

She started crying and Charlene took her hand across the bed.

"I'm alright," Ursula said, trying to compose herself. "I suppose you see a lot of bad stuff. You must get used to it."

"I do see bad… stuff, but I'm not sure I get used to it. I don't sit in on all cases, you know."

Ursula smiled and wiped her eyes.

"I guess not," she said.

"I feel for you all. I feel for her," said Charlene, looking at the sleeping Naila. "I'm not supposed to, but there you go."

"How do you deal with it all, then?" Ursula asked.

Charlene said, "It's different when it's work, you don't get drawn in, or you're not supposed to. Some things make me mad, though. I can't take kids being hurt, that really gets to me. I see a lot of kids in bad situations, growing up way before they're ready, pretending to be adults at twelve or thirteen. It's all topsy-turvy. They're just so lost."

"I think," said Ursula, "that's why Michael was so close to Kath. She gave him meaning. She was his guide when he was small, and a good one, the best!"

"He was lucky then," said Charlene. "A lot of parents don't have a clue. They shout, threaten, hit their kids, and the kids do the same when they're big enough. I look around sometimes and wonder what I'm doing, just putting plaster on the wound, I think."

"I'm sure it's more than that," said Ursula.

"I wonder," said Charlene. "I feel I'm more useful here than I am on the beat with my partner."

"The one who was with you before?"

"Yes, him." Even to Ursula, whose mind and heart were strained to the limit, Charlene sounded as if she was hiding something. "Maybe you all give me hope," Charlene said, pulling the subject away from Matt, "that people can care for each other. I don't see too much of that, you know. I see more talking the talk, not walking the walk."

Ursula almost laughed, but said, "I don't know how you do it. You must be really brave."

"I'm not," said Charlene. "I have kittens thinking about some of the nutters I've dealt with, and whoever killed your friend...well, they frighten me. They'd frighten anyone, but we'll get him all the same."

"You think so?"

"Inspector Faraday is good. He's quiet, not The Sweeney or the rubbish you see on TV..."

"Don't watch," said Ursula.

"...right, but on the ball, and works like a Trojan."

"What about your partner, Officer Davis?"

All roads appeared to lead to Rome.

"What about him?" Charlene asked, defensively.

"Oh, don't know. Is he good?"

Charlene gave a rueful smile and said, "I hope so. We've been together a while now. Maybe we can help on this case. Neither of us like the idea of a killer on the loose."

"No," said Ursula. "You think whoever killed Kathryn could do it again?"

"No idea," said Charlene, "but we have to assume he might. Faraday won't rest until he's caught."

Ursula thought it scary, that no one had any idea who had done this. She might pass the murderer in the street, ask him directions or get into some kind of conversation, and she'd have no idea who he was or what he'd done. It was both the blessing and curse of human isolation.

"You've seen us all tonight," she said, "do you think one of us could have done this?"

"One thing I've learned," said Charlene, "is never to be surprised, and another, never to make assumptions about people. We're all a bit crazy and anyone can do anything given the motive."

"Even so ..." said Ursula.

"Look," said Charlene, "I haven't met all her friends or the people she knew. It might not be one of them, so don't worry – it might well be a random attack or some obscure connection." Even an obscure connection worried Ursula. "We'll follow up everything," said Charlene, "we have to. Just tell Inspector Faraday anything you think might be important."

"I doubt I'll think of anything," said Ursula. "We're just a bunch of friends getting on with our lives, nothing special at all. I'd never think of anyone in a million years who could do this, never."

"You already have," said Charlene. Ursula was taken aback. "You told us that you had a call from Mrs Hargreaves last night?"

"Oh, right. So?"

"Kathryn met someone there who bothered her."

"Yes, right again. Sorry. I never met him, though. It was just what Kathryn told us."

"Those are exactly the things we need to know," said Charlene.

Ursula remembered the call from Maggie, and how anxious she was on the phone. Poor lady, she was fond of Kathryn, she'd be distraught. Ursula made a mental note for the three of them to go around there – although, the idea that her grandson or whoever was somehow implicated unsettled her.

Naila moved, moaned, half opened her eyes then closed them again.

"She'll need care," said Charlene. "I don't think she's going to be strong enough to get on with life for a while."

"No," said Ursula, "but we'll all help out."

When Elena and Jasmine arrived, they peeked through the bed curtain first, then came in, both looking exhausted.

"How is she?" Jasmine asked.

"Drugged to the eyeballs," said Ursula, "didn't take it well."

Charlene said, "Ladies, I have to go. Duty calls. You've got our number if you think of anything," she said to Ursula, told them to take care and left.

"'Think of anything'?" said Jasmine, sitting down, "like what?"

"Anything," Ursula answered.

"And 'take care'?" said Elena, "does she, you know..."

"Just wants us to be safe," said Ursula.

The two pulled up chairs and sat beside Naila, Jasmine holding her hand and stroking her hair.

"She's so beautiful," said Jasmine. "What happened when she found out?"

Ursula told them and they listened, full of pity. They'd returned from the night-time rowing but had barely settled before Faraday called to tell them of Michael's suicide. Ursula had gone with him but they'd been desperate to join her.

"What are they going to do?" Elena asked, gesturing to Naila. "They'll have to wake her at some point."

Ursula didn't know, but hoped it wouldn't be for a while.

They sat close to each other, and close to Naila. The shock of losing Kathryn had been hard enough, but Michael's suicide pushed them to the limit. They were struggling with their own fears and needed each other more than ever in a world spinning out of control.

For the moment, they simply had to ride the storm. They wanted be near Naila and the epicentre of the insanity. Whether this was right, or whether they ought to have got on with their lives was debatable, but they couldn't be apart. Their flat was filled with Kathryn's absence and they needed to fight for life, take on the force that was harming them and defeat it, if only by sticking together and caring for each other.

A nurse, looking more anxious and concerned than a detached carer ought to be, came by to see how Naila was doing.

"We all knew Kathryn," she said. "We can't believe it, none of us. The whole hospital is in shock."

They commiserated as best they could and watched as she went about her business. When she left, they made a chain of hand-holding over Naila's sleeping figure, as if it would afford some protection to her and to them from the malevolent force which seemed determined to punish innocence, wondering whether there would ever be an end to the madness and whether they would ever know safety and security again.

## 5

Faraday drove to Richmond Road and to the home of Jerome Reed. The tiredness of a sleepless night had vanished as Friday dawned and the investigations developed. Viv Fowler sat beside him, looking through some papers, still sharp despite the lack of sleep.

Hackney was already frighteningly busy, Queensbridge Road, like most of the routes into the city, thick with cars. The borough was up and coming, a gateway to the city of London, but it had been up and coming for decades without ever having up and come. In this respect it was unlike its richer neighbour Islington which wore a mantle of respectability, even though both boroughs faced similar problems with areas of great wealth alongside those of shameful poverty.

Richmond Road was a long, typical Hackney Road full of impressive brick houses built to last a thousand years but already in need of some TLC. There were no shops and few distinguishing features, apart from the bridge itself, and that was hardly Golden Gate, yet Faraday knew this was Hackney and could probably have said so even if he'd been blindfolded. There was something in the layout of the roads, despite the fact that Queensbridge was arrow straight, in the style of the houses and in the very air of the borough that he recognised. He'd played in these streets when he was a boy, gone to school at Homerton and imbibed East London into his veins. And yet he felt as if he were a stranger, as if his thoughts didn't quite tally with the locals, assuming there were any 'locals' in this pot of cultures, melting or otherwise.

"Hopeful?"

Fowler asked him in her usual quiet voice, flicking through the papers their team had given them.

"Always hopeful," he said.

"Not a lot to go on," said Viv.

"Not a lot, but they already have the DNA."

"So it's just a question of matching?"

"Just."

"You okay sir? You've had a long night."

"Long and sad, Viv. This is different, more intense, and it's nothing to do with the usual nonsense, gangs, drugs and petty squabbles. This is deeper."

"How do you mean, sir?"

"Well, unless Kathryn was living a double life, which I suppose is possible, there's someone out there who hated her, and I can't see it."

"You've discarded the random theory?"

"Not totally, but you've read the reports, it was like she knew what was happening. If she was meeting some secret lover, he had a strange way of showing his affection."

"You believe Robert?"

"I do. We'll check it out but yes, I believe him. Lucky he was there."

"Too lucky?"

"You mean too fortuitous to be true? Could be, but why bother telling us at all, why not just clear off. No, I don't think he did it. He's not a violent man, just a victim. Whoever did this is the hardest sicko to find, Viv, pure malice but totally rational, so we won't even know when we look him in the eyes."

"Like now?"

"Like now. Just do the usual, watch and listen. Hopefully we'll get some inkling. Have you checked his file?"

"I have. You going to challenge him right away?"

"About the murder?"

"No, about Maggie."

"Hmm, let's see what he says first, assuming he's there, of course."

They arrived at the address of Jerome Reed, a terraced house in Richmond Road. They parked, reported their position and approached the door, a basement entrance but not seedy, in fact in good shape, clean and tidy. Viv opened a black cast iron gate which swung back on oiled hinges, and at the same moment the basement door opened and a man came out. He was in his early thirties, smartly dressed and carrying a briefcase. Just before he closed the front door he saw the two of them standing by the gate and said, "What do you want?"

The two officers were in plain clothes, so it wasn't obvious who they were or what they wanted. Faraday showed his identity and said, "Detective Inspector Faraday, Hackney Police. Are you Jerome Reed?"

"I am."

"We need to speak with you for a few minutes, sir."

"I'm just off to work; we've got a meeting. Can't this wait?"

"Afraid not, sir."

Jerome Reed, if he was guilty, showed astonishing coolness. At first, Faraday thought he had the characteristics of American Psycho, calm, collected and deadly, but first impressions weren't always reliable, especially when you really wanted the impression to fit a template.

"What's it about?" Jerome asked.

"Might we come in," said Faraday, "don't really like to discuss it out here."

Reed looked peeved and said, "This is really inconvenient. I've got an important meeting and..."

"Hopefully we won't take up too much time. Can't you call in and tell them you might be a little late?"

Reed scowled at them. He had a mask of a face, self-satisfied and a touch heartless, if not openly cruel, but also with the potential of charm. He beckoned them down, pushed the door open and led them in, taking out his mobile as he did so.

"Veronica, hi, it's Jerry. I've been held up, can you tell the others I might be late. I'll call in as soon as I'm free...sorry? ...No, I'll tell you when I see you...yes...that's fine...buzz me if it's urgent, okay? Got to go." He turned to Faraday and Fowler but didn't offer them a seat. "What's this about?"

Faraday and Fowler had taken the few seconds Reed was on the phone to study at his home. With a few glances they could both get a feel for the lifestyle he led, superficial but useful. The flat was simple, even minimalist, but with expensive items focusing attention. A Bang and Olufsen system took pride of place, faced by a black leather sofa, all on a plush wine coloured carpet. There was truly little else, no books, no trinkets, just a small coffee table with a single fashion magazine and an arched entrance to the kitchen area and a doorway to what was probably the bedroom. At the rear there were French windows looking out on to a small garden. This was a bachelor pad par excellence. The bed, Faraday thought, was probably king size with a Canadian goose down quilt, fifteen tog, warm but light.

"It's about Kathryn Hudson. Did you know her, sir?"

Reed didn't flinch. "No. Who is she?"

Either this was a barefaced lie or Faraday had missed something; then he realised what he'd missed.

"Nell. Maggie Hargreaves called her Little Nell."

Reed's face darkened.

"Was that her name, then? I didn't know."

"But you knew the girl?"

"You know I did, you wouldn't be here otherwise would you? What's the problem? Has she reported me or something?"

"Why would she do that, sir?"

Reed looked even more uncomfortable for a second, then composed himself and said, "No reason, except for Maggie Hargreaves. I suppose she put you on to me?"

"Again sir, why would she do that?"

"And again, you know as well as I do. Look – Inspector Faraday – will you stop treating me like a dumb ass criminal and be straight or are we going to play cat and mouse all the time?"

"I would just like to know why you think Mrs Hargreaves should have put us on to you, sir."

"She did it because, as you already know, she thought I was hounding her precious Little Nell."

"And were you?"

"No! I liked her, is that a crime?"

"No sir, but she seemed to think you were rather, how shall we say, over-zealous?"

"I'm no shrinking violet inspector, but surely this can't have brought you out so early in the day? Don't you have more important things to do than harass citizens because of one senile old woman?"

If Reed had had any chance of getting Faraday and Fowler on his side, this lost it.

"So you think Mrs Hargreaves is senile? I met her earlier on. She seemed pretty sound to me," said Faraday.

"Well, whether she's sound or senile it doesn't matter. She's sent you here because she doesn't like me, isn't that right?"

"No sir, it isn't right."

"Then why did she send you here?"

"She didn't send us, sir."

Reed started looking fidgety.

"Is this about work, then?"

"Work?"

"For God's sake, are you going to keep answering questions with questions? We really will be here all day."

Faraday didn't look at Fowler but knew she was studying Reed with keen interest. He was hiding something, they knew that, but what?

"Do you mind if we ask what your work is, sir?" Faraday asked.

"You mean you don't know?"

"If you don't mind," said Faraday.

Reed told them he was in the insurance industry, shipping and various heavy freights. He gave them his address in the city near Broadgate.

"Now may I ask what you were doing last night?"

"Last night? Why, what was I supposed to be doing?"

"Sir, if you could answer directly this will be over quickly."

"I worked till late, got home late, went to bed late and am late again now."

"Alone?"

"Unfortunately yes," said Reed.

"No witnesses?"

"What, to being alone?"

"...to your schedule."

"You can ask my colleagues at work, if you must. Inspector, I hate to repeat myself, but why are you pestering me with all these questions? What was I supposed to be doing last night?"

Reed was unfazed by having two police officers in his home. He was abrupt, even rude, and trying to establish some control. Faraday decided it was time to break the news, even if Reed secretly already knew it. The man's reaction would be critical.

"Last night, Kathryn Hudson was murdered, Mr Reed."

They watched him, he watched them back. He tried to be inscrutable but his eyes flickered slightly.

"Are you sure you can't be more specific about where you were last night, Mr Reed?"

Jerome Reed didn't answer. He looked down and clasped his hands together.

"Is that the truth?" he asked quietly.

"Yes."

"Jesus wept!" he whispered to himself.

Faraday and Fowler looked at each other. They weren't sure; he might have been innocent, he might have been guilty, he was certainly a sharp customer, intelligent and wily.

"How?" he asked. "What happened?"

"No need to go into details," said Faraday. "You'll find out soon enough, I daresay. For the moment we'd just like to clear your name..."

"Blacken my name, you mean."

"Sorry sir?"

"You think I had something to do with this, that's plain as pie."

"Did you?"

"No, I didn't." No hesitation at all. "What makes you think I did, the fact that old blabbermouth mother Hargreaves told you."

"She says you've visited her, Mr Reed, yet you sound, if I might say so, a touch hostile."

Reed shifted uncomfortably.

"Do I? She's an old bat."

"Really? I didn't think so, sir."

"She is to me."

"Why is that?"

"I just wanted to call the girl. Girls like that don't come your way every day, you know."

"Girls like Kathryn?"

"Yes of course girls like Kathryn. We're not talking about Mother Theresa are we?"

"But you didn't see her again?"

"No."

"Not at all?"

"No. I wanted to but the old fuddy-duddy wouldn't help."

"Did you know what she did for a living, Mr Reed?"

"She was a nurse."

"She told you that?"

"Why shouldn't she?"

"And you didn't try to trace her?"

"How was I supposed to do that? She was introduced to me as Nell, a silly game she and the old lady were playing. She was a nurse at a hospital, I didn't even know which one. What was I supposed to do?"

"You met her just the once?"

"I told you, yes."

"You never called her?"

"Might have done. Is that illegal?"

"Would you mind at some point coming for a blood test, sir?"

"A what?"

"A blood test; it would help us clear your name."

"Isn't it clear already?"

"It would help us, sir."

"How would it help you, inspector?"

"No need for details, Mr Reed, but it certainly would be invaluable for the investigation. You can pop along to the hospital at any time. Here's a card," and Faraday handed Reed a card with a contact at the hospital. "They'll take a small sample of blood. It would..."

"...be of great help, yes, I heard. I'll think about it."

"That's good of you, sir."

There was an uncomfortable pause, but Reed didn't seem to want them to go. Rather, he was itching to say something, and when he did it rather surprised the two police officers.

"She was ... involved, wasn't she?"

"Yes, she was."

"I knew it. She was the loyal type."

"I get the impression she was rather exceptional in many ways," said Faraday. He was trying to hide his instinctive dislike of Reed. He'd seen the type before, sharp, greedy, ruthless and very self-centred. The man was lying, too, perhaps about Kathryn but definitely about work. Reed was about as much in the insurance field as Faraday was a ballet dancer – the man was a loan shark, nothing more, nothing less. They'd checked – they always checked.

Faraday tried to hide his instinctive dislike of such a trade, but he knew the ways of the world and saw its failures. Money was the lifeblood of the modern world, probably of ancient and future worlds. If people were denied it, they would find ways to tap into it, legal or otherwise. This wasn't rocket science, it was common sense. You couldn't have a society so dependent on money then make it scarce for some, easy as water for others. That way chaos lay. People like Reed were only doing what the system, in a way, led them to do, survive by any means available. That didn't, however, make him a sympathetic character. If Kathryn had been half the woman Faraday thought she'd been, Reed would have had as much chance of attracting her as a fly to a spider.

"Is that all?" Reed asked. "Am I free to go about my business or am I going be taken in for questioning?"

"Not right now, sir," said Faraday, "but we'd appreciate it if you stayed local for a while."

"Stayed local?"

"Don't leave the area. I'm sure we will need to speak to you again. It is, as you can see, an important matter."

"Important or not, it has nothing to do with me," said Reed, "and I have meetings around the country. It's important that I travel."

"Then if you leave your contact numbers with us, that will have to do," said Faraday. "All we ask is co-operation, not coercion."

"I'll co-operate up to a point," said Reed, "but I resent my name being dragged through the mire because of a muddle headed old biddy."

Fowler glanced at Faraday, wondering how he kept his calm.

"We ask for any information," said Faraday evenly, though Fowler sensed a slight irritation, "from anyone. We're talking about murder, sir, so a slight inconvenience on your part shouldn't be too unbearable. We won't drag your name through the mire, just follow up all possibilities. I'm sure you can understand that?"

Whether he could or couldn't, Reed stood and said he had to get going.

"I'm afraid I'm not finished," said Faraday softly.

"I am," said Reed.

"Be that as it may, I have another question to ask you. Please sit."

Reed sat down with a dark expression. Actually, Faraday didn't have another question at all, he just disliked being dismissed by a mean, small-minded creep like Reed.

"Well?" Reed asked.

"What exactly is your relationship to Mrs Hargreaves?"

Reed turned a darker shade of pale and said, "Is this one of those questions you know the answer to already?"

"I'd just like an explanation," said Faraday.

"She's a relative," said Reed.

"Distant?" Faraday asked.

"Of course, bloody distant," Reed said, "she's hardly my mother is she?"

"Grandmother?" Faraday asked. "I'd just like to get a clear picture of how you got to know her."

"Family tree," said Reed, slowly, "came across her name, realised she lived locally, went to see her; great great aunt or something. Happy?"

"Can you be more specific?"

"No."

Faraday stood up slowly, preparing the usual goodbye speech, but he didn't hurry. If he was to leave any impression at all with Reed, it was that he couldn't and wouldn't be rushed. Reed looked at him, unabashed, unfazed and unfriendly.

"Whatever you're thinking, it wasn't me," said Reed. "I may not be Mr Likeable, but I didn't kill the girl."

"No," said Faraday, "I appreciate the time."

If there was one impression Reed wanted to leave with the Detective Inspector it was that he was straightforward and honest, which was about as possible as Faraday thinking endearing thoughts of Dr Crippen.

Outside, Faraday took a deep breath of morning air.

"Did you get all that?" he asked Fowler who had taken assiduous notes. She had.

"What do you make of him, sir?" she asked.

They got into the car and drove away, not waiting for Reed to leave his home for the second time.

"Disliked him intensely," said Faraday. "He's conning the old lady, he's probably making a hundred people miserable, he's living a decent life on a nasty occupation, he's a self-absorbed, self-serving waste of space."

"He charmed you, then?" Fowler asked and Faraday forced a smile. He was feeling the tiredness from a sleepless night begin to roll over him, and he desperately wanted to close his eyes for a while, but there was too much to do.

"He didn't charm me," he said, "but I'm not sure he's guilty. How about you?"

Fowler shook her head. "Tricky one, sir. I suppose we'll know if he checks in at the hospital and gives blood."

Faraday desperately wanted Reed to be guilty, but he even more desperately wanted the truth. He'd hoped for a quick resolution but he had a feeling that it might be protracted. Quite unprofessionally, but totally understandably, he felt immensely sad at the two lives lost during the night, a sister and her brother, good people who had hurt no one, just victims of life's unconcern. He'd seen good people hurt before, that wasn't unusual, but these two were different. Michael had had a rare quality about him and he guessed that Kathryn had been the same, if not more pronounced. He felt a deep sense of grievance that this kind of thing should happen, that people like Jerome Reed were alive and well to greet the new day whilst these two poor souls were gone forever. If Reed was guilty, Faraday would know soon enough, whether or not Reed trotted along to the hospital to give blood, like any innocent citizen would have done.

## 6

About the same time as Faraday and Fowler were interviewing Reed, Daniel arrived at the hospital to see Naila. He'd always had a deeply religious sensibility, in the spiritual sense of the word, but with the added touch of Jewish ritual, tradition and culture. It really didn't matter where he went, how far he ran from home or who he tried to be, the seed of who he was, or who his people wanted him to be, grew inside him. His race had been through hell and had come away with some measure of pride and independence. For two thousand years they'd been the pariahs of almost every culture, eking out the barest living in every corner of Earth, unwanted, unloved and misunderstood. That deep rooted resentment, implanted millennia before, in one of Creation's greatest acts of irony, by the followers of one of the most ardent and aware Jews of all time, had exploded in genocide, humanity's ultimate barbarity, and from it a new generation had been born, with hope, ideals and a range of experience unknown to any other creed.

All this, though, seemed a trifle empty in the face of these events lacking rhyme, reason or the slightest hint of divine concern. He felt, if anything, the same bitterness hounding him, imaginary or not, despite all he could do to deflect it. Worse, the ill luck he felt following him was wreaking havoc amongst those he loved. He felt, instinctively, that there was a connection, that the cause of this misery was locked in his identity and in something that he was, regardless of what he wanted to be, but he couldn't be certain and he didn't want to appear paranoid.

Michael was gone. The thought was harder to reconcile than the loss of Kathryn. Neither were part of the Grand Scheme. Both deaths were anathema, insults to reason and an abomination of order. The Old Testament language licked around his mind, all the epic lives and deaths of ancient time made him dizzy, instructing him how to deal with this new evil. He listened, but the voices would make him mad. What possible voice of reason or learning could explain this? He couldn't believe that such sadness had engulfed him and his friends. The sense of dream pervaded everything he did and saw, as if he were dealing with the horror by distancing himself from a reality which was too cruel to contemplate.

Compounding all this was the fact that Naila was, by birthright, heritage and contemporary politics, supposed to be his enemy. They had both known it, though they both did all they could to ignore it. She had been so affectionate in the hospital, had done all she could to reach out to him. She had been fond of Kathryn, never close, but through Michael they had a bond, and her own love for Michael told her something of Kathryn's love for Daniel. Hours later, here he was, on his way to see her, to offer her the same comfort, but wondering whether he had anything left to give.

They were in conflict by the sheer weight of history, from races destined to face each other over the battlefields of belief, yet doing what they could as individuals to master the biblical psyche of tribal rivalries. They were twenty-first century people with pre-Christian heritages and minds wired, like computers, with different Read Only Memories, tainted or enriched, depending on your standpoint, with epochal visions of the world and of each other.

He resented the intrusion. All he ever wanted was to be free of his past, but the world would never let him have that freedom, and again he felt the guilt of complicity, somehow, in these deaths. His mind was in a fractious state and his heart heavier than he'd thought possible when he arrived at Naila's bedside.

"Daniel!" said Ursula. "You came!"

"I did," said Daniel. "Hello," he said to Jasmine and Elena. "How is she?"

Naila lay like some mystical beauty, a Persian princess from the time of Xerxes. She had the dark skin, the jet black hair, the bone structure and countenance of an ancient queen. Yet here she was, two thousand years out of place, suffering horribly, her life wrecked and unrecoverable.

"Stoned," said Jasmine. "They've filled her with drugs. She was going nuts, Daniel."

Going nuts just about summed up what was happening to him and what was unavoidably happening to Naila.

"I wasn't sure whether to come or not," he said gently.

"It's fantastic that you came," said Jasmine. "Isn't it, Urse, El?"

"Ursula and Elena hugged Daniel. They were all fond of him and would have done anything to ease his heart, but there was nothing they could do, except be there.

"You didn't have to," said Ursula, "I mean, we all would have understood if you'd rested. You must be dead beat."

"I'm tough," he said, half joking, half in earnest. "Really, how is she?"

They told him what had happened, how she'd swung from sanity to insanity and back again, how her body had started to rebel and how she'd been brought to the hospital. A thought passed through Daniel's mind that he hadn't reacted in the same way, that he'd been less volatile, much calmer, at least on the outside, and he felt concern that he didn't feel as much as he ought. But when he asked himself what he ought to feel, he had no answer.

Naila was at a disadvantage. She had a volatile, artistic soul, a mind burning with passions and ideas, so an act of God or the Devil such as this was insupportable, it would destroy her if she couldn't find something of what Daniel had in him, whatever that was, something more stable than lurching human passions.

He sat and held Naila's hand. Her palm lay in his, warm and gentle, but Daniel felt uneasy. Though he tried not to think it, he wished it was Kathryn lying there, exhausted but alive. Life was everything, death was nothing, an extinction from which there was no return. He couldn't quite convince himself that it was Naila whose hand he was holding. It made no sense to think that this was happening, that he was sitting beside Naila who had lost Michael as he had lost Kathryn. The world seemed to lose shape and form and he wondered at his own ability to move, to see, to use his senses and his mind. How was he to use them sensibly in this chaos?

"Dan?" Jasmine had moved next to him and was holding his hand and Naila's. He hadn't even noticed. "How are you doing?" she asked, touching him on the shoulder.

"I suppose you know?" he said to all three of them, "about Kathryn?"

At first they wondered what he meant, that of course they knew she'd been killed, but Melissa had called them about the pregnancy. Jasmine put her arm around Daniel and lay her head on his shoulder.

"Mel told us," she said.

Daniel felt an increasing sense of panic, as if a monstrous abyss was opening up in front of him and that all he had to do was let himself fall into it. There was no point trying to deal with this craziness, sitting beside Naila with Kathryn's friends, trying to hold things together when life had fractured so badly.

"I didn't know," he said.

"We'll find out what happened, Dan," said Jasmine, "don't think bad thoughts, sweety."

"I won't," he said, "thanks for being here, with me, with Naila. You're good people."

His words sounded awkward, but he was awkward himself, even in the best of times, and this was the worst of times. Words shaped sense out of the world, but there was no sense to be had from this.

"She wouldn't have done anything wrong, not Kathryn," said Elena.

"Never," said Jasmine.

"She should have told me," said Daniel. "All this might have been different."

"But we don't know why," said Ursula. "Trust her. She had her reasons."

Daniel felt Naila's hand move slightly. He looked at her and the others followed his gaze.

"She's miles away," said Jasmine.

"Best place," said Daniel. Jasmine squeezed his hand.

"I can't believe you came here," she said. "You're an angel, Dan, you really are!"

Daniel didn't know whether it was kind or not, it had just felt right to visit, to let the tide of the night's events sweep him along.

"We're not disturbing her, are we?" he asked.

"Not with methadone instead of blood," said Ursula, pointing at the tubes. "I could do with some of that myself. What's going on, Daniel? Do you understand?"

He didn't. He wondered if there was any understanding to be had. The girls looked exhausted. They each had jobs but morning had come and here they were putting friendship before work.

"We ought to have a rota," said Jasmine, "making sure there's someone with her all the time. She shouldn't wake up alone."

They did this, even Daniel said he'd come and sit with her.

"What about Michael's parents?" Elena asked.

"What about them?" said Ursula. "Pretty useless lot, if you ask me."

"Well, I don't think Naila would want to wake up and see them anyway," said Jasmine. "We can do it ourselves."

It wasn't that they knew her, they didn't. She was a mystery, an Eastern enigma who had fallen into their lives in this mad moment. They fell silent, afraid of their own thoughts but unable to chase them away. In a peculiar way, Naila's plight gave them a focus, someone who needed their help, and ironically the one who had appeared most unlikely to need help, the strongest, the most passionate, the most independent. Here she was, laid out before them like the sleeping beauty, victim of a wicked spell.

"He shouldn't have done it," said Ursula. "Not now. Not ever, but not now."

"Don't say that," said Jasmine. "You don't know what was going on in his head. It must have been unbearable."

They looked at Daniel. If anyone knew what unbearable meant, it was him, yet there he sat, still holding Naila's hand, showing astonishing resilience. He said, "I'm sure it was. Kath told me he was fragile. I didn't realise how much."

Naila lay in the induced stupor looking as stunning in sleep as she did awake, but she would have been touched that people who, in truth, she hardly knew, were sitting beside her, keeping vigil, and especially that one of them was Daniel. If some small particle of truth had reached her, she might have cried that he was there, but she appeared to be in absolute oblivion, her face an impenetrable mask, her body lifting and falling ever so slightly with each breath. Now and again her eyes twitched and her skin trembled, but the four friends couldn't tell if this was the effect of dreams or a physiological reaction.

They set a rota so that there would be someone there most of the time. None of them wanted to leave. The night had bound them together, the deaths, the hospital, the boating and now this vigil. Though they wouldn't say so, they dreaded being alone again, even Daniel who stayed with them a while, uncertain what he was supposed to do with his time now that everything had fallen away. It was only when the nurses had work to do and the ward emptied did they leave, aimless and exhausted, almost envying Naila's catatonic isolation.

7

Ivan Orlich was reading a paper at the kitchen table when there was a knock at the door. Margot was out and Milly was at school so he opened the door himself, irritated at being bothered.

"Mr Orlich?"

"Yes."

"I'm Detective Inspector Faraday, this is Inspector Fowler; can we have a quick word with you?"

"What about?"

Both officers wondered if manners had gone out of fashion; this was the fifth call, including Jerome Reed, and they hadn't had a civil reception yet.

"It's about one of the nurses at the hospital... where your son is being treated?" Faraday added as Orlich looked bemused.

"What nurse?"

"Is it possible to come in to discuss this, Mr Orlich?"

Orlich let them in, though he looked to be in a foul temper. He didn't offer them a seat so they stood facing each other in the lounge, a very different room from Jerome Reed's. This had no Bang and Olufsen, nor any fancy equipment. There was no sign of wealth at all and only a modest attempt at keeping the place in order. The furniture and furnishings were all drab, the carpet stained, and there was a musty smell, but different from the one he remembered in Maggie Hargreaves's home; this was not so much age as hygiene - the lack of it.

"How is your son?" Faraday asked.

Orlich looked puzzled.

191

"You didn't come here to ask me about William," he said suspiciously, "and how do you know he's in hospital anyway?"

"I'm afraid we have some sad news," said Faraday.

"Will?" Orlich perked up for a moment- a good sign. Concern.

"No, as I said, it's about one of the nurses."

He waited, so did Orlich. Neither gave anything away. Orlich seemed to look at the officers with a mixture of trepidation and anger. He might have been hiding something, but they couldn't be sure.

"I'm afraid to say one of them was murdered last night."

Orlich's eyes opened a little wider. He really did appear, at least for a moment, shocked.

"Who?" he asked.

"Nurse Hudson. Kathryn Hudson. Did you know her?"

Orlich sat down and the two policemen did likewise.

"Yeh, of course I did. I saw her every day. She was Will's favourite."

His expression was as dark and unreadable as Reed's. Faraday waited, then said, "You'll have to forgive our intrusion, but obviously we need to make enquiries. We have a team out there talking to neighbours and people who knew Kathryn."

"Right," said Orlich, his voice low, gruff and angry.

"Because at the moment we're not sure who did it."

"Yep, I get it," said Orlich.

"We're wondering if you noticed anything unusual about Nurse Hudson over the past few weeks."

Orlich thought for a moment then said, "Not really. She weren't as perky as she had been but nothing more than that. She was a good lady. Will liked her a lot."

"Did you speak to her at all?" Faraday asked.

"Margot did, I didn't. Margot will be upset."

"You didn't speak to her then?"

"Not really, just hello now and again."

"And you didn't notice anything untoward?"

"In the hospital? Like what, inspector?"

"Well, at this stage, anything you can tell us might be useful, whether you saw her with anyone she looked uncomfortable with, whether she was unhappy at any time, things like that."

Orlich took a deep breath and looked down at his knuckles which he squeezed and released every now and again. Faraday sensed the man's anger - it wasn't easy to miss, and there was a good chance it came from the usual frustrations of a life not quite working out – money problems, marital problems, problems of self-esteem and the like.

Despite the name, Orlich was English through and through, his family having been in East London for a few generations. He thought his great grandparents might have been from Eastern Europe but he'd never bothered to find out. He'd worked as a labourer, digging roads in Hackney, Tower Hamlets, Islington, Brent, Haringey and every other London borough until he thought he'd dug every road it was possible to dig in London, but all the money he'd earned from the hard slog had gone on his family and on drink. Evidence of one was in the room, and evidence of the other was in his breath. Orlich had precious little to show for his efforts except a giant chip on his shoulder.

But was he a killer? Faraday was keeping every option open. He'd got his team on to families of children in Alexandra Ward, not because he suspected any of them, but because it was a connection and any connection just might lead to a vital piece of information. These families were vulnerable and not to be pushed too hard, but Orlich appeared at first to be a bit of a brute and Faraday decided to push just a little further.

"I hope you won't mind me asking," he said, "but can you tell me where you were last night, around midnight?"

Orlich looked at the policeman with a mixture of malice and frustration, as if being victimised was expected. He still hated the world for doing this to him.

"You making me a suspect?"

"I have to ask," said Faraday.

"No you bloody don't," said Orlich. "I bet you wouldn't if I were some fancy yuppie living the life of Riley, would you?"

"Actually," said Faraday, "I just have."

Orlich snorted some response and said, "I was here. We all were."

Faraday knew that his family, whatever the truth, would stick by him. Families were like that, most of the time. He'd seen tougher nuts than Orlich give their wives and children hell, yet they'd support each other. Humans were, in the case of families, essentially predictable despite being put together from the most uncertain bits of the uncertainty principle. They lived brief, sometimes brutal lives, and violence was at their heart, one way or another. It wasn't cynicism, it was the truth. The violence might be physical or it might be emotional, but it was there, protecting as well as attacking, and surprisingly a force for good as well as for bad. Faraday saw it as part of his life's work to impose the law of the land to keep the violence in check, but families and their volcanic emotions worked against him.

At that moment of contemplating the human condition, Faraday heard the front door open and Margot came in. She stopped short when she saw the two strangers in her home. Ivan, rather abruptly, told her who they were.

"Are you here about the murder?" she asked.

'There you were,' Faraday thought, 'barely twelve hours had passed and the world knew.'

He said they were, and Orlich added, "They think I did it, Margot."

Margot shook her head in disbelief, looking from Faraday to Fowler to her husband.

"Is this a joke?" she asked.

"No joke," Orlich said.

"I must put you right on that," said Faraday firmly, before Margot could speak, "we don't think that at all. I'm sorry, Mrs Orlich, your husband has got the wrong end of the stick."

"He better have," she answered, with an edge to her voice.

Faraday introduced himself and Fowler to Margot Orlich, explaining that they had no choice but to speak with everyone connected to Kathryn, no matter how tenuous the connection. He had an easy way about him, even in testing situations, and Margot accepted the explanation. She looked exceptionally tired and told them she'd paid a quick visit to the hospital after taking Milly to school. The place was in shock, she told them, sitting down and pulling back her hair. Not too many years ago, Margot Orlich would have been a handsome woman, and she still could have been, with care, but life more than age was taking its toll.

"How is it there?" Faraday asked.

That wasn't the question she was expecting.

"You could feel it," she said, "everywhere. Poor kids! She was so popular. I don't think Will's got it yet, Ivan."

"He wouldn't," said Orlich. "I hope none of them kids get it."

Faraday and Fowler were doing what all trained detectives did, listening and watching and trying to piece together Kathryn Hudson's world. Faraday could see, as he'd expected, that Margot was fiercely loyal to her husband, that they were a tightly knit unit. Margot was clearly distraught by the murder and Faraday decided it wasn't in their best interest to stay longer, but Margot said, "I suppose you need to know where we were last night?"

"Well, yes, but not now. I can see you're ...."

"Now is as good a time as any," said Margot.

"You were together all the evening then?" Faraday asked.

"Not all," said Margot, "Ivan went out for a drink."

"What time was that?" Faraday asked.

"After we got back from the hospital, around nine."

Orlich looked embarrassed. He hadn't mentioned going out to Faraday who asked "And you got back around what time?"

"Eleven," said Margot. "Just before Paula called."

"Paula is?" Faraday asked.

"Our neighbour," said Margot. "She called to see how William is."

"A bit late to call, isn't it?" Fowler asked.

"She knows we're late birds," said Margot, "we don't mind. She's a nice lady."

Orlich turned away and Faraday noticed the expression on his face, almost of contempt. He was an oddball, Orlich, and Faraday hadn't yet made up his mind whether he was a battered teddy or a dangerous grizzly; Margot didn't look at all afraid of him and put her hand on his shoulder when she answered Faraday's questions. He also asked her what he'd asked Orlich earlier, whether she'd seen anything untoward at the hospital, but she hadn't. She mentioned that Nurse Hudson had been a little off colour – "off colour?" – "distracted," said Margot, "for a few weeks. She was normally bright and breezy but she'd been down in the dumps for a while. Yes, I did notice that."

"Well," said Faraday, "that's something."

"Listen," said Orlich sharply, "I don't want you leaving here thinking I had anything to do with this, inspector."

"Neither of us do," said Margot.

"I don't think that, and I hope I'm right."

"You are right."

After the officers had left, Margot sat down next to her husband and said, "Ivan, tell me the truth now, when you went out last night, you didn't..."

"I went for a drink. I always go for a drink. There's no smoke here, Margot, don't let them tell you that."

"I do know it," said Margot, "I just wanted to hear it from you."

"You shouldn't need to," said Ivan. "I ain't a murderer!"

"I know love, sorry."

Ivan took out a beer from the fridge. Even at mid-morning he liked his drink, especially when he felt the world closing in on him again. He'd felt that more and more, especially with Will in hospital, no job, no money and a sense of waste consuming him. He'd always thought he was special. His name was different, he felt different and he'd worked hard, but somehow nothing went right. Whether that was true or an excuse, it didn't matter, he believed he was a victim and played the part. Maybe he had enough anger in him to kill someone, he often felt like it, and there were people in his past he'd like to have put away, but could he have done this? Just for a few moments he wondered whether he'd drunk too much the night before and done something too terrible to remember. People did that, he'd heard of it, and there were many times he was so drunk he couldn't remember details ... but this wasn't one of them, it couldn't be, it mustn't be!

"Bloody nerve," he said to Margot.

"It's their job, Ivan, don't take it personally."

"They bloody think I did it!"

"They don't. Lay off it, Ivan. You get a bee in your bonnet and it stays there forever. They don't think you did it, they're just asking around."

"Doesn't matter what they're doing, it's what they're saying and what they're thinking. Bloody nerve!"

Margot despaired of her husband at times. Obsessive wasn't the word – half the reason he messed up so often was that his brain got stuck like a broken record. It was already too late, she could tell. She'd just have to weather the storm. Besides, there were more important things than Ivan's mood, like William. When she'd seen him, she hadn't known what to say about Nurse Kathryn. No one had known quite what to do. The staff were shaken but they had to keep going. A few children asked where Nurse Kathryn was but no one told them – how could they? Margot guessed it would have to be something that the children learned slowly and...

"I'm going out," said Ivan.

"No you're not," said Margot, "we're going to the hospital together. Will needs us."

"I'll join you later," said Ivan.

"I said Will needs you."

"And I said I'll see you later," said Ivan, hastily slipping on a pair of battered shoes then grabbing a shabby old coat, watched in disdain by Margot who, at moments like this, didn't know how to cope. She saw the door bang shut, wondering whether her husband had such a foul temper he might really and truly hurt someone. But this? No, surely not. She looked both sad and defiant, hurrying into the kitchen to prepare a little food for William before heading back to the hospital.

She doubted suddenly how much she actually knew Ivan, how much anyone could know someone else. It wasn't unheard of for murderers to have unknowing wives. Did she know? Was he really at the pub last night? He knew Kathryn; she'd even seen him look at her! God!

She cried out as the knife she was holding pressed into her forefinger. Damn! She cleaned it under cold water, strapped it then stared at the knife, uncertain for the first time in her life about just who her husband really was.

## 8

Faraday and Fowler, heading towards the next house, exchanged looks.

"Fun visit," said Fowler.

"Indeed," said Faraday.

"You sure it was a 'J' that Hudson tried to trace?" she asked.

Faraday wasn't sure whether she was being serious or ironic.

"Not a hundred percent, no. You think it might have been an 'I'?"

Before she could answer, they saw Ivan Orlich storm away. He might have seen them standing at the neighbour's door but he didn't acknowledge them and went the other way.

"Angry man," said Fowler. "Shall we follow him?"

"No, not yet, but we'll keep him in mind; we'll keep everyone in mind, Viv."

"Indeed sir. Wicked world. Who's next?"

"Paula Taft," he said. "Late night wanderer," and he rang the bell.

## 9

Chaim Levinson put down the phone and stared at his desk. His faith was never critically questioned, but at times he wondered why the world was the way it was in that inexplicably bad things happened. It was an unspoken tenet of his religion never to doubt its fundamental truth, although six Jews might have given seven opinions about what that truth might be. No matter how wicked the ways of the world, you stuck to the rituals and beliefs, and nothing would change that. You might get away with tampering around with them a little, but the overall shape and fundamental belief never changed, not without morphing into something entirely different.

And what was that fundamental belief? It was that a single, righteous, omnipotent, unfathomable God instructed mankind in its early years to observe certain laws so vital that absolutely nothing, not even the most hellish atrocities, could undermine it. Such faith led inevitably to suffering, but suffering had become such an intrinsic part of the religion that it was questionable whether Judaism could survive without it. Amazingly, though, it was a happy religion, full of joy and celebrating life at every opportunity. As Job himself might have said, though probably not, go figure.

Chaim had suffering genetically encoded into his DNA. After two thousand years of homelessness and brutality, the Jewish people had developed a profound sensitivity to cruelty and injustice but also a profound sense of victimisation. This was no exaggeration. History had proved that wickedness knew no bounds, so just because you thought everyone was out to get you didn't mean they weren't. Chaim was a strong, funny and loyal man, loyal to his family and friends and deeply appreciative of the culture in England which allowed him to live the life he wanted without persecution.

This was why he was shaken to the core when the police officer on the phone had asked to come and speak with him about his son in connection with a murder.

"Lilly?"

His wife was getting ready to go to the hospital to see their other son.

"What is it Chaim?"

She came in and saw immediately that he was white as a sheet.

"The police just called," he said. "Sit down."

"Is it Sam...is he...?"

"Sam's okay - I think."

"You think! Chaim, what...?"

"Sit down, Lilly."

"I don't want to sit down."

"Take my advice, sit down," said Chaim. Lilly sat. "There's been a murder," he said, "someone we know."

Lilly put her hand to her mouth, thinking of all the people in her family and amongst their friends who she might never see again. When Chaim told her it was Nurse Hudson, one of the nurses who looked after Jonathan, she stared at him in disbelief. Why, she had seen her only a couple of days ago! She was full of life, a good lady, young, beautiful and caring – a mensch!. Lilly couldn't take it in, but before she had time to consider it, Chaim said, "There's more, Lilly."

"What more could there be?" she asked.

Chaim had to be very careful, but the more he pussyfooted around the more suspicious Lilly would become.

"The police are coming to speak to us."

"What, now?"

"Yes now."

"Why, Chaim?"

"Because, Lilly, they think that our son is involved?"

"What, Jonathan?"

Chaim had noticed this in people. They sometimes subconsciously avoided the blindingly obvious if it was not what they wanted to know; it was called selective hearing and Lilly was doing it now.

"Not Jonathan, Sam; they think our Sam might be - implicated."

Lilly looked at Chaim with a blank expression and then, unexpectedly, laughed out loud.

"Oh really, Chaim, be sensible!"

"It isn't me that's not being sensible, Lilly. This isn't a sensible situation. The nurse has been murdered, Samuel was out last night and he was picked up on camera in the area."

"But there are thousands of people in the area! This is our Sam, Chaim! He wouldn't hurt a fly!"

"They don't know that, do they?"

"We'll tell them! Chaim, this is ridiculous; maybe you misheard them?"

"No I didn't."

Lilly pulled a number of faces and rubbed her hands together frantically.

"We'll call his friend, what's his name, Jemmy..."

Jemal."

"Yes, and his sister, and their parents, we'll call them. I told you he shouldn't mix with them, Chaim! I told you, they would only get him into trouble."

"He isn't in trouble, Lilly, not yet."

"Not in trouble! The police want to talk to him about a murder and you say he isn't in trouble! Now who's not sensible? Oh, what a boy he is!"

"He's a good boy, Lilly. He's just trying to find himself."

"Find himself! Find himself! What's there to find? We know who he is, he knows who he is, there's nothing to find! We should have been more strict, Chaim! Everyone told us that we were spoiling him and we were! We've let things get out of hand. We..."

"Lilly," said Chaim gently, holding her hands, "nothing is out of hand. We know his heart, we know he would never hurt anyone..."

"I don't know that," said Lilly, "he has a vile temper and he's a strong boy!"

"He's not a boy, he's a young man," said Chaim, "and however bad his temper is, he would never in a million years hurt anyone, let alone do something as horrible as this. Don't fret about Sam, Lilly, he'll be fine. Think about what has happened to that poor nurse!"

"I am thinking, I am thinking, Chaim, but I don't know what to think! It's all too horrible! Oh, the lovely lady! And to think they suspect our boy of doing such a thing! How could they, Chaim, how could they?"

Lilly was in a terrible state. Their religion organised their lives completely. It told them how to live, how to pray, how to eat, how to act according to hundreds of rules. There was no deviation from routine; routine was the bedrock of the religion, as it was for many religions. Routine, ritual and traditions were the time fillers that allowed people not to think too much about the human condition. They were often beautiful and wonderful and full of historic implication, but they could also be a kind of opium which held more adventurous speculation at bay. This news threatened the routine; it threatened them as Jews, as citizens, as people. If − no, when - others got to hear about this, they would turn smoke into flame. There would be such a fire in the community that would scar them forever. It was horrible, beyond consideration.

"Lilly?"

"Yes, yes, I'm all right! Where is the boy now?"

"He's at college. Shall we call him?"

"Of course call him! Here, I'll do it."

Lilly fumbled with the phone and their address book, trying to find Sam's number with shaking hands, whispering as she did so, "We'll be different from now on, Chaim, no letting him off the leash! He's got to settle down. We'll find him a nice girl. Oh, that poor nurse!" She stopped dialling and wiped her eyes. "Who would do such a thing, Chaim, who?"

Chaim shook his head, sickeningly afraid in the depths of his soul, that Sam was involved. Chaim had always known that Samuel was not quite the good Jewish boy they'd hoped for, but he was still good, Chaim was desperate to believe that. The tiniest suspicion that he could have done something as terrible as this was monstrous, but Chaim owned up, in his most secret heart, to the equally monstrous doubt. He had never been able to relate to his son, nor to get inside his head. Sam was a mystery. He hid so much from his parents and the world. He mixed with heathen friends, played violent computer games, went out late at night, and sometimes - yes sometimes - even broke the laws of the Sabbath! Chaim had seen him turn lights on, seen him sneak off to some illicit liaison and knew, even when he hadn't seen him, that he'd been breaking the Jewish laws. All this was, in Chaim's view, totally demoralising, but not the end of the world. Sam was his son, he loved the boy, had faith in him and believed he would come good in the end, even if that good wasn't exactly what he and Lilly had in mind. But could Sam be bad at heart? Could he be a taker of life? That was beyond consideration and Chaim had words with himself, annoyed that the thought had dared raise its ugly head.

"Chaim?"

"Yes Lilly, sorry, I was dreaming."

"Dreaming, at a moment like this!"

"Thinking Lilly, I was thinking ... about Sam."

"Thinking won't help us, Chaim. We have to do something. Here, you talk to him. I'm too distraught.

She handed him the phone when it started ringing.

"Sam?"

"Hello dad."

"Where are you, Sam?"

"I'm at college, you know that."

"Have you heard the bad news son?"

"About Jonathan's nurse? Yes, I have."

For a moment Chaim wondered how Sam had heard and his heart skipped a beat or two.

"How did you hear, Sam? Who told you?"

"My friends told me, dad. Their aunt works at the hospital."

"Oh, good, I mean, well, it's terrible news. Are you alright Sam?"

"Course I'm alright. Why shouldn't I be?"

Lilly was listening intently and began whispering in her husband's ear, 'tell him, tell him!'

"No reason Sam, but listen..."

"I'm listening dad."

"We want you to come home please Sam, right away."

"What for dad? I've got classes. Is it because it's Shabbos tonight? I won't be late, you know that. I finish at three, I'll come home straight away."

"No Sam, we need you to come home now."

"Why, is something wrong? Is mum alright?" Lilly nearly broke into hysterical tears when she heard her beloved Sam worry about her. Sam heard her cry and said, "Is it Jonathan? Nothing's happened to Jonathan, has it?"

They both heard the concern in his voice. One thing Chaim never doubted was that Sam loved his little brother. Elder brothers didn't always love their younger ones – take Joseph for a perfect example – but Sam, Chaim believed, would have given his life for his little brother.

"No, it isn't Jonathan. I'd rather not tell you on the phone, Sam. Can't you just trust me and come home now?"

"Dad," pleaded Sam, " just spit it out, tell me what's up."

Really, Chaim thought, Sam didn't speak like a Jewish boy ought to speak. Chaim decided that firmness was needed, not pleading.

"Samuel, I'm not asking, I'm telling you, come home now."

"Dad, I'm not a little boy any more, I'm a man."

"I know that, but I'm still your father. Listen to me, Sam, I want you here right away, then we'll tell you everything. Yes?"

Sam grunted something at the other end of the phone and hung up.

"Well," said Lilly, "is he coming?"

"I hope so," said Chaim. "You know Samuel, stubborn as a mule."

"Oh," said Lilly, "this is too awful, too terrible. My son! The police! What have we done to deserve this, Chaim? Haven't we been good parents?"

Chaim wondered if they had indeed been good parents. Well yes, they had, they'd done all they could for their children, but some things were God's Will and you had to accept it. Judaism was nothing if not acceptance of God's Will, and this was a testing moment for all of them.

Lilly tried to calm down, but failed miserably. Friday was the busiest of days. She had to prepare the Friday night Shabbos meal and get the home in order for the holy day itself. Even when things were running smoothly, this kept her busy, but Jonathan was in hospital and now...now Samuel had to be interrogated by the police! The thought appalled her! She could barely accept the fact that the police were coming into *her* house, to talk about murder and to ask whether her darling son was guilty! It was enough to make her weep with shame.

## 10

Nurcan left Nilgun early in the morning, supposedly for home, even though Nilgun told her to stay, that she was too tired to drive. She had the reputation of being fierce in her independence, but reputations are often mistaken. Such fierceness as there was came from a deep-seated insecurity, the cause of which she'd told no one, until now. She was devoted to her work, and if anything was fierce inside her, it was the determination to do her difficult job as best she could.

As she drove, she realised that she wasn't heading home, that she didn't want to go home, wasn't strong enough to do so, and that if she didn't, then it might be time to face up to certain issues. She had never felt particularly Turkish or particularly English. She had her own solitary way of doing things and held on to those ways with a grip of iron. This life choice had made her strong, when it was working smoothly, but at this critical moment it felt like nothing at all, a choice that wasn't a choice, a dizzying void. She'd seen death before of course, that was unavoidable in the Accident and Emergency department of a hospital, but Kathryn's murder was more than just another loss of life.

She drove to Stamford Hill, then turned towards Tottenham. She wanted to keep driving forever, never have to leave the car and face the madness of this murderous world. Outside, people were going about their business, rushing across roads, darting into and out of shops as if there were no tomorrow, and for Kathryn there would be no tomorrow. The scene through the car windows felt unreal, as if she were watching a play with neither plot nor meaning, but there was meaning, only it was deeply personal and deeply hidden.

What Nurcan Celik had hid from herself as much as from her family, friends and colleagues was that she had never been attracted to men, that she had always been attracted to women and that for the past two years she had been in love with Kathryn Hudson.

Even in a liberal society there are countless souls ill at ease with themselves. Passionate and intense, Nurcan had kept her desires in check, but doing so had cost her dearly in energy and anxiety. She sublimated these desires through work, focusing all her energy into her profession. When, just a few hours earlier, she had seen Kathryn's dead body, something inside her began to collapse, and it had been continuing to fall away each moment since.

She'd first met Kathryn through Melissa, two years ago. They were introduced in the hospital cafeteria. Nurcan was transfixed by the girl's eyes, so blue, so clear and full of joy, and by her voice, resonant with harmonies that span a web around Nurcan's heart. It was all she could do not to stare or make a fool of herself. She was probably more than ten years older than Kathryn and she was locked in a closet of adoration with triple padlocks.

For weeks after their first meeting, all Nurcan could think about was Kathryn. The high point of most days was driving her and Melissa to work, or seeing her in the cafeteria, but at the same time this delight was cloaked in exhausting secrecy. She dreaded these feelings somehow leaking out, terrified that Kathryn might realise how she felt and hate her.

It wasn't as if there were other women and ways to release the insupportable tension inside her; she simply couldn't bear the idea of anyone knowing her inclinations, despite the ease with which London appeared, at least on the surface, to deal with sexuality. She couldn't explain it; it was just the way she was, brought up with certain cultural mores that she didn't know how to leave behind. She thought she'd done it, until Kathryn turned up.

Those two years of seeing her were both the happiest and the hardest of her life. Her soul seemed to soar when she was near the girl, but at the same time tore her apart. She was always on guard and it never became easier. She couldn't understand why she felt this way or why she didn't know, at her age, how to deal with such feelings. It was a vicious circle in the true sense of the word - she couldn't bear to see Kathryn, but not seeing her was worse.

The situation might have been eased if she'd had a friend to confide in, but she'd kept it under wraps from everyone, even her sister, fearing they might condemn her true nature. There were moments when she feared a look or a word or a gesture had escaped, but no one ever mentioned it. Nurcan knew this obsession wasn't healthy, but she simply didn't know how to tackle it. Love wasn't a one-way process, a selfish 'must-have' thing that you could take because you wanted it. She saw that in others, an egotistic demand which had no regard for the mutuality of feelings, as if a one way passion were sufficient for love. Nurcan had disturbing visions of pouring her heart out to Kathryn, telling her how she felt, and that the strength of her desire would transform the girl, but her reason told her otherwise, and after a few weeks this reasoning was justified when she found out about Daniel.

Until that moment, a routine night-shift tea break, Nurcan had wondered whether there was anyone special in Kathryn's life, hoping beyond hope that she could be The One. When Daniel's name was mentioned, Nurcan felt a sudden dizziness. She raged inside, torn apart by fantasy and reality tormenting her so cruelly. She tried with all her heart to accept the truth and to think good thoughts of this Daniel who had everything in life that she wanted, everything that could make her complete. She obsessed about him and doubted she could ever face him, but was totally disarmed when she'd met him a few weeks later. He'd come to the hospital to see Kathryn and he was everything Nurcan feared he would be, gentle, kind, handsome and clever. He and Kathryn made a beautiful couple.

When she got home after that first brief encounter, Nurcan didn't sleep. She sat by her living room window drinking coffee and watching the world, figuring out a way to put Kathryn out of her heart, but knowing that this was impossible. She cried such lonely tears and was as close as she'd ever been to confessing, but she was in too much of a state. She preferred to let her family and friends think that she was the strong, silent, independent woman which she so clearly was not.

It would have been easy for her love to turn to hate, but Nurcan had a good heart and didn't want it to become unfeeling. The desire remained. Worse, the more she saw Kathryn the more she loved her, the way she moved, the things she said, every nuance of the girl. It wouldn't let her rest, ever.

When she'd seen Kathryn's body that night, she thought the gods were taunting her, making her world the most miserable of all worlds. During the whole sequence of realisation, contact with her friends and family and sharing the grief, she feared her heart might explode. As much as Daniel loved Kathryn and as much as Michael loved her, Nurcan couldn't believe they felt more for the dead girl than she did. An intense anger filled her, to endure such powerful, useless emotions and to suffer them all alone!

And then she'd told Nilgun. It was a collision of worlds, the real and the imagined, the feared and the desired, but there was no violence, only affection.

She parked the car, unable to concentrate. Across the road was a homely little cafe. She headed for it and sat down, blanking out the sights and sounds of north London. There were half a dozen tables, but only one was being used, a woman with a mug of something hot, engrossed in a book. Nurcan sat at the opposite side of the cafe and ordered a strong coffee, her mind and heart ablaze, even in such banal surroundings. When it arrived, she cradled it in the palm of her hands as if it offered the only source of comfort.

What was worse, she asked herself, not to see Kathryn again or to know that Kathryn herself would never see anything ever again?

Ever!

The word frightened her. How was it possible that someone so full of life could be taken from it without warning, so cruelly? What craziness underpinned the world to let such things happen? And what malicious spirit had allowed Nurcan to feel the way she did, and now to have those feelings exacerbated and amplified to breaking point?

Her thoughts were locked in this despairing mode when her mobile rang; it was Nilgun's number. She answered the call, her voice cracking.

"Nurcan, are you okay?"

"Fine; what's happening?" and Nilgun told her about Michael.

She listened impassively, ever more sure that the world lacked meaning. When she hung up she sat as if nothing important had happened, yet her eyes were full of tears. That night had been the first time she'd met Michael, even though Kathryn had spoken about him in such affectionate ways. Nurcan found him unusually quiet, more like a flower than the kind of man she was used to in her family and at work. She'd seen his pain, but she'd also seen the way Naila Shahidi had tended to him and felt sure that that comfort would be enough to see him through, but apparently it wasn't. Michael was gone, taken his own life Nilgun had said – 'taken his own life'. Nurcan said the words over and over in her mind, but couldn't make the image real. Nothing seemed real, or else too cruel to be understood.

"Are you okay?" The words came from nowhere, drifting into her consciousness and hanging there, unanswered. "Are you?"

She felt a light touch on her shoulder and looked up. The woman opposite had come over and was looking at her in a concerned way.

"Sorry?"

"Are you okay? You ... well, you look ... unwell."

Nurcan felt her head – it was hot, and her eyes were watery.

"Just tired," she said. "Long night."

The woman smiled hesitantly, unsure what to do, half turned away, then turned back and said, just as hesitantly, "Do you need to talk to someone?"

It was such an odd question from someone she'd never seen before, and the whole situation was materialising out of thin air, intruding on her emotional introspection.

"I don't think I can ... not right now ... not to a stranger."

"My name is Angela," was the answer. "There, I'm not a stranger anymore."

Nurcan wiped her eyes and said, "Even so."

"Can I talk to you, then?" she asked.

Nurcan was puzzled. What did this woman want?

"I suppose so," she said, unsure whether she was glad or not for the unexpected company.

Angela sat down and said, "I won't lay anything heavy on you, promise. I hate to see people in distress, and it's obvious that's where you are. Look, I don't jump in every time I see someone struggling, I'm no do-gooder, and I'm not nosey, I just acted on instinct. Is that okay?"

It seemed to be. Angela took out a notepad and pen from her bag, opened the pad and wrote down her name and telephone number. She tore off the paper and put it on the table.

"Sometimes it's worth taking a chance," she said, "even at the risk of looking foolish ... or desperate. Call me, if you want, any time, night or day. I'm a good listener."

"I don't understand," said Nurcan.

Angela said, "There's nothing to understand. We pass a thousand people a day and never say a word to them, what difference if you break the silence, just once."

"You're not some sort of missionary, are you?" Nurcan asked.

Angela gave a light laugh and answered, "No way."

"Then why?"

"Why not? I saw you and I just had this feeling you were in trouble. I acted on impulse. I'm sorry if it was the wrong thing, really."

Nurcan looked at the slip of paper lying on the table between them, but she didn't touch it.

"You took me by surprise," said Nurcan.

"Life isn't worth much without surprises, is it?"

"Some, not all."

"Okay, good surprises. I meant no harm."

Nurcan looked up. Angela held her eyes with an easy calmness.

"I still can't talk now. It isn't the time."

"That's fine," said Angela, and she meant it. "I didn't think you'd pour your heart out over a cup of coffee, even in a pleasant little cafe like this. I mean you can, if you want, but I didn't expect it."

"What did you expect?"

"No idea. Like I say, spur of the moment. Don't be angry with me." Angela touched Nurcan's arm and Nurcan trembled, pulling away sharply. "Sorry again," said Angela, "that was clumsy of me."

"No, I'm a bit tense right now," said Nurcan, "probably best not to talk."

Angela's eyes seemed to shine for a moment and she said, "I'll leave you then. If you change your mind..." and she gestured towards the paper with her telephone number, then stood up and turned to go.

What made Nurcan do what she did next was a mystery, she didn't think about it, she just reacted. Quite possibly, in the split second it takes for a few thousand learned experiences to prompt a response, her mind decided enough was enough and that in this particular situation she had nothing to lose.

"Don't go," she said, reaching out and touching Angela on the hand. The touch was electric, to Angela as much as to Nurcan. She turned and sat down again. "Sorry," whispered Nurcan, when Angela sat quietly, saying nothing.

"No need to be, really."

"It's just...hard to put into words."

"I'll just sit," said Angela, "if that's alright?"

Nurcan ought to have felt awkward, but it was strangely comforting to have someone there, on the fringes of her world, but there, in her space, but Angela wasn't an intrusive presence.

"Yes," she answered, "please, sit, though I'm not much company right now."

"I understand," Angela replied, "but it isn't company I want."

"What do you want?" Nurcan asked.

Angela thought for a moment and said, "To help, nothing more. That's a promise. I'll vanish the moment you say the magic word." She sat opposite Nurcan who risked a look into the woman's eyes. "I'm no evangelist," Angela said, "but don't you think the Lord works in mysterious ways?"

Nurcan hesitated what seemed like a lifetime before saying, "Yes, I think she does."

## 11

"Paula Taft?"

Paula was half asleep when the doorbell rang. Faraday and Fowler rang twice and were about to leave when they heard sluggish movements inside. The door opened and Paula looked out, clutching her dressing gown around her waist, her eyes bleary.

"Sorry to bother you," said Faraday, showing his identity card to the bemused woman at the door. "We're investigating a crime that took place last night. Do you have a few moments?"

Paula seemed to wake up quite suddenly. What Cassie did for a living wasn't exactly kosher, but it wasn't something the police would go round the neighbourhood investigating, unless they knew about her policeman client.

"Trouble?" she asked.

"I'm afraid there was a murder in the neighbourhood."

Paula became even more alert. Her first thought prompted her first reaction.

"It isn't Cassie?" she asked, alarmed. She had the sudden fear that, after leaving her, something terrible might have happened.

"The victim's name was Kathryn Hudson. She was a nurse at the local hospital."

"Oh," said Paula, relieved. "I don't know her," then realising what she'd said and how it sounded, added, "I mean ... sorry," then she clammed up.

"That's alright," said Faraday, "it would have been coincidence if you had. We're just trying to place people in the area, see if they noticed anything unusual. Can you tell us where you were last night?" he asked.

"Working," said Paula, "then I met Cassie. That's who I thought you ... never mind."

"What time did you arrive home?" Faraday asked.

Paula was nervous, afraid that the police would dig too deep.

"Early hours," she said, "that's why I am as I am now."

"That was straight after work?" Faraday asked.

"No, I told you, I met Cassie, my friend. We went for a bite to eat. We often do."

"Around here?"

"Yes," and Paula told them where she and Cassie had met. She felt like saying 'Don't come over all self-righteous with me, officer, I know you and your type, you're not all squeaky clean,' but she wisely held her tongue.

"Did you see anything or anyone at all unusual?" Faraday asked. Paula didn't answer, remembering the creepy feeling she'd had on the street as she and Cassie were walking home. "Miss Taft?"

"Oh, no, nothing," she said.

"Are you sure?"

"Well, if you can accept being unnerved as evidence," she said, "then yes, something."

This woman was definitely hiding something, Faraday thought, but then he was used to people being secretive; they chattered on about nothing and kept quiet about things that mattered. He asked her to explain.

"I can't," said Paula, "not without coming across as weird."

"Try," said Faraday, "if you don't mind."

Paula wasn't sure how much she could explain. She was into the unknowable, a creature of the New Age but not without some substance. She truly believed she had a gift.

"I get vibes from people," she said, "always have done, especially the deeper sides of the spectrum." Fowler held back a sigh and tried hard not to look up to heaven. "Look officers," said Paula, "you'll only think I'm crazy , so why bother? It's getting cold here and, as you can see, I'm only half dressed. Is this really necessary?"

Faraday had to make a quick decision. There were crackpots galore in Hackney as there were in the rest of the world, but he felt inclined to follow this up, so he said, "May we come in, Miss Taft, just for a few moments?"

This wasn't what Paula had intended. She'd thought they'd thank her and go on their merry way. A little anxiously, she let them in.

Her home was a treasure trove of trinkets, countless figurines and mystical objects in a purple haze of New Age shopping. You didn't have to be on the ball to see inside Paula Taft's mind. Fowler almost smiled but managed to retain her professional poise. They sat and sank in crimson armchairs.

"We passed some guy on the street," said Paula. "He gave me bad vibes, but that's hardly useful to you is it?

"Can you describe this man," Faraday said.

"You know, inspector, this is really nothing at all. I'm sorry I mentioned it."

"You never know, Miss Taft, it might be a useful lead, and if it isn't, there's nothing lost, just a little time. Can you describe him?"

"It was dark," said Paula, thinking that a blindingly obvious thing to say, "and we passed him quickly. I just felt the way he walked, the way he moved, was odd."

"In what way?"

"It's hard to put into words, he just unnerved me."

"How?"

"Like I say, inspector, it's really hard to put into words. He carried an aura with him."

"An aura?"

"You can scoff, but it's true. I see them, sometimes. It's like a manifestation of the inner self, and his was disturbed."

Faraday feared that he'd might well be wasting precious time here, but Paula Taft didn't seem to be a chatterbox or completely doolally, just a little eccentric.

"You felt this?" Faraday asked.

"I did, yes, briefly. And I saw his eyes." Fowler looked up, from writing notes, expecting some details, but Paula was sitting still and thinking. "He wasn't a good man," she said.

"It would be useful if you could give us a physical description," said Faraday, "height, weight, what he was wearing..."

Paula surprised them by answering immediately and factually, "About five ten, quite slim. He wore a green anorak..."

"You could tell it was green, even in the dark?"

"I could tell, yes."

"Colours can be deceptive, Miss Taft."

"I'm good at colours, inspector. It was green."

Fowler wrote this down and waited for more, but Taft said nothing.

"You mentioned his eyes," Faraday said.

"I did," said Paula. "They upset me."

"Can you explain?"

"No, I can't."

"Anything else?"

"You mean like did he walk with a limp, carry a walking stick or wear a top hat?"

The woman had a sense of humour, so Faraday said, "That would be grand."

"I'm afraid not," said Paula. "I don't normally react to men wearing green anoraks but ..."

"...his aura?"

Paula smiled patiently and said, "I'm sure you have hunches, inspector. That's all this was, an intuitive reaction."

Faraday waited a few seconds and checked Fowler's notes before saying, "Your friend Cassie..."

Paula tensed up. She was unafraid of giving evidence that might help catch a killer, but she'd say nothing against Cassie.

"How do you know about Cassie?" she asked.

"You mentioned her. She was the friend you were with last night."

"Right, yes, she's my best and only friend, inspector."

"Do you think she'd be able to give us any more details?"

"I doubt it. It was me that got the heebie-jeebies."

"Does she live near here?"

Paula really didn't want to head in this direction. Cassie was already in deep water with her policeman client, and if this inspector got any whiff of trouble, he seemed the type to latch on like a limpet and never let go, but she had no choice. It wasn't as if she could pretend that Cassie lived miles away, so she told them Cassie's address, emphasizing that she saw and felt nothing amiss last night.

"Perhaps after she left you," suggested Faraday. "We'll speak to everyone we can, Miss Taft, you never know what will turn up."

Paula thought how right that was.

Outside, Fowler asked Faraday, "Auras? Vibes?"

"She had a point," said Faraday, "we work on hunches and intuition."

"Yes, but based on experience and knowledge, not passing someone in the street in the middle of the night, sir."

"I know that," said Faraday, "but she seemed eminently sensible."

"She seemed, if I might say so sir, a little nuts."

The morning was wearing on. They'd already spoken to a good number of people, others in the team were covering the area and forensics were still as busy as ever. This was the critical time. If they could make a breakthrough now, they might be able to close in and bring the case to an end quickly, if not, then it might drag on and the killer would remain on the streets. Faraday couldn't take the chance that whoever had done this would not kill again; it was his responsibility to close this case as soon as possible and he needed to follow every lead, no matter how bizarre. He wasn't a religious man, but he believed in order, and unpunished crimes broke that order. Even the smallest injustices bothered him, an obsession traceable to the endless bullying he'd witnessed at school. Now, it was who he was. He needed to repair the fabric of moral order when it was torn apart by greed, anger and hatred. There was little point in the human race being around if they didn't live in a lawful universe. The best human laws reflected something noble, kind and generous, pretty much summed up by The Ten Commandments. At a time when tribes had few laws and when there was nothing in place to enforce them, it wasn't really surprising that they needed some basic instructions on what to do and what not to do. Faraday was a well-read man and had taken a keen interest in how laws had developed over the centuries, particularly working, as he did, amidst the Jewish communities of Stamford Hill, so close, ironically, to Murder Mile. He wanted to feel part of something useful and civilised, upholding the law, but there were moments when he felt he upheld nothing at all, that wickedness was winning and that evil was mocking his puny attempts to keep it at bay.

"Sir," Fowler was holding his arm, "are you alright?"

He snapped out of his reverie and said, "How many more visits on our list, Viv?"

She checked the addresses their team were calling at; there seemed to be an endless number left, even though they'd already made a decent start. Other officers weren't far away, doing the business, as it were, asking the questions that just might give them the key to the case.

"Quite a lot, sir," she said.

Faraday looked at the notes and said, "I think we ought to check out the Levinson family. Don't want some rookie putting his foot in it with the Jewish community, and I know Chaim, he's a freelance reporter, a friend of Patrick Connelly, Melissa's partner."

"Bit of a network, sir," said Fowler.

"People knowing people knowing people, Viv, that's the way it works."

"Glad you can get your head around it, sir."

He smiled and said, "Ask Matt and Charlene to do the rest of our calls," he said. "Tell them to visit this Cassie Logan first, check on Taft's story. We'll go see Chaim and his family."

Faraday was aware of much more than most officers in his unit, and in any unit for that matter. He was clever, determined, analytical and logical, but he was also a victim of the fates as much as anyone, and had inadvertently sent Matt Davis on the mission to hell.

## 12

Despite its reputation as a poor borough overwhelmed by urban blight, Hackney had some of the greenest, most pleasant spots in the city, possibly in any city. Springfield Park and Victoria Park were amongst its gems, then there were the marshes, part of the Lea Valley, Millfields, the Lea Navigation, London Fields and many other gems that belied the borough's lowly status. It was in Springfield Park that Daniel, Ursula and Jasmine were walking, he in the middle, Ursula holding his right arm, Jasmine his left.

Though not the largest, Springfield Park had a variety of contours, all overlooking the impressive Lea Valley and Walthamstow Marshes. It was on the higher level, close by the Upper Clapton Road, that the three of them were walking. To an outsider, Daniel might have appeared as some kind of gigolo, but he was anything but that. He had a relaxed air about him that didn't reflect the turmoil inside him, and despite the madness of the night, he still looked handsome and dignified.

"Michael, Michael, Michael!" whispered Jasmine. "Why did he do it?"

"We know why," said Ursula, "but he was wrong. He shouldn't have. Dan's still here, aren't you?"

"Just about," said Daniel.

"You won't do anything, will you?" Jasmine asked.

"Don't ask him that, Jas," said Ursula. "What can he say?"

In truth, the girls were afraid of letting Daniel go off by himself. When Melissa had arrived to keep vigil, Elena, being Elena the Teacher, had gone off to work, but the other two stayed with Daniel. They dreaded anything happening to him and decided to keep him company, whether he wanted it or not.

"You shouldn't worry about me," he said. "You've got to get your lives into order. What about work?"

"Screw work," said Ursula. "They can do without my unique skills for the day. I'll make it up to them."

"And me," said Jasmine. "We just want to be with you Dan. You don't mind, do you?"

"I don't mind," he said, "it's nice of you."

It was partly selfish too. Neither of them wanted to go back to their flat and see Kathryn's empty room. Despite all that had happened, it was less than twelve hours ago that she'd been alive and well. Every degree of turn, the world changed; it was an alarming, humbling thought. They were also afraid. It was irrational, but they thought that whoever had killed Kathryn might be after them, too, and that keeping together, or with Daniel, would offer them some level of protection.

"No probs, Dan," said Ursula, squeezing his arm.

"We used to walk here a lot," said Daniel. "She would talk about you all, say what you were doing, what was happening in the house, all the rowing gossip, stuff like that."

"And she'd talk about you to us," said Ursula.

"Good things?" Daniel asked.

"Only the best," said Ursula. She suddenly stopped and held him back, saying, "This is all insane, you know. I don't think in a sane world the three of us would be walking in Springfield Park on a Friday when we should be working and ... and that..." She couldn't say that both Kathryn had been murdered and Michael had taken his life and everything was in ruins around them. "What are you going to do Daniel?" she asked, trying to regain her composure.

"You mean today or for the rest of my life?"

"Both," said Ursula. "Just tell us you'll keep in touch and that you won't do anything silly."

Daniel didn't know if he was going to do anything 'silly' but he didn't think he would. He owed it to Kathryn to get his life back on track, but he wasn't sure how he was going to do this. The key for the time being was to get through the day. Every moment weighed on him, and as they walked he kept expecting to see Kathryn come round a corner and greet them. She was strong in his mind, and he would keep her that way, never let her truly die, whatever he did in the future. He wasn't sure how to do this, but if he kept her face, her voice, her touch, her mind and her presence strong, then she would stay strong and still be with him, despite the noise and distractions all around.

"I'll keep in touch and I won't do anything silly," said Daniel, "scout's honour."

Ursula rested her head on his shoulder as they walked. "We should all make the same promise," she said. "Jas?"

"No, not me; if things get tough, I'm off. I'll promise for El, though, she won't do anything stupid, she never does. She's a teacher, for God's sake."

Trying to be light didn't work. The pall of loss and shock gripped them and they struggled to find a way out of the depression which threatened to overwhelm them, each in their own private and unbearably lonely ways. For the moment, Ursula and Jasmine found comfort in comforting Daniel, and they did as good a job as was possible in the impossible circumstances and in spite of his natural reserve. How were they supposed to be hopeful and to offer hope to each other? Anything they did felt like papering over cracks – more than cracks, great gaping crevasses.

They walked down the Eastern side of the park towards the river, then along the paths in between dense clumps of trees. There was a bench and they sat for a while, Ursula putting her feet up on Daniel's knees and Jasmine resting her head on Ursula's shoulder. In the shadows of the foliage they looked like a mythical creature with three heads and sprawling limbs.

"Maybe we should all get a house together. How about that, Daniel, you come and live with us?"

"Maybe," he answered, but he couldn't see it happening. Possibilities of what he might do beat about his brain, uncontrolled, and following Kathryn had been one of them, but now that Michael had pre-empted him, it didn't seem right any longer. How close Michael and Kathryn must have been for him to do that! Daniel felt an undignified pang of jealousy, not so much because brother and sister had been so close, but that Michael had somehow undermined his own love. This was all cock-eyed and selfish, he knew that, but it was what he felt.

"We'll look after you," said Ursula.

"I know you would," said Daniel. "I'll give it some thought, promise."

"It will keep her alive," Ursula went on, "in a way. I mean, if you bugger off somewhere, Daniel, there'll be nothing left."

"I'm not planning to bugger off anywhere," said Daniel, though in truth the idea had occurred to him and he hadn't put it to bed yet. All three of them were struggling to understand the events of the night and each moment was an effort of will to alter their take on this new reality and shape their particular futures.

The reality of the moment was surprisingly peaceful. They sat beneath an arch of leaves, not yet fully formed but still bathed in shadow. A variety of trees grew in the park, oak, plane, sycamore, beech and many others, often growing in clumps which created tranquil pockets, well away from the workaday world, almost like fairy dells if they hadn't been frequented by an equal variety of undesirables, none of whom, thankfully, were there now.

Daniel still hadn't cried. Tears wouldn't come, though his heart was heavier than he thought possible and his thoughts desolate. Jasmine and Ursula let their tears flow freely and the more one cried, the more it set the other off, though they also laughed softly at each other's tears, uncertain what to do with these precious moments of being alive.

"It isn't like this when you hear stuff on the news, is it?" Jasmine said. "I mean, there are murders and killings every day, but you don't think, do you, what it means?"

"You can't," said Ursula, "we're not built that way, are we Daniel?"

They seemed to want to involve him and turn to him, as if to make sure he was still with them in mind and spirit. He said no, they weren't built that way. People let so much slip by them, unfeeling, unknowing and unaware. That was one of Kathryn's strengths, to empathize in ways that others couldn't see. Daniel feared that his own life might revert to what it had been before he'd met Kathryn, killing time in any which way because that was how you dealt with time. She'd showed him something else, but he wasn't sure if he could hold on to her passion and commitment; all ways appeared equally meaningless in the choices before him.

"Tell you what," said Jasmine, "we should go off somewhere together, leave the rat race, find somewhere like this," she said, gesturing at the trees and shrubs around them, "somewhere peaceful, start our own commune, in memory of Kathryn."

"That's such a silly idea, Jas," said Ursula, "but I like it! What about you, Daniel?"

"Maybe," he said.

"Daniel's saying 'maybe' to everything," said Jasmine.

"That's because he doesn't know what he's going to do, does he, Dan?"

"No, he doesn't," said Daniel.

"This is impossible, guys!" said Jasmine, sitting up and wiping her eyes, "it really is!"

They talked for a long while, going over memories of Kathryn, making each other laugh and cry, trying to fix these images in their minds so they would never be forgotten. They would have gone on for longer but Daniel's mobile rang. He only spoke a few words but they could tell it was partly to do with work. When he hung up, Daniel said, "Agency guy, just to say he was sorry."

"We're all sorry, Daniel," said Ursula. "No one knows what to say to you."

"That's alright, I wouldn't know what to say to me either. Listen, it's lovely here, and you've been great, but I have to go."

"Go where, Dan?" asked Ursula, then added, "I mean, you don't have to tell us, I was just...erm..."

"Worried?" Daniel said. "I know you are, but I won't do anything stupid. It would be a bit much if three of us kicked the bucket in twenty-four hours." The two women stared, unable to fathom his humour or state of mind. He smiled dolefully and said, "You'll have to forgive me. It's the way I cope."

"Is it the Jewish way, Dan?" said Jasmine. "I mean all that suffering and stuff, do you just make jokes about it to fend off the devil?"

"Yes," said Daniel, "I think we do – they do – I do – whatever. Did it sound cruel?"

"You couldn't sound cruel if you tried, Dan," said Ursula. "Do you want any help doing whatever you're going to do?"

He didn't. They walked together to the park exit. Ursula and Jasmine were heading back to the hospital to see Naila. Daniel had his own secret assignation.

"You will be alright, won't you?" Ursula asked.

"Do my best, scout's honour," said Daniel. "Don't worry about me, you look after yourselves."

They watched him go, as unsure as ever what to make of Daniel Hart.

## 13

Daniel headed back to his office, thinking the call had come from there, but when he arrived it was empty, so he guessed it was either from the Wick workroom or a job. It didn't matter. Nothing much mattered to him at that moment. A few hours ago he didn't think he'd be back at all, but here he was, duty calling whilst life unravelled around him.

He jotted down some notes and put them next to the unopened envelope for the temp. He glanced at his computer, saw about twenty emails, all work, and was about to leave them when he noticed one from little Frankie Davis. He decided to answer just that one and sent the boy a funny message, telling him to make sure he didn't crash the computer again, but that if he did, then he should use a different email address for a while. Just as he'd done earlier, he looked around before leaving, only this time he felt uneasy about something, but assumed it was anxiety about nothing and left.

He made his way to a synagogue in Clapton, an old one that barely had a congregation, just a handful of die-hards. He'd been in two minds whether to go, but he needed some space and time to himself, and although he hated to admit it, he also needed some contact with his roots. The synagogue door was firmly shut, as expected - few places of worship were left unattended these days, but being a Friday the warden was around, getting things ready for the Sabbath service. Daniel knocked on the door and the warden opened a shutter and looked out.

"Daniel! Welcome, my boy!"

He'd been there a couple of times before and the warden had never forgotten him. Daniel was looking a little rough, unshaven and a touch dishevelled, but he spoke gently, telling him something of what had happened. The warden, a man in his seventies, listened attentively and then allowed Daniel some time alone, inside. The synagogue itself needed attention but there was no money or interest to put things right. It didn't bother Daniel who wanted only to sit, think and question the God who had so carelessly allowed yet another brutal wickedness to stain the beauty of the world.

Most synagogues have a formulaic design much like any place of worship or, for that matter, any high street store. This gives a sense of familiarity and security; it wouldn't do to be hit by revolutionary new designs too often. The bible gives clear architectural measurements for a temple, and although builders no longer work in hands, the general structure is much the same as it was a couple of thousand years ago. They are found in most cities of the world and vary from the simple to the ornate but still keeping to the basic design, capturing the essence of the religion, no matter how much they differ in detail, with a representation of the Ark of the Covenant at the front, the Ten Commandments displayed above and hand written scrolls of the Old Testament inside. Some synagogues, and this was no exception, also have archives, either in a separate building or basement, where documents, scrolls and various artefacts are stored. Daniel had been there a couple of years before, interested, despite his determination not to be, by the history. This particular one was in the basement. It was infrequently used now but a few interesting relics were stored there and it was still a place that had registered with him because it was so forlorn and forgotten.

Ancient and modern laws are not dissimilar - no killing, no stealing, no sleeping with the neighbour's wife and so on, although the neighbour's wife rule was for some reason always under greater pressure. Despite the passing of millennia, these laws haven't lost their edge. The connection with God might have become more tenuous, but there is still a formidable sense of authority when facing the Ten

Commandments - they are, after all, still the bedrock of most societies.

Despite trying to separate himself from his roots, at a couple of crucial moments Daniel had visited the synagogue, driven by a need to re-connect. He wasn't sure whether it was right or wrong, a sign of strength or weakness, but it was a chance to think. Over the past twelve hours he hadn't had much of a chance to gather his thoughts, though he feared there was no longer anything of meaning to gather; Kathryn was gone, a brutal reality that mocked all else.

He sat on a cold wooden seat thinking of his history, his duty, his obligations and wondering whether what had happened was all due to his negligence. This was guilt, pure and simple, but it was still real, and probably not understood by anyone who hasn't had guilt hardwired into them since birth. He tried to make sense of his past, his present and his future, but his thoughts spiralled into a depressing cycle of recrimination and sadness. He was quite relieved when he felt a tap on his shoulder and looked up to see the warden's wife standing over him with a concerned expression.

"Come to our house, Daniel," she said. "I'll feed you."

He tried to say that he was fine, but she was insistent. The warden locked the synagogue doors and they took Daniel to their home a block away. Both were very concerned about him, although they would have been more concerned if he'd told them everything that had happened during the night, but he didn't want to go into detail. He didn't think he could, or wanted, to explain Kathryn, Michael and the collapse of the little universe he had been building for the past few years; he didn't think he could talk about love, feelings and the emotions that were tearing him apart; he definitely couldn't talk to them about Ursula, Jasmine and Elena, or about Naila lying heartbroken and sick so close by. There was nothing he could talk to them about because if he tried to put anything into words it would sound less than it demanded. Besides, he knew how they would approach it, in the time honoured tradition of any religion, offering the comfort of ritual, prayer and acceptance. And they would be right. What was this loss in the grand scheme of things? However horrible it was, it was nothing that couldn't be overcome. This is what gave him the strength to endure, something that Michael, for all his sensibilities never had. He disliked the thought, and the idea of using religion as a crutch for tackling truth, but that was what this horror was all about, seeing how the world worked and finding an emotional consistency to face the huge fluctuations of fortune. Nevertheless, he was glad of the time they gave him. He listened to them with affection because they were good people who wanted to help, but they wouldn't pry, and he appreciated that. He thought of Kathryn's friends, wondering how they would get by, lacking this ancient psychological support structure. He admired them, worried about them, but felt apart from them, as if Kathryn's death separated him from all that was hers.

The warden invited him to the service that evening. "We need a minyan," said the warden. "You know what that is, Daniel?"

"I do," he said. "Ten men."

He felt again the power of this religion, the huge gravity that was Jewish faith, pulling him into its arms, taking some of the suffering away through companionship, security and the sheer weight of tradition. He said he would think about it, but at the same time he didn't want to suffocate in the tidal wave of ritual. Would everything that Kathryn tried to be, and everything he'd learned from her vanish with her passing? This saddened him, as if he weren't strong enough to carry her memory forward in the way she would have wanted.

He was extraordinarily tired, but he still had things to do, despite wanting to hide away and regain some balance, but he feared he would never be truly balanced again, that something precious and vital had been lost which could never be replaced. He had to try to keep a clear head. He felt that in his tiredness he'd already missed something important but hoped it would either come back to him later or be nothing at all. For the time being, he thanked the warden and his wife, told them he would consider coming back to the service if he could and left them, heading back to the hospital to see Naila.

## 14

Melissa had been sitting with Naila for about half an hour. Coming back to the hospital had been hard enough, but seeing Naila drugged, pale and out-of-it was even harder. Naila was about as full of life, ideas and imagination as it is possible to be, and to see her so still and broken was a shock.

First, though, she'd gone to Alexandra Ward where the gloom was almost tangible. No one was unaffected but they were all trying not to let it affect the children, some of whom had asked where Nurse Kathryn was; none had been told the truth. The ward sister and hospital administrators were discussing how best to do this, but the last thing they wanted was the children upset. Melissa went to see some of them, including Milly Orlich and Jonathan Levinson. Milly's mother was there, but Jonathan only had an aunt by his side, which was unusual – either mum or dad were generally visiting, and their oddball son Sam was often around too, but he also was missing. It was a tough but necessary visit.

Afterwards, she sat with Naila, holding her hand - there was no reaction, nothing at all. Naila was in a world of her own.

Melissa took out her mobile and called Pat who'd gone into work a couple of hours earlier. The story had already broken, but Patrick wanted a handle on it as quickly as possible, insisting that Kathryn's name not be released yet. Apart from anything else, Faraday had asked him to do this, just for a few hours, so they could keep close tabs on the investigation. The news report said that a nurse had been killed but that her name wouldn't be released until the family had been informed; it was standard procedure. However, people talked, and there was little chance of Patrick keeping Kathryn's name from being broadcast for long. Faraday realised this too and decided to arrange a press conference for mid-afternoon.

"How's it going, Pat?" Melissa asked.

"Pandemonium," he answered. "We're having a press conference at three o'clock. You don't have to be there, but it would be a good idea if you were," he said, "and the others."

"What will you say?" she asked.

"The truth, ask for witnesses, leads. Faraday's out talking to people now but he'll be there. What do you think, Mel?"

"I'll be there," she said.

"It'll be tough," said Patrick.

Melissa remembered some of the press conferences she'd seen on television. It was an impossible line to tread between over emotional and stoic, between stiff upper lip and mawkishness.

"What about Daniel, will he come?"

"No idea. I spoke to him before, he's even more enigmatic than usual. I wouldn't be surprised if he vanished."

"Where would he go?"

"Anywhere, Mel; he hides it but he's in a terrible state. How's Naila doing?"

Melissa looked down at the sleeping beauty and shook her head, as if Patrick could see her.

"Not great, but then she's fast asleep. God knows what she'll be like when she wakes. Oh Lord!"

"What's up, Mel?"

"Kathryn and Michael's mother is here! Pat, can you come and help me out? I'm not sure I can cope with this."

"I'll be there," he said.

A few hours ago, Michelle and Gordon Hudson had lost their

daughter; now they'd lost their son. They looked bewildered as they came in with the ward sister to join Melissa.

"How is she?" Mrs Hudson asked, her voice stretched.

Melissa felt protective of Naila who had collapsed under the weight of Michael's suicide whilst his parents were there, at her side, asking after her.

"Under sedation. How about you?"

It seemed like such a trite question in the circumstances.

"Not very good," said Michelle Hudson. "We're going to have the funeral for both our children together," she said, "next Wednesday. The police need time for the post mortem, otherwise we'd do it sooner. Will you let her friends know?"

For some reason, the idea of a funeral shocked Melissa. Despite all that had happened, it had been a short time since the death of both brother and sister, and the finality of a funeral disturbed her, unreasonably she thought.

"We can discuss the arrangements with you and their friends later," Mrs Hudson said, then added, "They were very close."

"Yes," said Melissa. "I know."

"We probably weren't the best parents," Mrs Hudson said. "We know it, but we can't change it."

Melissa wasn't sure whether to sympathise or blame them.

"It brought them together. Michael worshipped his sister. We should have guessed last night what he might do."

"Don't blame yourselves," said Melissa, and instantly regretted saying it. They obviously did blame themselves, and what was worse, they were probably right.

"We'll stay in town for a while," said Mrs Hudson. "There's a lot to sort out. We'll need your help, and the girls in the flat. The police don't want us to touch anything yet, just in case there's some evidence ... you know."

She sounded hesitant but Melissa understood. No one was holier than thou in these situations. The police believed that Kathryn knew her attacker and there might be some evidence in her room. The idea was disturbing. If Kathryn knew her attacker, then Melissa probably did too, but the thought of it being someone she'd seen, spoken to and maybe even laughed with was appalling. Yet what other alternative was there? Kathryn had been pregnant, and it wasn't by Daniel, and unless the attack and the rape – assuming it was rape – were unconnected, then this was the only alternative.

"Do you have any idea..." Mr Hudson began, "I mean ... someone ...

that could have done this, Melissa?"

"No, I don't, none at all."

"I hope they rot in hell forever," he said in a whisper that was surprisingly ferocious. Melissa couldn't believe he'd said it. She stared at him and for the first time realised how little she knew people. She might chat and jest with the best of them, but you couldn't tell what was going on, not for sure. Mr Hudson seemed rather unassuming, but these few words hissed out so venomously that she was unnerved.

"The police will find whoever did it," she said.

"You don't think ..." Mrs Hudson said with hesitation, "that ... her boyfriend ... Daniel ... that..."

"Absolutely not!" said Melissa. "Don't think it, really, it's wrong!"

"He's a strange one, though," said Mr Hudson. Melissa felt like saying 'So are you'. She was in danger of losing sympathy.

"Not that strange," she said, "once you get to know him. He's the kindest, loveliest man in the world."

They didn't look convinced. They knew he was Jewish and somehow that associated him with all manner of devilry, but Melissa was his champion.

"We're all fond of him," she said, "and so should you be. It wasn't Daniel."

"But it was someone," said Mr Hudson.

She couldn't argue with that. Yes, it was someone. There was an awkward pause before Mrs Hudson said, "They were good children, both of them. We didn't deserve them and they deserved better than us. They certainly didn't deserve this."

"No," said Melissa. "They didn't."

"We didn't want them to live here," said Mr Hudson, "but they wouldn't listen. They never listened."

Melissa's first impulse was to champion Hackney as well as Daniel, and although she sensed a potential argument, she couldn't seem to stop herself.

"They were independent people," she said, "and Hackney is fine, more than fine, it's a lively and lovely place to live. This could have happened anywhere."

She had no compunction saying this because it was true, she lived and loved this part of London and, argument or not, Kathryn and Michael had not died in gang or drug warfare – theirs was a different story.

She couldn't make out Mr and Mrs Hudson. They were older and supposedly wiser, but there was something 'not quite right' about them, as if they were too self-absorbed and full of unspoken resentments, but at the same time, it was hard to be angry with or critical of people who'd just suffered such a monstrous loss.

Melissa wished they would leave. She couldn't offer them comfort and she was beginning to feel useless. She hoped Naila wouldn't wake up to see Michael's parents; that would be even more uncomfortable, but they didn't seem to want to leave. They looked as if they weren't quite sure what they were supposed to do next.

"Kathryn spoke about you on the telephone," said Mrs Hudson, "told us how close you were, and about all her friends. She was very fond of you all. Michael never spoke so much. He didn't call often and when we called him he said little. We'd only met Naila a couple of times. We didn't realise how serious they were about each other, only... she's ... well..."

"Older than Michael?" said Melissa.

"Yes, but we hoped she'd be able to look after him better. He was a vulnerable boy."

"She loved him as much as it's possible for anyone to love," said Melissa who had the disturbing feeling that they might blame Naila for Michael's suicide. "She couldn't have done more, no one could. This was Michael's choice."

"If he'd come to us," said Mr Hudson, "we could have talked it over."

"Michael knew his own mind," said Melissa, finding herself in the odd position of championing son and daughter against parents, "and he wasn't so vulnerable, at least I don't think so. He was strong in his own way. He was lucky to have met Naila and she was lucky to have met him. I don't know how she's going to survive this."

Mr and Mrs Hudson looked at the sleeping Naila but their expressions mixed pity with recrimination.

"How long are they going to let her sleep," asked Mrs Hudson.

"I don't know, as long as necessary. We want to be here when she wakes up, but ... but..." Melissa hesitated, then told Mr and Mrs Hudson what Patrick had told her, about the press conference.

"Yes, we know," said Mr Hudson. "The police called us a little while ago." Melissa saw how fast the wheels of communication turned. "It will be difficult. You'll be there?"

"If that's okay with you," she said. "We didn't want Naila to wake up alone."

Melissa had the feeling that such a thought wasn't high on the Hudson's priority list.

They talked a little about the press conference, how they should deal with it and what they wanted to ask of the media. They actually looked, thought Melissa, a little self-important, as if the moment would cast them in the spotlight for fifteen minutes of fame, but she banished the thought, sure it was misplaced.

They stayed for about half an hour, and might have stayed longer if Patrick hadn't arrived. Thankfully, Naila had remained insensible to their presence. Melissa couldn't help but feel some negative vibes from them to Naila, as if they might be jealous that, as unwell as she was, she was still alive whereas both their children had gone. Again, she banished the thought, sure she was misreading them.

She was utterly relieved when Pat arrived and the parents left. If they hadn't been in a hospital ward she would have wanted to make love as slowly and as perfectly as could be. Life was a fragile thing at the best of times, but now it seemed more delicate than ever. Melissa was strong, she had to be, but surrounded by this level of uncertainty she felt an overwhelming need to be with her man. Love was even more fragile than life and Melissa had to fight both her desires and the fears all this sadness and confusion had created.

"Tough with the parents, was it?" Patrick asked.

"Mildly," she answered, then added, "very."

"Listen," he said, "I can't stay long. There's such a lot going on, but I wanted to see you." Melissa wondered whether Patrick felt what she felt, whether the need in him was as great as in her, whether he was even aware of how desperate she was. As men went, Patrick was pretty receptive, but even if he was totally in tune with her, there was nothing they could do, not there and then. "Why don't you come with me, back to the office, then we'll head to the police station for the press conference. I don't want to leave you alone here. You look – I don't know – agitated."

"I am," she said, but she didn't say why. If Patrick was in the slightest bit aware, he'd catch on. "It means leaving Naila alone," she said. "We didn't want to do that."

Patrick thought for a moment then said, "Doesn't she have family?"

"No, but I'll call Ursula. Maybe one of them can come back for a while. I really don't want Naila to wake up by herself.."

"Kath and Michael's parents, couldn't they have stayed?"

"Not a good idea," said Melissa. "Look, Pat, I think I'll stay. Do you mind?"

He sensed she was upset and asked her what he could do. What she wanted him to do he couldn't, but it was more the fact that he wasn't even aware of it that upset her.

"Pat, I don't suppose..?"

"What?"

"Oh, nothing," but the light suddenly switched on. Patrick took her hand and said, "Is all this getting to you, love? Look, if you don't mind leaving Naila, we could go back, just for a while, if it would help."

Melissa thought 'just for a while' didn't suggest the slow, everlasting lovemaking she needed, and 'if it would help' ... this wasn't some kind of medication! But Patrick was a good guy, she told herself, one of the best, so what could he say that was word perfect?

"I think it might," she said, trying not to look too desperate. "I just feel," she whispered, looking at Naila, "a little guilty."

"Don't," said Patrick firmly. "You're a rock, Melissa Cochrane. Let's go back and celebrate life for half an hour."

Melissa laughed with tears in her eyes.

"Half an hour," she said, "that much celebration?"

"I know," Patrick answered. "Maybe we can stretch it. Proof of life and all that."

Melissa was exhausted, shocked, in danger of losing it completely, but she had a man, she was still here, for whatever reason, and all she wanted, even for half an hour, was proof of life.

She tidied the sheets on Naila's bed, brushed a coupled of loose dark curls off the sleeping beauty's head and whispered, "We'll be back soon, promise," then left with Patrick to find some comfort and release from the madness which had come into their lives.

## 15

"That is true madness," said Angela, "and if the Lord really works in mysterious ways, these are about as mysterious as they get."

Nurcan had related the night's events but she hadn't told Angela the most important thing of all. She might have told her sister how she felt, but this was different. To everyone else it was absolutely secret, and always would be, so she heard Angela's next words with incredulity.

"And you loved this girl?"

Nurcan was worldly wise, or thought she was. At thirty-nine she'd seen many things and thought she understood most things, but she didn't understand this mind-reading act.

"What? ... I mean ...Why did you say that?"

"Am I right or wrong?" asked Angela.

"Wrong, of course! I ... I worked with her. I liked her. I ..."

Angela stopped her and said, "Methinks the lady doth protest too much. Look, I'm a stranger, telling me the truth is like talking to the wind. Your words will never be heard by anyone else, but it could be important for you, whoever you are, to be truthful, just this once. The soul can't feed off a lie, it really can't."

Nurcan was scared on so many levels that she hadn't even given away her name, but Angela had seen through this deepest of secrets as if it was open to the world to see. She wiped her eyes, not knowing what to do.

"I ought to leave," she said, but made no motion to go.

Angela moved her hand to Nurcan's as if to hold it, then pulled away.

"You'll have to forgive me if I'm a bit brutal," she said. "I can't seem to stop myself sometimes."

Nurcan dared look up at this woman's face and was caught by her eyes.

"No," she whispered, "I did love her. I did," then she looked down again and held her own hands, one on top of the other.

There was silence for a few moments, then Angela said, "You see, the world is still turning. Life goes on. There are no fingers pointing at you. How do you feel?"

Nurcan wasn't sure how she felt. She hated to admit it, but there was a sense of enormous relief, absolutely out of proportion to what she'd done.

"Dizzy," she answered, "but I've been up all night. I'm tired, very tired."

There was another silence until Angela said, "This is the point where I get a little nervous. I'll ask you something, and you can say no if you want, of course you can, but would you ... would you come back with me, to my home ... I don't live far ... you can tidy up, have a rest ... I won't bother you ... we can talk more ... I ... gosh ... I like you ... I'd feel ... I don't know ... upset, really upset if I never saw you again ... I ... well ... will you ... please?"

Nurcan looked again at Angela and again was caught by her eyes which were bright, happy and beautiful and more, they expressed a deep anxiety on many levels, about what she'd said, about Nurcan's grief and about her possible reaction. They were, in a way, brave words.

Nurcan couldn't look away. It was one of those rare crossroad moments when you decide who you are and what you want. A thousand fears and habits charged up to her brain, warning her, telling her to say no, to leave, to be what she was, a hardworking, dedicated, respectable woman, but another voice, of longing, yes, but also of an honest desire desperate to find expression spoke to her and would not be denied.

"Shall I?" she asked, as if Angela would say 'no'.

Instead, Angela stood and said, "On one condition." Nurcan looked puzzled. "You tell me your name."

Angela's home was in easy walking distance of the cafe but on the way Nurcan had second thoughts, third thoughts and an unending feeling of falling. She was so close every moment to turning back, apologizing to Angela who walked beside her with a steady, unrushed step, and hurrying back to her car, her home, her little, organised, independent, secret, meaningless life.

But she didn't.

She kept walking, unsure whether this was through courage or foolishness. What she felt and what drove her was a longing that, even in the streets of London, even though they might be cruelly treated or ignored and even after the night to end all nights, coursed through her as if her whole life had risen in rebellion and was saying 'Enough!'.

Angela said nothing, occasionally touching her arm, a touch which transmitted a million messages.

She could barely stand, let alone walk the short distance. Angela seemed aware of it. She seemed aware of everything.

"Not far," she said softly when Nurcan was close to stopping and giving up the whole crazy encounter.

It was an ordinary house in an ordinary street but the front door looked to Nurcan like a door between worlds, full of implications. She had never felt so tired in her life, nor so anxious nor so exhilarated. As they approached, she once again fought the urge to turn and run. The voices in her head pulled her one way then the other, but she was so exhausted and so distraught that she had little strength to fight.

Angela gave her every opportunity to go. She never rushed her, led her gently to the door and before she opened it said, "I hate myself for saying this, but there's still time, if you want to change your mind, I'll take you back."

Nurcan shook her head. She was thinking of Kathryn and of all the good that had gone out of the world. She thought of the rules by which she'd tried to lead her life and how they suddenly seemed so foolish, so unnecessary.

She watched Angela open the door and followed her inside.

She had no idea what to expect or what to do. She thought that Angela might offer her a drink, make her comfortable, talk for a while, anything except what happened.

Within the passing of a mere moment that transformed her life, she found herself pinned against the wall, not harshly, not even firmly, but as if her own willingness held her there. Angela stood in front of her, brushing her hair aside, closer and closer, looking at her, touching her cheek, her eyes, her nose, her lips.

When their lips met, Nurcan froze. A panic seized her, the like of which she had always feared but never experienced. It was as if all the demons of past nightmares suddenly broke through the barriers which had held her down for so long. Tears rose to her eyes, thinking of Kathryn, of the face she'd wanted so much but never dared admit, of the body she'd loved but dreaded, of the woman she would never see again.

"I'm not Kathryn," said Angela, "I never can be, no one can ever be. Let me just be me, yes?"

Nurcan buried her head on Angela's shoulder and held her as if she were a lover she'd known all her life. She clung to her, uncertain, desperate to be led on this wild adventure.

She felt Angela's lips on hers and a thrill shot through every nerve in her body as if all reserve were cast aside and the body was master at last. She felt Angela's hands hold her gently, touching her gently, never rushing. She closed her eyes, letting herself fall into the darkness of a sensation she'd hardly dared dream about ever since the realisation of who she was had dawned on her so many years past.

She felt a change.

Angela was leading her away from the door. Nurcan looked back as if she would never be able to pass through again it in the same state. She'd made a decision coming in and she would not be the same going out. Her old world fell away as Angela led her into another room.

A bedroom.

She allowed this other woman, this Angela, this stranger, to undress her. She, so independent, so strong in her desire to hide herself, was in this woman's bedroom, allowing a seduction which she might regret forever, but she couldn't fight it. She no longer wanted to fight it. Kathryn was gone, her fantasy was gone, but the gift Kathryn left her was this encounter, this enlightenment, telling her who she was and that there was no need to fear it.

Angela's nakedness shocked her, but she felt as if a light had blasted away the darkness.

She felt the body next to her and shook with desire. Tears came to her eyes, remembering all that had happened during the night, hoping that the sadness and despair could be washed away in this unexpected embrace. She sunk into the void that was Angela's kiss, desperate to lose herself, even for a few moments. Let her forget the night, please, let her forget the night!

Oh so gently, Angela's hands caressed the frustrations of her life away, atom by atom, cell by cell.

It must be, she thought, a little like dying, but with pleasure, not pain, slowly losing yourself like this. She recalled an eldest child always in charge, the one others looked up to for support; she recalled the same child at school, trying to do what the teachers asked of her, but never quite at home there, no matter how hard she tried; she remembered that endless feeling of being different, but not understanding why, of being aware of unthinkable attractions but forbidding them to take hold, of trying her heart out to be like the others at school and then at college and finally at work. She saw a soul struggling for freedom, to gain its liberty amidst a host of rules, misguidedly learned but well-meaning. And then she saw a face, Kathryn Hudson, a nurse whose presence shocked her into realizing for the first time who she was.

As their bodies began the slow dance to the rhythms of love, Nurcan saw her old life drift away to vanishing point, like a slow moving panorama. It was an astonishing sensation, something more mystical than she could ever have imagined.

Angela's body curved into hers, finding the perfect form. She responded, at first consciously, uncertain if she was doing the right thing, fearing that Angela might stop, might throw her out as a useless lover, but gradually her body began to act of its own accord, knowing when to move and how to shape itself, moulding into the contours of the other. Slowly she drifted into that rare territory where the mind is at rest and all disturbing thoughts forgotten. She reacted to every touch and every kiss, sure beyond all possible doubt that this was who she was and that, for whatever reason, something wonderful was released in an embrace with another woman.

When she climaxed, Angela gently laid her hand over her mouth to hush the scream. Nurcan's body lifted upwards, holding tightly to what felt like its mirror image, pulling Angela into her own body as if to make them a single entity. She cried and laughed and turned her head, coming back to herself in slow moments, aware again of this woman's eyes looking at her, amazed.

"My goodness, Nurcan, are you sure you've never done this before?"

"Never," said Nurcan. "Was it ... alright?"

Angela brushed Nurcan's hair aside, looked into her with such affections and said, "I don't think 'alright' quite covers it."

Nurcan breathed deeply, sensing her body, examining each nerve, wondering if she could ever lose herself in such a way again. And then Kathryn's face came back to her and she turned, her eyes shining.

"Is it this poor girl that you love?" Angela asked.

"It is."

"Do you feel guilt that this moment was with me, not with her?"

"I don't know. It wasn't real with her, was it? And now she's gone."

"Look," said Angela, turning Nurcan to face her and settling the duvet around them both. "This is what I think. I think this is her gift to you, that I am her gift to you. The dead can do that, you know."

"Can they?"

"Yes, they can bestow gifts on those they love."

"She never loved me."

"Not in the way you wanted, but she does now. You can't believe this was just coincidence?"

"I don't know what to believe."

"And I can't tell you, but to me it seems obvious. When I saw you in the cafe I knew, I absolutely knew that I should talk with you. I could see your distress, Nurcan. I can't with everyone but I could with you. It was impossible to let you go without a word. Life is too short to allow these moments to pass."

"What if I'd said no?"

"You did say no. I would have gone, I would never have pressed you. Some people would have done, but I'm not like that. I would have come home and thought about you for the rest of my life. I still will."

"Isn't it wrong to make love after such a crime? How can I make sense of this?"

"I don't think life allows much sense to be made of it," said Angela, "and there is no way you must ever think of this as wrong – *that* would be a crime. This was a miracle, Nurcan, nothing less."

"Truly?"

"Truly, truly, sweet thing that you are!"

"I forgot her, for a while, I forgot all the horrible events of the night. How shallow am I?"

"Not shallow at all! You are as deep as the deepest ocean! It isn't possible to feel any more than you do. Do you think you should have taken your life like her poor brother?" The thought had passed through Nurcan's mind. "Don't you dare!" said Angela with mock severity, tracing Nurcan's eyebrows with her finger. "You are a rich human being, one of the richest. You have so much goodness in you!"

"But you don't know me."

"I know as much as I need to know. No one could make love like that without depth and passion and goodness."

Nurcan felt Angela's hands touching her again, her arms, her breasts, her stomach. Every touch was a delight and she started, impossibly, to respond again.

"I think I'm exhausted," she said.

"No," said Angela, "you're sad still, and you'll always have that sadness. What happened to Kathryn is a blight against us all, a terrible thing. I didn't know the girl, but my heart goes out to her because she must have been special for you to feel about her the way you do. I don't understand why such horrors are allowed. I think the universe can be a beautiful but cruel place, inexplicable but fundamentally good, it has to be."

"Does it?"

"Oh yes, for sure. I don't mean it's sweetness and light, but there is light and sweetness somewhere, we just have to open ourselves to it, even in the roughest moments."

Nurcan wanted to believe, but all she could do was feel. She was afraid, desperately fearful, of the sorrow that might haunt her when all this was over, that she might never be able to forget Kathryn, that she would hate herself for this pleasure at such a time. But she looked into Angela's eyes and saw no selfishness.

The look lasted and turned into another kiss, then the kiss into more sensations as their bodies slid into each other, beginning to know the places where most delight lay. To Nurcan it was like losing consciousness, only the deepest part of her aware of what was happening, and then even that faded as they began to move in perfect unison. Joy flooded through Nurcan's body. She let herself slip further into this absorbing mystery, aware enough only to imprint each sensation into memory. Each nerve bristled with fire, tautening and tightening, ready to explode with whatever magic Angela's spell was casting. And when it happened, it happened together and they held on to each other as if they might fall into an abyss and vanish from the world.

"Tell me again Nurcan," said Angela as they relaxed for the second time, "are you sure you've never done this before?"

"Never, I promise."

Angela caught the edge in her voice and said, "Whatever we do, you know, the sadness won't go, not yet, not ever, but maybe you'll have something to balance the loss."

"Yes," said Nurcan, "maybe. I'm sorry if ... if I'm still..."

She was conscious of there being something left to give, of her past life even now exerting a restraining influence in this coming together.

"You are wonderful," said Angela. "Maybe the sadness of what's happened adds to you, as long as you don't let it master you. I guess there'll always be something of Kathryn in you, but something of me, too?"

She asked this in a light but urgent way. Nurcan didn't answer in words, but cuddled up close, holding on to the other woman and resting her head in her breast as Angela stroked her hair. Tears flowed again as the visions of Kathryn in life and death drifted into her mind. She was afraid Angela might realise this and lose patience, but she held her tight and smoothed her hair like a child with a new doll.

"Should I leave?" Nurcan asked. "I mean, do you have to go somewhere, you know, work, business, anything?"

"Nowhere."

Nurcan thought for a moment then said, "Do you sit in that cafe every day and wait for likely women to roll up?"

"Every day, yes, that's right."

"So I'm not unique?"

"No. This happens all the time."

Nurcan looked up and said, concerned, "Truly?"

"No, not truly at all! I've been there once before."

"So why did you go there today?"

"I have no idea, but it was just about the best little decision I've ever made," said Angela, kissing Nurcan's head. Nurcan looked up and said again, in a lighter way, "Truly?"

"Listen," said Angela with sudden seriousness, "all my life I've dreamed about finding you. That's what humans do, dream about the perfect partner. I don't know if it's you, and I don't want to frighten you off with silly talk like that, but believe me, this is special ... for both of us and for all kinds of reasons. You have to believe that."

Nurcan believed it, though the way they had met and the bizarre coincidences of life were too complex to unravel. For a third time she felt a shiver of need and possibility sweep through her. She thought she would never have her fill of this lovemaking, as if her whole life had been waiting for the moment and the rest of her life would be built upon it.

Their eyes caught fire again and for a third time they moved into each other, even more deftly and knowing than before, slow, patient and perfect, and at last Nurcan left every thought behind, aware of nothing except an overwhelming, unremitting ecstasy.

# 16

Despite forty plus years of living and working in Hackney, Faraday still wasn't sure whether the borough worked or not. It had once been a green and pleasant land, the retreat of lords, ladies and rich folk seeking sanctuary from the rigours of the city. Few people sought sanctuary there any longer, but it could still be found in the legacy of those green and pleasant days, the local parks and the river bank. The real rough spots of nineteenth century London were around the Docklands and Wapping, often the first port of call for immigrants from all areas of the globe and a thriving, if thoroughly dangerous, haven for those who time and a disinterested divinity forgot. Eventually the pressure was so great that communities escaped to the New World of Hackney, at which point the borough became the focus of Victorian builders. Since then it had struggled to find an identity, home to many people of many nations. Even the graphic designers of the late twentieth century failed to find a logo and colour scheme that encapsulated Hackney.

The Jewish communities allowed back into England by Oliver Cromwell in the seventeenth century were typical, settling in the East End where the Huguenots had arrived before them, but it was not until the twentieth century that they started moving onwards and outwards, including a lengthy stay in Hackney, but the orthodox groups, for reasons best known to them, remained, and, in Faraday's view, added stability and calm to an area which might otherwise be both mad and bad. They were rarely, if ever, trouble and took an active part in helping the borough grow. It was therefore with some trepidation that Faraday entered the Levinson's home to talk about their son's possible involvement in the murder of Kathryn Hudson.

Lilly and Chaim welcomed him and Fowler, offered them some refreshment and then sat and waited in complete terror.

To Lilly Levinson, the mildest breaking of the mildest law was unacceptable. The Jewish religion was based on hundreds of laws and the many happy hours of interpreting them. Its followers had devised some of the earliest systems of civil laws and built on them to create a mind-boggling array of regulations by which their lives were governed, but the basic divinely given commandments brooked no interpretation, they were clear and simple and you didn't mess with them. The thought that her eldest and thoroughly loved son could be in any way associated with such a horrendous crime was anathema, a thought as impossible as Mount Everest taking an evening stroll in the Himalayan sunset.

"All I want," said Faraday, "is for Sam to tell us what he was doing late last night. We have to follow up all leads, and this is just another one."

Sam sat in between his parents, fuming. He didn't think it was any of anyone's business to know where he went, especially when he knew his mother and father wouldn't approve. It was a weird kind of double think, to be fiercely independent and fighting against a whole host of desires, and at the same time not to want to upset his mum and dad who he knew were good people, even though they irritated him immensely in the way most parents irritate their teenage children.

He resented being implicated in this, of all things, because he'd liked the nurse very much. He'd hardly every spoken to her because he was a little in awe of what she did, and she looked so clever and classy, but she'd been excellent with Jonathan and always been kind to him. The thought that the police considered him a suspect was infuriating.

"I didn't do anything," he mumbled. "She was a nice lady."

"You see," said Lilly, "he's a good boy, he wouldn't..."

"Lilly," said Chaim, holding her hand, "let the inspector speak."

Faraday asked Sam to tell them exactly what he did the night before.

"Why should I?" asked Sam. He had the nasty suspicion that he was the only 'lead' and that the police were on to him because he was Jewish. He suspected everyone of suspecting him of everything, but this was an inherited trait of a people so long condemned for a million things they'd never done. He made light of it with Feriha and Jemal, but he couldn't make light of it now.

"We're following up some camera images of people out last night in or near the area where Kathryn Hudson was killed," said Faraday, "that's all, Sam. I have a team of people talking to hundreds of people."

Sam humphed and said he was 'just out'.

"Can you be a bit more specific?" Faraday asked.

"What do you mean?" Sam asked back. He wasn't feeling in a helpful mood, in fact he was bristling with righteous indignation. He was, like most teenagers, struggling to find himself, but what made it harder was this massive gravitational pull towards something he had grave doubts about - his religion. Denying this would, in his parents' view, be as heinous a crime as murder, almost, but Sam was suffering the seeds of doubt. He didn't know where they came from and didn't know where they were leading. All he knew was that his religion was stopping him being who he wanted to be, and he couldn't bear that. He thought of Jemal and Feriha and wondered if they were being questioned, too, but he doubted it. The police were having a go at him because he was..."

"Sam, please tell the policeman what you were doing," said his father.

"Just out," said Sam. "It's my business where I go."

"Yes," said Faraday, trying not to ruffle the boy's feathers too much, "and I'm sorry we have to ask, but as I say, we're asking lots of people. Were you seeing friends?" Sam nodded. "Friends in the community?" Sam shook his head.

"He has some Turkish friends from coll..."

"Lilly!" said Chaim.

"Yes," said Sam rudely, "let the policeman speak."

If Faraday hadn't had a teenage son of his own, he might not have recognised this fight for independence, but he did have a similar age son and the similar aged son had similar gripes so Faraday saw beyond the gruff exterior. Nevertheless, he needed clarification.

"Were these the friends you went to see, Sam?"

"Might be."

"Yes or no?"

"Yes. Happy?"

"Sam," said Lilly, "be polite! What have we taught you all these years?"

Sam wondered about that and would have answered back if the policeman wasn't asking him more irritating questions.

"Can you give me their names and addresses?"

"Why, so you can bother them like you're bothering us?"

Even Chaim, who rarely lost his temper, was becoming agitated at Sam's manner, but he held back. He didn't want the inspector to see his family arguing.

"No, so we can take your name off our list..."

"...of suspects, that's what you mean, isn't it. I'm on your list of suspects."

"We don't have a list yet," said Faraday, which was the sad truth, and he didn't believe for one moment that Samuel Levinson should be anywhere near such a list, but the boy was obstinate, "and I doubt you'll be on it, Sam. Now, these friends you saw last night."

Sam took a deep breath, scowled and gave Faraday Jemal's address.

"And what were you doing there?" Faraday asked.

"You see," Sam said, "I told him but he still wants more." Sam didn't want his parents to know that he was a deft hand at hacking computer systems; he preferred them believing that he went out to talk important points of law with his Jewish friends. For a moment or two, Faraday had the sinking feeling that Sam might be involved in drugs, but those few moments passed, even though Samuel Levinson was hardly exonerating himself honourably. "If you must know, I was using a state-of-the-art 3D Graphics package on a home-built computer with 8 gigabytes of memory and a four-core chip with a two megabyte Supreme Graphics Card and..."

"Okay, I get the picture," said Faraday. "Nice machine, then?"

This took Sam back a bit, but he said, "Yes, nice machine."

"You're good at computer games are you?"

"I'm not a kid, Mr Policeman, and yes, I am 'good at these games'."

"Sam!" exclaimed his mother, "What is wrong with you? I'm so sorry, sir, he's never this rude."

Faraday quite liked Samuel Levinson. The boy was bright and showing healthy signs of independence. Although he doubted that Sam had anything to do with the murder, he asked him to go along to the hospital to have a sample of DNA taken, like Reed, or for someone to come to the home, whichever was easiest. Sam looked like he was on a leash the whole time. Faraday thought of buttering him up with offers of a visit to the station to see the computers in action, but Sam was indeed 'not a kid' and Faraday didn't think he could be easily persuaded. On the other hand, he wasn't a typical streetwise teenager. He had more a touch of the child in him than most, probably because he'd been closeted away with such an unusual world view. Whatever the reason, he had an interesting mixture of assumed tough guy and innocent child.

Once Faraday had the information he needed, he asked if he could have a word with Chaim and Lilly alone. Sam didn't argue with that. He went to his room and called Jemal to tell him what had happened.

"They don't really think you did it, do they?" Jemal asked.

"I don't know; they'd better not," said Sam. He was both upset and angry, probably more the former than the latter. He hadn't just liked the nurse who'd been killed, he'd liked her a lot. She and Feriha had had equal space in his confused head. The world seemed to him a complicated place with no easy answers, and he was beginning to think all the laws he followed hid the truth rather than revealed them. He told Jemal that the police might call them to confirm he'd been there which didn't bother Jemal at all, in fact he liked the idea of having a visit by the police. Jemal asked if Sam was going to come over that evening, but it was Friday, the beginning of the Sabbath, and Sam couldn't. Friday night was *the* night of the week, a family occasion. Normally, it was a happy celebration, but tonight, with Jonathan in hospital and Sam interviewed by the police for murder it wasn't promising to be the best of nights.

Downstairs, Faraday and Fowler were talking to Chaim and Lilly, trying to reassure them that all would be well. No matter what Faraday said, Lilly was shocked by the remotest connection of her son with such a crime. She tried to understand Faraday's point of view, that he had to investigate all leads, but Sam was beyond reproach, in her eyes. He wasn't, however, beyond reproach in his father's eyes, Chaim having a different and more realistic perspective, and the interview left him disturbed.

He was even more disturbed a little while later when he saw Sam again.

One of the binding features of a sect is clothing, a uniform by which followers can identify each other and be comfortable in a society where choice is infinite, and the dark, unobtrusive, unfashionable suits and long coats were recognizably this branch of orthodox Judaism, so both Lilly and Chaim were speechless when Sam appeared ready to visit his brother at the hospital in jeans, trainers and a jokey tee-shirt.

## 17

Another interview was about to take place not too far away. Matt Davis had joined his partner Charlene for the regular morning updates. He was still tired from the demanding night, so the very last thing he wanted, and the very last thing he would have expected, was a professional interview with Cassie Logan. When he saw her name on the list he thought he was seeing things. Coincidences like that just didn't happen unless this was some kind of fate-inspired retribution.

"Do you want to do these alone?" he asked Charlene who looked at him as if he'd spoken an alien language.

"What kind of dumb question is that?" she said. "If you're too tired to work, Matt, you should have called in sick."

If he'd known he'd have to knock on Cassie's door for the second time in a few hours, he might well have phoned in sick, but he could hardly get out of it now.

"You do the talking he said. Why, exactly, are we interviewing all these people?"

Charlene again looked at him as if he were Mr Gormless.

"You do remember there was a murder last night, followed by a suicide?" Matt didn't think this needed an answer. "We interview everyone."

"What, everyone in the world?"

"Don't be so weird, Matt," said Charlene. "You know the procedure. What's the big deal?"

He couldn't tell her so he said they should just get on with it.

Charlene went through the notes Faraday had left, then knocked on the door whilst Matt stood back, trying to hold himself together.

Cassie opened the door in her dressing gown, much as Matt had left her just hours earlier. She'd been asleep and her eyes were bleary, but she sharpened up when she saw Matt standing behind the black policewoman. Cassie rarely, if ever, lost her composure. She was the most self-assured woman Matt had ever met, and she didn't fail him now. He'd feared that she might blurt out something embarrassing, but Cassie wasn't the type. She stood there, looking sensual as hell, and said, "Yes, officers?"

Charlene did the talking.

"Sorry to bother you madam. Are you Cassie Logan?"

"I am."

"I'm Police Officer Charlene Okoru and this is Police Officer Matt Davis. We're speaking to everyone in the neighbourhood about a murder that took place last night."

Cassie caught on straight away. Not only was she composed, she was also bright as a button. Matt felt his body begin to move again, despite the uniform and despite the huge awkwardness of the situation.

"Another murder," said Cassie, "that's bad news. Who was it?"

"A nurse," said Charlene, "at the local hospital. Miss Logan, may we come in for a few moments. It's awkward talking at the door."

"Am I a suspect?" Cassie asked, as if she knew it was a ludicrous suggestion. She wasn't, and she let them in. Matt felt his face turn red with either embarrassment or shame as he stepped inside. The flat was as he had left it. He could almost smell the lovemaking in the air. Charlene didn't look at him but was taking in the ambience of the place.

"Sit down," Cassie said.

Matt preferred to stand, but Charlene sat on the very same chair ... Matt looked away, desperate to get out. He felt he couldn't breathe in there. The gods had ganged up against him to put him in this predicament.

Cassie sat and crossed her legs slowly, pulling up her dressing gown in a modest way, not looking at Matt but holding a steady gaze with Charlene who seemed unfazed by the woman's sensuality.

Charlene asked her a couple of standard questions then said, "We spoke to Paula Taft..."

"Paula's alright, isn't she?" Cassie asked, slightly worried.

"Fine, yes. She said you passed someone in the street late last night who spooked her. Is that right?"

Cassie thought back and remembered the incident.

"Yes, but Paula's like that, she's got this peculiar gift. I didn't feel anything myself, hardly saw the guy."

"That's a pity," said Charlene. "We thought you might be able to give us a description.

Cassie pushed back her hair. Matt tried not to look but he couldn't help himself. After he'd left her, he'd gone back home but Eileen was fast asleep. He'd climbed into bed with a conscience heavy as lead, swearing he would try to be a better husband, but here he was a few hours later knowing that he was a weak and foolish man and that Cassie held sway over him.

Cassie said, "If I remember, he wore an anorak – green, I think, but I only saw him from behind and it was dark, of course, so I can't be sure. I turned when Paula told me he'd given her a creepy feeling, but I thought she was imagining it."

"You don't remember anything else about him, height, weight, hair, anything at all?"

Cassie sat back and looked for the first time at Matt who looked away. Cassie never blinked but stood up, walked slowly around the room, thinking hard.

"Nothing exceptional, no. Are you really asking me these questions because of Paula's reaction? That seems a bit desperate, if you don't mind me saying."

"We're not desperate," said Charlene, "but we're thorough."

Matt listened to the conversation with acute embarrassment bordering on shame. He was sweating beneath his uniform and kept stealing glances at Cassie who steadfastly refused to look at him. She really was the most self-assured woman, astonishingly composed. She showed no sign of being in discomfort, despite Charlene's intimidating presence. If Charlene knew, or ever got to know, that this woman was the centre of their conflict, Matt balked at the possible reaction. On the other hand, the two might have a chat about the foibles of men, which were too numerous to list, and become fast friends; anything was possible, though this did seem a touch like wishful thinking. For the moment, Charlene continued to ask questions, where Cassie and Paula had been the night before, what time, who they had seen and whether Cassie might have any other information that might be of use. She didn't.

They stayed about fifteen minutes, but it was one of the longest fifteen minutes of Matt's life. He was shifting around, watching both women and trying to stay professional. He felt as if he were being squeezed to death by worlds colliding, his own personal world with

Eileen, the children and his work, and this mysterious other world he had fallen in to, blindly and foolishly but to which he was bound by a powerful passion. It didn't let up, this passion, not even as he stood behind Charlene trying to be the regular bobby on the beat. He had no idea how it could all be resolved without some seismic event, and in this respect he was dead right.

"Interesting woman," said Charlene when they'd left Cassie's home, and without waiting for an answer added, "femme fatale, don't you think?"

Matt wondered if Charlene had guessed and was testing him, or rather prodding him, but decided she was just making light of the interview and said, "I didn't notice; where next?" Charlene glanced at him as if he'd answered too quickly, but there was no dawning realisation on her face, at least none that Matt saw. She pointed next door and said, in the easy way they'd spoken to each other before he'd told her of his affair, "thataway, cowboy."

## 18

The press conference was held at Stoke Newington. Although the Hackney Station was nearer the scene of the crime, Stoke Newington was set up for such invasions by journalists. They weren't that regular, but unfortunately they weren't that uncommon either. This was an unusually large gathering with national reporters and photographers and also a host of TV crews. Faraday disliked this part of his work, but it was essential not only for the news broadcasts but also for the information and leads they could initiate.

He sat at the centre of a long table with Fowler on one side and Daniel on the other. Daniel looked as though he would rather be anywhere but there. Melissa sat beside him and next to her sat Daphne Rowe, the Homerton Registrar. Beside Fowler sat Kathryn and Michael's parents and next to them a grey-suited, serious looking woman.

The room was buzzing with concern, anxiety and anticipation. Those who were closest to Kathryn and Michael and who had been up all night each felt they were part of some interrupted drama where normal service would resume presently. Whilst the day before had been routine, the night and now this new day were the shards of catastrophe. Their own lives had been thrown into confusion and they could hardly believe where they were and why they were there.

Apart from those sitting in the glaring light of the front table, others close to Kathryn and Michael were in the room too. Of the three flatmates, Ursula was there with Elena who had gone to work but promptly been sent home as she was constantly in tears; Jasmine had stayed with Naila. Belinda, the staff nurse of Alexandra Ward was there. Nurcan had received a text about the conference but wasn't there – she watched it with Angela holding her together, literally and metaphorically, on a twenty-four hour news channel from Angela's home.

When Faraday started to speak, the buzzing died down immediately. Notebooks and pencils were readied, tapes switched on and cameras activated. It was a circus, but the kind societies seemed to need for these dreadful moments. Faraday talked well, despite acute tiredness . He introduced himself and then said, "Thank you for coming. As you know, there was an incident last night around midnight in which a young woman was murdered. This took place..." and he started giving a brief description of the 'incident'. Pencils and pens scraped across notepads, a few bulbs flashed and the press conference was underway.

For most of those closest to Kathryn and Michael, this was the inside view of something they'd seen many times on television, but the inside view was a radically different experience from the broadcasts. Truth depends on perspective, and watching whilst uninvolved is not the same as being interrogated under scrutiny with the pressure of a suffocating grief closing in, but from whichever perspective the people in that room were considering Faraday's description, the truth remained elusive. Everyone had their reasons for being there and their own interpretation of the events Faraday was describing. There was no way to pin down the meeting in simple terms because it was a complicated thing attempting simply to inform, but it also reached out and touched people, mutating into countless personal experiences.

Daniel sat stony faced, listening to Faraday's description of the 'incident', trying to get his head around the word. It sounded inadequate, but it was necessary police talk. In this 'incident' he had lost his soul mate and was in danger of losing himself. Faraday didn't mention that Kathryn was pregnant, and for that Daniel was grateful. It was hard enough being stared at with, he felt, suspicion, without the rumours that would follow such a revelation. He had a feeling that he looked guilty, that his religion was weighing on him heavier than ever, drawing the wrong kind of attention. He remembered the family and friends of people he'd seen on television in similar situations, how they cried or pleaded; he couldn't do either. He was just himself and his emotions were thoroughly private. He'd only attended the conference because Faraday had advised it, but now, sitting there in front of what appeared to be a frightening array of faces, he was sorry he'd agreed, and he was even sorrier when some questions were directed towards him.

"Mr Hart, can you tell us how you feel?"

Daniel knew it was coming. He wished again a thousand times over that he'd stuck to his gut feeling and stayed away, but now that he was there it was make or break time. The temptation was to say what they expected, to cry because they thought he should cry, and to plead for information because that was the thing to do, but he couldn't do any of this. Instead, he whispered into the microphone, "Kathryn Hudson was a beautiful and special lady. I was lucky that she loved me. We were all lucky," he gestured to Melissa and the others, "that we knew her, even for such a short time. I hope whoever did this knows what he's done now and comes forward before anyone else is hurt."

He said it in such a dignified way, and meant well, but the press latched on to the "anyone else is hurt" bit and questioned the police about whether they had witnesses or suspects and did they think this might be the first victim of a serial killer.

"We have a possible witness, but unfortunately he hasn't been able to give us a clear description. We have teams out in all the areas asking questions, so may I thank everyone who's been approached and tell them we appreciate their time. As for the nature of the crime, time will tell, but I'm hopeful we'll catch whoever did this quite soon."

This also sparked off questions about whether they were close to catching the killer. Daniel was not unaware that in similar situations the killer had been there in the room, a father, a friend, anyone in the victim's circle was suspect and he dreaded the eye of the devil being turned his way. Those in the room from so many media channels had their own agenda and would take from the press conference what they wanted. Some, more sensitive, would understand the loss and write about it in gentle terms, but most would turn the whole thing into a selling spree, perverting honest feelings into something harmful to the human spirit. Anything could, and usually was, diminished by vast outpourings of emotion and the need to create a story, and however quiet Daniel, Melissa, Michael's parents, Naila, and all their friends would have wanted to keep this, the media wouldn't let that happen. There would be a stampede to interpret the night's events and to squeeze the last drop of sentiment from what were essentially private passions. Daniel hoped that he and the others would be able to navigate the storm without being shipwrecked, but he doubted it; the waves were already rough and the winds beginning to howl.

Faraday was doing his best to keep the ship upright and true, sticking to the facts and avoiding speculation. He asked the public to come forward if they'd seen anything unusual the night before in or around the area of the murder. He showed photographs of Kathryn which were enlarged on the Press Room screens. At this point Daniel began to feel dizzy and disoriented. It made no sense to see this image of his love on display for the world to gawp at. He tried telling himself that she was alive and this was some dreadful mistake, but that just made him feel worse. People were staring at the picture because Kathryn was gone forever, and he had to be strong, to remember who she was and not let the mania of the moment destroy his precious, private memories.

When asked about the witness, Faraday mentioned Robert, but not by name. He told the press that a man said he'd seen an incident from a distance and his story was being checked. Faraday knew that if the press got hold of Robert's name, they would tear him to shreds. The public would convict and hang him without a shred of proof and, as much as Faraday wanted an outcome to the case, that was not the right one.

He gave precise times and even mentioned the possibility of the killer wearing a green anorak, but he didn't say where this information came from. He could hardly tell the press that a passing mystic had had one of her psychic turns as she crossed the killer's path in the street. In fact, Faraday had little hard evidence to offer and was wary of appearing both desperate and dopey. He'd been working flat out, and so had his team, but the leads were few and there were no real suspects. He couldn't give away any hard information because, as he feared would happen with Robert, the press would have a field day with anyone linked to the murder, like Reed, Orlich and particularly Samuel Levinson. Faraday was well aware that he had touchpaper in one hand and a match in the other; all he had to do was make a slip and the press would strike the match, light the touchpaper and watch the fire of repressed resentments begin to burn. Faraday imagined the result with horror so did what he could to avoid it happening. If the truth, when it was finally discovered, soiled a good name then so be it, but gossip, prejudice and tribal instincts were unwanted features of his investigation.

Melissa spoke with feeling about Kathryn when she was asked. Daniel listened and watched with awe, wishing he could come across half as emotional, but at the same time he was who he was and they either understood or they didn't. Melissa held his arm as she spoke and he loved her for doing this. She told the press as much as she could, but was never so emotional as to reveal the things that Faraday had advised her to keep quiet. Like Daniel, she felt that she was in some demonic drama, forced to act out a nightmare, but she did really well and the press took to her kindly, Faraday could see that and was impressed.

Kathryn's parents were a different matter, but they would have had to be monsters for the press to turn against them so soon. They didn't have Melissa's warmth or Daniel's unself-conscious charm, but they were the parents of two young people who had lost their lives in a single night, and for that alone they had the sympathy of everyone in the room, as well as of a few million people watching. It might not last. If the public got to hear about their parenting skills, it could turn nasty in an instant, but for the time being they were safe, and whatever their failings as parents, they were visibly and truly devastated.

Elena sat in between Ursula and Patrick with a face lined with tear marks. She'd returned from an aborted hour at school unable to focus on anything. She felt exposed and vulnerable, not so much to a killer on the loose, but to something which she wasn't quite sure about, a kind of threatening confusion, as if she might lose her moral balance and no longer know right from wrong, good from bad, where both were rewarded or punished by chance more than by direction. She held Ursula's and Patrick's hand, watching the conference unfold with disbelieving eyes. She was the quiet one of the foursome – now the threesome – the one closest in spirit, she thought, to Kathryn. They'd sometimes talked about their work and how "people-centred" jobs were so much more tiring than plain old money-centred ones. As with everyone that had known her, Kathryn had been a great listener and good friend. When times were rough at school, it was always Kathryn that had had the sympathetic ear, not the others. Now the dynamics were all changed, Elena feared the friendships falling apart. She doubted that any of them would stay – this was a sea change, if ever there was one. A tidal wave had swept away their history and everything was tempest tossed. She tried hard to pay attention to what Faraday was saying, but her mind was wandering horribly.

Despite the great swell of sympathy and compassion, the questions revolved around the murderer and how close Faraday and his team were to closing in on him – or her. A reporter from a tabloid paper had asked the gender question and Faraday had no definite answer as the witness wasn't a hundred percent sure. Why wasn't he a hundred percent sure, came the response, and Faraday repeated the difficulties of observation in the dark and the distance.

Patrick should have been taking notes. As the crime reporter for the local paper this was his big day, but it felt like nothing of the sort. He was there for Melissa and Kathryn's friends. He had more in his head and in the experiences of the past twenty-four hours than would fill half a dozen notebooks, and he'd done his best to tone down the sensational side of the story rather than hype it up. He had his heart in two worlds, partly in the journalistic, partly in the emotional, and it was the latter which took priority. He listened and watched as he'd done many times before, but for the first time he felt uneasy with his work, as if he were part of something not quite right. But then, nothing was 'right' at such a moment. The word had lost its meaning with Kathryn's murder. Crime had taken on a whole new perspective for him. He'd become entangled and he didn't think it would be easy to disentangle himself, even to the point of continuing with his 'cops and robbers' journalism when the dust settled. He stole glances at Elena and Ursula sitting beside him, saw their pained expressions and took courage in their courage, laying aside his personal dilemmas and focusing on the questions.

"How many officers are involved, Inspector?"

"Have the door to door questions been useful?"

"Was anything recovered from the crime scene?"

"Can you tell us the name of anyone in custody?"

and so on. Faraday answered them all with great care and dignity, but he was struggling. The thought tormented him – this murder had happened on *his* watch, near *his* old school, and he was getting nowhere fast. Critical moments were coming and going and the murderer was still at large, probably watching, possibly in that very room. The thought appalled him, but such things weren't unknown, villains could disguise themselves with impressive composure. His mind raced as he spoke, despite the careful wording, thinking what else he could do, what else he could have done. More than anything else he wanted the guilty caught. That was his job, but he'd allowed himself to be drawn in to this case. As an officer of the law it was his role to uphold that law, but he felt there was real wickedness involved in this case, something beyond the normal banality of human drama, and it touched him deeply.

When the time came to round up the conference, he promised to leave no stone unturned and assured everyone this had been the case to that very moment. He meant it and wanted to believe it, but he knew, of course, that he had left a stone unturned, otherwise the murderer would have already been in custody. He would spare no energy in tracking down the killer, but at the same time was already aware that he'd missed something. He hoped this self-doubt hadn't been noticed by the press who would soon become desperate for points of contention, but for the moment they played along, demanding information but not yet judgemental. Faraday knew this would change if time passed and nothing happened, but he still believed he could solve this quickly, only the belief was changing into hope at a rate of knots.

The press conference lasted almost forty five minutes and at the end of it Faraday was drained, balancing so many conflicting pressures. Despite all the words and assurances though, he feared what he had thought moments before, that a stone had indeed been left unturned, that the murderer was not even on the radar and that the killing might not yet be over.

## 19

A few days later people were gathered again, not at the press room of Stoke Newington Police Station but at the East London Cemetery where the bodies of Kathryn and Michael were to be cremated. There'd been no arrest and precious little progress. Faraday was at the funeral, not because he had to be but because he wanted to be. Professionally, he needn't have attended, but he liked these people and wanted to show respect. Law and order wasn't solely statistics and not all professionalism meant emotional detachment. He wanted to go, so he did. Viv Fowler, who had immersed herself in the case in a similar way, accompanied him. Both were equally disappointed that they hadn't made a breakthrough. They'd gone through past unsolved cases, talked to suspects of previous crimes, even discussed behind closed doors the inner circle of friends, knowing never to exonerate anyone without proof, but they'd got precisely nowhere, and that hurt.

About a hundred people filled the room where the service took place. Special arrangements had been made to carry two coffins into the room, an unbearably poignant moment. The crowd was huge, family, friends and colleagues. Although he tried not to be the detective at such a moment, Faraday saw how many more people he could interview and how many might have known Kathryn who had somehow escaped the net. They were planning the investigation as carefully as they could but despite the attention to detail there were many faces amongst the mourners that he'd never seen before. He made a mental note to follow this up. It was an awful thought, but it wasn't unheard of for killers to be at the funerals of those they'd killed.

The atmosphere was intensely sad. These were two young, talented and passionate people with so much to offer. There was nothing understandable about their deaths and everyone felt the fragility of their own lives as well as the uncertainty and cold impartiality that seemed to underpin nature itself. For the religious minded, this was a test of faith because there was no rational explanation. Religious faith for those who had it was a gift, like Job, holding on to an accepted belief no matter how cruelly the world fell away from them. Those without this emotional support were faced with extraordinarily challenging questions, even if the answers to those questions might better reflect the truth of the world.

Kathryn and Michael's parents sat in the front row, along with other family, Daniel and Naila. Naila had stayed in hospital three nights, but though discharged she looked more spectral than corporeal. For someone so beautiful, radiant and full of imagination, it was heart-breaking to see her so anxious and empty, as if all her vital energy had been drained away. She sat beside Daniel who remained as enigmatic as ever, wondering whether he should hold her hand in support, but she had separated herself from him and from everyone.

Melissa and Patrick sat near the front along with Ursula, Jasmine and Elena. They each looked bewildered, as if the murder had been repeated and they were just hearing the news. Melissa's eyes were shiny bright as she fought to cope, holding on to Patrick's hand with an almost painful grip. The flatmates wouldn't leave each other, afraid that if they split up something terrible would happen and they'd never see each other again. Next to Ursula sat Margaret Hargreaves who, as old as she was, looked remarkably strong, as if she'd seen so much that now she saw nothing but The Bigger Picture. Behind her sat the Levinsons along with Sam, looking uneasy, forced by something beyond teenage rebellion to dress in his dark suit again.

Close to Melissa sat Nurcan Celik. She'd contemplated not going because she didn't want to make a fool of herself in front of all these people, but there she was, looking for some reason much stronger and calmer than those who'd seen her on the night of the murder expected.

Belinda and Daphne were there, next to Faraday and Fowler. They were already planning a memorial of some kind for Kathryn, possibly a fountain or a small garden area in the hospital grounds, but it was hard to look beyond the present.

Despite the undeniable reality of the service, there was still a sense of disbelief at the sheer unnaturalness of events, as if it were all some cosmic mistake.

Kathryn and Michael's family had asked Daniel, Melissa and their friends to organise a humanist service rather than hold anything overtly religious with words and music that brother and sister had loved. Keith, the second registrar, took the service and did it perfectly, calm, kind and unobtrusive. There were readings by colleagues and friends except those who didn't feel sufficiently strong enough to stand in front of such a crowd at such a time, but when it came to the eulogy they insisted it be given by Daniel.

When the time came, he spoke without notes, memorising three pages of carefully prepared material for both Kathryn and Michael. He was gentle, affectionate and even funny. He captured the essence of Kathryn's unique nature and the beauty of Michael's imagination; even for those listening who hadn't known them, he conveyed a vivid image of the two lost siblings. He was never mawkish and never angry but disarmingly vulnerable.

When he'd finished, it was as if he'd managed to bring this part of the nightmare to an end. People began to believe that this was indeed real, that for whatever reason, these two young people were gone from the world, but Daniel had been so simple and straight that he'd left a little of Kathryn and Michael in everyone who heard him and changed them forever.

Near the end of the service, the two coffins were slowly drawn into the furnace beyond a small crimson curtain. Naila suddenly held on to Daniel's arm as if her life depended on it. Ursula, Jasmine and Elena put their arms around each other and stared. Melissa squeezed Patrick's hand and fought back tears of distress. There was a silence that seemed to challenge whoever had carried out this horrendous deed, as if to say the battle might be lost but the war was not over and there would most certainly, sooner or later, be retribution.

# 5:    **Retribution**

### 1

Frankie Davis stared at the computer screen, not quite understanding what he was seeing. A woman lay on the ground with a thick crimson liquid spreading unevenly around her, but on reaching a certain point it suddenly shrank, then began to grow all over again. The cycle took about fifteen seconds and in that time the woman hardly moved. Her hand twitched a little and her body might have shifted slightly, but nothing more. Frankie, however, was hardly being analytical; he was scared and started crying, though he wasn't sure why. He'd seen many horrible images on television and they meant nothing, but this meant something; it wasn't normal and he knew it.

He was eleven now. It was a year since he'd fouled up the computer and Mr Hart had come to fix it. Lots of things had happened in that year, the worst one being his dad leaving home. His mum had tried to explain why, but Frankie didn't understand. His dad had "been silly" his mother had told him with tears in her eyes. She said he wasn't himself but Frankie didn't know what this meant – if he wasn't himself, who was he? His mother told him that his father hadn't behaved and that he wasn't good. Again, Frankie didn't know what this meant, but the fact was his father wasn't at home any more. He wasn't even a policeman any more. Everything had gone wrong in their lives and now something else horrible was happening. Frankie wished his father was there now; he needed him both as a dad and as a policeman.

He switched the monitor off so he didn't have to look at the nasty video, but he left the computer running, then he went into the kitchen where his mother was making supper. She didn't look the same bright woman who had called Daniel a year before. She was tired and nervous and had lost weight; she had been slim but now was positively waif like. As young as he was, Frankie worried about her and didn't want to upset her, but at the same time he needed to tell her what he'd seen.

"Mum?"

"What is it?" said Eileen without looking up. Her voice was as tired as her expression, but she tried not to lose patience with Frankie or Kylie who was hovering around the kitchen table, attempting to complete a wooden jigsaw. She stopped when she saw her big brother's tear-stained face.

"It's the computer, mum," said Frankie.

Eileen breathed a sigh of frustration. A broken computer was the last of their problems, but the littlest thing could push her over the edge, her nerves were so stretched.

"It'll have to wait till tomorrow Frankie," she said. "I can't deal with it right now. Just switch it off if it's broken and do something else."

"It isn't broken mum," said Frankie, his voice cracking.

Eileen paused and looked at her son. Everything that had gone wrong in her life seemed to stem from the last time the infernal machine had gone wrong, and here it was happening all over again. In the intervening year, Matt's relationship with the call-girl had caused her world to fall apart; it was only her children who held her together.

"Well, what is it, sweety?" Eileen asked, seeing Frankie's distress.

"There's something on it," he answered.

"Frankie," said Eileen, "Is it that serious? Can't you just leave it to the morning? I need to get on and cook. You're a good boy, can't you do that?"

How she wished Matt was there! But how galling it was to wish that, too! She couldn't bear to be with him. The knowledge of all he'd done made her dizzy, defied all decency and loyalty. She cursed him, had hit him, cried tears of frustration and wanted nothing more to do with him. Neither did the police. They'd suspended him on full pay, then on half pay, then on no pay. He was living in a Hackney bedsit, trying and failing to put his life back together.

Frankie shook his head and was about to turn away when something about his upset touched his mother.

"Come on, Frankie!" she said. "Surely 'something on the computer' isn't as bad as that?"

"It is," he said.

Kylie looked on keenly, aware that something was about to happen.

Eileen dried her hands, sighed and said, "Frankie, if this is something stupid, I'll be really angry with you. Alright, let's go and see."

She hated herself for sounding so fed up with him, but she was losing patience more often and more easily. The littlest aggravation could be the last straw. Frankie tried to sniffle up his tears. Kylie watched him then got down from the chair and held her mother's hand.

"No," said Frankie.

"No what?" Eileen said, puzzled.

"Not Kylie."

"Yes, me!" Kylie said.

"Don't be silly," said Eileen.

"No!" said Frankie, sounding unduly agitated. Eileen felt a touch of alarm. She was normally good with her children, quick to sense danger and to respond, but her reflexes were worn down from anxiety and tiredness.

"Kylie, be a good girl," she said. "Wait here. I won't be a minute."

"Why?" said Kylie, angry at being left out of something that looked really interesting and grown up.

Eileen turned on her daughter and said in a way that wouldn't brook argument, "Kylie, stay here! Understood?"

Kylie froze while Eileen followed Frankie to his bedroom, closing the door behind. She rushed up behind and tried to peek through the keyhole, but she couldn't get Frankie's computer table into view, though she tried hard. She squinted for about three or four minutes and when she decided she couldn't see, she put her ear to the keyhole instead. It was quiet, but not just ordinarily quiet, frighteningly quiet. She had the horrible suspicion that something had happened to her mother and her brother. She was afraid of standing there alone and turned the doorknob slowly, peeking inside. They were there, huddled over the computer, but she couldn't see what they were looking at.

Hearing the door open, Eileen turned, her face white, and with an expression her daughter had never seen before.

"Get out!" Eileen screamed at Kylie who turned and ran to her room, confused and scared. Eileen punched the off switch of the monitor and said to Frankie, "Don't touch it! You hear? Don't touch it! Go into the kitchen, now!"

Frankie didn't argue but shuffled into the kitchen, followed by his mother whose eyes were blazing. She sat down and held Frankie's hand, then clutched him to her as if someone might snatch him away.

"Sorry darling," she whispered, "I'm really sorry! You alright?"

Frankie nodded, trying to be brave.

"I told you," he said.

"Yes, you did," Eileen said.

"What is it?" Frankie asked.

Eileen said she didn't know but told him again not to touch the computer. They both heard a sound and looked to see Kylie peeking at them from behind the kitchen door.

"Can I come in?" she whispered.

Eileen pulled Kylie towards her and hugged both her children. Kylie thought this was strange behaviour. She couldn't imagine what had happened in the bedroom to make her mother act like this so she asked.

"Nothing for you to worry about," said Eileen. "I'll sort it out," but in all honesty she wasn't sure how she would sort it out. She would have called Daniel Hart, if he'd been around, but the company had closed and Daniel gone. She thought of calling the police, but something prodded her to call Matt first. He knew a fair bit about computers and might be able to sort this out without a fuss, and despite all that had happened, he knew the way the police worked and could get things done quicker than if she'd phoned the emergency service to report a nasty video. Calling Matt would also, she had to admit, be cheap. Since he'd lost his job, money was scarce and she dreaded calling someone who'd charge her more than she could afford, so she said to Frankie, "Frankie, don't go in that room again tonight. I'll bring what you need, you can sleep in the spare room. Kylie, you don't go in there either. I know what you're like. Curiosity killed the cat, remember? I'm going to call dad."

Here was another reason for calling Matt. The children didn't understand what had passed between their parents and they missed their father. Seeing him rather than strange policemen might make them feel more secure. They were both looking anxious, especially Frankie.

Matt arrived within half an hour. When the children saw him, they ran to him with a mixture of joy and puzzlement, unsure whether he was a good or a bad man. He was certainly different from the father they used to know. Then he was smart and self-assured; now he was unkempt and uncertain. Every movement and every look was full of regret and shame, though the children couldn't name these things, just aware that he wasn't what he should be. He greeted Eileen with a nervous smile but she didn't smile back. She didn't even greet him, just told the children to make themselves scarce and took him into Frankie's bedroom.

Matt Davis was still a policeman at heart. He'd made a dreadful mistake and was paying for it heavily, but he felt that this was a moment of restitution, that depending on what he did here, he could make amends ... or screw things up forever.

He watched the video a few times, then said, "Did Frankie see it all?" He had. "Damn! What about Kylie?" No, she hadn't seen it. There was some relief. "You know what this is?" he asked. Eileen had a suspicion, but hoped it was just a horror flick, a cheap import from some rotten, obscure part of the world. She feared, however, that it might be what she knew was called a snuff movie. Matt said it wasn't just any snuff movie, "it's the girl that was killed last year," he said, "Kathryn Hudson."

Eileen held on to a chair, unable to connect all these things.

"Are you sure?"

"Damn right I'm sure," said Matt. "I saw her body, remember. This is her. The killer took a video of her dying, sick bastard."

"Jesus, Matt!"

"I know. Question is, what's it doing on our son's computer?"

They stared at the screen until Matt slowly leaned over and switched off the monitor.

"Will you tell Inspector Faraday?" Eileen asked.

This really was a crossroads moment. If he could nail this sick creep, he'd be a hero. Everything, or nearly everything, would be forgotten, or at least forgiven. He could do it, he was sure. Just telling Faraday would achieve nothing, even though he felt it was the right thing to do. Eileen would want him to, so he said, "Yes, I will, but I'm going to take the computer with me. Don't want this place to become the focus of unwanted attention, not with the kids around."

"No," said Eileen, "thanks Matt. I..." she stumbled over her words, full of conflicting emotions. She loved and hated this man, was grateful to him for helping out but angry with herself for asking him. She was also fearful of what the children had seen and what it all meant.

"Don't worry," said Matt, "Frankie will get over it. Tell him not to say anything to Kylie. I need a few minutes to make sure I can access this nasty again when I take it away. Good thinking not to turn it off. This might work out well, Eileen, for all of us."

Eileen saw that her husband was still a policeman and still essentially a good man, not completely beyond redemption.

Matt spent a while sorting things out before dismantling the machine and loading it into his car. When the time came to leave, he hugged his children who said, "Daddy, can't you stay, just for tonight?"

He looked at Eileen but she was wary of letting things slip back to the way they were. "Not now. Maybe another day. Frankie, you okay?"

Frankie nodded but said, "Was it real, dad?"

"No," said Matt, without hesitation, "but I've got to deal with it. I'll get the computer back to you ASAP. Alright?"

Surviving without a computer wasn't so simple as it once had been but Frankie said he'd be alright, for a while, and in truth he didn't want the machine back if it threatened to show him more such horrors. The boy was still upset and held on to his mother's hand tightly.

"You two be good to mum," said Matt.

"You weren't," said Kylie.

Matt took a deep breath, turned and left. As he drove away he saw them still standing at the door, looking for all the world like a grieving family watching their father leave for the last time.

**2**

Maggie Hargreaves, ninety-two and counting, was sitting in an armchair, browsing through various albums of family photographs. Every now and again she would take up some papers from an occasional table beside her and check something. When she was younger she'd been able to focus on tasks, but during the past few decades she'd been struggling, either because her memory was failing or she was losing interest in the world. She'd heard and seen everything there was to hear and see, and it was all just a variation on the single theme of human foolishness. However, she was focused now because, almost as if the decades had fallen away, she was motivated again.

She'd taken the word of her long lost relative Jerome Reed that he was indeed a long lost relative, but now she was checking him out, which was the expression she'd heard on every police programme from Dixon to The Bill. If she'd known how to use a computer she might have hurried things along, but she had to resort to photographs, her diary and the book she and Nell had begun together. It was astonishing and worrying how much she'd forgotten. Names cropped up she thought she'd never forget, people who were once so important to her, but the passing years had seen them drift into obscurity, and now they were at vanishing point. Aunts and uncles, first cousins, second cousins and cousins removed any number of times popped up as Maggie gradually compiled a family tree.

And Jerome wasn't on it.

He hadn't been convicted of killing Nell, but the nice inspector had asked her questions about him and ever since she'd felt so uneasy that she wouldn't let him into her house, and when he phoned, which was rare now, she would say, "I'm still alive, Jerome, so no will yet, I'm afraid. Goodbye."

Many people Maggie had known had wanted something from her, sex when she was young, money now she was old, though not much in the middle. She would have liked to think that such cynical thoughts were due to age, but they weren't, they were true. Whether it was her cantankerous nature or whether people were simply too self-obsessed, she didn't know, but here she was in her nineties trying to reconstruct a life which had been long, but lacking incident.

Except one.

It haunted her still, after all these years. You were, in the end, the sum of all your actions, great and small, and this was on the great side, but on the other hand, people could drive you to distraction through their own blinding selfishness, so she wasn't, she told herself, totally to blame. If she'd continued with the autobiography, and she hadn't touched it for a year, she might have felt obliged to go into more detail, after all, once she'd gone, what would it matter? But she wouldn't continue, it was too late for that and the motivation had died with Nell. Her confession would take another form and maybe change things for the better, just a little.

This was comeuppance time, right now, but not just for her, it was also the moment of reckoning for Mr Jerome Reed.

She'd double checked and triple checked, considered and reconsidered, but Jerome Reed wasn't family. She was ready for a fight and surprisingly less afraid than she thought she would be; after all, what could he do to her that nature wasn't already doing to her, only slowly and tortuously? Besides, she would take him by surprise; he wouldn't be fearful of an old biddy; who would be?

She picked up the telephone and dialled.

"Hello?"

A gruff, rough and tired voice.

Maggie said nothing, just hung up. He was in, that was all she needed to know.

She packed the papers into a battered school briefcase, the very one she'd used in 1925 when she was eight years old to go to her school on Millfields Road - it seemed fitting to close the circle like that. She opened a drawer, hesitated, took out a smallish brown package and slipped it into the bag, checked her watch, then put on a coat and shoes, studying herself in the mirror to make sure she was presentable, then called a taxi.

"Where to, my dear?" the driver asked when he arrived.

Maggie took out a slip of paper with an address in Richmond Road.

"Here," she said, "and step on it. Five pounds is the limit. Don't go around the houses trying to fiddle me, understand?"

"Wouldn't dream of it," he answered

It wasn't far, but there was time enough for Maggie to consider many things, particularly the rights and wrongs of what she was about to do. Nothing changed her mind. She felt quite comfortable; this was the right thing to do.

She gave the driver five pounds ... and a hundred pounds tip.

"Treat yourself," she said, "you're a nice man."

He stared at the money as if it might fade away, asked her if she was sure, then drove off, delighted.

Maggie checked the door number and rang the bell. Her hearing was still good and she could make out the sound of a television inside. Jerome opened the door and looked at her as if she were a ghost.

"What the devil are you doing here, granny?"

"Nice to see you too, Jerome. Can I come in?" she said, stepping inside.

The room was much the same as it had been a year before when Inspectors Faraday and Fowler had come calling. This time the television set was on and Maggie said, "Very nice. Better than mine. Rubbish programmes, though, don't you think?"

"Not all. What are you doing here, granny? I thought you didn't want to see me."

"I don't."

"Then..."

"Oh, do turn the set off, will you. We need to talk."

"I was watching football, granny. Is this really important?"

Maggie thought for a moment, then reached inside her bag, took out the package wrapped in brown paper, undid it and revealed a rather splendid old fashioned gun. She aimed it at the television and pulled the trigger. The Bang and Olufsen exploded and, after a few moments, all was quiet.

"There," said Maggie, "that's better. Sit yourself down, Jerome. I will," and she sat down aiming the gun at Jerome who stood stock still, frozen to the spot.

"You shot my television!" he whispered.

"And I'll shoot you too, you cheating little bastard," said Maggie, "now sit and talk."

Jerome sat opposite Maggie, his eyes on the gun which seemed to rest remarkably comfortably in her wrinkled hands.

"You're mad," he said.

"Sane as sane can be," said Maggie. "I've been doing some homework, dear boy," she said. Jerome tried to look at her, but he couldn't take his eyes off the gun. This was some kind of nightmare; he'd overdosed on drugs and was hallucinating. There had to be an explanation, but then again, the Bang and Olufsen was definitely smoking and the old witch had definitely blasted it. "About you."

"About me?"

"Yes, and me – us – our family, or should I say, *my* family."

"I don't understand, granny."

"Okay," said Maggie, playing with the gun, "let me explain. I wasn't born ninety-two years old, I've had a life and that life is all done now.

Many things have happened, good and bad, beautiful and terrible, but the most terrible was the death of my Little Nell."

"Who?"

"Kathryn Hudson, you idiot. Now, in these final moments of my life, I need to clear up two points, and you are going to clear them up for me. Understood?" He nodded, still staring at the gun, afraid she would pull the trigger more by accident than intention. He was sweating and deathly pale. "I must warn you," said Maggie, "that if you lie, I'll know, and I'll shoot you without warning. Do you understand?" He nodded again. "Good. Well, first, are you or are you not a member of my family?"

Jerome's mind worked at lightning speed. Something had happened to his "granny". She'd changed, more than anyone of that age was supposed to change. If she was asking him such a question, she must know the answer, and if he lied she might well blow his brains out, but if he told the truth she might do the same thing anyway.

"No," he said, "sorry."

He closed his eyes, waiting for another explosion, but nothing happened.

"Good boy," said Maggie. "The homework I've been doing was very interesting, mostly because you never showed your ugly face anywhere. I've been a foolish and fond old woman, Jerome. I let my guard slip, but what happened to Little Nell woke me up. And do you know why?" He didn't. "Because, at the end of my life, she was the most beautiful thing that ever happened to me. Can you believe that? After ninety years of nonsense, I suddenly meet an angel, and she convinced me that maybe the world isn't altogether a nasty, brutish place. There is, I think, the chance of salvation for us all. What do you think of that?"

Jerome still thought she was mad, bad and dangerous, but he said, "Yes, gran... I mean...Mrs Hargreaves."

"You're agreeing because I've got this gun pointing at your empty head," she said. "I doubt whether you'd agree if I packed it away, but nevertheless, think about it as I ask you the next, and most important question. Did you or did you not kill my Little Nell?"

This time, Jerome didn't have to think at all.

"I did NOT!" he said. "You know I didn't! Jesus!"

Maggie studied the man, then said, "Inspector Faraday came to see me the day after she was killed. He asked about you because, as we both know, you pestered her."

"I did not ..."

"Shut up and listen," said Maggie, waving the gun in front of him. "You liked her, which is all very well, but you stalked her..."

"I did NOT!" There was another heart ripping crack as the gun went off and a mirror on the wall fractured. "For fuck's sake, granny!"

"Language Jerome. Right, I am going to ask you once again, did you kill Little Nell?"

"No! NO! What do you want me to say, granny...Mrs Hargreaves? I didn't do it. I didn't do it! I'm not a murderer, unlike you!"

"Careful," said Maggie. "Well, you're doing alright so far. I think I know you a bit better now, Jerome. You're a con man and a bully and a coward, but perhaps you didn't kill the poor girl."

"I told you I didn't," he said, "now will you please put that gun away. Where did you get it from anyway?"

Maggie looked at the gun, then said, "I'll tell you, as it doesn't matter now. I got it about ... hmm, let me see ... sixty eight years ago, during the war. I used it to kill my husband."

Jerome stared at the old woman, trying to take this in.

"You didn't," he said.

"Allow me to know just a little more than you in this respect," said Maggie.

"Why? When? How?" Jerome asked.

"Why? Because he was a two-timing, cheating scoundrel and a bully, like you. He hit me and he hurt me so I killed him. When? 1940, during The Blitz – you've heard of The Blitz, have you?" He had. "And how did I do it? Well, that's obvious, isn't it? I shot him, one bullet in the head. Then I burned his body. Bombs were dropping all around so no one noticed."

"Jesus!" whispered Jerome again, mortally afraid now.

"Jesus has had nothing to do with my life," said Maggie, "unless sending Nell to me was his one good idea." Jerome noticed that Maggie wasn't exactly crying, but her eyes were very bright. "I've thought about him at times," she said, "my husband, not Jesus, but I never felt sorry for what I did. The world was well rid of him. There are shits like him all over the place, and you're just like him." Jerome was going to say something but Maggie aimed the gun at him and he sat back in terror. "However, there's still time to change," she said.

"Yes," he said, "I can...."

"Oh leave off!" shouted Maggie. "You'll say anything to stop me shooting you, but the best thing you can do is hold your tongue. If you don't cotton on to what I'm going to say I really will blast you out of this smart little bachelor pad. Got it?" He got it. "Listen," she said, "I know the world is a bad place, I know how tough it is and how hard it is, but even so, there's a place for goodness."

Jerome thought of saying 'I can be good,' but he kept shtum. He was actually listening.

"I don't believe you killed her," said Maggie. "Little Nell, Kathryn Hudson. If I did, your brains would be decorating the walls by now. But I know what you are, and I want to do you a favour."

Jerome thought the favour might mean shooting him dead, but this wasn't what Maggie had in mind. She pointed to her schoolbag and said, "This is the same schoolbag I used when I went to school, not far from here, almost a hundred years ago, Jerome. Inside it I have two confessions and a will."

Jerome was puzzled, but he carried on sitting, staring at the old woman and the gun.

"In the first confession I tell nice Inspector Faraday what happened to my husband, just to get it off my chest you see, leave no loose ends when I go. And in the will, I'm leaving you my house and my all my money."

Jerome thought he was hearing things, or that the nutjob opposite had already shot him and this was some crazy afterlife experience.

"You what?" he asked.

"Don't be slow," said Maggie. "I'm leaving you what you tried to take from me by lies. It's what you wanted, isn't it?"

"Well..."

"For heaven's sake, boy, is it or isn't it?"

"Yes, but..."

"Listen, Jerome," said Maggie, "there's still time to change my mind. If you dither and convince me you're a complete loss, then I'll shoot you, got it?"

"Yes. Got it, got it!"

"There's a condition," said Maggie, "and that condition is, you change your ways. I know a leopard can never completely change its spots, but you can camouflage yours a little. My house is worth about three hundred thousand pounds and I have about the same amount put away, that's over half a million. It's all yours if you promise to do good with it. Now, shut up before you answer and listen. When you speak, I'll know if you're telling me the truth or not. If I think you're buttering me up, I'll kill you without another word. If you're not sure you can change, then say no, you don't want it, but if you think you can do better than con old women, then say yes, and mean it, and it's yours."

Jerome Reed was in torment. He was not a man of good character and he doubted he could change, yet he wanted that wealth, very, very much! However, was he brave enough to lie and risk being blown to kingdom come to get it?

"I see you're in doubt as to what to say," said Maggie, "and that's good. If you'd popped out with certainties I would have killed you. What I suggest is that you never forget Little Nell. I don't mean just stick her in the back of your mind, but remember what she was and let her guide you, just as she's been guiding me. Can you do that?"

"I don't know, Maggie, I really don't know..."

"No," Maggie said, a little more reassuringly, "it isn't easy, is it? Good people like that are rare, but it would be criminal to let everything that she was die with her, so maybe she can touch you and change you, even in a tiny way. What do you think?"

Jerome thought hard before saying, "Mrs Hargreaves, I can't accept this. I want what you've offered, I mean who wouldn't, but if I say I'll change, you'll pop me, I know you will. I think the best thing is for you take your will and your confession and rethink it, give it to someone better than me."

"That won't be hard," she said.

"No, it probably won't," said Jerome, "but I'm not going to take the risk. Sorry."

Maggie was quiet for a while, then smiled and said, "Nothing to be sorry about. All will be well. Now, as I said, I have a second confession."

"Two?"

"Yes, two. The second one is for what I'm about to do."

Jerome panicked again. He tensed up, thinking that he was going to be shot, but Maggie gently laid the bag down on the floor, a little way away and said, "Ninety-two is old enough. If you get there, Jerome Reed, you'll know what I mean. I've seen too much, and seeing what happened to my Little Nell told me that I didn't want to see any more. This is a cruel world, Jerome, but amidst all the cruelty there are better things, and she was the best of all. I'll never forget the time she gave me, the kindness and the laughter, and she wanted nothing, do you hear, nothing at all. Isn't that astonishing? Can you imagine, giving all that to someone and not wanting anything back? Well, it was true, and some sick dickhead fucker kills her. It wasn't...?"

"NO!"

"Alright, alright, I believe you. So now, everything's in order. If you misbehave with what I've left you, be it on your head, though I may come back and haunt you, Jerome Reed."

"Come back from where?" he asked. "You're in pretty good shape," he said.

"Not for long," said Maggie. "Goodbye, Mr Reed."

Jerome tensed again, afraid she was going to fire the gun.

And she did, only it wasn't his head that exploded, it was hers.

## 3

Lori Ellerman had gone to school and been friends with Kathryn Hudson, but like most children, they'd lost contact after primary school. It was only by chance, when Lori, now a teacher, had come to see one of her pupils, William Orlich, in hospital, that she'd met Kathryn again. At first they'd glanced at each other, then they'd looked a bit harder, then Kathryn had said, "Lori?" and Lori had said "Kathryn?" and then they almost screamed, but being a hospital ward they controlled themselves, at least for two minutes until Kathryn took Lori into the staff room where they laughed at how small the world was and started to catch up. When the excitement had faded, Lori told Kathryn why she was there.

"I'm worried about William," she said. Kathryn told her that William would be fine. "Here, yes," said Lori, "but I'm worried about him at home."

Kathryn was quick to catch on. She'd not taken to Ivan Orlich but was as professional as possible with him. It hadn't occurred to her that he might have hit William but this was what Lori Ellerman feared. She promised to keep an eye on him and they also promised each other to meet again, but before they could, Kathryn was gone.

When Lori found out about the murder, reading it in the local paper, her reaction was, like all those who knew Kathryn, a mixture of shock and disbelief. At the same time, she also found out that a colleague, Elena Imrie, was Kathryn's flatmate and friend. They hadn't spoken much till then, but afterwards they spent more time together, not just in the staff room but out and about in the wine bars of Hackney and the city, as much for support as for friendship.

By the time Lori met Ursula and Jasmine, the three friends had moved into a place on Spring Hill, not far away, but somewhere different where they didn't have Kathryn's empty room disturbing them each day; the new surroundings were a temporary relief. There was an amiable rapport when Lori met them, but they were all peculiarly aware that the vacuum left by Kathryn had changed the group dynamics. This made Lori a little uncomfortable, as if it was her impossible role to fill Kathryn's shoes, but she was easy company, especially for Elena who found a kindred spirit, even if she didn't like rowing.

They swapped endless stories about Kathryn and Lori told them what they didn't know, about when they were at primary school together. All the time they were trying to get the better of the devil which had settled on their shoulders. They thought the creature would hound them forever, but as the anniversary approached it seemed to get tired and left them occasionally and they started to feel a little like their old selves, even though they knew their true old selves had gone forever.

All four were sitting together one night in a bar on Mare Street. Ursula, Jasmine and Elena had never gone back to the one they'd been in the night Kathryn died, thinking that the place brought them bad luck. This one was okay, with quiet corners where they could talk. They hadn't spoken about the murder for a while, but sometimes, no matter what they'd been talking about before, the blues would roll over them.

They were all feeling reasonably okay and chatting about this and that when Lori stopped in mid-sentence, staring at a group of men a few tables away. The others followed her stare, but Lori was ducking down, trying not to be seen.

"I know that man," she said.

"A man!" said Ursula. "She knows a man! Tell us!"

"No," said Lori, "it's not that kind of man. It's to do with ... well, you know."

They knew, and they listened.

"Who is it?" asked Elena.

"It's William's father," said Lori, "William Orlich? The boy in my class who was in hospital."

She nodded towards the table and Elena saw a face she vaguely recognised. The man wasn't aware of them looking. He was deep in drink and looked in a foul temper. Two empty beer glasses sat on the table in front of him.

"That's weird," said Lori.

"What is?" asked Elena.

"Seeing him. That was how I met Kathryn again, when I went to see Will. I'd never have known she was there otherwise. And when I did see her, I told her I was worried about Will."

"Why?" asked Elena. "He wasn't seriously ill and they were looking after him. He's been back at school for ages now."

"I know," said Lori, "but I'd seen some bruises on him and I thought..."

"You think he hit him?" suggested Elena, shocked.

"I did. Kath didn't, but she was always upbeat and positive about people."

"You don't have to speak to him, Lori," said Ursula. "Just ignore him. He's never bothered you, has he?"

"No, not directly, but I know the Head has spoken to social services. He's got a criminal record, but that's in confidence, I'm not supposed to say anything about that to anyone."

"We won't tell," said Ursula, and then added with a whispered sneer at Orlich, "Creep!"

They all looked daggers at him and their fiery gaze somehow burned into his consciousness as he turned their way.

"It's alright, Lori," said Elena, "he didn't see you. You're not thinking what I'm thinking you're thinking, are you?"

"Probably," said Lori.

"Hey, you two," said Ursula, "don't mind read each other, tell us."

Lori was reluctant to say what had popped into her head, but Elena wasn't.

"She thinks he might be the one," she said, "isn't that right, Lori?"

"The one who...", Jasmine began, then said, "oh, right. God!"

It startled them to think they might be looking at the murderer.

"But surely the police would have spoken to him, wouldn't they?" said Ursula.

"Probably," said Lori, "but that doesn't mean he didn't do it."

It was true. Whoever killed Kathryn was still out there. He hadn't struck again, but he might, and even if he didn't, the thought that he remained free was anathema.

"What's his name again?" Ursula asked.

"Ivan," whispered Lori. "Ivan Orlich."

"Only I remember in the investigation," said Ursula, "they said something about Kath trying to make out a letter in her ... oh God, I hate to think of it!"

"It was the letter 'J'," said Jasmine. "I would remember that, wouldn't I?"

"Well then, it can't be him," said Lori.

"It could," said Elena. "Kath might have been trying to write 'I'; they're not that different, are they?"

If looks could have killed, Orlich would have been dead four times over. Even one glance from Elena would have done the trick.

"What do we do, then?" said Jasmine. "Do we tell the police?"

"Tell them what?" said Ursula, "and what would they do? They haven't done anything so far."

"Come on," said Elena, "let's get out before he sees Lori."

She hurried away, closely followed by the others, double checking to make sure Orlich wasn't watching them – he was still drinking and seemed unaware of much else.

Over the next few weeks, they couldn't get the idea out of their heads that Ivan Orlich was the killer, and even if he wasn't, he'd hurt his own son, and that even if he hadn't done that, he had a criminal record which meant he was basically bad. As sane and sensible as they were, they seemed to forget all logic and became judge, jury and executioner.

"Did you bring it?" asked Ursula.

They were sitting around a glass topped coffee table in their lounge. Lori was visiting but looking unsure of herself. She said, "I did," and poked around her bag, taking out a notepad which she opened and showed the others, saying, "If school gets to hear of this, my career goes down the pan. You know that, Elena."

On the first page of the pad was Ivan Orlich's home address. This wasn't top secret information but Lori had taken it from school records. What was more, they intended to use it to persecute the man until he owned up. They couldn't let Orlich live his violent life without letting him know that someone, somewhere knew.

Elena took out a box in which she'd cut out a range of letters from various newspapers. It was a  primary school teacher thing to make collages, so Elena felt comfortable enough doing this, even though what she was about to do was hardly national curriculum.

Wearing thin rubber gloves, Elena took the letters one at a time from the box and glued them to an A4 piece of paper, watched by the others. They did it all in a whisper as if they might be overheard, sometimes laughing in between words, but the laughter must have been brought on by nerves because what the letters spelt out wasn't particularly funny. It read,

"wE know WhAt YOuvE done. tEIL thE PoLicE nOW Or yOu'll be in tRouble."

When it was done, they looked at it with a mixture of satisfaction and dread.

"Are we really going to send it?" said Jasmine. "I mean, it's a bit criminal, isn't it?"

"It's totally criminal," said Elena who seemed, oddly, to find the whole thing more exciting than any of the others. They stared at the paper spread before them on the glass topped table as if it wasn't real.

"This is crazy," said Ursula.

"Mad," said Jasmine.

"What else can we do?" said Elena. "If we scare him, maybe he really will go to the police, and if he doesn't, they'll never trace this. We owe Kath something. It's been a year, nothing has happened. What can we lose?"

"Well, our home, our reputation, our jobs, our lives, apart from that, not much," said Jasmine.

The paper lay there, the focus of their attention, harmless enough for the time being, but if it was posted it would make a commotion. All they had to do was fold it, slip it in an envelope, post it and wait. That was all. And yet, it was an unexpectedly a major step to take. It was like lighting the touchpaper of a firework, or worse, setting off the detonator of some nasty explosive. And all it needed was the most innocuous action.

"Let's think about this girls," said Ursula, "you know me, I'm not a wimp, but I'm not sure this is the right thing, really. What would Kath want us to do?"

"I'm not Kathryn," said Elena, "I'm me. She was my friend and if things were the other way around, I wouldn't want her walking the streets with a killer on the loose. And I wouldn't want to think my friends weren't doing anything. A year, girls, a whole year and we've done nothing! This is such a small thing; let's just do it."

There was silence, though they could almost hear each other think.

"I've never known you like this before, El," said Jasmine. "You're normally the docile one."

"Thanks. I'll ignore that."

"What she means," said Ursula, "is that you don't normally push for us to break the law like this."

"This isn't a normal situation," said Elena, "is it? And I resent being called docile."

"Sorry," said Jasmine, "but you aren't the same as usual."

"Good," said Elena. "This man is a menace and he deserves a fright. We should give it to him."

They looked at Elena, normally the sane and stable one who was now prime motivator for breaking the law. She was red faced and angry and her eyes were shiny. They all felt rather nervous of her and felt sorry for the children in her class if she was often in this mood.

"What do you think, Lori?" Ursula asked.

This put Lori in an awkward position, if she wasn't already in one. She felt responsible for getting them into this predicament and she was still the outsider, aware of upsetting the balance that held the group together. She worked with Elena and didn't want to sour what was a friendly relationship, but on the other hand, she didn't want to end up in prison.

"Don't put me on the spot," she said.

"We are on the spot, Lori," said Elena, unrelenting. "Do we send it or not?"

"I can't decide that," said Lori, "maybe we should vote on it."

They agreed, but as expected the votes were three to one against, Elena being the one in favour. She looked remarkably fed up.

"Come on, El, it wasn't a good idea," said Ursula. "We'd get into trouble."

"That wasn't the point," said Elena. "The point was to tackle this beast who probably killed our friend and hits children."

"We don't know that," said Lori, gently, "I mean Kath never said anything definite to me."

Nothing seemed to placate Elena who screwed up the letter and threw it into a bin.

Early the next morning, unable to sleep, she crept downstairs and made herself a cup of tea, pacing round the kitchen. Her head was in a spin and she wasn't thinking clearly. She was a teacher because she believed strongly in right and wrong, and when these were muddled she wanted to unmuddle them. She was the quietest of the three flatmates but the deepest, and she felt the injustice of the murderer evading the law more personally than the others. It grated on her, and she desperately needed to do something. Being a teacher, she also liked to get her own way, and though the vote was fair, it annoyed her that her friends were prepared to sit and do nothing.

In a fit of pique, she retrieved the letter, smoothed it out and stared at it for a while, but not long enough to doubt what she wanted to do. She went to her room, took an envelope and prepared an address label – Lori had taken the address but Elena remembered it. She stamped it, slipped on jeans and a jacket over her pyjamas and took it to the post box at the end of the street. She hesitated, but only for a few seconds; she didn't want to be seen there by anyone, especially at three in the morning, but looked around and was sure the coast was clear. The girls would never know what she'd done, after all, she wouldn't tell them and the incompetent police would never find out. The worst that could happen would be that Ivan Orlich realised someone was on his case and held back from doing anything else, but the best was that he would own up – in her naivety, Elena really believed this.

She posted it and then, blushing in the dark, hurried home, head down, hands in pockets, fighting an annoying sense of guilt and shame.

## 4

They sat near Bomb Crater Pond on the Walthamstow Marshes. It was a warm April Day so they'd decided to abandon college for the afternoon and take some quality time together. Bomb Crater Pond was exactly what it said on the tin, though the marshes weren't exactly marshes and the Walthamstow tag was confusing being so close to the more famous Hackney Marshes. The green areas appeared to merge here but were so extensive that they shared their part of the world quite amicably and gave the borough a surprising sense of space.

Sam lay with his head on Feriha's lap. She played with his eyebrows and ruffled his thick, dark hair. They'd kissed a few weeks before, in an amusement arcade of all places, whilst Sam was on a winning streak. They were aware that flirting had changed to something deeper, and so had Jemal who was a bit shell shocked by the revelation. Sam was supposed to be *his* friend and they were supposed to be computer geeks against the world. Jemal knew that Feriha flirted with Sam, but she flirted with anyone in trousers, which didn't mean that she had to kiss them all. He felt a bit cut off from the two of them, and was finding this hard to handle, which was why he often telephoned either his sister or Sam to make sure they were "okay", in other words not having babies together. He couldn't face that and neither would his mum or dad. This didn't seem to bother Sam or Feriha who seemed pretty happy in each other's company.

"How's your mum doing?" asked Feriha. "Is she talking to you?"

"Just," said Sam. "It isn't easy."

"Not for me either," said Feriha. "Parents, eh?"

Sam smiled. He was actually smiling quite a bit more than he used to do, despite having the whole community on his back. Any ethnic minority has to fight to hold itself together and often reacts badly when children look like being lost to the fold. Both Sam and Feriha appeared to be going astray; the pull of the modern world was greater than the gravity of the old.

"They'll have to deal with it," said Sam. "How about yours?"

"They'll probably lock me in a cupboard without food or water for a year then take me out when they've found a suitable boy."

Sam lifted his arm and stroked Feriha's hair.

"Aren't I a suitable boy?" he asked.

"You are, for me," she said. "Am I a suitable girl?" she asked.

"You are for me," Sam answered.

Although Sam was outwardly cavalier towards his parents, he hated hurting them. It troubled him whenever he felt he upset them, but he didn't see what choice he had. He felt an unstoppable force drawing him towards Feriha. All he could think about was her, and when he was with her the rest of the world and all its worries vanished. Feriha leaned over and kissed him.

"What are we going to do?" she asked.

"Stay here," he said. "I'll buy a tent, we can camp here forever."

"Nice idea," she said, "but a bit cold in winter."

"We can keep each other warm," he said. Her eyes held him, so deep, so dark, so different from anything he'd ever seen or imagined. It was weird to defy everything he'd ever been taught was important for this girl who hypnotized him. It made no sense, three thousand years of history, five if you took things literally, a whole world of pressure to conform, to believe, to follow, to be what there was no question you had to be, all thrown away for this enchantress who had stolen his heart. She stroked his head and said, "You're very brave, Sam."

"Am I? Why is that?"

"Well, going against everyone, for me. They must hate me."

"Probably. But I love you, so it doesn't matter."

She kissed him again, then asked, "Do you really?" He nodded. "How do you know?" she asked.

"I don't know how I know, I just know."

"But supposing you don't love me tomorrow; what if you wake up tomorrow and you realise I'm a witch and I've put a spell on you?"

"You *have* put a spell on me."

"No, seriously, what if it all gets too much, our parents and your Jewish stuff."

"My Jewish 'stuff'," he said. "I'll handle it."

"Will you? It might be harder than you think."

"Trust me," Sam repeated. "What about you?"

"Don't think they're too fussed," she said, "they think I'm just a kid."

Sam sat up and they kissed until time seemed to stand still around them. It was only Feriha's mobile ringing that broke the magic.

"It's Jemal," she said.

"Don't answer it," said Sam, feeling a touch guilty for saying it.

"I have to," Feriha answered, "he's my pesky brother. If it wasn't for him we wouldn't be here now."

Sam couldn't help but listen as Feriha spoke to Jemal, or rather as she lied to him. She didn't tell Jemal where they were, only that they were together somewhere. Sam felt the pressure and the uncertainty from Jemal who was supposed to be his friend, but friends and family were all topsy-turvy at the moment; no one gave him what he needed except Feriha and no one gave them what they needed, full stop. They were alone against the world, which was oddly exciting. Sam had never felt so grown up. He wondered how long he'd be able to stay at home, before his mum and dad did what other parents in the community had done and cut off their children. It happened, he knew it did, and though he didn't want it to happen to him, he didn't care, so long as Feriha was with him. He looked at her talking on the phone and wondered how he could ever have seen her as the silly sister of his best friend. Now she was his best friend, and much more besides, but Sam couldn't find a name for what she had become. She was everything. Her beauty stunned him and her voice entranced him. When she moved, every movement fascinated him. And when he touched her his whole body came alive. He was so happy when he was with her, happier than he ever thought possible, locked away in his peculiar life, full of expectations and planned pathways. When he was with her he felt a joy that no religious experience had ever brought him. He truly didn't know if it was right or wrong, whether he was being led astray or not; all he knew was that he adored her. When they parted he felt dismal and depressed; when he saw her again his life lit up and all was well.

He listened to her on the phone; even that made his heart beat faster. When she'd finished, he looked at her enquiringly and she said, "Don't worry, he doesn't hate you, not that much anyway," and she laughed. "He'll get over it," she said, then added, "he's more interested in our auntie."

"Which auntie is that?" Sam asked, letting Feriha's hair drift in between his fingers, like some dark, magical, wonderful liquid.

"The one that came out," said Feriha with a touch of mischief.

"Out where."

"Of the closet."

"Which closet was that?"

Feriha laughed and said, "Are you being thick or have you really forgotten?"

"I'm being thick," said Sam with a straight face. "I don't suppose it's the same auntie that likes other aunties?"

"Other women, yes," said Feriha with her own enigmatic expression.

"Is Jemal alright about it?" Sam asked.

"Why shouldn't he be?" said Feriha.

"No reason. How about you?"

"Why shouldn't I be? How about you, Mr StraightDownTheMiddle, are you alright about it?"

"She's not my aunt," he said, "but I would be, if she was. Why not?"

Feriha made herself comfortable lying down with her head on Sam's stomach, looking up at the sky.

"No reason, but it was still a bit of a shock. I wondered why she never got married."

"That wouldn't make her gay."

"No, but there was always something different about her. Poor old Auntie Nurcan, she must have been so wound up."

"What about?"

"Come on, Sam, wake up! Wound up about sex, what else? All those years she was locked away inside herself, blimey, that would drive me crazy. I don't know how she didn't go nuts. She must have fancied so many women and couldn't do anything about it."

"She could have, if she wanted. Why didn't she?"

Feriha turned her head slightly and tickled Sam's nose with a piece of grass, saying, "Coming from you, that's a laugh. Because she couldn't. I mean, if it wasn't for me, you'd probably have locked yourself away, too."

"I'm not gay."

"No, dummy, in your religion. Aunt Nurcan was always a bit distant; I never really talked to her. I thought she was a bit off sometimes, but really she was just screwed up. She's much better now. She was nervous when she knew I knew, really nervous. I could see it in her face. I thought she was going to cry again."

"Again?"

"Yeh, you know, the night the nurse was killed. In fact, I'll tell you what I think if you promise not to tell anyone."

"I'll tell everyone," said Sam, and Feriha tweaked his nose.

"I think my auntie had a crush on that nurse. I do. Just like you."

"I didn't."

"Yes you did. I wouldn't blame you, she was lovely, wasn't she? But the way Aunt Nurcan came to our house and cried that night, I thought it was a bit odd at the time, and maybe it was just shock, but I bet it was something more."

"You think they were having a thing together?"

"No! Come on, Sam, wakey wakey! Auntie kept it all secret, from everyone. That must have hurt. I couldn't do it. If I like someone, I let them know."

"I noticed," said Sam.

"Well there's no point in beating around the bush, is there?" Feriha said. "waste of time. I remember we did Jane Austen at school – did

271

you?" Sam hadn't even heard of her. He'd gone to a religious school and Jane Austen hadn't reached him. "Well, every woman in her book plays this long winded game with men. I only read one book, but all the women were the same, kept everything locked up inside them."

"Were they gay, too?" Sam asked.

"No, Sam, they weren't gay! You really ought to read more, now you're not so Jewish anymore."

"I'm still Jewish," he said.

"Yes, but not so much. Anyway, they weren't gay, but they go round the houses with what they want. Takes them forever to land a bloke."

"Well," said Sam thoughtfully, "if they got their bloke straight away, there wouldn't be a book, would there?"

"True," said Feriha, "but my auntie wasn't writing a book and she's not in a book. This was her life. Do you know how old she is? Forty one! Sam, can you imagine that, forty-one, and she was in love with women the whole time and didn't do a thing about it!"

"So what happened?" said Sam.

"She met someone," said Feriha. "I'm glad. I know it's a shock, my auntie turning out all weird, but she's happy, so that can't be bad, can it? You approve, don't you, Sam?"

Sam wasn't sure if he approved or not, but even if he didn't he wouldn't have argued with Feriha about it. He was having a tough enough time coming to terms with his own life, let alone condemning someone else's way of dealing with theirs, and from what he gathered from Feriha, this auntie wasn't someone you'd argue with.

"So you think she might have liked that nurse, the one who was killed, then?"

"I do, but I'll never know. I can't ask her, can I?"

"Why not? She might like to tell you."

Feriha thought about this. Her aunt made her a bit nervous now because she wasn't the auntie Feriha had known since being a girl. It was alright people being whatever they wanted if you didn't already have them in your head as something different, but once they were in your head, it was hard to shift the image of what they were then to what they were now. But still, if the chance came, Feriha might ask her. She trusted her auntie a lot, and if she really had liked that nurse, God, she must have been devastated.

"I'll see," she said. "Sam?"

"Hmm?" Sam was looking up at the sky, feeling Feriha's head on his tummy, rising and falling gently as he breathed. It was unsettling to think that everything which made this diamond called Feriha was resting on his tummy, so small and fragile.

"Would you be upset if anything happened to me?"

He sat up, slowly, holding her head in his lap as she'd held his. "Course I would," he said. "Why?"

"I was thinking of auntie, if she really liked that nurse and she was killed, what my auntie must have felt."

"You're not going to get murdered, are you?" Sam asked.

"You shouldn't joke," said Feriha, "after all, he's still out there, whoever did it, the police haven't caught him yet. But suppose it did happen, what would you do?"

"I can't answer that!" he said. "Why do you have to talk about death?"

"Because it happens, and it's forever. Would you kill yourself if something happened to me?"

"Would you want me to?"

"You always do that," said Feriha, "answer a question with a question."

"Do I?"

"See? You did it again. All I want to know is how much you love me."

Sam thought, but he couldn't find the words, and he certainly couldn't imagine Feriha not being around. She was as firm as the Earth itself. It made no sense to think of a world without her.

"Well?" she asked again.

"I can't tell you that," he said. "There aren't the right words to say it."

Feriha laughed with delight and stroked his cheek saying, "Oh, Sam, that's the best answer you could give!"

"That's a relief," he said. "I tried to imagine it, I mean you being all dead and gone, but my mind won't let me. You're too real to be murdered."

Feriha hugged him and said, "You're a romantic, Sam. I knew you were, but it was locked away inside you. It would be horrible, though, wouldn't it, one of us being dead?"

"Suppose so. You're being morbid, Feri."

"I'm just trying to understand my auntie," she replied. "You know, I think I really will ask her. She might want to talk about it, like you said."

"Or she might not."

"Then she'll say so. I wonder if she was jealous."

"Of who?"

"Of the nurse's boyfriend of course. Who else?"

Sam felt a little unwanted discomfort here. He'd been a touch jealous himself, but that all seemed like a long time ago. He didn't want to talk about the dead nurse or anything to do with her; that was all someone else's world, not theirs, even though it had touched both his and Feriha's lives in different ways. He was about to say this and not answer the question when his own mobile rang. Thinking it was Jemal checking up on him he was going to switch it off, but when he checked the number he saw that it wasn't Jemal; it wasn't anyone he knew. Feriha watched him, amused.

"Not another girlfriend?" she asked.

He shook his head.

"Shall I answer?" he asked her.

"Don't mind me," said Feriha, kissing him, "you go ahead and talk to all the girls in your life."

Sam pressed the talk button, but when he spoke, Feriha sensed that he was becoming tense again. He just kept saying yes or no or maybe, so that when he hung up, Feriha didn't have a clue about who he was talking to or what had been said.

"Was that the Chief Rabbi," she asked, "checking up on you?"

"Not quite," he said. "It was the police."

Feriha sat up sharply, worried.

"You're not in trouble, are you Sam?"

"Yeh, I'm a secret drug dealer and gun runner. They want to know when it would be convenient to come and arrest me."

She slapped him gently and said, "You never take things seriously, Sam. What did they want, or is it private?"

"No, not private," said Sam, "but weird."

"You don't have to tell me," Feriha said, but she was dying to know.

Sam looked at her and said, "It was about the dead nurse."

"Seriously? They don't still think you did it, do they Sam?"

"I did do it," he said with a straight face. "I lied."

"Flip, Sam! You've got such a warped sense of humour!"

"Sorry," he said, playing with her hand, looking at it as if it was some precious jewel, which it was, so delicate, but warm and soft. "They want me to help them with their enquiries."

"Sam, that's bad! That's what they say when they want to arrest you."

"I know," he said, "but it isn't that. It was a policeman named Davis. He said he's found something on a computer and he wants me to help him trace where it came from."

Feriha looked suspicious.

"Something?" she asked.

"A video," Sam explained.

"That sounds a bit fishy to me, Sam. Are you sure he's a policeman?"

"He spoke like one."

"Did he? How was that then?"

"Dunno, but he did."

Feriha was suspicious. She asked him where they'd got his name from.

"This is the police, Feri, they know everyone and everything."

"But why don't they go to a proper company. Why you?"

Sam guessed there were reasons. He'd find out and tell her but Feriha wasn't happy.

"Sam, this doesn't feel right to me."

"The girl's worried!" he said, kissing her head and gently squeezing her fingers.

"I am!" she said, pulling her hand away. "You be careful Samuel. You're my one and only and I don't want anything happening to you."

"Really?" he said. "Am I your one and only?"

Feriha looked more serious than he'd ever seen her.

"You are," she said, and he saw how much she liked him.

"It's the police," he said. "I'll be safe as houses."

Feriha put her arms around him and said, "Samuel, if you really, really, really like me, you have to take special care of yourself." He said he would. "And you have to trust me." He said he did. "And I've got a weird feeling about that call."

"You want me to phone him back and say no? I will, if you tell me."

Feriha didn't want Sam to think she was a killjoy or a nag, not as they were getting on so well, so she eased up and said no, do what he wanted, just take care.

"Maybe you can come with me," he suggested.

"I hate computers," she answered.

"You can still come with, if you want."

"Let Jemal go, he'll be pleased. I'll let him have a bit of you, just not too much."

Sam lay back and Feriha knelt down beside him, looking intently into his eyes.

"It's still strange," she said, "being like this."

"But you like it?"

"You know I do."

"And you know I do."

Feriha brushed his hair back and smoothed his eyebrows.

"We mustn't let anyone muck it up," she said.

"Like?"

"Like anyone. My mum and dad. Your mum and dad. Jemal. Anyone. This isn't a teenage crush, is it Sam? I mean, it's the real thing, isn't it?"

"Now who's being romantic?"

"Say it is."

"Alright, it is."

Despite the flippant exterior, Feriha was a passionate girl with a fiery heart. She wondered if Sam really knew what she was about. It felt so special, even unique. Surely no one, ever, at any time in this history of the universe, had felt like this! She couldn't get him out of her mind and now she was suddenly worried about him and she couldn't say why. Maybe the talk about the dead nurse had freaked her, or the weird telephone call, but whatever the reason, she didn't want to let him out of her sight.

She lay down next to him and hugged him tight, tucking her head into his neck, getting as close to him as possible, Turk and Jew, Jew and Turk, it didn't matter; nothing mattered except they cared for each other and didn't let the stupid world get to them. She closed her eyes, felt the warmth of the sun and the warmth of his body and tried to throw off the fears which had seized her.

"You alright, Feri?" he asked. She didn't answer. "Feri?"

"I'm alright."

"You went quiet."

"I was thinking."

"What about?"

"About you, dummy."

He turned to face her, saw again the eyes that sucked him in, that showed him an infinite vision of longing and mystery. They held him, serious and still, until he smiled, but she didn't smile back. Instead, she raised her hand, opened it and stroked his lips with her forefinger, unable to shift the unease and the sense that someone, somehow was about to break them apart, maybe forever.

## 5

Hackney had many hearts, not just the human ones which beat to so many different rhythms, but physical ones, sprawling as it did over such a vast and varied landscape with geometries and structures recogniseable at any point, at least to the practised eye. Charlene Okoru knew every street and feature of this borough which she cared for with surprising zeal. Considering what she'd seen happen there, and what had happened to Matthew Davis, she ought to have had grave doubts about the place, but she lived and worked there and had much affection for it. Sitting in a Portuguese cafe on the Upper Clapton Road waiting for her ex-partner, she mused over all that she'd seen, heard and done there and wondered whether it was time to move on. The murder of Kathryn Hudson had been a blow, to innocence as much as to her faith in humanity. Unsolved, it was also a blot on the police crime books, not to mention the police conscience. They solved most of their cases and Detective Inspector Simon Faraday had expected to solve this case too, and quickly, but it hadn't been solved and the murder festered in all their minds like an open wound. If it wasn't for that, she wouldn't be sitting there now, waiting for Matt to show up.

When he'd been dismissed, she thought it best not to meet up with him socially, more for his sake than hers. He needed a new start and she didn't want him hanging on to her, remembering the good old days. They were both young and hopefully had a lot of good old days ahead of them, even though Matt had made a pig's ear of his life so far. He'd called her saying he needed her help and that it was to do with the murder, but he wouldn't say more. She was tempted not to turn up in case he just wanted an excuse to meet, but she was there anyway.

The Portuguese restaurant was quite typical of the untypical eateries of Hackney. Cosmopolitan wasn't the word; indeed there was no word for the astonishing range of nations offering ethnic food from the most distant points on the globe. This one was relatively new having replaced a Jewish fish shop that had stood on the site for well over fifty years. Such was the nature of this borough where little gems were to be found in the most obscure spots. It was well decked out in the reds and greens of Portugal, decorated with pictures of the Portuguese football team, very clean and very relaxed.

Charlene, however, wasn't particularly relaxed. Doubts entered her mind as to why she was there and what Matt wanted. She was on duty soon and would have to leave, but she might get up and go sooner rather than later if he didn't turn up.

But he did.

He arrived rough shaven and looking a pale shadow of the confident man he'd once been.

"You look a mess, Matt," she said.

"I'm not my best, am I? Thanks for coming."

He sat down and ordered an espresso.

"I've been saving up," he said.

"My treat," Charlene replied, and he accepted. She felt sorry for him, despite all he'd done. She wasn't so hard hearted as to judge him without compassion, but she'd warned and him and he hadn't listened. She wished he had, for all their sakes. She didn't know what he was doing now or how he was providing for Eileen and the children, if at all, but part of her didn't want to know. This was history, or at best a present that was no longer her business. She watched him sip the coffee and felt both pity and irritation. He'd been such a fool, and what was more, he'd lied to everyone who cared for him. He'd lied to his wife, to his children and to her. And with her, he'd had the gall to interview the very woman he'd been seeing and not say a word! She still couldn't believe it, but she should have guessed. Looking back, there was a definite 'something' in the room that day. When Cassie Logan had been arrested for soliciting and Matt had been incriminated, Charlene had to reconsider so much of her time with him, and this one incident astonished and angered her more than any other. She thought she wouldn't be able to forgive him, but here she was answering his plea for help. He sipped the coffee and stared at it, reflecting on past days.

"We were good together," he said. "Good coppers, I mean."

"I know what you mean, Matt. Yes, we were."

"How's your new partner?"

"Equally good."

This hurt him. He hoped she'd say he wasn't up to scratch and she wanted him back, but no, he was as unnecessary at work as he was at home. He seemed to have excommunicated himself from everyone and everything that meant anything.

"Why did you call me, Matt?"

"I need your help."

"You said so – about the murder?"

"Yes. I've got a lead. A bloody good one, Charlene."

"What is it?"

"Can't tell you, not yet. I need a tech guy to help me, someone not police."

"I don't know any tech guys 'not police'. I'm not going out on a limb for you, Matt. If you really have got a lead, you should tell Faraday."

"I will, I promise, but not yet. I've got to follow this up myself first, make sure it's legit."

"So how do you intend to do that?"

"Like I said, with your help."

"And what can I do, Matt?"

Charlene sounded peeved. Matt had let himself, his wife and family and the whole police force down. His story had been told in national as well as local papers, and although the newspaper reading public had short memories, his family, the Force and Charlene would never forget. They might even never forgive. He'd gone beyond the pale and now he was asking for help. Charlene doubted his motives.

"They'll never let you back in."

"They might," he said, "if the reason is big enough. They've let worse people back into the force. I'm not a bad person, Charlene."

Charlene shifted uncomfortably in her chair and sipped some coffee, giving herself time to think.

"What exactly do you want me to do?" she asked.

"I need a whizz kid, someone who knows computers inside out. This is a techie problem."

"And you're sure it's to do with the murder?"

"Believe me, Charlene, it is."

She thought for a moment then said, "How about Daniel Hart? He's got reason enough to help you."

Matt breathed out and shook his head.

"You know where he is, don't you? You think he'd leave all that stuff and open old wounds, just because I say 'please'."

Charlene knew where Daniel was and no, she doubted he would leave all that stuff and open old wounds; in this case Matt was right. She knew people in the force, but she daren't ask any of them; no one there would want to get involved with Matt Davis – it would be professional suicide.

"I know someone," said Matt. "Faraday interviewed him and we met him."

Charlene thought back and then said hesitantly, "The Levinson boy?"

"Bullseye," said Matt. "You could either ask him, or ..."

"Or what?"

"Get me the boy's number. No one would know. If it goes belly up, I'd say I had it from previous records. I wouldn't blame you, you know that. Never. He's a genius. He could do this, I know he could. Charlene, this is a way back for me, I feel it. I just need one small favour."

"There must be hundreds of computer anoraks who could help, Matt. Why not go to some local company?"

"Well, for a start I can't afford them; second, I can't trust them, not with this; and third, the boy liked Kathryn Hudson, remember? He'll be motivated and he'll keep it secret."

Charlene recalled the boy, a rebellious teenager, quite rare in the orthodox Jewish households of the borough. She'd read his notes, along with every other vaguely implicated suspect, knew he was bright but also that he was hard to handle.

"Let me think about it," she said.

Matt looked restless. He was so desperate to get the boy on board and track the images which had been haunting him for days. He was sitting on vital evidence, he knew that, and if Faraday found out, Matt would could be imprisoned – this was withholding evidence, a criminal offence. Charlene knew that, too.

"You know Matt, I think you've got the devil sitting on your shoulder," she said. He looked puzzled. "You just make wrong decisions. Some people do that, I've seen it again and again, but I don't understand why. They're bright, like you, and rational, like you, but they keep making the devil's decisions."

"This isn't the devil's anything, Charlene, this is right. It's my way back in."

"If what you've told me is true, you're sitting on vital evidence."

"It is true, and yes I am, so the sooner I hand it over the better, but not before I know exactly what it is. If I'm wrong, I'll look a fool, can't you see that?"

Yes, she could. "I'll think about it," she said again, and wouldn't talk about it anymore.

Charlene might not have been convinced, but she had a soft spot for Matt, despite everything he'd done and apparently planned to do. She met him the next day in the same place. It was almost a surprise to herself to see her hand over Samuel Levinson's mobile number. The condition was that she could hear the conversation and Matt was happy to oblige. He called the boy and Charlene listened, anxious and not at all sure she'd done the right thing. Perhaps the devil on Matt's shoulder had jumped on to hers. But the conversation was just as Matt had said, no games, no change of direction.

"Well?" she asked.

"He'll do it," said Matt. "I knew he would. There was someone with him, a girl, I heard her."

Charlene stared hard at Matt and said, "Promise me this isn't dangerous."

"I promise," he answered, and he meant it, she could tell, but whether he knew what he was promising, that she couldn't tell.

## 6

It had been tough for Melissa returning to Alexandra Ward, a combination of sadness and disbelief. People told her time would heal, and indeed it did heal, but not enough for her to be happy there. After three months she changed ward and three months after that she moved to another hospital. No one wanted her to go, and Belinda fought hard for her to stay, but the absence of her friend was too much to face each day.

"She'll be absent wherever you go," Belinda said. "You can't run away from what's happened."

"I can try," said Melissa.

Moving to the new hospital helped, and it would have helped more if Nurcan had moved there too, but the newly out-ed Nurcan Celik stayed put, unwilling to leave Homerton. She and Melissa had talked a lot after the funeral but Nurcan still behaved as if there was something left to tell. This puzzled Melissa who wondered what other revelation could follow the opening of closet doors. She kept in touch with Nurcan, but couldn't rid herself of the suspicion that Nurcan was hiding something. When, eventually, she told Patrick, he hit the spot in an uncanny way at the first attempt.

"You want to know what I think, Mel?" he said. "I think she probably loved Kathryn."

As soon as he said it a light switched on in Melissa's mind. She knew he was right. It suddenly all made sense, every smile, every word, every gesture Nurcan had ever made when Kathryn was around. She slapped herself for not seeing it and wanted to hug Nurcan who must have been in torment for years. 'Poor girl!' she whispered to herself.

She relied on Patrick more and more. They made love every day and called each other when they were apart as if they'd become acutely aware of the fragility of being. For a few months after the murder, at least until she moved jobs, everything had an ethereal quality, as if nothing was substantial, neither people nor places. Melissa felt as if she were walking on quicksand, that the Earth could swallow her up any moment, and for no reason. She had panic attacks when she could hardly breathe. She lost weight and confidence and much of her natural joy faded. Her energy levels were low, and though she threw herself into her new job, she was often tired and unhappy. Patrick suggested seeing a counsellor, but she didn't want to, not yet. As soon as the year passed, if she was still feeling unwell, she promised him that she'd go, but for the time being she wanted to try and cope in her own way.

Now the year was almost upon her, she still had frequent bouts of depression with little idea how to deal with them. The memory of that terrible night haunted her and often overwhelmed her. She was desperate to forget, but at the same time she tried hard to remember, caught in a struggle between sadness and survival, afraid that in a short while she'd remember Kathryn with a little nod of the head, a smile and nothing more, but she didn't know how to survive unless she allowed the shock and sadness to dissipate.

They'd made love early one Sunday morning, a few weeks before the first anniversary of Kathryn's killing. Each time they'd been together that year, Melissa had tried hard to lose herself, but that part of her which was still grieving refused to hide. She was painfully anxious, looking for a way out of the deepening gloom which threatened to engulf her. Patrick turned towards her, concerned that he wasn't any help. He was taken aback when Melissa suddenly sat bolt upright.

"Mel, are you okay?" Patrick asked. "Did I hurt you?"

"You never hurt me," she said gently. "I've had an idea."

"Share it?"

Normally, Melissa would have shared her thoughts with Patrick straight away, but this time she decided to keep it to herself. If she told him, he'd be worried and try to stop her. And the telling would lose some of the momentum that had started to build.

"Sweety, do you mind if I don't?" she said. "Not yet."

"Whatever's best for you love," he said.

Melissa hugged her knees to her chin, trying to hold on to the idea and not let it escape. She'd suddenly seen what was wrong, what was upsetting her. She'd known it all the time, but taken it for granted. Yes, Kathryn was gone, but the murder remained unsolved. She suddenly saw the injustice of this and how it was affecting her, a wound that had been allowed to fester. She assumed the police were working away, but nothing had happened, and the reason for her chronic depression was that she was doing nothing to repair the damage. Retribution, that was what was needed, good old fashioned eye for an eye. Something had sparked inside her, the need for action! Somewhere out there a killer walked free. This miserable, despicable human had taken the life of a very special person, and whilst everyone who'd known Kathryn struggled to come to terms with the loss, this fiend walked free and easy. It wasn't right, and Melissa felt a sudden, huge burst of anger.

"Mel, are you sure you're okay?" Patrick asked.

"Not completely, no," said Melissa. "Sorry, Pat, I'm still me."

She sat there, deep in thought, trying to focus the anger, making sure it didn't explode and die. She needed to channel it, to let it drive her. She could do this, she knew she could, if she put her heart into it she could do what Detective Inspector Faraday hadn't done, not yet and probably not ever. And even if she failed, it was action. What had been driving her to despair was not just loss, but the acceptance of wrong, the crime of omission. She wasn't that type of person. She had so much energy, but it had been turned inwards, eating itself with its own impotence.

Over the next few days she became increasingly distracted, sometimes frantic, sometimes intensely quiet. Patrick grew concerned for her, as if she were in danger of losing balance; she wasn't the Melissa he remembered.

The following Sunday she was so restless, they couldn't relax, not even after trying and failing for the first time to make love. In the evening, after a meal she barely touched, she said, "Pat, do you mind if I go out for a while, just to clear my head?"

Patrick had been, and still was, all accepting. He trusted her and never put obstacles in the way because of what he wanted rather than what Melissa needed, but this worried him.

"Now?" he asked, bemused.

"Yes, now."

"Can I come with?" he asked.

"Not now, sweetheart, sorry. I won't be long."

"I'll die of loneliness," said Patrick, touching her shoulder. He watched her anxiously, even when she kissed him goodbye. "Take care," he said.

She took a bus to Cambridge Heath, which was where she needed to go. She'd been thinking about this, and decided to start with the one man the investigation had forgotten, the mysterious witness named Robert. She'd never really talked to him so there might be something the police had overlooked, in fact she felt sure there was and that she could find it out. A tremendous excitement gripped her and all the depression suddenly lifted. She could do something, take matters into her own hands and get the investigation moving again. It was no good having a killer on the street. He could be there, standing at the bus stop with her. She might already have passed him a dozen times in the street that year. No wonder she was depressed! Her best friend had been killed and the police had done nothing, the murderer was still free. And it was not just her best friend who had died, it was Michael and, just a short while ago, Mrs Margaret Hargreaves had blown her brains out. The story had been all over the papers, local and national, but Melissa felt something different to the general morbid interest – she felt both sadness and despondency that the ripples from Kathryn's murder were still spreading.

She could end it. She'd never felt anything so certain as this. It was as if a light had clicked on in her head and she saw the way forward, talk to Robert, talk to all the people the police had spoken to and think this out herself. She was bright and she'd share it with Patrick who would help her. They'd end this madness and bring the murderer to justice!

A bus arrived, fairly full, but not overloaded for a Sunday evening. Melissa sat upstairs where there were fewer people and she could think more clearly. Upper decks let you sit above the world for a while, gave you a clearer perspective. Melissa had a chance to think through the questions she'd ask Robert, about what exactly he'd seen, whether he'd heard anything, whether he thought that he'd seen the killer since then and also what emotions he might have sensed, apart from fear. Melissa believed that if only she could get some kind of fix on what happened in that dreadful alleyway, she might be able to understand what went through Kathryn's mind, to see what made her go there at that time of night. She'd given this so much thought over the year, but neither the police nor she had an answer, and once again the anger rose inside her because the monster who had carried out the attack had not been punished.

She tried not to look around the bus – that was often a mistake, people being too easy to provoke – but she caught sight of them from the corner of her eye. She felt elated that she had such a special purpose whilst they were probably doing nothing more than the normal banalities of life. There was a woman with a child who was fidgeting on the seat across the aisle; a teenage boy listening to some music, bobbing his head in time with a beat that leaked out a little from his smart headphones; a couple were sitting next to each other but staring in opposite directions; a man in his early thirties wearing a green anorak sat a few rows in front with his head buried in a book; a girl was chatting on a mobile, engrossed in trivia and a boy of twelve or so was sitting alone, fixated on a game machine clutched in his hands. All this Melissa was aware of without actually looking, she just let the information filter through.

She tried to keep a lid on her excitement but she did think that Kathryn would be proud of her, knowing that after a year Melissa was going to actually do something. They'd all been lazy, waiting in expectation, but days had turned to weeks and months, and now the year had almost gone and nothing was resolved. If there were such a thing as ghosts, Kathryn's might be wandering the Earth, seeking out the one who had taken her life.

The journey to Cambridge Heath took about twenty minutes and passed through the spine of the borough. Melissa watched with a detached interest. For the orthodox Jewish people this was just another day, the first of the new week, and they were busier than most. Seeing them made Melissa remember Daniel now that he'd signed on the dotted line, but he was back home and she hadn't seen him for months. Daniel didn't want to be seen. Her heart went out to him, but as generous as she was, she wished he hadn't decided to do what he'd done. He must have felt the same as her, frustrated at the lack of progress, unless he'd immersed himself so deeply in his new life that he didn't care anymore.

She had to admit, she was a little angry with him for going, but people were affected in so many ways, and they were all legitimate. Remembering Kathryn was sad enough, but remembering Michael and Margaret Hargreaves and Daniel and Naila and the endless distress to all of them galvanised her. Anger fuelled her determination to do something. She wondered how she'd managed to sit and wait for so long. That would change now.

The bus arrived at Cambridge Heath, close to The Salvation Army building. She ought to have phoned and checked first, that would have been wise, but wisdom had got Faraday nowhere so this was the time for adrenalin and action.

The place had a forlorn air. A couple of men hung around outside chatting to each other and hardly noticed as she went inside. A receptionist smiled and asked if she needed help.

"I'm looking for a man called Robert," said Melissa, and she described him as she remembered him from the last time she'd seen him, almost a year ago.

"I'm new," said the receptionist. "Can't help you, but I know a lady who can."

She called on an intercom and a woman came down, probably younger than Melissa but with a tough demeanour. She introduced herself as Gail, the duty superintendent.

"May I ask who you are and what you want?" Gail asked.

Melissa felt a little uneasy with this hard-edged woman, but Gail seemed to soften when she heard Melissa's explanation.

"I know who you mean," she said. "I'm sorry to tell you, but Robert passed away two months ago. If you're a friend of the family, such as it was, or you were involved in that murder case, you should have been informed. I really am sorry. Are you alright?"

Melissa felt faint and asked to sit down. The receptionist brought her a glass of water and Melissa sipped it, trying to fathom out what was going on in her head and heart. Another death? Would it never end?

All the anger and determination which had fired her suddenly seeped away. She suddenly felt empty, a hollow shell. No amount of will power could confront this vacuum. It was as if all the gods were laughing at her, telling her that the world was an open house for evil and that nothing she did would make the slightest difference. Good people would die horrible deaths and the wicked would go unpunished. That was the way things were and no matter how fierce you were about righting wrongs, the world was simply too vast to change.

"Would you like me to call a doctor?" Gail asked.

"No, thanks, I'll be okay," said Melissa, but her voice didn't sound like her voice, it sounded distant and weak, the stupid, pathetic voice of someone who thought they could make a difference.

She stood up feeling as if she'd stepped into a different universe. A moment ago she was sure this was the right thing to do, that Robert would be there, that he would answer all her questions and that she'd be able to tell Patrick and Faraday that she'd discovered something they'd missed. How foolish! How arrogant! She spat the words out in her mind, deflated and despondent.

Gail was surprisingly compassionate as Melissa left, even asking if she wanted a taxi home. Melissa thanked her but preferred to walk. She needed air, space and time.

Outside, the two men had gone, but the world was still there, still taking no notice of her, mocking her childish efforts.

The walk home took over half an hour, but it gave her time to think. She couldn't bear being on a bus again with people. She felt terrible, demoralised and depressed, and the drab landscape of Hackney didn't help. It really was time to leave, try something new, somewhere new.

Melissa drifted into Springfield Park, close to home but not wanting to see Patrick in this state. The disappointment was immense and she could barely put one foot in front of the other, but she found her way to a bench in a secluded area and sat down, taking out a handkerchief to wipe her face, trying to breathe slowly. Had she known, this was the same bench Ursula and Jasmine had tried to comfort Daniel the morning after the murder.

She would call Patrick, hear his strong voice, tell her what she'd tried to do and how she'd been foiled at the first hurdle. Robert, their one and only witness, was dead.

A year might have passed, but the shock was still there, biding its time, waiting for the right moment, and here it was again, her spirits lower than they had been for months, her stupid plan fallen apart at the first puff of opposition.

Unexpectedly, she felt something else amidst the disappointment and frustration, a presence. She wasn't sure how she knew, but she knew that someone was close by. At first, with a mixture of trepidation and expectation, she thought it might be Kathryn, come to offer comfort and hope, but this was no ghost. A man approached from around a shaded corner, speaking on a mobile phone, in his early thirties, casual, wearing a dark green anorak.

Something made Melissa uneasy, but he wasn't looking at her and was evidently distracted on the mobile.

Passing by the bench, he ended the conversation and stopped, saying in a light, scornful tone, "Women!"

Melissa couldn't smile and hoped he wouldn't linger.

But he did.

He was looking at her, relaxed, half smiling, half something else, hard to define.

Something stirred in Melissa's mind, but she couldn't recall it – was it something to do with the evidence a woman had given?

"Such a beautiful evening," he said.

She didn't answer. She was staring at him because she remembered the man on the bus.

Jesus! Had he followed her there and back?

And she knew. She didn't know how she knew, but she did.

Paralysed, all she could do was stare back, her lips slightly apart, her mind beginning to race. 'Go!' it screamed. 'Run!'

But she had no time to act.

His hand move fast, holding something white which banged hard into her face, dimmed her senses in a second. Fear and confusion gripped her. She'd wanted to solve everything but she understood nothing, least of all this.

There was no pain, just a sudden, smothering and almost welcome darkness.

## 7

"Daniel?"

"Inspector, welcome. Come in."

Faraday had travelled all the way to Salford to meet Daniel who'd moved back into his parents' house, a smart, detached home in the suburbs of the city. Daniel led Faraday into the living room, a tidy, traditional room in a tidy, traditional home. Daniel's parents were there, together with his younger brother and three sisters, all from the orthodox

Jewish community. Faraday had to admit, he liked the sense of safety and security of these people and respected the values that kept them going from generation to generation, but he was still puzzled by Daniel's reversion.

Daniel's family made themselves scarce after the youngest sister had introduced herself to Inspector Faraday and asked him if he wanted to play Scrabble with her. He politely refused saying that even at eight years old, she would definitely beat him.

"How are you, Daniel?" Faraday asked.

"Well," he replied.

"Good. Your family were pleased to welcome you back, then, I take it?"

"That's an understatement," said Daniel. "They were never relaxed about me going to London, especially to the dreaded Hackney, so now all they want to do is fix me up with a nice Jewish wife and all will be well."

Faraday smiled and said, "Are you ready for that?"

"Not in the slightest," said Daniel. "Any news, inspector?"

Faraday told him how the investigation was going, or rather how it wasn't going.

"I thought we'd crack this quickly," he said, "but I was wrong. We missed something, we must have done, but I don't know where or how. We've been meticulous, or at least I thought we had. That's partly why I came here, to see if we could trace this missing link. It must be there."

"You think so?" said Daniel. "You still don't think it was random?"

"I don't, no," said Faraday. "Our chief witness died, you know, Robert Thomas, but he couldn't have told us more than he did. And of course, there was ..."

"The baby, yes," said Daniel. His face, now heavily bearded, took on a deeper, darker expression. "I suppose that ... diminishes the random element."

"It does, but it hasn't helped us, I'm afraid. No one we've tested has the same DNA and there's no clue in Kathryn's records, no phone calls, no letters, nothing that explains it. Can I ask you, Daniel, and I know I've asked before, if you have a theory, even a guess?"

"A theory, no, but lots of guesses, all of them dreadful. Either she was raped or she deceived me. Both options are hard to live with. You know, inspector, I didn't make this move here lightly. I loved Kathryn as much, I think, as any man can love a woman. She was everything to me, my link to the real world. This, by the way," he said, gesturing to his parents' house, "isn't real."

"Isn't it?"

"No, not the kind of reality Kathryn wanted for me. It's a bolt hole, a microcosm that keeps us safe, nothing too exciting. It cuts out a lot, but it offers a lot, too. I'm grateful that it was here when I needed it."

"Yes," said Faraday, "I'm sure. No more computers then?"

"No. I could do, if I wanted, but I don't. I've lost interest. A lot of Jews are very nifty with them, you know. Israel is one of the hotspots of development."

"Why is that, Daniel?"

"Because it's such a precise and cerebral activity, and we're a precise and cerebral people."

"But it isn't for you anymore?"

"No."

"What do you do, Daniel?"

"I study, at a local shteeble, that's a seminary. I drown myself in the Talmud."

"Right," said Faraday, not really understanding, but trying hard to fathom this man who had lost everything and morphed into his past. "You enjoy it?"

"Actually, I do. It keeps my mind busy, away from ... other things."

"Yes, I can understand that. Your friends back in Hackney miss you. I see them occasionally, as part of the on-going investigation."

"Are they all okay?"

"Up to a point. The girls are in a bit of trouble, though I think I can handle it."

"Trouble? Not serious, I hope?"

"It could be. They wrote an anonymous letter to someone we thought might have been a suspect, threatening him unless he gave himself up to the police."

"Really? Well, that's hard to imagine. They're all good souls."

"Very, which is why I'll try and keep this quiet."

"What made them do such a thing?"

"Desperation," said Faraday. "They're frustrated and anxious that the killer is still out there. They wanted to do something, but this was the wrong thing to do."

"You traced them?"

"We did, yes, quite easily as it happens - they put their address on the back of the letter."

Daniel took a moment to digest this, then burst out laughing. He hadn't laughed in a year, and this was a weird reason. "Truly?" he asked.

"Truly," said Faraday. "Mr Orlich the man they sent it to, brought it to me. He's a rough sort with a lot of chips on his shoulder, but he isn't a murderer, just one of life's victims."

"And the girls wrote to him?"

"Yes. Stupid thing to do."

"But not as stupid as putting their address on the back?"

"No. It was Elena Imrie who did it, apparently, the teacher. She obviously knows how to write letters. Always a good idea to put your name and address on the back," and Daniel laughed again. His youngest sister, Sarah, heard her brother's laughter and popped her head in to see what was happening. Daniel let her come in and she sat on his knee, staring at Faraday.

"And you are?" said Faraday.

"Sarah," said Sarah.

"Nice to meet you Sarah. My name is Simon."

Sarah looked at Daniel as if to say "is he safe to speak with?" or "is that a real name?", but whatever the meaning of the look, Daniel seemed to understand and said, "Simon is a policeman, Sarah. He's come all the way from London where I used to live."

"Is it to do with Kathryn?" she asked.

Faraday was taken aback. He thought – though he didn't know why he thought it – that the family wouldn't talk about Kathryn, but evidently they had.

"She asked me and I told her," said Daniel. "She's very grown up, aren't you Pumpkin?"

"Yes," said Sarah, who glowed when Daniel praised her. "It's very sad, isn't it?" Sarah said to Faraday.

"Indeed it is," he answered, "one of the saddest cases I know. Your brother is very brave," he added, "but I suppose you know that."

"He was very naughty to run away," said Sarah.

"I didn't run away, Pumpkin, I was just trying something different, but it didn't work and I came back."

"Will you go away again?" she asked.

"Maybe, maybe not. Do you want me to?"

"No."

"Then I won't go," said Daniel. Faraday asked him if this was true, that he was settled now. "For the moment," Daniel replied. "I don't know what can bring me back to London, especially Hackney."

"Naila's back from Tehran," said Faraday. "You know she also went back home for a while?" He did. "She would like to see you."

"Would she?" said Daniel. "Maybe one day. How is she?"

"Better, but different. Hard to describe. I don't see much of her but she's part of the case so we have to keep track. Besides, we all like her."

"Who's Nailer?" asked Sarah, thinking it might be someone who did a lot of woodwork.

"She was Kathryn's brother's boyfriend."

Sarah had to work this out for a few moments, then said "Is he the one who drowned himself?"

"Yes he was," said Daniel.

"Because he was unhappy," said Sarah.

"Exactly."

Faraday listened to them, amazed at how close they were, but also how much Sarah knew. Daniel registered this and said, "She really is quite grown up, and there's no point hiding things from you, is there Pumpkin?"

Sarah shook her head and looked at Faraday in a very adult way that made him smile, despite the subject.

"No more ideas then Daniel?" Faraday asked.

Daniel shook his head and said, "Nothing, but on the other hand, inspector, I haven't been thinking too much about it. Self-protection, you see."

"I see, yes of course. I hope my visit hasn't upset you?"

"A little, yes, to be honest, but I can cope, although I'm not sure why you came all this way."

Faraday said, "I think personal contact is important. It's all very well talking on the phone, but you never know what a meeting might do, more time to think and remember. And also, I want you to know how disappointed I am myself that we haven't solved this case, Daniel. By coming here, I hope you'll believe me when I say we haven't let it drop, not by any means, but I do feel we've missed something. Obviously we have, otherwise the ..." he hesitated, looking at Sarah who listened to every word, "... person who did it would have been caught by now."

"Is it difficult to catch bad people?" Sarah asked.

"It can be," said Faraday.

"Is that because they're cleverer than you."

Faraday turned slightly pink and said, quite honestly, "They may be, but I hope not. It's sometimes like looking for a needle in haystack, Sarah, so it isn't easy. Haven't you ever lost something and no matter where you look, you can't find it."

Sarah thought for a while and said, "I lost teddy once."

"Did you find him in the end?"

"Oh yes. He was hiding in the garden."

Faraday laughed and said, "Well, our bad people hide too, and not just in gardens, so we have to look everywhere. It can take time."

"I understand," said Sarah, sagely. Daniel looked and listened to his sister with great affection, even though it was about something which tore him apart. "I hope you find this bad person. They deserve to be punished."

"Yes, indeed they do," said Faraday.

"Come on now, Pumpkin," said Daniel, "you're getting heavy and my leg's going to sleep."

Sarah climbed down and said, "I'll leave you in case you have grown up things to say to each other."

Faraday watched her go and said, "No wonder you came back home, Daniel, she's adorable."

"Yes, isn't she, but not all the time. She has her moments."

Faraday wondered whether he would have a job if all children came from the same manufacturing company.

"So, Daniel, can we find this bad person?"

Daniel took a deep breath and stood up, stretching the leg that Sarah had been sitting on. He walked to the French windows looking out on the garden where Sarah was playing with the same teddy that had once been lost.

"There's one thing that popped into my head when you told me about the letter Elena wrote, but it's probably nothing."

"Tell me," said Faraday.

"Well, I was in the park – Springfield Park- with Ursula and the others. We were trying to deal with the whole thing, you know, and they were very kind, when I had a call from my temp."

Faraday frowned.

"Which temp is that, Daniel? I don't remember there being a temp. I thought you were a one-man band."

"I am ... I mean I was, but sometimes, when the workload was heavy, I needed help from a local agency and they'd send me a tech guy."

"The same one each time?"

"Not always, no. The last one was with me a couple of months. Anyway, I'd left a note for him during the night. I would have called but it was late. Besides, I hardly knew the man. I couldn't very well ask him to run the business for me while I was away so I just told him what had happened and said he should finish off whatever jobs were scheduled and go back to the agency. I'd call them as soon as possible. That was all."

"And?"

"I went back to my office later that morning but he hadn't been in and the letter was still on the desk. Something bothered me at the time but I never really thought about it till you told me what Elena had done, but it must have registered with me, otherwise I would have forgotten about it completely."

Faraday's frown deepened. "What you're asking yourself," he said "is how this chap came to call you if he hadn't read your note."

"Yes, but by then the news would have spread anyway."

Faraday stood up too, pacing the room.

"What was his name, this temp?" he asked.

He kept his fingers crossed behind his back, hoping that it would begin with the letter 'J'.

"Jud," said Daniel, "with one 'd'. Odd name, that's why I ..."

"And his second name?" Faraday sounded unusually impatient.

Daniel shook his head.

"Sorry, but you could call the agency, they'd know. He was a good guy, knew his stuff. He was the best of the ..."

"What time did you get the call?" Faraday interrupted, uncrossing his fingers, uncertain whether to hug or chastise Daniel.

"Around midday. You can check with the girls, they'll know."

"I will. You're right, the news was out by then, but we'll chase it up. What was the agency called, Daniel?"

For the first time, Daniel noted a hint of impatience in the inspector's voice. He told him the agency which had supplied him with technical whizzkids over the years. Faraday immediately called Fowler, gave her the information and asked to call back as soon as she had the man's name.

"How long did you say this chap had been with you?" Faraday asked.

Daniel did some mental arithmetic and said, "Off and on for about two months, maybe a little longer."

"But you never mentioned him to me," said Faraday, the irritation showing more keenly.

Daniel looked bewildered. "No, but I never gave him a thought. Why should I? I rarely saw him. He worked part time and only with repairs. We communicated by email or phone and that was that. He worked fast and well but never hung around. He wasn't part of my mind set, inspector."

Faraday tried to calm down. He couldn't be angry with Daniel, of all people, but he wondered why, time and time again, people who should know better, bright, sharp and well-meaning, left out critical pieces of information. It was as if some perverse censoring process made them disregard the most crucial memories. He'd known it before and he might well have stumbled on it again now. Alternatively, the guy might turn out to be all that Daniel made him out to be, an itinerant techie with nothing to hide, but it didn't matter, information was knowledge; the judgement would come later.

"Sorry if I was a bit snappy, Daniel. You really are the last person I'd want to upset. The thing is ... well, you know what the thing is better than me. Can you remember what this chap was like, anything odd about him?"

"Nothing," said Daniel. "He was fine – polite, hardworking and good at the job. I wouldn't have kept him otherwise, although..."

"Although what?"

"A touch arrogant, but so are many people. I've had it said to me, and I know I'm not, so it's easy to make a mistake."

"Arrogant in what way?" Faraday asked, ignoring Daniel's self-doubt.

Daniel didn't like criticising others so he said, "My imagination probably, but there were moments when he seemed to look down on me. I laughed it off. Lots of people do that, insecurity probably, but other than that he was excellent."

"What about looks," said Faraday. "Rough description."

"Taller than me," said Daniel, "and handsome as hell; knew it, too."

Faraday listened with surprising intensity.

"Interesting," he said. "I wish ... okay, I won't say it again. These things happen, and it may be nothing. Did Kathryn mention him at all, Daniel?"

Daniel thought, keeping very still and stroking his beard like some wise old guru, even though he was still young and with no pretensions to guru-hood. "No ... Oh ... God, maybe she did."

"Maybe?"

Daniel turned red, but it was hard to know whether it was with embarrassment or anger.

"A while before ... before ... yes, she said she'd popped into the office to see me and she'd met "this bloke", that's what she said. She told me he'd made her laugh and said I was the best boss he'd ever worked for. That was it."

Faraday wrote this down as if it was crucial, but it was so hard to sift out evidence from the millions of tiny events that marked a day in the life of a life. So much is said and so much is done, but most of it oils the wheels of social interaction, nothing more. To pick out a word or a gesture that could signify intent to murder is a refined skill, but Faraday had it, and something about these unexpected, innocuous recollections chilled him. It may have been hope more than experience, but over the years he'd developed a sharp sixth sense in his work and he often relied on it in the best traditions of detecting.

Fowler's return call came in about ten minutes. Faraday said 'yes' a few times then thanked her and instructed the team to keep checking. Ending the call, he turned to Daniel and said, "Does the name 'Rekin' ring a bell?"

At once, Daniel said, "Yes! Rekin! That was it. Sorry, I..."

"No problem," said Faraday, though it was anything but. "The agency are still there but your temp has flown the coop."

"That's not unusual," said Daniel. "Most part-timers are here today, gone tomorrow."

"Yes," said Faraday, "but we'll chase it up. It's a lead, and I haven't seen one of those for months."

Faraday got to meet Daniel's family, and felt both the love and the pressure; they were an intense group. He didn't know whether to feel sorry for Daniel being thrust back into the bosom of his family and his religion or to be angry with him for giving up the fight for freedom. People made their choices and lived by them; it was the beauty and tragedy of life.

More pertinently, Daniel had given him something new to follow, which was the main reason for travelling all that way. He was fed and watered by Daniel's parents and interrogated by Sarah, but he managed to keep a vestige of professional distance. He couldn't relax though. Instinctively he felt something promising in this lead, and where there was hope there was justice. He hadn't found it easy to live with himself the past year, knowing some heartless, brutal villain was out there, probably sneering at police efforts, but now he had a name and a glimmer of a chance.

After an extended visit, he was about to leave when another call came in. He assumed it was headquarters saying they'd tracked Rekin, but it wasn't.

The room went quiet as he listened to the voice at the other end of the line. When he closed the call he turned to Daniel and said, "I need a private word, Daniel."

He appeared reluctant to talk in front of anyone else and took Daniel aside.

"This may be nothing," he said, "we're not sure yet, but your friend

Patrick Connelly called us this morning, in some distress, apparently."

"Distress?" asked Daniel. "Why?"

Faraday took a deep breath and spoke as if the words were being forced out of him , "Because Melissa Cochrane is missing."

## 8

"You want a drink while you work, Sam?"

Sam grunted something which resembled 'no'. He wasn't comfortable in this detective's excuse for a home, but he was being paid, minimally, and the job was interesting so he got on with it. He had no idea that Matt Davis was no more a detective than he or that Matt had been dismissed from the police force for inappropriate behaviour. Sam thought the flat a bit pokey for a proper place to live, but he didn't doubt that Matt was who he said he was, a plain clothes detective, especially as the black police lady had been there when they'd met. Charlene had wanted to keep out of the whole thing, but foolishly fond of Matt to the last, she was there when he met Samuel Levinson and added credibility to the story, though she disappeared as soon as she could, and before she knew exactly what Sam was going to do.

Sam, wondering why he wasn't doing this technical investigation at Stoke Newington or somewhere grand, nevertheless went along with the 'undercover' story. When he was away from Feriha, Sam reverted to his grumpy monosyllabic self, and that was the mode he was in now, especially as the police detective undercover guy looked nervous and even more especially once he'd seen the video.

It wasn't a real video, just five images strung together in three second cycles. Matt hadn't wanted Sam to see the damn thing but there was no way to avoid it. The whole purpose of this clandestine visit was to trace its origin and that couldn't be done without Sam seeing it. Matt had given him a gentle lecture beforehand, warning him that what he was about to see was disturbing. Sam, used to a thousand violent games on Jemal's whizzbang machine couldn't imagine that this would be worse, but it was, and it shook him. If Charlene had known she would never have let this happen, but she didn't know and she did let it happen. Matt insisted it was his way back into the force and that it would be okay, promise. This was his big moment. If he could locate the source and track it down, then he'd call DI  Faraday and all would be well. It was a misguided and disastrous idea, but he was so far down the misguided trail that he wasn't thinking clearly any longer, and he was desperate, all of which muddied his thoughts.

Sam busied himself with the technical side, trying to ignore what he'd seen, but it kept popping into his head like some nightmare he'd had when he was a boy. He wanted to see Feriha, to put his head on her lap and look into her eyes again and to tell her about this, but at the same time he wondered if he could or should tell her. This was beyond anything he'd seen and the whole thing made him sick, especially as he had a horrible feeling of recognition. He couldn't be sure because the footage was fuzzy, but something told him that the face, half hidden and totally contorted, was familiar, but nothing more registered and he ploughed on with the technical wizardry.

A client-server relationship definitely existed between this machine and the source machine. Something allowed access to the source computer and Sam had to trace it. He took the URL and typed it into the command prompt at the operating system level using a tracer command. He'd done this before and found a whole host of IP addresses, but this was direct, nothing in between. He took the address and typed it into a standard IP finder then clicked the Lookup button when a location was found.

Hackney, London.

The location was regional rather than specific, but there was no way he knew how to pinpoint a real address directly. What the detective guy would have to do would be to call the ISP provider of the source machine and request the information – not easy for Joe Bloggs but dead simple when you were a detective policeman bigshot doing undercover work, thought Sam.

Unless...

He tried pinging the machine and lo and behold he got a response – it was online!

"What are you doing?" Matt asked.

"What you asked," grunted Sam. He didn't like to talk when he was immersed in computer stuff.

"Tell me," said Matt. He was edgy and impatient and didn't particularly take to Sam's teenage angst. He was beginning to wonder if he really ought to have gone to a professional.

"Pinging him," said Sam.

"Meaning?"

"Testing the line and he's there."

"You can tell that?"

"Yes."

"Can you find out where he is?" Matt asked.

"Not unless I ask him?" said Sam.

"Well ask him!" said Matt, with a touch too much impatience.

Sam's mind was working furiously. He had the IP address and used a program he knew to find the MAC address. He then set about hacking into the other computer, not at all sure that he could do it, but he did, surprisingly quickly.

"It's almost if..." he started to say.

"As if what?" Matt asked, increasingly impatient.

"... that he wanted me to find him," said Sam.

He loaded Notepad then used the connection they'd made to send messages.

"Can't you just get his email," Matt asked, "or use one of these messaging systems?"

"Gives too much away," said Sam. "He's waiting, Mr Policeman. What should I say?"

"Ask him if he knows about the video."

Sam looked uncertain; it seemed too close to the bone to get a truthful answer, but he asked it anyway. "No," came the sparse reply, then, "Explain."

"He wants to know more," said Sam.

"I thought it was us asking the questions. Ask him where he is?"

'As if', Sam thought, but he just followed orders. He got 'LOL' in response.

"Can't you locate him?" Matt asked. "You're supposed to be the genius here."

"I can't work miracles," said Sam, and added silently, 'not on this crap equipment'.

Matt was increasingly agitated. He felt that he was on the right track but going about things in the wrong way. For a start, he wasn't in control, nor was Sam. There was something tense and unnatural about the replies as the two techies echoed minimal language over the connection.

"Keep pressing," said Matt. "Get a location."

Sam thought that this detective policeman guy was a bit uptight. If the techie at the other end of the line was a nutter, he'd have to be a dickhead as well to send back his address. Why should he? There were a few short bursts of Q and A with Matt peering over Sam's shoulder, telling him what to ask.

'explain video.'

'video?'

'explain.'

'show video.'

'where are u?'

Nothing.

"We're not getting very far," said Sam, but Matt felt the vibes in the answers. They were just too tricky to be innocent.

'where'

'find me.'

'need location. will send vid after'

'lol. ok. address.'

And an address did come back, only it wasn't unknown, it was Matt's.

"Did you give it to him?" Matt asked, annoyed.

"No! He just knew it. What's this about, Mr Policeman?" Sam asked.

Matt stared at the screen. This wasn't email, it was ultra-fast pure communication along one of the IP Protocols and it was all wrong.

"End it," said Matt. "Now."

Sam terminated the connection and sat back.

"He knew what he was doing," said Sam. "Better than me."

Matt was pacing the room, agitated.

"How come that video turns up on this machine?" he asked. "Where's the connection?"

Sam shook his head. He searched through the registry looking for a clue. Matt let him work in quiet, desperate for an answer. After what felt like forever, Sam said, "There is something here."

"Something like what?"

"A client server relationship. This is the client, the other machine is the server. There's a tiny program here that would let him do that. It's called ... Hart, that's H..A..R..T not H..E..A..R..T."

Matt stopped. A memory jumped into his mind and he whispered "Daniel?"

"Sorry?" said Sam, thinking the nuthead policeman was talking to him.

Matt didn't answer. He was remembering a year before when he had a wife and children and everything was in some kind of order. The very night of the murder! Little Frankie had wrecked the computer and Daniel had come to fix it. Daniel Hart! But what the hell had Daniel to do with this sick video? This was crazy, and what was even crazier was seeing his own address echoed on the computer screen, mixed in with a whole bunch of gobbledygook. Was Daniel at the other end of the line? But Daniel had buggered off to Manchester, hadn't he? And this connection was in Hackney, if the brainbox here was to be believed. Just what was going on?

"Am I done or what?" Sam asked.

"I don't know," said Matt, "are you?"

"You tell me," Sam answered.

Matt tried to calm down and said, "You did a good job Sam. Thank you."

Sam nodded, not sure whether to go or wait for more instructions.

"It's called 'peer-to-peer'" he said.

"What is?"

"That kind of connection. But you can't establish it unless both parties want it. It's hard to force your way in, but if two or more people have the software, then you can do it."

"Do what?"

"Share stuff," said Sam. "Like music, films, videos, anything really. That's why there's so much piracy. Don't you know that?"

Matt was only half listening. Had Daniel set up some software on their computer a year ago? Why? He was hardly going to share 'stuff' with Frankie.

"Or you can do remote connection, repair things from a distance," added Sam. "Save travelling."

"Right," whispered Matt, "that was why!"

"That was why what?" Sam asked, unable to tune in to the distracted detective.

"Why Daniel set up a connection between our ... this computer and his. That makes sense."

Sam heard the word 'Daniel' and something twigged.

"It was her, wasn't it?" he asked.

"Her who?"

"The girl, on the video, it was Nurse Hudson, wasn't it?"

Matt seemed to snap out of his dreaming.

"No."

"But Daniel was her boyfriend. My dad knew him."

"I said no."

Sam didn't argue the point, but he was feeling a little uneasy. The images were bad enough, but if it really was that nurse he'd liked, the one who looked after Jonathan, then that stank.

"I think I'll go now," he said.

Matt nodded and said, "Sorry if I was snappy. You've done brilliant, son."

"I'm not your son," said Sam, "but thanks. Do you want me to print it?"

"Print what?"

"All the stuff on screen, otherwise you won't be able to use it in court in evidence and all that stuff."

Matt said that would be great and Sam printed out the entire session.

"Do you reckon you can catch the guy that did this now?" Sam asked.

"We'll try," said Matt. "Here." He took out twenty pounds from his wallet and gave it to Sam. This didn't feel right, even to Sam. The police surely wouldn't go about their work, even undercover work, like this.

"Are you for real?" Sam asked.

"What do you mean?"

"A real policeman," said Sam.

A hundred thoughts passed through Matt's head. His life had been the police force. His whole reason for being on Earth was to enforce the law of the land. He loved the work and desperately wanted to get back into it. Just because of one stupid weakness he he'd been excommunicated.

"Yes," he said, "I am a real policeman. Don't I look like one?"

"Not particularly," said Sam. "Anyway, thanks for the job. If you need me again..."

"We'll call," said Matt, seeing the boy out. "You did good."

Left alone, Matt read through the printouts of the weird communication. Now was the time to call Faraday, but still something held him back. If he did what the boy said and contacted the guy's provider, he could get the address, but he'd need bona fide credentials and he didn't have them anymore. Dare he ask Charlene? He's asked her so much already. Before long she'd be in this mess as deep as him and he didn't want that. What he wanted, more than anything else, was re-instatement and redemption. What drove him, though, was something else, something he didn't accept. He picked up the phone and made a call, but not to Charlene. He called Cassie.

"Not now, Matt. I'm working."

"I need to see you. Let me come over."

"Not now, Matt. It's over. Let it go."

He didn't even argue. He'd argued before and never won. Cassie had taken him down, body and soul, and when the world had discarded him, she didn't pick him up and comfort him, she abandoned him to the wolves. He hung up, called another number.

"Charlene?"

"Matt, how did it go?"

"Good, but I need your help again. Sorry."

Silence, then, "What kind of help?"

"A call. I need you to make a call."

"Who to?"

"Let's meet. I'll tell you."

"Matt, I can't. Not for a while. I'm on duty soon. What did the boy find out?"

"Stuff," said Matt. "Can't tell you on the phone. Please help me, Charlene. I'm almost there."

"Listen, Matt," said Charlene. "Take my advice, go to Faraday. If you don't, I will. You mustn't do more alone. Give up what you've found and tell the DI. That's the way to go, Matt."

He listened, but it didn't register. He was in a world of his own shaped by rejection.

"Just this last request, Charlene, promise, nothing more after this. All I need is a call to company, locate an IP address. That's it. Then we've got him."

"Got who, Matt?"

Matt held back. He didn't want to say too much. "Never mind. I'll tell you if...when we meet."

"Matt, I have to go. Sorry. We'll talk later. You take care."

Matt heard the line go dead.

This was a world of rejection. For some reason the gods had turned against him. He'd always thought of himself a good man, but he'd fallen from grace. No doubt why, but he was only human, after all. Policemen were all only human.

He sat and read through the printout as if it was the bible, his route to redemption, though most of it was indecipherable. What he ought to do was take it right away to Faraday. This was crucial stuff, he knew it. Why not, just for a change, he asked himself, do the sensible thing? He could end all this failure, make amends and get back on track. But at the same time, he was so close to cracking this thing alone, the hubris that would go with such a success would be enormous, immeasurable. He wouldn't just be back, he'd be back with a vengeance.

He lay down with the paper on his lap, holding on to it for dear life. It was his passport back to reality, and even in sleep he gripped it as though the devil himself might be coming to take it away.

And in a sense, he was.

A knock on the door woke Matt.

It was dark when he opened his eyes and for a moment he was disoriented. The curtains were open so it must have been dark outside. Sam had left around seven so it had to be well into the night by now. He sat up and the printouts fell to the floor. The knocking came again, not loud or aggressive but insistent. The only visitor he had now was Charlene, coming to see how he was doing, once a fortnight whenever she was off duty. She was the only one that cared; to everyone else he was already a leper. But Charlene never called by surprise, she always telephoned first so he could make himself half presentable.

He stood, aware that he was looking a little rough and feeling even rougher. He was also aware that the battle he was fighting in himself was a losing one. He felt a conspiratorial fate driving him down, as if he had broken a fundamental rule of nature and the consequence was disaster, in whichever form that would take.

For a moment this despair faded as the thought occurred that it might be Eileen at the door, come to forgive him and ask him back. Frankie and Kylie would be holding her hand and they'd come in, help him pack and take him back where he belonged, home.

But the shadow at the window was not Eileen's. It wasn't even Cassie, come to apologise for abandoning him after luring him onto the rocks. The silhouette was of no one familiar, but as Matt feared nothing except his own weakness he opened the door and saw a smiling stranger, young, good looking, casually dressed. He had no badge, no obvious sales pitch, no clipboard, nothing. He stood with one hand in his pocket, perfectly at ease.

"Matthew Davis?"

"Yes. And you are?"

The man didn't answer. Instead, Matt was aware of something bright and silver whipped out from the man's pocket and heading his way. He tried to step back but the knife had already passed through most of his neck when he began to move. The step turned into a stumble as a thousand thoughts crowded into his mind, the most prominent being that Kathryn Hudson probably felt like this the night of the murder, both surprised and angry. Surely, Matt thought, his life had more meaning than to end in this ignominious way? He tried to right himself but the killer gently pushed him in the chest and he fell backwards, aware that the killer had come into the house and closed the door.

Matt was on the floor, trying to stem the flow of blood, but though his hand was crimson from fingertip to wrist, he could do nothing as the world span around him. He turned to see the killer ignoring his spasms, looking around the untidy, forlorn room.

"Ah!" he heard, as the man picked up the printouts, checking them then folding them neatly and putting them in his pocket.

He moved over to the computer but didn't even switch it on. He prised open the cabinet with the blood-stained knife and ripped out the hard drive.

"You can't get these for love nor money," he said, as if Matt was interested. "Amazing how these things never hold their value. But the information, now that's priceless."

Matt heard the words as if from a distance. He was impressed. The killer was cool in the freezing cold sense of the word. Matt wanted to ask him why, how, all the questions the entire police force had been unable to ask over the past year. All that came out, however, was a sad, indecipherable gurgle and more blood. He could see it, pooling around him just as he'd seen it pooling around the nurse. History really did repeat itself. He could see the crimes scene team examining his body, saw Eileen in unredeemable tears, heard his children crying for him, felt Charlene curse, heard Faraday blame himself and saw the whole sorry scene unfurl itself before his dying eyes, just as he'd seen it in the crimes he'd witnessed.

He felt a closeness and saw the silhouette of the killer squatting down close to his face, looking at him. Matt tried to ask again 'why' but nothing came out.

"How you doing?" said the killer. "That's a lot of blood you're losing there. I've give you another ... hmm ... let's see ... five minutes? But you'll black out before then. I wouldn't fight it if I were you, just accept it. Won't be so painful."

Matt's spasms and groans seemed to say otherwise.

"I'm loathe to leave you," said the man, "seeing as though you've all been looking for such a long while, it feels rude to rush off, but needs must. Oh, okay, just to help you on your way."

Matt felt a sharp, almighty and indescribably painful pressure in his head. He had time only to think that this was grossly unfair before the pressure burst and all his thoughts vanished, such light as there was dimmed to darkness and everything that ever was fell into oblivion.

## 9

The incident room at Stoke Newington exuded a tangibly heavy atmosphere. Faraday stood by the window looking tense and ill at ease. By his side, Viv Fowler held on to a mug of tea as if her life depended on it and next to her was Charlene Okoru, in uniform, stony faced, her eyes fixed to a spot on the ground close to her feet. Sitting on simple wooden seats were Samuel Levinson with his father beside him whilst pacing in the centre with eyes of fire was Patrick Connelly. A couple of other detectives and policemen were also in the room, standing discreetly at the back.

"Officer Okoru," said Faraday, "has told us all she knew of Davis's attempts to track the video. Davis's widow has described it in more detail and it matches Sam's description, so we know pretty well what it shows."

Faraday's voice wasn't assured. This case had dragged on for a year, and now, suddenly, everything had exploded – the bizarre suicide of Maggie Hargreaves, the abduction of Melissa Cochrane and now the death of a policeman.

"Our priority..." he began...

"...is to find Melissa," Patrick interrupted. "She's alive, I know it."

Faraday didn't know it, but of course it was possible. Confidence was everything, but the loss of life and the threat to more lives was sapping everyone's faith, in him and in the system. He just didn't seem able to end this nightmare of shocks and was struggling to fight a growing sense of failure, annoyed beyond description that he'd missed Daniel's vital link to the man they were now seeking and wondering what else they'd missed in their supposed thoroughness.

"Yes," he said, "that is our priority. We have a large team on it, Patrick, I promise you, and we're closing in. Sam?" Sam looked up. "You're sure you've told us everything about the communication?" He nodded. "And you're sure you left the printouts behind?"

"I told you, he took them."

"You didn't make a copy?"

"Why should I? It was just a job. That's what she said," he added, looking at Charlene Okoru as if the whole thing was her fault. Charlene looked back at him without anger, though she was furious with herself for going along with Matt's stupidity. But blame wasn't the issue now, tracking the killer before he struck again was everything.

"I'm sorry, Sam," she said. "I had no idea."

"No," said Sam, "no one has any idea of anything, do they?"

Although he was petulant, he was also frightened. He hadn't felt comfortable with the detective who he now knew wasn't a detective at all, just an ex-policemen in disgrace, but to be so close to someone who only hours later would be murdered, this shook him. He didn't like being afraid and he fought it, but he sensed that everyone in the room was afraid. And Sam had actually spoken to the monster who'd created all this havoc, not voice to voice, but as good as, and that scared him, too. He felt too close to something that shouldn't have involved him at all, or his family or Feri. The thought that Feri might get drawn disturbed him even more. This killer was hounding them, for whatever reason. Sam was involved in something too deep and terrible to comprehend, but he feared even more dragging Feriha into it. He wouldn't mention her, wouldn't see her unless he had to, just to make sure she was safe. Sam's father Chaim tried to comfort his son, but Sam pushed his arm away. Chaim looked bewildered, caught in this alien world of hatred, mystery and murder.

"We have a name and we have a face," said Faraday. "The agency that employed this man last year have given us everything they know about him, so unless he can render himself invisible, he'll be caught soon."

"Right," Sam said softly but cynically, "like another year."

"Sooner," said Faraday. In other circumstances he would have told the boy to watch his tone, but he felt sorry for Sam. He'd been dragged into the mess by Matt Davis's foolishness but he'd done well to recall almost every line of the lost communication. The computer itself had been taken, at least it's heart and soul, but Sam, for all his anger and rebelliousness, had a sharp mind and given the police every detail he could. Faraday noted this and had a secret wish to offer the boy work when this whole sorry saga was ended, assuming he himself was still there, neither sacked nor resigned.

He took a deep breath and said, "My guess is that Melissa was taken as a hostage. This killer seems to know who we are, but that's no mystery as almost everything we do is freely available in the media."

Patrick looked uncomfortable, but he wasn't going to feel guilty. Melissa came way before any self-indulgence.

Faraday continued, "He might have sensed we would close in and has acted accordingly. I can't see any other reason."

"Unless he's a psycho," said Patrick, his voice husky and tired. He'd hardly slept since Melissa had gone missing and all he could think about was finding her. He believed with a lover's irrational belief that she was alive. He couldn't see her as they had seen Kathryn. This wasn't the same – it mustn't be the same!

"That's a possibility," said Faraday. "I'm not saying it isn't, but he's had a year to act, so why now, unless he feels hemmed in?"

Patrick couldn't argue logically. Logic had little to do with any of their states of mind, except the police who were doing their utmost to stay rational in an irrational situation. There wasn't one person in the room who didn't see this unfolding nightmare from a unique perspective. It gave the lie to there being a single world view, or even a single comprehensible world. They were bound together in a knot tied by a murderous creature freely walking and stalking the streets of Hackney. When he was caught, as he must surely be, the knot would unravel, but so, in all likelihood, would their lives. For the moment, only the necessities of moral and practical support held the knot in place.

They'd each seen Faraday, Fowler and the other officers involved separately. This was the first time they'd been together since the news broke of Matt Davis's murder. It was Charlene who'd found him, checking in the next day to see how he was doing and to explain again why she wouldn't help with his solitary manhunt any longer. Now she felt guilty as hell, wondering what would have happened if she'd agreed to call the network provider, or if she'd simply gone to Faraday and told him what was going on. Maybe Matt would still be alive; maybe the killer would have been caught. She clenched her fists in anger at her own poor decision making.

Faraday, however, hadn't blamed her, not outwardly, but she knew she'd made errors of judgement. Who hadn't though? No one was spotless in this flawed case and it sometimes felt as though they were all being prompted by some malign influence to head in the wrong direction.

Charlene, who was a most upright woman, found herself flailing around, searching for faith in herself and an order in the world, so much seemed to be falling apart. She had always liked to think herself as a cohesive force in a society tending to disorder, but she was losing confidence. She'd seen so much violence, and the murder of Kathryn Hudson was heart-wrenching, even to an outsider, but to see Matt dead drained her of hope and energy.

Faraday had been a rock. There wasn't the slightest hint of condemnation; instead he offered her anything she needed, including time off, but she couldn't rest, she had to be in the midst of the investigation, even though it was struggling to find the devil at the heart of it all, still evading them with what felt like contempt.

"Inspector?" The voice was Chaim Levinson, and everyone turned, Charlene too, lost in her own thoughts, was taken aback by what this quiet man had to say. "Is it possible to go back to first principles?"

"Sorry?" Faraday said. "What do you mean, Chaim?"

Chaim Levinson, who had said very little and been distant for much of the year, let alone in this new turn of events, said, "I mean human nature, inspector. This less than human man who has taken lives is in hiding, yes?"

"Yes."

"He will find a place that he knows and that you don't suspect, yes?"

"Dad, for God's sake!" said Sam, exasperated that his father was sounding like a rabbi giving a sermon to his flock. "Why don't you let them do the detecting and you do the praying?"

"Shall I go on?" inspector, Chaim asked, squeezing his son's shoulder in affection. Jewish teaching taught parents to love that much harder the deeper their children's obstinacy. Faraday nodded. "I'm trying to get into the mind of this beast," said Levinson, "and it isn't easy, but we have a saying, 'a friendless man is like a left hand without a right hand.' "

Sam looked up to heaven, muttering, "You have a million sayings."

"True, and that's because we've been around a long time under some considerable pressure, Samuel, the worst kind. We've had time to think. Thinking and feeling are our strengths. This man is alone, he is probably hiding the girl, and if my son is to be believed, he is not far away. The technical wizardry that has so captivated Samuel tells us so, isn't that right Sam?"

"You mean he's in Hackney, yeh, I told you that. So what? It's a big place, dad. Even God could hide here."

"The foolish despise wisdom and instruction, Sam; fear of the Lord is the beginning of knowledge. Don't be so hasty to condemn me."

Sam didn't want to get into an argument with his dad, or rather he did, but not there with others watching and twitching with so much at stake.

"Keep going, Chaim," said Faraday, interested in the man's train of thought, though not sure that it would lead anywhere useful.

"He wouldn't hide away somewhere that was totally unfamiliar, that would put him at a disadvantage. He would want to know where and how he could escape, and the local landscape, as much as possible."

"Where might that be, Chaim?" Faraday asked.

"This man has had limited experience of the borough, from what you say," said Chaim. "Wasn't he an itinerant worker, a temporary specialist?"

"He was."

"And you've checked all his known addresses?"

"Of course we have." Faraday was beginning to feel that he was the criminal and Chaim Levinson the investigator.

"Then we are missing something vital," said Levinson.

"We gathered that, dad," said Sam.

"I am thinking that this goes back to Daniel and to Kathryn, that the missing link is there."

"This is a bit vague, Chaim," said Faraday, starting to lose hope with the man's train of thought. "Have you got something or somewhere specific in mind."

"How can I," said Chaim, "when it is you that has the information?"

Faraday felt a bit aggrieved, but Chaim was right, the information was there, it had to be.

"This creature knew Daniel, you believe?"

"If it's who we think it is, then yes, he worked with him for a while."

"Then the link is probably there," said Chaim.

"Where dad, can't you ever stop speaking in riddles?"

"No, son, because this is a riddle. Inspector, was there anything in Daniel's office?"

"Well, it depends what you mean by 'anything'. And it isn't his office any more. He gave it up a year ago and it belongs to another company now, but we've been there and no, there wasn't 'anything', and if there had been, it was lost months ago."

Chaim looked dissatisfied, as if he knew his first principle idea was right but that the inspector hadn't latched on to it.

"Inspector," he said, "I don't mean to sound stubborn..."

"Well you do," whispered Sam.

"...but if we assume, rightly or wrongly, that the poor nurse was killed by this man, then he either knew her or knew of her, and if their fateful meeting the night she was killed was planned, it must be the former, he knew her, and where else could he have met her but at Daniel's work?"

Something started to rumble in Faraday's mind. He could have ended Chaim's Sherlock Holmes imitation there and then, but he didn't. Instead, he took out his mobile, checked the address book and dialled. The room was quiet. Fowler looked at Faraday questioningly, but he was impassive. Fowler thought he should do this away from the madding crowd, but she supposed that he realised time was of the essence and there was no room for delay.

"Daniel?" They all listened, totally focused. "It's Faraday here. No, not yet. Daniel, when you were here, in Hackney, I take it your Homerton office was the only place you worked?"

Silence. Everyone could hear the tinny voice at the other end of the phone but they couldn't make out what was being said.

"That's what I thought. So you had no other .. I don't know ... bases?"

This time, the silence came at the other end of the line. Daniel wasn't speaking.

"Daniel?" Faraday asked. They heard Daniel's voice again and saw Faraday's face turn dark, and it looked like the darkness of a controlled anger. "Can you give me the address?" Faraday said in rather too soft a voice. He scribbled down something as Daniel spoke. "Daniel," said Faraday, "there are people here now so I can't speak, but I'll call you later. Goodbye for now."

Faraday closed the call and looked at Chaim.

"I think I'll convert to Judaism," he said, but though he made light of the situation, his face showed the controlled anger even more. "That was Daniel," he said. "Apparently he had a rented work space in Hackney Wick." Silence for a few seconds as to why this should be so important. "If you don't mind," Faraday went on, "we'll end now. Sam, stay with your dad. Patrick, I'll be in touch. Officer Okoru, will you come with myself and Inspector Fowler."

That was all. He left the room in something of a hurry, leaving Sam staring at his dad as if he was seeing him for the first time.

## 10

Melissa opened her eyes, the awareness of consciousness slowly growing on dimmed senses. She hardly knew she had opened her eyes as the blackness was much the same, if not deeper. Only the pain in her limbs, all bound, and around her mouth, tightly gagged, told her she was still alive.

And her mind was rapidly clicking into gear, the man in the park drifting into memory, the smell – chloroform? – which still lingered in her nose and the cold, damp and dark of her surroundings.

She started to panic, but ropes held her down, curled, foetus-like by a brick wall in a rough space whose dimensions she couldn't make out in the dense darkness.

There was no light at all, not the slightest hint of the outside world.

She tried to sit up but whoever had tied her had fixed the bonds to an iron frame screwed into the brickwork, the remnants of a broken cupboard, and she couldn't move. She lay still, forcing herself to keep calm, to breathe slowly through her nose and not to cry – tears would hinder her vision and she needed every sense that was available.

She'd always hated closed spaces. The only times she felt free was when she out walking with Patrick or jogging with Kathryn. The thought of her friends triggered a fresh rush of anxiety.

Patrick! She conjured his image in her mind, sending him telepathic waves of distress, sure that he would sense her presence and come for her. Nothing happened. The silence was profound, menacing.

As her eyes adjusted, the darkness turned to a thick but penetrable gloom. She blinked, trying to clear the tears that had formed but not fallen. She started to make out the space around her, an area the size of a garage. It wasn't empty. A few cartons lay here and there, and some uneven shelves were just about visible, steeped in shadow, but nothing was clear. She thought she could make out a chair in the far corner, but she wasn't sure. There was no movement. She listened hard, and outside, far away it seemed, she could hear the sounds of life, but within this prison she heard nothing.

The panic returned as thoughts of being left to rot forever overwhelmed her. She would have no food, no water, nothing, not even sleep until she fell away, lost and abandoned. Who would do this? Who wanted her dead, or as good as dead? She was neither rich nor famous, in no way connected to anything on Earth that mattered. Why had this happened? The only answer was Kathryn, something to do with her dead friend, but even that 'something to do with' made no sense. Kathryn had died a year ago; what had this nightmare to do with that?

She tried to move, ever so slightly, but the knots were firm and cut her if she shifted. Every bone in her body ached and her muscles cried out for exercise, to be stretched and set free. She was viciously thirsty. There was dust in the stale air and it drifted into her nose, clogging her throat and forcing a cough, but whatever material covered her mouth stifled the cough and it was all she could do not to choke. What would she have given for a glass, even a sip of water, and a single breath of fresh air! This was hell, like being buried alive, and she doubted she could deal with it for much longer.

How much time had already passed? There was no way of telling. She couldn't see her watch and there was nothing around to give any clue. She might have been unconscious an hour, a day, maybe more than a day. She was hungry as well as thirsty but the hunger was tempered by a sickness of spirit trying to come to terms with this horror.

She lay still, remembering Patrick, remembering Kathryn, her friends and her family. She tried to fill her head with the people who loved her and whom she loved in equal measure. It was hard. The isolation and confinement, the sheer cold blooded emptiness of her abduction weighed on her, threatening to drown the love she lived by beneath a vast, dark and terrible sea of fear.

Madness threatened. She couldn't bear the idea of being left to rot. Who could? It was inhuman, bestial to do this to someone else! It made no sense to her whose whole life was directed by kindness and healing to be bound, dumped and discarded as if there were no laws in the world to prevent such things. She felt her faith in goodness threatened. Surely, surely, surely there had to be some answer to this travesty?

She tried again to calm herself, to keep rational, but the irrationality of the nightmare diverted her efforts, like some powerful gravity pulling her into confusion.

She tried to dismiss the face of the man who had taken her, but it was impossible. It persisted, drawing her attention, taunting her. Who was he? She gave way to its insistence, let it become a focus for a while and tried to match it to her past, a thousand faces in a thousand places. None of them matched. It was a handsome, unthreatening face.

Unless...

Suddenly she realised. It was the absence of expression that revealed the truth. There was nothing there, no soul, no moral compass, no joy, no variety of human feeling, no compassion, sympathy, benevolence; no awareness except of self. She saw it as clearly as if she were looking at him again now. How was it possible to understand such a void? Everything she knew in life was measured according to her own standards, who she was and how she saw the world. This ... thing was alien. She doubted she'd be able to talk with him, let alone reason with him - you couldn't reason with nothing.

She froze.

A noise.

A chink of light appeared, vertical, about thirty feet away at a slightly higher level. It grew, a single vertical line slowly expanding.

A door opening.

A figure entering.

Melissa watched, wide-eyed, dreading who she feared she would see, hoping beyond hope that she might see who she most wanted to see.

She waited to hear Patrick's voice. If it was him, he would call her name. "Melissa?" he would call, gently, and all would be well. But each second that passed was a silent second and there was no calling of names. Instead, the chink of light faded and the door closed.

She saw the silhouette of the man who'd entered. Oh God, oh God, it wasn't Patrick, it was him! It was him!

He didn't look at her. He didn't even cast a glance her way. For another moment Melissa thought that this was someone else, a stranger, or the owner of the building who didn't know she was there. He would turn and see her in astonishment and she would be saved. She murmured through the cloth that covered her mouth, capturing his attention with stifled cries from her stomach. He must have heard, but he didn't turn. Was he deaf? Why wouldn't he see her?

What seemed like a blinding light lit the room. All at once the shadows turned to substance and she saw that she was in a storeroom of some kind, about thirty feet square. The light was from a bare bulb, no more than forty watts, but sun and life in the miserable darkness.

Yes, it was him! The same face, the same presence, a man with an air of single minded purpose, handsome as she remembered, strikingly so.

She feared his look and some terrible, final action that would end her time on Earth, but he ignored her, as if he had no interest or had even forgotten she was there.

Melissa watched him, an invisible bond tying her gaze to his every movement.

He pulled out the chair, a simple wooden one, and sat down, resting a portable computer on a rickety table. Whilst the machine booted up he looked away, but not at her, never at her. She feared his seeing her. She lay perfectly still, afraid that the change might attract his attention, but he ignored her and settled intently to whatever he was doing.

How much time passed she couldn't be sure, but he'd been busy for a long while when he stopped, stood, stretched, then set to work again. She'd never seen anyone so focused, hardly moving at all, like the surgeons at hospital.

After an immeasurable time, he stopped, stood and, at last, looked at her.

She had never taken her eyes off him the whole time and now, unexpectedly, she met his gaze. She tried not to show fear, but she was petrified, and he knew it.

He came towards her and she thought of Kathryn and the knife and started to sweat, but all he did was to loosen the rope and say, "Let's sit you up."

The world had been lopsided ever since she regained consciousness so she was grateful for this small mercy. Once sitting, he tightened the rope again with her hands locked behind her back, her shoulders pulled backwards and taught to breaking point. She found herself about six inches from his gaze.

"Here," he said, "you must be thirsty."

He loosened the gag around her mouth and offered her a sip of water from a glass tumbler. She let him pour a trickle of it at a time down her throat.

"Brave girl," he said, as if he was rescuing her from danger.

"What are you going to do with me?" Melissa asked, her voice husky and edged with fear. She wished she'd never asked.

"Same as Kathryn, probably," he answered. "We'll see."

She trembled at the coldness in the answer, as if it might be the solution to some simple question or a comment on the weather.

"Why are you doing this?" she asked. "Who are you? What...?"

The gag was tied again, tightly as before, the material cutting into the corners of her mouth. He looked at her for a second and took something from a pocket.

With horror, she saw it was a knife.

He ran his finger along the edge and said, "It was an act of charity, you know, nothing more. You can't fraternize with the devil and not expect some retribution."

Melissa's eyes were wide with terror. His words scared her, more because they hid as much as they revealed.

She pleaded with him not to do whatever it was she thought he was about to do. Drops of sweat fell from her and she felt a terrible tightness in her stomach. Her mind seemed to reel as she stared at the knife.

"Not yet," he said gently, and he put it away, then turned from her as if she had vanished from his consciousness altogether and continued to busy himself with his work.

Melissa watched him, not understanding any of this bizarre behaviour. She was measuring him by familiar human standards, but those standards didn't apply here. He might as well have been alien; nothing she thought, spoke or felt would register with him, she saw that, and that was more unnerving than anything else. He moved with such ease, totally unfazed by the life and death fluctuations of the moment. What, thought Melissa, had Kathryn had to do with this maniac? Who was he and how had Kathryn become his victim?

He worked away silently for another half an hour or so. All the time, Melissa never took her eyes off him, afraid that any second he would turn, pick up the knife and end her life for no other reason than a whim. The arbitrariness scared her as much as anything else, though she still tried to reason out why she was there and what he wanted. She failed, miserably - nothing was even vaguely evident.

She watched him work, and whilst he busied himself on the computer she felt safe, but when, eventually, he stopped again, the panic returned. She froze, afraid he would turn his attention to her, but he picked up his coat from the back of the chair and headed to the door. He gripped the door handle and she prayed he would just go without acknowledgement, but at the last moment he turned towards her and said, "Did you really think I would leave without saying goodbye?"

She started to tremble and prayed to whichever god might be listening, 'Make him go! Make him go! Don't let him hurt me, please!'

Her eyes opened wide; there was no way she could hide the fear.

"Back soon," he said, then without waiting for a response he turned out the light and left.

She listened for any sound of his return and, on hearing nothing, ever so slowly, she let go a breath that had been held for eternity.

Plunged into darkness, Melissa ached to scream, but the gag tore into her mouth and all she could do was make the most useless, plaintiff sounds, like a beaten animal, knowing its master had abandoned it for the night with neither food nor water, just an unkind word and the threat of a beating yet to come.

## 11

Despite Faraday's instructions for Sam to stay with his father, they were hardly out of the police station when he excused himself.

"No Sam," said Chaim, "you stay with me."

"'fraid not, dad. That was impressive, it really was, thinking deep like that, but I've got to go."

"Go where? To see your girlfriend? There are more important things, Sam."

Sam couldn't think of any and said, "Dad, I'm sorry, I really am. I don't mean to be a pain, but this is important."

"More important than doing what the police tell you?"

"They don't know everything dad. I've just got a feeling about something. Trust me."

Chaim shook his head. He couldn't see a single reason why the girl, who he'd never met, shouldn't be a nice, decent even if non-Jewish girl, but he was angry with Sam for disobeying the inspector. He was a patient man who rarely got angry, but Sam was a frustrating teenager and this was a particularly frustrating thing to do.

"You're going to have to choose, Sam," he said. "You can't live in two worlds. Everyone has to decide."

"Later," said Sam, in a hurry to do what he had to do. "We'll talk about it dad, promise. I'm not being a rebel for nothing, I like her. I love her. I want to make sure she's okay."

"You don't know what love is, Sam. You..."

"Dad, I've got to go, really. Tell me later. I won't be long. Just want to check things out. Don't panic, dad. I'll take care."

He dashed off leaving Chaim staring after his son as if he'd just been robbed.

Sam took out his mobile and called Feriha. No answer. Faintly anxious, he called Jemal.

"Jem, it's Sam."

"Oh, right, my sister's boyfriend."

They hadn't seen much of each other in the past couple of months so the friendship was a little cold, bordering on icy.

"Don't be a pratt," said Sam. "I can't help the way things are." Jemal grunted something on the other end of the phone. "Is Feri there?" Sam asked. "I tried to call her but there's no answer."

He heard a sigh, then Jemal said, "Is that all you're ever going to call me for, to find out where my drop dead gorgeous sister is?"

"No," said Sam, "but where is she?"

"Not a clue," said Jemal. "Am I my sister's keeper?"

"No," said Sam. "I am. Listen Jemal, this is important. There's loads of stuff going on. I just want to make sure she's okay."

"Stuff?" Jemal asked. "What kind of stuff?"

"Listen," said Sam. "I'm coming round to see you. I'll tell you then."

"Suppose I don't want to see you."

"You have to, Jemal, this is serious. And I need your computer. See you."

Jemal might have sworn at his almost-ex-friend, but Sam had hung up.

Their meeting was predictably awkward.

"Watcha Jemal."

"Yeh."

"Come on, Jem, don't be sore at me. I'm your friend, I really am."

"And you need my computer."

"Yeh, I do, but you'll understand."

Sam wasn't sure whether or not Jemal would understand, but he was in dynamic mode and his friend's feelings came second to the urgency of the moment.

The 'job' he'd done for the dead policeman was worrying him, just as it was worrying his father and Faraday, and though he couldn't change what he'd done, he might be able to finish what he'd started. Something about the communication was wrong and something about the new lead the police had was wrong, too, and Sam needed Jemal's computer equipment to resolve it all, if it was resolvable.

"You dumped me," said Jemal, obstinate to the end. "Why should I bother with you?"

"I didn't dump you Jemal, I just like your sister better than you - I mean I like her different to you. I can't help what's happened but you're still my friend." Jemal didn't look convinced. "And this is to do with Feriha," Sam added.

"I thought it might be," Jemal said, glumly.

He let Sam in and they went upstairs to the bedroom which was more like the US Defence Headquarters than ever.

"Is she around?" Sam asked.

"I told you, she's out. She's visiting our gay auntie."

Sam remembered the talk he and Feriha had had and smiled to himself, but didn't say anything to Jemal whose feathers were easily ruffled right now. In a way, he was glad Feriha wasn't there; he'd need to concentrate, and he couldn't seem to do that when he saw her. He told Jemal all that had happened and Jemal's antipathy slowly began to fade. He'd heard about the policeman being murdered but he didn't know Sam had been involved. He was impressed, especially when Sam told him about the weird communication.

"With the killer?"

"Yeh, I think so. It has to be."

"And they know where he is?"

"That's the thing," said Sam, "I'm not sure they do." He told Jemal about the murdered nurse's boyfriend giving them an address in Hackney Wick, but something about the Notepad communication stuck in Sam's mind. "My dad was brilliant," he said. "I hate to admit it, but he was. Regular Mr Spock, all logic, and it got me thinking about the contact. Something didn't fit, Jemal."

"Like what?" They set up Jemal's computer, along with a GPS system. "You're not going to contact him from here, are you?" Jemal asked, worried. "I don't want the freak knowing about me."

"No," said Sam, "but what I want to do is check the MAC address and the IP."

Jemal watched. He was good at the technical side, but he'd always known that Sam was better. It wasn't that Sam knew more than he did, it was that Sam was more creative, able to break through problems quicker than Jemal. Whenever they hit brick walls in their hacking efforts, Sam cracked the problem first – always. He watched as Sam loaded a MAC finding program and set about tracing the information again, all of which he'd written down.

"I'll tell you what I think," said Sam. "This MAC address is fake."

"You can't fake a MAC address," said Jemal.

"Yes," said Sam, "you can. You can put up a dummy address, and that's what he's done, and that's what I'd do if I was trying to hide."

"But even so, Sam, there's no way you can find out where the freak is just by knowing his MAC. It'll be like looking for the proverbial needle, mate."

That was a good sign, Jemal calling him 'mate' again. It told Sam that all might be well between them soon.

"What I think," said Sam, "logically, like my dad, is that this guy is arrogant. He'll hide alright, but I don't think he'll use regular stuff that anyone can break into. He's cleverer than that."

"So what will he do?"

"Dunno, Jemal, not for sure. Let's see..." and Jemal watched as Sam began a sequence of scans and searches using a range of commands, most of which ended up with "Search Aborted" messages flashing up. Jemal knew better than to interrupt when Sam was in full flow, so he watched, only making suggestions when he thought Sam needed a prompt, which wasn't often.

An hour later, a circle lit up on the GPS system.

"That was easy," said Sam, sweating slightly.

"Hackney?" said Jemal, looking at the map.

Sam looked more closely and frowned. "Yes, but..."

"But what?"

Instead of answering, Sam re-checked his routing, through scores of hubs and switches. After this solid checking he said, "but not where it's supposed to be."

"Where's that then?" Jemal asked. "I don't understand."

Sam told him what had happened at the meeting with the Inspector who was off to Hackney Wick where they thought the missing woman was being held.

"And?" Jemal asked again.

"Look," said Sam, pointing at the GPS, "this is Hackney, but it isn't Hackney Wick."

Jemal looked again and said, "Maybe your trace isn't a hundred percent accurate, brainbox."

Sam sat back and stared at Jemal.

"It is," he said simply. "It doesn't make sense though, unless..."

"Unless what? Come on, Sam, spit it out."

Sam wouldn't be rushed. In fact, he couldn't be rushed. He remembered what his father had said and what he had always been taught, to think in terms of biblical law, precisely and with attention to detail. His father had been right, go back to first principles, but maybe they'd missed the true connection, something so tight between the mysterious Daniel Hart, who Sam had never met but heard of too many times, and this nutjob roaming the streets of Hackney, that it would take a twenty-first century whizzkid as well as biblical analysis to sort it out.

He stared at the GPS location and google-mapped it and enlarged it to maximum.

"Sam? Are you okay?"

"No, I'm not."

"Why? What's up, mate?" Jemal looked at the enlarged area into which Sam had traced the true origin of the video. "Oh, right. I see. That's a bit odd, Sam, don't you think?"

Odd wasn't the word. Smack in the middle of the map, pointed at in a rather incriminatory way by a little red arrow, was the symbol for a place of worship that was neither church nor mosque, but somewhere deep in Sam's struggling soul ... a synagogue.

## 12

"So," said Nurcan, "I'm glad we've had this talk. Are you, Feriha?"

"Yes, auntie."

"But you're still fazed by it, aren't you?"

"A bit, yeh."

They were walking in the eastern area of Victoria Park. They hadn't spoken much the past year and Nurcan felt that she wanted – that she needed – to speak with her niece.

"I don't want to feel like a leper," said Nurcan.

"What's that?" Feriha asked, and Nurcan laughed. She was laughing more often than she ever thought possible.

"I don't want to feel like I'm unwelcome," Nurcan said, "especially by you. Jemal, well, he's a boy, his head is wired differently, but you Feriha, you're my favourite niece..."

"I'm your only niece, auntie."

"Yes you are, and I couldn't ask for a better one."

"And I do understand, I really do. I mean, it isn't something I want to be myself..."

"It isn't a question of want," said Nurcan, "it's who I am. I fought it for so long, but this is me. I don't understand it myself, not completely, but I don't think anyone understands what drives them. I'm happy now, much happier than before, don't you see that?"

Feriha remembered the stiff, anxious, severe auntie who had been replaced by this chatty, friendly and supportive version.

"Yeh, I do," she said. "It's nice of you to talk to me, auntie."

"Sometimes," said Nurcan, "I feel you are the auntie and I'm the niece," which made them both laugh. "Anyway, how are things with you and Sam?"

Feriha hadn't seen Sam for a day, and although absence made the heart grow fonder, it also made her grow more anxious. She feared his parents and his religion might pull him away from her.

319

"Great," she said, uncertain how much to tell her aunt.

"Great is good," said Nurcan. "I won't pry, Feriha, it's none of my business, but I guess it isn't straightforward, nothing that's a tiny bit different is straightforward."

Even Feriha, as young as she was, saw this. She knew how much of a pull Sam's religion was on him, even though he denied it, and how wary her mum and dad were of her getting 'too involved', so she could hardly imagine what hell it must have been for her aunt to 'come out'. It was much safer to tread the path most followed, she'd got that message pretty clearly already.

"He makes me laugh," said Feriha, "which is strange because he doesn't seem to make anyone else laugh."

Nurcan stopped walking and looked at her niece.

"That," she said, "is deep insight, Feri. Most people see their lovers as universally irresistible."

"I don't think he's that," said Feriha. "He's nice looking and all that, but he can be a bit strung up, only not with me, at least not any more. He used to be, but he's changed, like you."

"This sounds serious, Feri."

"Does your ... erm ... Angela ... does she make you laugh, auntie?" another question which made Nurcan appreciate and adore her niece.

"Yes, she does."

"Well, that's good too, isn't it?" said Feriha. "Can I ask you something, auntie. It's a bit nosey, and you can tell me to mind my own business if you want."

"You can ask me anything, Feri. What is it?"

Feriha hesitated because she had a feeling that this might be a tricky subject, but she asked anyway. "It's about the nurse who was killed."

The silence told Feriha that her instincts were right, this might well be a tricky subject.

"What about her, Feri?" Nurcan asked, her guard up slightly.

"It's just ... that night ... when you came round ... you were so upset ... I mean really, really, really upset. I told Sam."

"Did you?"

"Yes, sorry, shouldn't I?"

"Well, it's best for you two not to have secrets. What did he say?"

Here, Feriha hesitated again, but she was in so deep she had to keep going.

"He thought ... I mean considering that you're out now, auntie, he wouldn't have thought it otherwise ... that ... you might have liked her in your way ... a bit special."

For the third time, Nurcan stopped, and this time she didn't know whether to laugh or cry. What she really wanted to do was hug her niece, but she daren't. Everything she did, especially everything physical or emotional, was looked at in a different way now, and no matter how accepting people were, she had to be careful.

"And what did you think, Feri?"

"I thought he might be right auntie, I mean you were so upset. I said I'd ask you."

"And will you report back?"

Feriha turned red and said, "I wouldn't put it like that, auntie, but if the subject crops up and he asks me, I might, unless you tell me not to."

Nurcan thought for a moment, then said, "I loved her, Feri. She was a beautiful woman and I fell for her as soon as we met. The highlight of my day was when I gave her and her friend a lift to work or when I saw her in the hospital. Sometimes I couldn't sleep, thinking about her."

"But you never told her, auntie?"

"No, I didn't. She was straight, if that's the right word, and it probably isn't, but you know what I mean, and she had Daniel – the boyfriend?" Feriha nodded. She'd obviously heard of him through Sam. "I thought it was an obsession that would wear off one day."

"But it didn't, did it?"

"No, not after weeks, months or years. "

"Blimey, auntie, that was tough!"

Nurcan burst out laughing again saying, "Feri, you really are a delight. No wonder this boy likes you."

"I think he loves me, auntie. So ... wow ... how did you deal with it when she was ... well..."

"...when she was murdered? I didn't deal with it, it dealt with me, Feri. I had to identify her and ... Feri, I don't think I can go into detail," she said, clearly disturbed by the memory, "but it was all I could do to hold myself together. That's why I came to your mum."

"Yeh, I can see that," said Feriha. "Poor auntie!"

"We were up all night, everyone involved, but I was on the edge of it all. I hadn't told anyone and so to them I was just the night nurse on duty who had identified the body, an acquaintance, too, but nothing more. My feelings were my own, and they were too much to bear. I cracked up."

"Did you, auntie? I don't remember that?"

Nurcan brushed her niece's hair and said, "No one would. When you pass people on the street you don't think 'oh, she's cracking up' or 'he's about to have a nervous breakdown'. You just don't know what's going on inside them, but I was cracking up, and I did do something peculiar."

"What was that auntie?"

"I didn't go home, I didn't go back to work, I drove around London trying to figure out a way to handle it. And this is where it gets bizarre, Feriha. I ended up in a little cafe in the middle of some godforsaken street, surrounded by noise and madness, and met Angela."

"I didn't know that, auntie, what on the same day!"

"Yes, the same day."

"Blimey again, auntie, this is a bit weird."

"Yes, isn't it. She saw me crying and wanted to help. Can you believe that? Doesn't it make you believe in God, Feriha?"

God wasn't part of Feriha's world view. Whenever God was mentioned she'd conjure up a conventional image, but to think of God making such incredibly intimate things happen in a cafe in North London wasn't easy.

"I don't know, auntie. Flip!"

Nurcan laughed again. 'Flip!' was such an innocent way of summing up what had happened to her on the day of Kathryn's murder and all the days since.

"I know what you're thinking, Feri, that this was so fast, maybe I didn't love Kathryn as much as I thought. Is that right?"

"I suppose ... but no, not really auntie. I can't imagine what I'd do if something happened to Sam."

"That's just it, Feri, we can't imagine. And every love is different. I think I'd repressed my feelings for so long, they suddenly exploded. Listen, you don't mind me telling you all this, do you?"

"Mind! No, auntie, it's about time someone talked to me like I was grown up. Mum and dad still think I'm a little girl."

"No, you're not anymore, but this is private, Feriha, just between you and I."

"Yes, I know, auntie. I won't blab about it, promise."

They'd walked quite a long way, but the Spring day was warm and Victoria Park was an abundance of green. It didn't have the contours of Springfield, but it was much larger and you could lose yourself there fairly easily. It also bordered on the canal and they had reached a fence with the waterway on the other side. A barge motored along, heading towards the Regents Canal, and there were boats moored here and there along the embankment.

"Do you still think of her, auntie, the dead nurse?"

"Kathryn, call her Kathryn, Feri. And yes, I do, every day."

"But you love Angela?"

"I do, very much. Confusing, isn't it?"

"It is a bit. Doesn't she mind?"

"I don't think she does. If she did, I couldn't love her. We're complex creatures, humans. I wish things were simpler, but they're not are they, Feri?"

"No, auntie. It does my head in trying to understand it all. I kind of thought that people loved just one person forever, proper love that is, not the temporary kind."

Nurcan laughed again, fonder than ever of her niece.

"It happens," she said, "look at your mum and dad."

"Do I have to?"

"Well, they get on. A lot of people just 'get on'. There isn't always much space in life for passion to last the course. Everything changes. You'll also change, Feriha. So, what are you going to do about Sam, or is that a stupid question?"

"No, it isn't stupid, but I don't know yet. Do you think it's proper love, auntie?"

Nurcan wanted to squeeze her niece and give her all the wisdom she would need to keep her heart solid gold in a corrupting world, but once again she kept herself in check and said, "If you love him now, that's proper love. You are a special person, Feriha, he's lucky that you like him so much. Will I ever meet him?"

"Don't know auntie. I'm not sure you'd like him. He can be a dickhead sometimes." Nurcan shook her head, stifling her laughter. "Will I ever meet Angela?" Feriha added.

"Yes, whenever you want. And I know she'd like you." Nurcan checked her watch. "I'd better get going, Feriha. Let's walk back together."

They headed towards Well Street where Nurcan had parked her car. They didn't speak much and though Nurcan wanted very much just to hold her niece's arm, she didn't, but she was delighted and relieved when Feriha took hers instead and rested her head on her shoulder. She remembered when Feriha was born, when she was a delightfully happy baby, when she grew to be an independent little girl off to school for the first time, and now here she was, Nurcan's favourite family member, listening to her auntie open her heart and soul and treating it so delicately.

When they reached the car, Nurcan said, "You're a treasure, Feriha, look after yourself. And if things get, as you say, serious, with Sam, make sure he looks after you."

"I will, auntie, and if he doesn't I'll kick him in the goolies."

"Right. Well, do you want a lift back?"

"No, it's okay, I'm going to see Sam the Man."

Nurcan kissed Feri on the cheek and drove away.

Feriha watched her aunt drive off, thinking a thousand thoughts. She waited at the bus stop, sitting on the ridiculously sloped and narrow red plastic strip which did all it could to make life uncomfortable.

"Stupid things, aren't they?"

Feriha turned to see who had spoken. A guy in a green anorak was sitting at the other end of the bus stop, handsome as hell and he knew it, but Feriha didn't spare him a glance.

"They're supposed to stop winos sleeping on them at night," he added.

Feriha didn't want to get into conversation and knew she ought to say nothing, but she hated the term 'winos' and said so.

"Lesson learned," said the man. "Apologies." He waited a few moments then said, "It's probably best not to talk to strangers."

"I know that," said Feriha, "so don't."

"Very sensible," said the man. He laughed lightly then stood and looked away.

The bus was coming.

## 13

A team of armed police officers was formed with Faraday in charge. He'd located the workshop in Hackney Wick which Daniel had, belatedly, told him about. He seemed to have to suck information from Daniel drop by drop, first the unread letter, then the fact that he had an agency temp helping out, and now this. He wondered what else Daniel was forgetting to tell him. Faraday knew it wasn't intentional, but Daniel was a deep chap whose mind had gone AWOL on religion, and Faraday could never forget that of all the people hurt by the death of Kathryn Hudson, Daniel was one of the worst affected, even though he showed it least.

They'd watched the place for a day, but though they'd seen nothing, Faraday decided it was time to act. The workshop was in an old block, most of the windows of which were boarded up. A single dubious firm still had rented rooms on the ground floor, but they had been quietly informed to make themselves conspicuous by their absence. The block was going to be pulled down for redevelopment, part of the all-encompassing Olympic Dream, and not before time. The brickwork of the three story building was dirty and the mortar holding the whole thing together was beginning to fail, so even if the demolition wasn't done on time, the building would probably demolish itself soon enough. Of the windows which weren't boarded, a few were broken. Faraday hoped there were no squatters inside liable to be caught up in any cross fire.

Hackney Wick lay at the convergence of the Lea Navigation and the Hertford Canal. Even if the Olympic wave hadn't touched it, something would have had to come its way sooner rather than later as it had become one of the bleakest parts of Hackney, belying its beautiful name. Already it was being transformed, and the last thing anyone associated with it wanted was a storming of the Bastille episode with guns blazing.

Faraday had told the team what to expect, although, as ever, they had to expect the unexpected. If Melissa Cochrane was being held there, her safety was paramount, and the team had to do everything they could, as trigger happy as some of them were, to make this a peaceful operation.

There were three doors giving access to the block, one at the front, one on the east side and one at the rear. The fourth side was solid, but there was an old iron fire escape built from a third floor window to the ground. Unfortunately, Daniel's old office was on the third floor so not only did the team have to operate on all four sides of the building, but they had somehow to navigate the entire internal structure to get to where they needed to be. Four members of the team were sent to each access point whilst a control team watched from a children's playground about ten metres away. A police helicopter had made a couple of passes above the building to check the flat roof, which was just as well as there was a skylight which gave access to it and thus to the fire escape. Unless there was a secret passage, which was highly unlikely, the building was secure.

Faraday led the team from the front, literally and metaphorically. He was comfortable with a gun, though he preferred, like most officers, not to have to use it. He'd only ever had to fire in self-defence once, and that was early on in his career. He preferred peaceful solutions to problems, but the world wouldn't always let its problems be solved peacefully – violence rumbled away at the heart of men and their machinations.

He was fed information by the control group and had decided to take the front entrance whilst Fowler took the back entrance and Charlene the side. It bothered Faraday that the suspect hadn't been seen there in the hours the building had been watched, but he might well be hiding there and, if Melissa Cochrane was indeed being kept hostage in one of the offices, they couldn't wait any longer; they had to go in. He wasn't expecting a great shoot out as guns hadn't been part of the equation so far, but they could hardly go in as if it was a Sunday stroll in the park.

On this warm Spring day the Wick had a touch of serenity about it, despite the massive building works going on all around. None of them had been asked to stop as Faraday wanted to cause as least disruption as possible and also to draw the least attention to what they were doing. It had been a moot point to ask the single remaining firm to go, but they'd done it as surreptitiously as possible. Besides, it was a mini-sweat shop and Faraday felt no remorse at giving three hard-done-by female workers the day off.

The teams entered the building at the same time, reporting back in muted whispers that there was nothing to be seen. Well, there was, in the sense that this was an interesting building almost eighty years old, once the grand ambitious dream of a rich entrepreneur, now cheap rental space for the financially challenged. Historians would have found the interior interesting, with its evidence of past glory and lost ambition. It had echoes of Ozymandias, though rather few and faint now.

"Clear here," whispered Faraday.

The three teams that had entered faced two stairwells, one at the front, one at the eastern side, so one team split, two members keeping guard on the ground floor, and the others joining the two teams climbing the steps, making their way to the first floor.

The area was also clear.

It was difficult to know what they expected to find. Faraday didn't think the murderer, if indeed it was the murderer, would do a Hollywood job on them; he was a secret, cowardly figure attacking those who couldn't fight back. Nevertheless, they were prepared.

"All clear on second," he whispered, and the same reply came from the other team. The guards on the ground floor said all was quiet.

The third floor was bound by iron railings with doors set along the top of the steps and along two corridors leading into each end of the building. The teams could see each other now and they could also see a few room numbers, although some were hanging askew whilst others had fallen off completely. Daniel had rented Room 323 which was in the western corridor. Faraday thought it odd that Daniel had wanted an upper floor to use as a workshop, but the place was obviously dirt cheap, and there had been a lift, though it was no longer in use.

The third floor was deserted.

Faraday made his way along, keeping in touch with the other team who were checking each of the rooms, just in case.

When he came to 323, Faraday split his team on either side of the door and knocked.

No answer.

He gently turned the handle. Locked. He called a beefy team member to do the Starsky and Hutch entry, kicking the door down and twisting to the side, just in case bullets flew their way, but all was quiet. Faraday signalled and poked his head around the corner of the door frame. The room was dark, it's boarded windows in shadow. There was absolutely no sound.

Faraday crept in, gun ready. On the inside of the wall was a light switch. He flicked it. Nothing. Electric for the upper floors had been turned off some time ago. They shone torches inside.

The workshop was about thirty feet by twenty. Three large tables stood in the centre and there were cupboard along the walls. A closed door faced them at the opposite end. Cautiously, Faraday went with another team member and checked it; it was open but revealed only a store cupboard, empty except for a couple of boxes left behind on an upper shelf.

The team started to relax. There was no one there, nor did it look as though anyone had been there recently. Faraday reported this to the control group who told him that nothing had been found by the other team and that the building looked safe. Nevertheless, Faraday sent officers to search each room, just in case Melissa, or her body, had been hidden in one of them.

They found nothing.

Faraday cursed. This had seemed so much like the missing link, a vital clue which had turned up at the very last moment and which would surely lead to resolution of the case. He felt thwarted, as he had right through the investigation. For a year he had devoted as much time as he could to finding the beat that had murdered Kathryn Hudson. He wasn't the type to give up, but he'd been at a loss to know what to do next when he'd visited Daniel and found out about Rekin. He would have sworn his life and soul that this was Rekin's hideaway and that Melissa Cochrane was being held here, but it wasn't and she wasn't and Faraday felt despair and anger taking hold again.

"Sir?"

One of the team had opened the boxes in the store cupboard.

The top box was empty, but the bottom box wasn't.

Inside was a piece of paper, blank side uppermost. On the reverse side, however, was a computer generated image of Kathryn Hudson, lying on the ground in the dim Homerton passageway where she'd been cut down.

Faraday was silent for a moment, then, "Must have left it behind, sir," said the officer

"I guess so," said Faraday. "Put it back. Don't touch it more than you can help."

He reported the find to the control group and to the other team. It made no difference to the rest of the search, nothing else was found and there was no more evidence. A forensic team was called in to check the picture and the rest of the workshop. Faraday waited outside the room, the teams standing down once the building was declared clear.

"Do you think he left it on purpose, sir?" Fowler asked

Faraday doubted it. There wouldn't appear to be any point, but he was losing faith in his own logic and intuition. He had ideas, but all his ideas had proved fruitless in the hunt for this killer. He also had a sick feeling that he'd tapped into a disturbingly deep hatred, one which reflected on society as well as an individual. As a police officer, his duty was to deal with law breakers and a lot of the time offences were trivial. Even when they weren't trivial, there were understandable personal motivations, but this was indicative of something intrinsically nasty and Faraday felt powerless to stop it.

"Possibly. I ..." he started to say when a call came in from a number he recognized only too well. He listened for a few brief moments then said something down the line in a strange voice Fowler had rarely heard, a mixture of panic and fierce determination.

"Where?" he asked, then, "Wait, watch, do nothing! We'll be there, ten minutes! Keep calm!" and he hung up.

"Sir?" Viv Fowler asked, sensing the connection.

He didn't answer but called to the teams in a voice of iron. They stopped dead and listened. He bellowed out an address and brief instructions.

"No questions!" he ordered. "Move!" he commanded. "Now! Go, go, go!"

He didn't stop for breath but shifted into gear with fierce determination, a man possessed.

## 14

"Sam, this is bananas, man," said Jemal. "Let's call the frigging police!"

Sam had that air of determination about him which Jemal recognised and knew he wouldn't be able to shift.

"Not yet. Let's just check it out ourselves first, then we can call them."

"Check what though, man? I don't want to tackle a flipping murderer, Sam."

Sam didn't listen – he wasn't the type to let the cat kill his curiosity. He didn't quite believe that a real live murderer was at the other end of his Notepad chat; it was more than likely a hacker, and when they met they'd have a laugh and swap stories.

They were close to the synagogue in a dense part of Hackney untouched by Olympic Fever. It was a half residential, half commercial area with little a stranger could distinguish from other parts of the borough, or indeed from other parts of any city. A familiar observer, however, would know the lie of the land, the colour of the brickwork, the design of houses and the style of shops. The initiated, just as Michael had said a year earlier, could be dropped anywhere in the borough and know exactly where they were.

Sam knew of the synagogue, but it wasn't one he'd ever been to. The Jewish people were as fussy about which sect they belonged to and which places of worship they attended as any other community. They were a strong minded people, too. A joke was told of the Jew stranded on a desert island who, when he was rescued after many years, had built two synagogues. 'One is mine,' he told his rescuers, 'one I wouldn't go in if you paid me.' Sam was not yet at that stage, but his parents were picky about their synagogues.

This one was down a side road, a little away from the main routes, but not isolated.

"If he is a murderer," said Sam, "he wouldn't choose a place like this, Jemal, would he? He'd be seen."

Jemal didn't know or care. All he wanted was to get away and tell the police, but Sam said they didn't have anything to tell them yet.

"We do," insisted Jemal, "otherwise what the heck are we doing here, Sam?"

Sam didn't answer but headed towards it.

"Tell you what," said Jemal with more than a touch of sarcasm, "let's stand at the door and sing Christmas Carols. That way he'll ignore us, especially if he's a Jewish murderer."

Again, Sam didn't answer. He was nothing if not focused, although the thought had crossed his mind that if this really was the killer, why had he chosen to hide in a synagogue? It didn't make sense. The only reasonable explanation was that this was a hacker, as obsessed as he and Jemal, and had tapped into the video. Maybe the guy was as wary of them as they were of him. And he might not be hiding in the synagogue, he might be living next door or close by – the GPS wasn't accurate to the nearest millimetre.

They walked around the synagogue but there was no sign of life.

"Okay, let's go," said Jemal.

Sam ignored him, thoughtful again. He could knock on the door, but what would he say, assuming anyone was there? It was an old place and the chances were that it wasn't even used any more.

"No," he said. "I want to look at something again."

"Like what, man? There's nothing here, Sam!"

Sam disagreed. Behind the Synagogue, easy to miss, was a narrow stairwell, accessed through an old iron gate. If you looked straight down it was nothing, just an innocuous rectangular area where litter collected, but to the side, beneath a jutting lintel, was a small, wooden door. It might have been painted black about three thousand years ago at the time of the first temple, but it hadn't seen much attention since. The paint was flaking and the wood looked as if it might be host to a civilisation of bugs, delighted at being left for so long to chew the door to dust.

"It's probably locked," said Jemal. "No one's going to go down there, Sam ... right ... except you, that is." Sam pushed the gate and it creaked open. "Come on, Sam, this is trespassing. We'll end up in prison."

Sam didn't want to keep arguing the point and said nothing. He walked down the stairs and inspected the door. An ancient lock stared back at him. There had once been a mortise lock but the weevils, or whichever creatures were living inside the wood, had eaten around it and there was now a half inch hole. He peeked through.

"There's nothing, is there?" Jemal said.

"Can't see anything," said Sam.

"Right, let's go then," said Jemal.

"That's because it's pitch black," said Sam.

"Well, it would be," said Jemal, more to himself than to his obsessed friend.

Sam looked at the door handle, a rusted black thing which seemed to be held in place by dirt rather than screws. He pushed it down. Nothing.

"Sam! Don't! For God's sake, mine if not yours, it's locked, leave it!"

Sam gently rested his shoulder against the door and shoved.

Jemal said, "Are all Jews as stubborn as you?"

"Certainly are," said Sam, pushing a little harder.

There was a sudden click and the door opened an inch or two.

"Oh, great!" said Jemal.

"Lock was broken," said Sam. "A baby could have opened it."

They waited, stepping back in case a mad axman jumped at them, but nothing happened. From inside, a deep darkness issued. Sam slowly pushed the door which did its best to creak with every inch it opened.

Jemal held his breath.

A musty smell seeped out, but there was neither sight nor sound of activity.

Sam stepped inside.

It took a few moments to adjust to the dark, even with the door open, for there were more steps leading further down where the darkness grew thicker.

"Don't go there, Sam. Let's call the police now."

"Just a quick look," said Sam. "It'll be okay."

Jemal didn't think 'okay' was the right word - scary as hell came close. What if the madman closed the door on them and locked them away forever? No one would find them. They would be discovered in thousands of years time, skeletons, rotten....

"Jemal?"

"What man?"

I think there's something here.

"Something like what?"

Jemal was inside the door, but at the top of the steps. Sam had walked down and was peering into the dark.

"Hard to say. Wish we'd bought torches."

"Good idea," said Jemal. "Let's go back and get some and bring a few policemen at the same time."

Sam looked around. The room was not particularly high and his head was only about six inches from the ceiling. This was definitely some kind of Jewish archive. There were things he recognised from synagogues, prayer books, chumash and even a sepher torah scroll holder – the wooden poles which held the sacred Pentateuch, the Five Books of Moses. In his own modest synagogue they didn't go in for fancy silver and gold trinkets, but he knew that wasn't the norm. There was nothing valuable down here, that was obvious, otherwise it would have been more secure, and he guessed it was for excess items no longer needed now that the community had moved to pastures new.

There was something else, though, something not quite in keeping with the layout of the land, as it were, a strange shape huddled on the floor at the far end of the room.

"Hello?" Sam whispered.

"What the fuck are you playing at, Sam?" Jemal whispered. "Why don't you just shout the odds?"

"Hey, Jemal, no swearing, this is a place of God. You know I don't like swearing."

Sam made his way towards the shape, watching it carefully, trying to make out what it was. He had to skirt a table and a chair and avoid some boxes placed, or fallen, on the concrete floor. About two metres from the huddled shape he stopped, or rather he froze.

The shape was a woman.

She was squeezed into a foetal position, lying on the cold ground, her hands and feet bound by ropes tied to old shelf supports fixed on the back wall. Her mouth was gagged and her eyes were closed. She was either asleep or...

Sam knelt beside her. He tapped her shoulder and flew back. The woman's eyes suddenly opened and she stared at him in horror. A pitiful sound emerged through the gag.

"It's alright, it's alright," said Sam. "I'm a friend."

The woman was trying to focus. Her eyes were wet with tears and dull with dust, but they also showed a fear that filled Sam's heart with pity.

"Here," said Sam, "sit up."

She was still afraid. He could tell that she wasn't sure of him or that she had so given up on a rescue that she couldn't believe he was there.

Gently, Sam raised her into a sitting position then put his hand to her mouth to remove the gag. He thought that she would calm down, but the noises from within the gag grew louder.

"Listen," said Sam, pausing a moment, "don't be afraid. Really. I'm a friend. We've found you. Just relax, honestly."

It made no difference, the sounds grew even louder and more manic, and Sam noticed that her eyes weren't looking directly at him but beyond him.

"Jemal," he said, without turning, "come and help. Quick, man. Don't worry," he said to the woman, "Jemal's a friend too. Jemal, where..."

When there was no answer, he turned and froze for a second time. It took a few moments to take in what he was looking at in the shadows of the basement.

Two figures stood at the bottom of the stairs but neither was Jemal. Jemal was nowhere to be seen, unless the crumpled heap lying close by was Jemal. He didn't know the man – it definitely was a man – standing and watching him, but he thought he recognised the smaller, frailer figure the man held close to his chest, only it made no sense to see her here, of all places.

"Feri?" he whispered.

"Sam! Sam! What are you..."

She stopped in mid-sentence. The man held her from behind, gripping a six inch knife around her throat.

Sam stood. He heard the pitiful cries of despair from the woman still tied and gagged. He could imagine how she felt, so close to rescue - then this!

"Make a sound and I'll slice her pretty head off," said the man.

"I won't say anything," said Sam. "Promise. Just let her go."

"Not yet," said the man. "Well, well, well. You are a bright little Jewboy aren't you?"

Sam felt the nastiness of the word. He'd experienced anti-Semitism in his life but whenever he did, he could take care of himself. This was different. He didn't know what to say or what to do. Jemal had been right. This was the stupidest thing he could have done.

"Let her go," said Sam. "She's a girl."

The man laughed.

"My, you are gallant, young sir. Brought up in the right way, were you?"

Sam didn't answer. He looked at Feriha whose expression he would never forget. The knife was pressing against her neck and he thought he could see, even in the shadows, a drop of blood. He felt a peculiar mixture of hatred and fear. He wanted to tear this man apart, wipe him from the face of the Earth. What kind of lunatic was he? All the passion of the Old Testament judgements flowed through Sam, but he kept control. He told himself, 'keep control, keep control', only there was no control to keep. This monster held lovely Feriha at knife point and Sam had the overwhelming feeling that the man could slit her throat without a blink. There was something missing in him, Sam felt it and saw it.

"What do you want?" Sam asked. "I'll do anything, just let her go."

The man looked at him with an almost amused expression.

"Get down on your knees."

Sam thought about arguing the point but was scared for Feri, more scared than he had ever been for anything, ever. He imagined the knife flicking and Feriha falling; he saw blood pouring from her neck and heard her screams – and it was all he could do to put these imaginings out of his mind.

He knelt down.

"Hands behind your back," said the man.

He did this, too.

The man walked up to him.

"You little Jewboys are all the same," he said. "All talk, no walk."

Sam felt the hatred, not his own so much as the man's. This wasn't dislike or animosity, this was a profound emotion that Sam couldn't match. His own feelings shrank before the supreme cruelty in every atom of this man's presence. He felt weighed down, paralysed by waves of hatred. His heart raced. What would happen? He would be killed, for sure, and then Feriha would be killed and all because he'd been so arrogant.

"Let her go," he said, "please."

"Right you are," said the man. "Never forget your manners. Did your Jewish mummy tell you that? Head down."

"What do you mean, head down."

"Put your fucking head down, you cretin. On the floor."

Sam didn't know what to do. He felt like such a coward, and yet if he angered the man in any way, Feriha would die. He cursed himself. He would happily take a thousand blows if this creature would just let Feri go.

"Feri," he said, "I love you. I'm so sorry."

She didn't answer because she couldn't answer, the knife was pressing hard against her throat. She could feel the cut skin and was starting to breathe heavily in sheer panic.

Sam bent his head down and felt the shadow of the monster approach.

"I love you Feriha!" he said again. "I'm really sorry."

"Say you despise her, Jewboy. Tell her the truth. Tell her that Jews can't love. Tell her she's nothing but a whore, a shiksa whore. Tell her!"

Sam couldn't. No matter how much it angered this creature, he couldn't say that. It was as bad as any blasphemy. He'd rather take the name of God in vain and break a commandment than say that about Feriha. She was beautiful and she loved him and he loved her and it didn't matter what this man did, nothing could take that away.

"I can't," he said. "She's my girl."

The man stood over him. Sam waited for whatever was going to happen to happen. He thought of his mum and dad, of his little brother, of Jemal and of Feriha, of everyone and everything he'd known in his short life. He loved them all in his own way, Feriha most of all, and thought his God a cruel God if He let her die. But he knew his history, knew that for whatever reason, that same cruel God had set the world against his people. There had been cruelty before and there would be cruelty in the future, he knew this but it explained nothing.

He tried not to cry, not to feel fear, to die bravely, breathing slowly and carefully, doing his best to go to heaven in the right way, and praying that somehow, whatever happened to him, Feriha would be safe.

He waited for the deadly strike and for the comforting words of God. Instead, he heard other words, unexpectedly soft.

"Jud?"

He looked up, but he had only a fraction of a second to take in what happened next.

A figure stood behind the killer. Sam couldn't quite make him out, or if he could, he didn't recognise him, but he did recognise what the man was holding in his hands – the wooden scroll holder of a sepher torah. These rollers were holy artefacts. They held the Old Testament, written in its original Hebrew, and were treated with reverence. The roller itself was a thirty inch carved wooden pole with eight inch plates set at either end to prevent the parchment slipping. The shadowy figure held a single roller by its oval handgrip, no parchment attached.

Rekin, heard his name and turned.

"Daniel! You clever..."

The wooden pole came sweeping towards him and the oak plate crashed into his temple. Rekin staggered, his eyes growing unfocused, looking through Daniel into some distant point. He tried to hold on to Feriha but Sam leapt up and pulled her away, just as Rekin dropped the knife which Sam snatched up, quick as lighting.

Daniel was going to strike again but Rekin sank to his knees. Blood was oozing from his left ear.

"Je...s....us, J..ew...b...oy!" Rekin managed to say through the spittle and vomit seeping from his mouth, "th.. a... hur..."

Daniel, full of a rage he had never thought possible, was close to beating the man to a pulp, but his reason told him there was no need, that a terrible blow had already been delivered. Rekin held his head and muttered incoherent sounds, his mouth a devilish imitation of a smile. He tried to stand but twisted and fell, face up, twitching violently, his eyes rolling, his teeth clenched, his head swinging madly from one side to the other as if shaking itself free of pain.

Sam turned Feriha away, barely able to look himself, only afraid that Rekin might somehow find the strength to stand again.

He couldn't.

Daniel lowered the wooden roller. His face was flushed but his gaze was fixed and firm. He watched Rekin shake and tremble as if a hundred thousand volts were ripping his soul and body apart.

Daniel turned his gaze away from the dying man to Sam and said in as gentle a way as he could, "Are you alright?"

Sam nodded, but he was shaking almost as much as Rekin.

Daniel hurriedly took out his mobile phone and called Faraday. Sam listened, holding on to Feriha who loosened her grip on him suddenly and said, "Jemal!"

Jemal was lying some feet away, still as stone. Feriha ran to him and Sam followed. Daniel turned to Melissa who had watched the horror unfold, gagged and bound. He released her and she clung to him, shaking.

"You okay?" Daniel asked. She sobbed a distorted 'yes', doing her best to compose herself.

They both stood over Rekin and he seemed to look back at them. His left temple was not so much dented as destroyed, his brain visible beneath the skull.

"Why?" Daniel asked, kneeling down and squeezing Rekin's shoulder, puzzled in his good heart by this creature of wickedness.

Rekin didn't, or couldn't, answer. He tried to mutter something, but nothing came out except bile. The only movements he made were reflexes from a lost nervous system, desperately trying and failing to send messages through broken pathways. His head lay at a peculiar angle and Daniel attempted to straighten it out, for no other reason than it looked untidy, and as he did so his eyes met Rekin's. He couldn't be sure, but he thought Rekin saw him. It was only for a moment, then all movement stopped. Rekin's eyes stilled and Daniel thought he glimpsed the terrible void that had hidden behind them.

"Is he dead?" Sam asked, coming towards Daniel and asking about Rekin.

An odd phrase from an old memory passed through Daniel's unexpectedly clear mind - 'Poor Jud is dead', but he didn't say it. Instead he said, "It's Samuel, isn't it?" It was. "Do you know, Samuel, I'm not sure, but I can't say I'm much bothered if he is. Are you alright? And your friend?"

"Think so. Bash on the head," said Sam. "Got to get him to hospital. Did you call ...?"

"I did."

Daniel went over to Jemal, felt his pulse, loosened his collar and raised his head. Feriha was holding Jemal's hand, crying. Her neck still showed the slight cut from Rekin's knife. Daniel, fighting all manner of emotions, put his hand on Sam's shoulder.

"I've heard about you," he said.

"Heard about you too," said Sam.

They both squatted down beside Jemal, waiting for the police and ambulance to arrive. In this forgotten hole beneath a symbol of something that both joined them and set them apart in equal measure, they found an unexpected brotherhood and both were glad the other was there. Moments turned to minutes as they waited for some sign of life from Jemal. They might have taken him out to the street, but they didn't want to move him or to leave each other – safety in numbers. Melissa, holding Daniel's arm for dear life, knelt down too, looking at the injured boy.

"Who was he?" she asked, motioning towards the still form of Rekin.

"Long story," said Daniel, "but a devil in disguise, I think. You okay Melissa?"

She nodded, still shocked, relieved and afraid in equal measure.

They relaxed a little, focusing their attention on Jemal who at last started to stir and open his eyes.

"How are you, Jem?" Sam asked.

"My head hurts," Jemal moaned.

"I should have listened to you," said Sam, "I'm sorry Jemal."

"I feel like I've been run over by a bulldozer," said Jemal, trying and failing to sit up, Feriha holding his shoulders and stroking his head, feeling a little blood seep from a cut.

"You'll be alright," said Feriha. "The ambulance is coming. Don't move too much, Jemmy."

She used to call him Jemmy when they were little, but they weren't little any more, they were grown up and seeing what the world could be like.

Jemal still tried to raise himself and looked around at the four faces staring down at him.

"Is this heaven?" he asked.

"Not quite, mate," said Sam. "Take it easy."

But Jemal didn't take it easy.

Without warning he suddenly sat up, his eyes wide with fear. They'd all been so attentive to him that they'd forgotten Rekin who was supposedly in the bowels of hell and therefore unlikely to be staggering towards Daniel with the blooded sepher roller dangling from one hand, but that was precisely what they saw when they turned to follow Jemal's terrified stare.

They froze, shocked and disbelieving. Rekin was no zombie, but what state he was in was hard to say. Daniel prepared to fend off a blow when he heard Sam give out an angry yell and saw him run at Rekin with the knife pointing straight at the man's heart.

"No, Sam!" Daniel shouted, not wanting blood on the boy's hands, but his shout and Sam's yell were both drowned by a commanding call of "Down!" followed immediately by an almighty explosion and a burst of light. Daniel, Sam and Feriha instinctively ducked, covering their ears.

When they looked up, they saw Faraday standing at the foot of the stairs, a smoking gun in his hand, and Rekin standing too, a smoking hole in his head.

Then he crumpled like a broken puppet.

Faraday, adrenalin pulsing through him, rushed towards the stunned group.

"All okay?" he asked.

"All okay," said Daniel.

Faraday called out and other officers rushed in, wary and ready, but this time Rekin was seriously dead.

Viv Fowler checked Jemal and other officers went to Melissa, Feriha and Sam. Faraday looked at them all in turn, feeling desperate that they'd all been exposed to such terror on his watch. He put his hand on Daniel's shoulder.

"You didn't tell us about this synagogue, Daniel," he said. "You don't mind me saying, but you're the world's worst witness."

Daniel shook his head. "I only remembered after you left, and it was such a vague memory. I didn't want to waste your time. I felt sure he'd be at the Wick office."

"But you still came down?"

"I did," said Daniel. "Instinct."

"Glad you did," he said. "Any injuries, Daniel?"

"No. I was lucky."

"Yes, you were. Tell me, how the devil did Rekin know about this place, Daniel?"

Daniel looked shamefaced.

"I told him," he said, "about two years ago. He seemed interested in my being Jewish."

"I bet he was," said Rekin, beginning to understand.

"Yes, I see that now," said Daniel. "He must have hated me, but I had no idea inspector, none at all. I can't believe he worked for me and I never saw it."

"No, well people often hide what they believe," said Faraday. "You sure you're okay, Daniel, you look a bit pale?"

"I'm fine," he replied, "just ... well ..."

"Wondering what happened?"

"Yes."

Faraday shook his head.

"Do you think ... I have to ask this, Daniel..."

"...that they were having an affair?"

Daniel recalled the Kathryn he knew, the kind, sweet, gentle, funny, loving, faithful, generous and honest soul. How in all the names of all the Gods could he believe that she had fallen for this monster? Of all the things that made little sense in the world, that made least sense of all. If he believed it, there would be nothing left to hold on to for the rest of his life. And yet, the baby? God, the baby!

"No," he said, "I can't believe it, inspector. I won't believe it."

Faraday felt such sympathy for Daniel. He was a kind and vulnerable young man in an often unkind world. If he'd been deceived it would be the most vile deception. Even Faraday baulked at the idea. The only believable thing was that this creature, and he cast a glance at the body now lying beneath a rough blanket, had forced Kathryn to his will, but they could never know for sure.

"Daniel?"

For the first time in a year, Faraday saw Daniel cry. He hadn't cried at the news of her death, hadn't cried during the long night following the murder, hadn't cried at the funeral or, as far as Faraday knew, any time since. Now, at this violent conclusion, his eyes were streaming with tears.

Faraday asked Fowler to help and she led him away with Sam, Feriha and Jemal looking on, not sure what to make of it all.

Faraday checked Feriha's neck.

"Close shave," he said, and she smiled at him, but her face was washed of colour.

Officers grouped around the three teenagers and helped them, then took them outside to where ambulances and police cars had gathered, not to mention a sizeable crowd, in fact more people gathered at the synagogue now than the poor place had seen for many a year.

A team was left at the archive to sort things out with the warden and the authorities. When the cars and ambulances eventually drove away, Faraday cast a wry look back. This was the end of the hardest investigation in which he'd ever been involved, and in truth he hadn't even solved it, it had solved itself. His shot had killed the monster, so he had served a purpose, but it was all chance and luck and the coming together of many lives. He wasn't Sherlock Holmes or a brilliant idiosyncratic TV detective, he was just a local boy doing his best in a chaotic world. But at the same time, however it had happened, Rekin was dead and no one else had died. This was a miracle. They were so close to death, all of them, and yet they were all well, scarred but breathing. For this, Faraday was grateful.

He turned and drove away, leaving behind that familiar sense of a mysterious justice, so evident when the vacuum left behind by defeated evil could be filled by something good, bright and full of hope.

# 6:     **Redemption**

Naila put down her brush, wiped her hands and went to see who had knocked at the door. It was late afternoon and she rarely had callers, except hawkers or missionaries. This was her favourite time of day, when she could concentrate on her work and not be bothered with the world, so when she looked through the spyhole and saw a bearded man in a black suit looking down at his feet, she called out, "No thank you."

"Naila?"

She was flummoxed for a moment, trying to put together the voice and the image in the spyhole.

"Yes?"

"It's me, Daniel."

Astonished, and surprised that she was astonished, Naila opened the door.

"Daniel! It is you!"

"Yes. In disguise," he said with a wry smile.

"Come in, Daniel. Come in!"

Naila was truly welcoming, forgetting that she was in the midst of absorbing, creative work. She was also a little thrown as Daniel was the last person she expected to drop by. Despite their mutual support, relations had always been tricky for many reasons, not least the weight of complicated cultural baggage, and a long time had passed since they'd been in touch.

"You're busy, Naila," said Daniel. "I should have called. Do you want me to go? I can come back another..."

"No, no, no! It's good to see you. It is you, isn't it?"

"You mean beneath the beard and funereal gear? Yes, it's me."

"Right," said Naila, somewhat hesitantly.

She didn't know quite what to make of Daniel in his new guise. Instinctively she was a free spirit and wary of anything institutional. Her life was art and little else mattered now that Michael was gone.

"I'm not sure I would have ever recognised you," she said.

"No. I feel like I'm hiding away beneath all this," he said, gesturing to his clothes and beard.

"Sit down," said Naila, "make yourself comfortable. We'll talk."

Daniel sat on a seat by the window. It was a seat Michael had often used to look out at Hackney and Naila felt an odd sensation when she saw Daniel in it, as if the world had been shifted somehow and she was in a parallel universe.

She offered him something to drink but all he wanted was water. She sat opposite, still adjusting to the fact that he was there, albeit different to the Daniel she remembered.

"It's two years since I saw you," she said, "three since ..." she hesitated, then asked, "Is everything alright, Daniel?" She was puzzled; she didn't understand why he'd come.

"Fine, or as fine as they can be. I'm in London for a few days. I wanted to see you, find out how you were."

"That's kind," said Naila. "I'm ... alright. I heard what happened," she said. "I was away though, back home."

"Yes, I heard. I was with you, you know, when…well, when you were ill. We all were. They were desperate days."

Naila looked embarrassed. Kath's friends had looked after her when she was in hospital then helped sort things out when she'd decided to go back to Iran. Daniel hadn't seen her since her illness.

"Of course you did! You all did. I haven't forgotten, Daniel."

"I know. You look ... beautiful ... and well. A little pale, but well." Naila smiled. "And you're back, here in Hackney, in the same flat. I was surprised, Naila. I thought you'd left forever."

"No, not forever. My family wanted me to stay," she said, "but I couldn't. I sub-let the flat and I missed it. I missed ... his ghost, Daniel."

She looked embarrassed again.

"So you couldn't resist the bright lights of Hackney?" said Daniel.

Naila laughed, a beautiful light laugh, not so often heard any more.

"No, apparently not, but it isn't the same. I knew it wouldn't be."

"You didn't want to try somewhere different?"

"I thought about it but there's too much of Michael here. I can't seem to leave it, whereas you..."

"Oh, me, I'm all over the place Naila."

"But you're here now."

"Just visiting."

It was a little awkward between them, as ever.

"I heard about what happened," said Naila. "Are you alright, Daniel? It must have been terrifying, in that basement .. and that creature!"

"I'm okay. Lucky, really. Samuel ... you know, the boy who found Melissa? He was the lucky one. So were his friends. They were close to disaster. But I can tell you about all this in time, Naila. I want to know how you are and what you're doing. That's really why I came. I haven't seen you for such a long time."

"I'm really fine," she said, knowing that 'fine' covered a whole multitude of sins. "Bit of a wet rag, wasn't I?" she laughed, although it was a laugh tinged with embarrassment; she was aware how fast and deep she'd collapsed.

"You showed your distress," said Daniel. "I didn't. I hide everything. And now, look at me, back in the fold, covering my tracks in religion."

"I don't know," said Naila, "I'm sure you're not hiding. It's obviously offering you something you need."

He nodded, but then there was a strained silence between them.

"Are you sure I'm not interrupting?" said Daniel. "I can..."

"No, really," said Naila, and she meant it. She was glad to see him. There were a million things to say, but they had to be said carefully and slowly, in their own time. She touched his hand in confirmation but he pulled away, too quickly.

"You're busier than ever," he said, looking around at the paintings, not just the ones on the walls, but piled up everywhere. "You need a gallery, show off what you do."

"Maybe, but I can't seem to galvanise myself."

"That's a pity. You've done so much."

"And you, you're back home?"

"Back home, yes, with mummy and daddy. Pathetic, isn't it? But I may go away, I have some ideas. I can't seem to galvanise myself either."

He seemed to want to talk but was anxious. Naila, aware of other people's sensibilities as much as her own, felt his anxiety.

"You're not blaming yourself for all this, are you?"

"Spot on," he said. "First time. I knew you'd see through me, Naila."

"Daniel! You mustn't think that!"

"Mustn't I? Why?"

"Because it isn't your fault, none of it. Why should it be?"

"Because he got to her through me. Because if Kathryn hadn't loved me she'd still be alive, and so would Michael. Because if I'd remembered to tell the police about Rekin they'd have found him, spoken to him. Because if I'd told them about the workshop and the synagogue archive they'd have found him. I'm culpable, Naila, and I'm finding it hard to live with."

Naila was wary of easy answers. She didn't jump in and say the obvious. Instead, she said, "It's a shame you feel that way, Daniel. You're the most innocent of all."

He looked at her, wondering what she meant.

"It isn't easy to love, and it can be even harder to accept love. Kathryn was a beautiful woman and she loved you, I know that. Just because there are monsters on this Earth who twist love and turn it into something else doesn't mean that love itself is bad. That makes no sense. You were lucky that she loved you, Daniel. So many other men would have given their lives to have her love. And don't say you didn't deserve it."

"I didn't."

Naila laughed again.

"Nor did I deserve Michael, but we aren't in control of who we love and who loves us. It just happens. I suppose it would have helped if ...what was the man's name?"

"Rekin. Jud Rekin. Short for Judas, maybe."

"Yes, well it might have made it easier for you if he'd lived and the police had had a chance to question him, to find out why he did what he did, but whatever the reason, Daniel, blaming yourself is wrong. Kathryn wouldn't have wanted it."

Daniel didn't look convinced.

"They don't know why and neither do I," he said. "I can only guess, Naila, and to tell the truth..." Daniel was very uncomfortable here, "some of the possibilities are unbearable."

"Like they might have been having an affair?" Daniel took a deep breath and nodded. "If you believe that, then you didn't deserve her, Daniel." He looked hurt, but he knew what she meant. "Could you even contemplate such a thing?"

"I can. It comes to me sometimes, even though I try to put it aside."

He looked out of the window and again Naila remembered Michael doing the same thing. The memory was so clear, and the alteration so vast, it made her dizzy.

"Try harder," said Naila. "Listen Daniel, I didn't know Kathryn that well, only through Michael, but I know enough to tell you that she loved you with all her heart, and that the world would implode under the weight of its own deceptions if she cheated on you. She didn't. You must never believe it."

"Then what about the baby? And the murder? Why did this happen, Naila? It drives me to distraction thinking about it."

Naila sat back and looked at Daniel as if she were about to paint him. He felt her eyes on him, but he liked the generosity of her spirit, trying to help him despite her own grief. Daniel hadn't spoken to anyone about his feelings. In the communities he now moved in, you didn't do such things. Life was life and you just got on with living. Death happened and you didn't make a fuss about it. With millennia of suffering, his people had found ways to deal with tragedy. It was self-indulgent to be so introspective. Nevertheless, he was bothered, and Naila was the one person his instinct told him he should see.

"I can only guess as much as you, Daniel. Did she ever come to see you at work?"

"Sometimes, yes."

"What if she came and you weren't there but he was? Who knows what might have happened?" Daniel looked tense and uncomfortable. Naila said, "How you must suffer, Daniel, but I can only say it once more, Kathryn wouldn't want it."

"I guess so, but I think of what might have happened, that he ... he ... raped her, in the office, or in the workshop, or somewhere. And I had no idea, none at all. How he must have laughed at me! There was I full of the joys of Spring and he'd done this wicked thing. It defies belief, Naila. Why didn't she say something to me? Why didn't she tell me?"

"I suppose," said Naila, "that she was scared."

"Of what? Of me? Did she think I would have blamed her or dropped her? What kind of man did she think I was?"

Naila considered for a moment and said, "There could be another reason, Daniel."

"Like what?"

"That she was scared for you."

"For me or of me?"

"For you, silly boy. Don't you see?" Daniel tried, but he was in the habit of blaming himself for everything that had happened. "You know now what kind of man this Rekin was. Kathryn knew too, and she was afraid, not for herself but for you."

A light dawned.

"You think he threatened to hurt me?"

"It's possible. It's even likely, yes. Didn't it occur to you, Daniel?

It hadn't occurred to him and he wasn't sure why. He'd agonized silently over what he knew had happened, but more, over what he didn't know. The not knowing was worse than the knowing. He'd tried to think of Kathryn as he had before she was killed, but the pregnancy loomed large and threatened to drive him mad. If Naila was right, it made sense, only he couldn't know for certain, ever.

"It didn't," he said. "I don't know why, Naila. I prefer to think the worst."

"Yes, I can see that," she said, "but you mustn't think the worst of Kathryn, that would be a mistake." She stopped, looked out at the unexpectedly lovely evening and said, "Shall we go for a walk, Daniel? Hackney's looking promisingly beautiful."

Until then, he hadn't looked directly at her, afraid of her hurt as much as he was afraid of his own, but he caught her eye now and said yes, with the proviso, "You don't mind being seen with me looking like this?"

"I should think you had more to fear than me," she said, arching her eyebrows slightly. "I mean excommunication."

"I'll risk it," he said.

Whilst she got ready, Daniel wandered around the room, admiring the paintings, muted but evocative, rich with colour and ideas. He lost himself staring at them and was surprised when he heard her voice.

"Verdict?"

"Beautiful. Really wonderful, Naila. You should be famous by now."

"Come on," she said. "Let's go."

Her voice was a touch strained and Daniel wondered again if he'd upset her by making this unannounced visit, but he said nothing. She was, in truth, glad he'd come, but at the same time, when she saw him admiring her work, she wished, with a wave of guilty feelings, that it had been Michael.

They walked without talking for a while, through Springfield Park and down to the river.

"Are you sure you want to come this way?" Daniel asked, aware that they were close to the place of Michael's suicide. "We could take a different route."

"No, I often amble along here," said Naila. "It helps me commune."

The Lea Navigation was remarkably calm even though there were more people than usual around, in the marina, the cafe, on boats, on the bridge and out in the marshes.

"I always liked it here," said Daniel. "Hard to believe this is London, isn't it?"

"Do you miss it?" Naila asked.

"I do, yes."

"Would you come back?"

"I doubt it, but nothing seems particularly fixed at the moment."

He said this with the same kind of sense of disorientation that Naila experienced every second of every day, a belief that nothing much mattered and that a noisy world confused more than clarified the way ahead.

"How about you Naila? I thought you might have wanted never to see all this again," and he gestured to the East London landscape.

"I didn't," she answered, "but I wasn't comfortable in Tehran. This is home now, as much as any home can be, and I like being near the river, I really do. I feel close to him here. Maybe one day I'll find where I belong, who knows, but it's still early days, isn't it?"

"Yes it is," he answered, "always will be early days. Not sure life will have enough days to squeeze in some kind of understanding."

They walked a while again without talking, aware of many unwanted tensions but not ready to part.

"So tell me the truth, Daniel," Naila asked, "what are you doing down here?"

"I came to see you, Naila, that's all. I was worried about you, honestly, and I still am, a little."

"That's sweet, Daniel, but I'll be alright. Different, but alright."

"Well, that's good news," he said. "I believe you ... a bit. I would have come to see you when you came back, but I wasn't sure what to do. I thought you might want to let the past go completely."

"I didn't know what I wanted, Daniel. I still don't. Except one thing. I'd like to hear what happened. I mean I read about it but I'd like to know from you, if you want to tell me?"

He told her the story and she listened, sometimes stopping in mid stride, amazed at the closeness to disaster for all of them, astonished, angry and puzzled at the inhumanity of the man who'd wrecked all their lives.

"After the denouement in the synagogue archive, I hung around for a while, you know, police interviews and all that, then I went back home. I wanted to see you but even if you'd been around I'm not sure I would have done." .

"Why not, Daniel?"

He said, "You're a very private person, Naila, and I didn't want to upset you. But you were away so there was no decision to make. Just as well."

"We'll never see each other again if we go on like that," she said. "I'm glad you disturbed me tonight, Daniel, it's good to see you. So what are you doing now? Are you working again? Back with computers?"

"Not like before. I'm in touch with a few people about certain ideas, but mostly I'm studying," he said. "Drowning myself in Jewish law."

She looked at him questioningly and said, "Are you enjoying it?"

"It's serving a purpose. I'm glad it's there."

She felt for him. Grief could eat you up in so many ways. It could destroy everything familiar, make a mockery of your life and abandon you to the wolves. Without some focus of attention it created a demoralising turmoil. She'd drowned herself in painting, not just her own, but learning and teaching. It helped, but the grief always followed her, ready to pounce like some wild predator.

"And you're okay at home again?"

"Definitely not," he said, "but it's support and familiarity ..."

"..and safety," Naila finished the list.

"Yes. I might have meant that," Daniel said. "I think I cracked up, Naila, only it didn't show. I'm not very good at showing how I feel, but I couldn't stay here. I couldn't concentrate on anything. Everything fell away."

"But you came back when you realised Rekin might be here?"

"I did, yes, and just in time. God, Naila, I felt - and feel – so stupid! Faraday had asked me what I knew so many times, and I thought I'd told him, I really did. And then a year later he comes to see me and I mention Rekin and the workshop in Hackney Wick and still I get it wrong! We went back together to London. I was supposed to keep out of the way whilst he and his team sorted out Rekin at The Wick workshop, but I had this intuition, from nowhere, and remembered the archive. It was so weird."

"Weird?"

"Yes. I mean partly that I remembered, but also that Rekin should have chosen that place, of all places. I guess it made some kind of perverse sense. You'd have to have got into his sick little head to know exactly what was going on. Not easy."

"Any guesses?"

"A few. I didn't see that much of him, he got on with his job and we talked by phone or emailed, but occasionally, really very occasionally, we were in the office together. One day I had a call from the synagogue and he was there, just coincidence, and he seemed interested. He said he'd like to do the job, so I let him. I suppose, knowing what I know now, he was just loading up ammunition. How could I guess what was going on, that  he hated me, that he hated all of us?"

"Us?"

"Yes, Jews. It isn't uncommon, you know."

Naila put her hands in her pockets, head down, looking intently at the grass, aware that their spiritual homes made a poor blueprint for world peace.  She looked perplexed, as all good hearted people do by the existence of evil.

"Didn't he give anything away to anyone?" she asked. "Didn't he wallpaper his house with Nazi flags or have piles of Mein Kampf by his bedside?"

"No, nothing at all. Except..."

"Except what?"

"Something Melissa told me. I don't understand, but it feels like it's important. You know he'd tied her up and kept her down there? He didn't speak to her much, but apparently he'd made some passing comment that it was an 'act of charity'. Does that make sense to you, Naila?"

Naila stopped walking and turned to him.

"Isn't it obvious, Daniel?"

"Not to me, no. Am I being thick?"

Naila looked suddenly anxious, but also full of pity.

"No, not thick. And maybe I'm wrong."

"Tell me," said Daniel.

"He was saving her from you," she said.

There were only half a dozen words but it took a full minute for them to register, and even once they'd registered, he didn't fully understand.

"Saving her from me?" he repeated.

"You have a kind heart, Daniel. Kathryn wouldn't have loved you otherwise, and you're probably not as worldly-wise as you should be, but then neither am I. I think it's hard for people like us to understand wickedness. I sometimes think it's impossible for any of us to understand another human being, we're all uniquely wired."

"But saving her from me ... why?" he asked.

"Because the man's heart was full of hate," she said. "He hated anything and anyone different, and you are different, in many ways, Daniel. I suspect he was insanely egotistical, that he saw the world revolving around his own inflated presence and I'd guess that he couldn't understand Kathryn preferring you to him."

"No, well I couldn't either sometimes, Naila."

"You might, one day. This Rekin, he was good looking, right?"

"Very."

"I don't even think it was jealousy," said Naila. "It's demented psychology. He was saving her from you."

They'd reached the end of the nature reserve, away from the river. It was evening now and the sound of roosting was quite clear, about a quarter of a mile away in the thick trees near the Leytonstone side of the marshes. It was all very peaceful, so to have to deal with this wickedness polluted the tranquillity.

"He never gave me any indication of what he was thinking," said Daniel. "I just remember a quiet, hardworking guy who kept himself to himself. I had no instincts at all, good or bad."

"That's because you trust people. Most of us do. We have to. No systems would function if we all went around suspecting each other."

"Maybe we should," said Daniel.

"No. It would be unbearable, and it wouldn't make any difference. Bad things would still happen."

"But how are we supposed to trust our judgement, Naila, if we're blind to something like that? I worked with him, spoke to him, shook his hand, laughed with him! It drives me mad, really!"

She took his arm and said, "You won't go mad, Daniel, you're not the type, but it's making you unhappy, and that's a pity. I don't have an answer. There's wickedness in the world, and it can be both clever and deceptive. Kathryn must have been deceived by him, too."

Daniel stopped, put his hands in his pockets and looked down, for all the world a rabbi in deep thought about a subtle point of religious dispute.

"I'm all over the place, Naila," he said. "You had your fall but you seem to have recovered. You're stronger than me. I'm hanging on to religion for dear life and maybe that isn't right."

"I'm not recovered, Daniel, and I doubt I'll ever be what I was. Don't you think there are many moments when I feel there's nothing holding me here any longer and all I want is to join Michael?"

"Are there?"

"Of course there are."

"But you wouldn't do anything?" he asked, worried.

"I might."

"But you mustn't," he said, "you have to promise!"

She was touched by his concern, pulled him on and said, "Let's keep moving, Daniel. Don't want your visit to be too heavy, do we?

They walked a while in silence till Daniel said, "How do you deal with those moments, Naila, when you're really down?"

"I'm not sure I do," she said. "I let the storm take hold, let it do what it likes with me. I seem to come out the other end in one piece, even a little wiser. I'm not quite sure how to approach life and people. I suppose I just hope that each day I can keep going and the light might dawn on me."

"What light is that, Naila?"

"You know, the light of understanding, a little wisdom."

"Assuming there is any to be had."

"Yes, assuming that."

They were side by side but separate in spirit. When the real light of the Spring sun began to fade, Naila said, "We should head back."

"Yes."

"When are you going back home?"

"Tomorrow."

"Oh. Quick visit?"

"Yes. Like I said, just to see you."

"Where are you staying?"

"Friends from the community. There's a strong social bond, Naila. Helps keep away the gremlins."

When they reached Naila's block, she said, "Will you come visit again, Daniel?"

He wasn't sure whether this was a wish or a fear.

"Not sure," he answered. "Don't want to become a pest."

"What would you like to do?" she asked.

He pondered for barely a second then said, "I'd like to talk to you again. I think we should."

"So do I."

"Alright. I'll call you first next time, promise."

She touched his cheek.

"Furry," she said.

"Yes. Can't be helped, I'm afraid. Dress code."

They said goodbye but he didn't head back immediately. He waited until she'd closed the door, felt a rush of grim moroseness about to descend and was tempted to ring her bell again to help stave it off, but took a deep breath, turned and walked away.

Months passed, but they didn't meet, not because they didn't want to but because they were afraid to. Then Daniel left. He went to Israel and made biblical research digital; she stayed in London and made emotional research pictorial. They wrote as often as time allowed, which was never enough. The passing time and physical distance meant nothing; the bond that bound them tightened every moment they were apart, as if some unstoppable physical force existed solely to assert life over death. Then she also left, heading back with very mixed feelings to Tehran, partly to see her family again but partly and privately to be closer to him, even though the politics of their lands made such closeness a crime. She spent time with her family, determined to hold on to her; he looked out over the hills, wondering when and how they would meet again.

She returned to London, painted with surprising passion, building a reputation, but he stayed on, passionate in different ways, all the while distracted, unable to put her out of his mind.

More months, more letters. An anniversary beckoned, the only one that mattered to them. He returned to London where they were to meet outside Hackney Town Hall on the fifth anniversary of Kathryn's murder.

As he waited, Daniel studied the noble building which had seen so much of the ignoble in its lifetime. It had, like many buildings created to impress, been designed on classical lines, complete with imposing white facade atop a grand set of marble steps. It might have served as a royal residence or stately home, but fate had had other plans. It seemed terribly out of place in a borough that witnessed poverty and problems, more a symbol of aspiration than achievement. Daniel hoped the borough might one day raise itself to the grandeur of its town hall, but he wouldn't hold his breath.

"Daniel?"

He turned and there she was, beautiful as ever, enigmatic as ever.

And there for him.

He wasn't sure how to greet her but she took his hands and kissed him on each cheek.

"You look lovely," he said. "I'm... glad you're here."

"I wanted to be here," she answered.

She touched his smooth face and said, "What a handsome man you are, Daniel, now that you reveal yourself."

She looked at him in a way he didn't think he'd ever be looked at again.

"Fine," he said, "but..." he hesitated.

"But what?"

"Are you sure about this, Naila?"

She thought before answering.

"If you are," she said.

He had to admit, he wasn't sure how he'd react, but it was certainly something he needed to do, and there was no one he wanted to accompany him more than Naila.

"I think so."

"Brave boy," said Naila. "Come on. We can talk as we go."

But they hardly said a word. Small talk was out of place and large talk was too large to handle, and Hackney remained as busy as ever and as opaque as ever to their mission.

It wasn't a long walk to the scene of the crime, but it was an emotional trek. The landscape was so banal it was inconceivable that something so terrible had happened there. It weighed on Daniel, this banality, as if the here and now had no place in such an immensity of feeling, but death and loss were ephemeral things, cracks in the fabric of daily life to be papered over. Kathryn, for all her qualities, wasn't celebrity so there would be no pilgrims keeping vigil at a holy site.

Except for the two of them.

When they turned a corner and saw it, they stopped, mesmerised. Naila held his hand and Daniel squeezed it, aware of time and space shifting, moment by moment. He thought the police cordon might still be up, that there would be fresh flowers strewn on the ground or even angels floating around, but there was nothing.

"You alright, Daniel?" Naila asked.

"A bit strange," he said. "Let's go closer."

He released her hand, feeling fragile as they drew nearer the spot where Kathryn had lost her life. If ever living felt like a dream, it was now, with the sturdy brickwork of the passageway enclosing such pitiful ghosts. There was nothing to be seen, but everything to be felt. They halted a few feet before entering the fateful space.

"Why?" Daniel said. "Why did she do it? Why not turn back, run away, tell me, tell anyone! It was such a foolish, foolish thing!" he said.

Naila held his arm. "Let's go inside," she said softly.

As they entered, Daniel felt as though he'd passed through some dimensional conduit. He could hear and see Kathryn and the monster that was Rekin. He felt Kathryn's terror but couldn't change it, echoes rippling down the years. He touched the wall as if it were a shrine.

"Do you sense anything at all?" he asked Naila.

"Of course I do," she said. "Poor girl!"

"Tell me why then," he said again, half to Naila, half to the imagined ghost of Kathryn.

"Because she didn't want to hurt you, Daniel. She thought she could handle this herself. She thought Rekin's mind worked like hers, like a rational, feeling human being. Good people can't put themselves in the place of villains, it's impossible. She made that crucial mistake. It's no mystery."

Daniel leaned against the wall and closed his eyes. No matter how much he tried, he couldn't see this. Anyone else would surely have known the danger, turned back and all would have been well. Those who had died wouldn't have died and those whose lives had been broken would be whole again. There was no need for murder and grief, it wasn't necessary, and yet it happened again and again, as if the violent core at the heart of man would always erupt, releasing some deep, volatile, amoral energy.

"It is to me," he said, "I knew something was wrong, I'd known for weeks, and that night I was going to ask her, truly, but I never got the chance."

"No," said Naila, "but she may not have told you. There's no point in regretting, Daniel."

For the first time, Naila saw anger in Daniel's eyes. She'd wondered if the emotion was alien to him altogether, but she could see it now. Who, she wondered, was he angry with?

She touched his shoulder and he said, "I can't help it, Naila, I regret not pressing her. I knew something was wrong but I didn't find out. And I regret employing that creature, letting him into my life and wrecking it, and yours, and that old lady's and the policeman and..."

"Daniel, Daniel," said Naila, "if Kathryn was to come back this very moment, she wouldn't want to find you so agitated."

"How would she want to find me?"

Naila squeezed his shoulder and said, "Full of love for her, remembering who she was and what a good life she led. Making sure you were managing your days thoughtfully, looking after yourself and the people who like you, doing the right thing..."

"Which is?"

"Whatever you think it is, Daniel. I never knew Kathryn that well, but you were her love and she'll always be here for you."

Daniel took a deep breath and said, "There's no mark at all, no memory for others to see. It's all so ... private."

"What other way would you want it?"

"I don't know, it just seems ... unfair. People will walk through here and not know. There should be something."

"It doesn't concern them, Daniel, it concerns you and I and her friends. This is just ... a place."

Daniel felt the brickwork again as though he were touching Kathryn through the wall.

"I was going to ask her to marry me," he said. "I wanted to share a life with her completely. I think she thought I was too hesitant, but I wasn't. If only..."

"Stop!" said Naila. "Things are as they are and the fault isn't yours. It isn't a question of fault."

"But the waste, the violence, the chaos of it all!" Daniel said. "And if I hadn't been the slow creature I am, I might have stopped it!"

Naila wanted to hold him close and comfort him but not sure herself now of the right thing to do.

"Don't be harsh on yourself," she said. "Be the way she would like you to be. You'll be doing her such an injustice if you keep this misery inside you."

Daniel felt as though Kathryn was pleading with him, desperately trying to get through to him, but he was too brutish and stupid to hear.

"I thought I was strong," he said, "but I'm not, Naila. Look at me! Pathetic, isn't it!"

Naila smiled at him. "Not a jot," she said. "I didn't know you well when Kathryn was alive," she admitted. "None of us see each other until certain moments allow it. I don't know why that is, but it's true. I suppose it would all be too much to take. But I see now what Kathryn saw in you Daniel, I really do, and I see her through you. Don't blame yourself, or her, she wouldn't want it."

Daniel stood and walked around the dismal little space, thinking how physically small it was but how infinite in what it had witnessed.

"I could live here," he said. "It's a kind of home."

"No, Daniel," said Naila straight away, "this isn't home. They should pull it down and build something beautiful, or grass it over."

The building works were still going on around. For whatever reason, progress had been slow, but there was every possibility the passageway would soon vanish forever. For the time being though, Daniel felt it exert a morbid pull on his spirits. The gravity of the place was huge. It had been hard reaching it, but now that he was there it would be even harder leaving it. There was a perverse comfort in the attraction it exerted on him, as if Kathryn was more here than anywhere else.

He covered every inch of the ground beneath the moss infested brickwork ceiling. He wanted to feel that he was treading in Kath's footsteps, to let her know he was there. He looked to either side and said, "I wonder which direction she came."

"There," said Naila, pointing.

"How do you know?" he asked.

"I read the reports," she said, surprising him, because of all people he knew, Naila appeared the least connected to reality. How many times did he have to learn that his understanding of others was so flawed? "That was where Robert must have been watching," she added, and pointed to a spot about a hundred metres away.

"She stopped first, didn't she? That's what the witness said, isn't it? She..."

His face was a mask of pain, full of dreadful imaginings.

"Daniel," said Naila, holding his arm. "You know I'd do whatever I can to help you, but this isn't good."

"What isn't?"

"To come here just to remember the suffering. Let's leave that side of it behind."

Daniel sank down by one of the walls. Naila squatted next to him and put her arm around him.

"What other side is there?" he asked.

"Her goodness, kindness, generosity, affection, loyalty, joy, wisdom…"

Daniel put his head in his hands, aware of the weight of Naila's arm around his shoulder, rubbing his back, full of compassion.

"Yes," he said. "You're right. She was all those things. I'm sorry," he added, looking up, "I really am. You've the same reason to grieve as me, Naila. I should be comforting you."

"You have comforted me. You still are."

"I just don't understand!" he said.

Naila lifted him gently and said, "None of us do, Daniel. We never will."

She waited for him to compose himself, which he did, as best he could. He shrugged, breathed deeply and said, "Will we ever be ourselves again, Naila?"

She laughed, a light and lovely laugh that brought a little cheer to the dismal passageway.

"I'm not sure what I was like before losing Michael," she said, "but no, I don't think we ever will be. Life is change and growth, Daniel, you know that."

"She was my link to the real world," he said. "She heard my thoughts, touched my heart, made me feel unique."

"Can't you hang on to that?" Naila asked. "If she made you feel that way, then there was truth in what she said whether she's here or not. Kathryn didn't see the world through rose coloured glasses. If she loved you, then you're still the man she loved, same qualities, same soul. And what she was is still alive, through us," said Naila, which was a beautiful thought. In a brash, noisy world so full of nonsense, it was a lifeline to know that someone like Kathryn had lived and added so much in such a brief time.

Naila had moved away and was leaning against the opposite wall. Daniel looked at her. She was so lovely, a bright light in this gloomy place of death. He was grateful that, of all Kathryn's circle of friends, it was, surprisingly, Naila who shared this precious moment with him. They had all been kind in their own way, and Naila had hardly known him, yet here she was, perfect company, despite everything that had happened, and in ways that the others could never be, no matter how hard they tried.

"Can you fight despair, Naila?"

"You know I can't."

"But you gained strength from what happened. I don't think I ever grieved properly, never emptied myself of it."

"You never will. But life is long, Daniel, we don't know how we'll feel in a year, two years, ten years."

"No, except that I'll never forget her," he said.

"And I won't forget Michael," said Naila, "but we'd be doing them a disservice if we stay unhappy forever. I'm trying to tell myself this as well as you, you know?"

She risked a smile and he saw how lucky he was that she was there. She pushed herself away from the wall and stood beside him. He felt the warmth of her presence seep through the cold and damp. He didn't move, reluctant to leave, the intensity of the moment pinning him to the spot. Naila was wary of pulling him away, but she was also wary of letting him slip too deeply into morbidity. When the moment felt right, she said, "Time to go, I think, Daniel."

He stared at the walls as if he were trying to see through the brick into the truth of what lay beyond them, to understand why they had allowed such a murderous act without rebelling in some way or showing the slightest evidence of what they'd witnessed. His attention was only broken when a figure approached, just a passer-by looking a little wary of them. He hesitated, but with no other option to get where he was going, hurried through the passageway on his own private, harmless mission.

"It's nothing, is it?" said Daniel. "Just a route from one place to another."

Naila took his arm and said, "That's all it is to the world, but not to you or me."

"I don't want to leave it with bad feelings," said Daniel.

"You won't. There's too much of Kathryn here."

There was everything of Kathryn there. Her lifeblood had been spilt here. All she was had seeped away in this miserable, lonely, godforsaken gloom.

"Naila?"

He seemed uncertain whether to speak or not.

"I think I know what you're going to say," she said, reading his expression, a mixture of concern and curiosity.

"She..."

"...tried to write something in her own blood?" said Naila. "Yes, I think she did."

"The murderer's name, Faraday thought," said Daniel. "It's just that..."

"You can't believe her last thoughts would be of him?" said Naila.

"No, I can't. It's too awful."

Daniel walked into the centre of the passageway and stared at the ground. Naila watched him, intrigued.

"He was wrong," she said.

Daniel looked at her in surprise. How would she know?

"What then?" he asked, digging his hands into his pockets, a picture of intensity, visualizing Kathryn's last moments and trying to reach into her mind.

"I saw the image, like everyone else," Naila whispered, "At first I thought he was right, especially after we knew who had done this. It made sense, but I don't think that was what Kathryn was trying to say." Daniel looked more nonplussed than ever. "You of all people should know," she whispered. Daniel shook his head. He didn't know at all. "It wasn't an English letter she was trying to write," said Naila. "It was a Hebrew letter. A letter for you, Daniel. In my childhood I learned a little of the language," she said, "even if it wasn't for the right reasons. Can't you see?"

A light dawned on Daniel's face.

"Aleph," he said, "the first letter of the Hebrew alphabet?"

"And the first letter of the Hebrew word for...?"

Naila smiled, moved her head in the faintest, most shy gesture of assent, gently took his hand and touched him on the cheek, then they turned their backs on the darkness and headed into the light.

**End**

## Acknowledgements and Author's Notes

To friends who have helped with this book, many thanks.

It occurred to me that the dedication might be construed by some as being suspiciously narcissistic – this is as far from the truth as Finsbury Park from Finsbury Square, if you get my drift; it's simply one of life's odd coincidences.

Finally, I must thank the London Borough of Hackney for simply being there. Its organised chaos is a joy to behold and its surprisingly green soul a light in the urban jungle. I miss you.

A. R.

Lightning Source UK Ltd.
Milton Keynes UK
UKOW021941121211

183657UK00001B/4/P

# Act of Charity
Aidan Rami

If

HB